RO
FAT MANS
SHADOW

PENGUIN BOOKS

# FAT MAN'S SHADOW

Robin Blake was born in Preston, Lancashire, in 1948. During the 1970s he taught in England, Bulgaria and Turkey. By 1979 he was producing and broadcasting programmes for Capital Radio in London, many of which were networked throughout Britain.

Since 1985 Robin Blake has been a writer. He is the author of *Mind Over Medicine* and (with Eleanor Stephens) *Compulsion*. He lives in London.

# ROBIN BLAKE

# FAT MAN'S SHADOW

PENGUIN BOOKS

PENGUIN BOOKS

Published by the Penguin Group
Penguin Books Ltd, 27 Wrights Lane, London W8 5TZ, England
Viking Penguin, a division of Penguin Books USA Inc.
375 Hudson Street, New York, New York 10014, USA
Penguin Books Australia Ltd, Ringwood, Victoria, Australia
Penguin Books Canada Ltd, 2801 John Street, Markham, Ontario, Canada L3R 1B4
Penguin Books (NZ) Ltd, 182–190 Wairau Road, Auckland 10, New Zealand

Penguin Books Ltd, Registered Offices: Harmondsworth, Middlesex, England

First published by Viking 1990
Published in Penguin Books 1991
1 3 5 7 9 10 8 6 4 2



Printed in England by Clays Ltd, St Ives plc

For FANNY

with gratitude and love

## *Acknowledgements*

My thanks are due to Frances Hegarty, who lent me her writing-house, and to Moris Farhi for so carefully picking nits out of my script.

It was the British Council who originally gave me the chance to know the incomparable city of Istanbul. For this I shall always be grateful.

# *Note on Turkish Pronunciation*

For any readers who are interested, the Turkish alphabet is pronounced phonetically, with the following additions to our twenty-six letters:

ı : as the short *u* in gam*u*t
ö : as the long *oeu* in *oeu*vre
ü : as *ew* in f*ew*
c : as the hard *j* in *j*udge
ç : as *ch* in *ch*in
ş : as *sh* in *sh*in
ğ : silent, but lengthens the preceding vowel

# I

Inside the disco, walls ran with condensation. The ground seemed to ripple, stirred by the tremendous decibel gain of the amplifying equipment.

Wedged in a corner, Dan Barry was watching a young woman as she danced peacefully on her own. She apparently wore nothing but a man's white shirt and a black Borsalino, which lay tilted back from her face. The shirt clung baggily to her sweat-damp skin, which showed through in pink patches. Her eyes were closed. He wondered how she had found this island of private space amid the turmoil. Many of the dancers were hooting and quivering, and jumping excitedly. The rest rolled their heads and yawed from side to side, fluttering their hands. They were all high as moon-birds.

It was a new resort, and barely coping with the tidal surge of tourists that had overwhelmed the place. This was the only discothèque for miles, and no one counted numbers through the door. A limit was reached only when no more bodies could be shoe-horned in. Then dancers had no choice but to writhe against each other, like a termites' nest on fire. The heat was intense and they wore a minimum of clothing.

Now Dan noticed the shaved heads of three men. They looked like bobbing corks in a seething river-race, as they moved among the closely-packed dancers. They'd raised their arms to chest a way through, their wrists mailed with chainstrap watches and name-bracelets. Each of them had a circle of gold threaded into his plump right earlobe. Jabbing drinkers aside with their elbows, they came to the bar and ordered half-litres of beer. These they drained simultaneously, then lounged back against the beer-slicked Formica to survey the cauldron of human bodies, boiling under the incessant bass rhythm and stroboscopic light. The young men exchanged glances, leering and laughing. They mouthed through projecting lips and bared teeth, and then lowered their faces into the next round of beers.

Dan tapped his partner on the shoulder and jerked his head towards the bar. Jack Bacon looked up and followed Dan's indication. He nodded, shifting the Nikon that was slung beneath his arm to a more accessible position.

Then the room was stunned by sudden silence, and the lights went out. Five hundred dancers paused in suspense, willing the power supply to resume. When it didn't, there was a splutter of breaking glass and someone yelled in English, 'Get on with the fucking music, you wankers.'

The shout was punctuated by more splintering glass. More ribaldries were called across the darkness, but the light-hearted mood soon faltered. The entire squash of bodies felt a common shimmer of anxiety, an eerie mood of suspended panic riding in the air above them. They were trapped inside a bubble of uncertainty.

When the bubble burst, as suddenly as the power-cut itself, the bodies started to struggle, and then scrabble in the blinding dark towards a door. With the music and flashing lights killed, there seemed nothing more desirable than moonlight and fresh air and the sound of sea on the beach. But the disco had only the one door and, at this stage, no one knew for certain where it was. Worse, the joint was a breeze-block shed pretending to be subterranean and sleazy-smart. So windows had been left out of the design.

Butane lighters and matches flared and were raised up. Dan saw one lighted match burn the fingers which held it and then tumble into someone's candyfloss bush of hair. The hair flamed briefly above a horrified scream. But by then half the room was screaming as, near the bar, new waves of breaking glass cascaded to the floor.

A series of dazzling flashes tricked some of them into thinking that the strobe lights had come back on. But this was Jack Bacon, standing on a table, taking flash-shots downwards and at random with the Nikon. Later the prints would show what the three young men at the bar were doing at the back of the mêlée.

In the early shots they were shouting and using the soles of their boots to push bodies towards the centre of the room. Then they vaulted the bar and were either upending bottles of spirits down their throats, or else sweeping the shelves clean with scything movements of the forearm. One of them – the one in shades – was holding the barman's head down on the bar and seemed to be working it over with his fist. The dark glasses had been shaken down almost to the tip of his nose by the vibration of his punches.

By the time the camera's evidence showed the room beginning to clear, the barman had been kicked to the floor. The yobbo with the dark glasses now started to grope for a fresh victim. He found a man in his twenties, dressed in natty casual clothes. He caught a bunch of material from the man's shirt in his fist and pushed him backwards against one of two massive loudspeakers. The man was not a package tourist, he was a Turk, and had emerged from behind the music system console. He was the evening's disc jockey.

Now he was having a finger wagged in his face. The rolls of flesh which rucked the shaven neck of the Englishman could be clearly seen in Jack's next photograph.

At this point the lights and music abruptly returned.

The music flourished again only briefly. With a vicious shove the Englishman sent the Turk juddering against the loudspeaker, which tipped backwards on top of the audio equipment. There were some incandescent sparks, a few fizzles and the music fell silent again. The Turk called out in alarm, and in English, 'Hey! What you guys doing? Are you mad?'

The disco customers had almost all left. Dan noticed, from the darkness of his vantage point, the girl in the soaked shirt. She was standing on tiptoe at the back of the diminishing ruck of dancers, pressing them to funnel faster through the door. As the strobe lights continued to flash, one of the English youths wandered over with a staggering gait and hooked a forearm round her waist. He dragged her back with him and Dan heard her voice for the first time, as she pulled and craned away from him. 'Let go, goddamn imbecile. Let go!'

She was an American. Dan looked questioningly at Jack, but was answered by a restraining hand on his shoulder.

The girl in the white shirt was pressed against the bar. Her hat had fallen to the ground and the imbecile was feeling her up, fingering her breasts and mumbling stupidly into her ear, using his weight to overwhelm her.

Dan could make out the words being mouthed by the one in sunglasses to the disc jockey.

'Someone was chatting up this bird here, wasn't they?' Still grasping the shirt, he worked his fists sharply back and forth into the disc jockey's chest. 'Don't shake your head like that. That was *you.*' He looked round to his mates, pulling a mock-goofy face. 'Well, *we* don't like Turkish wog bastards having it away with *white* women, right? That's dirty, that is. That needs a lesson, *right*? Okay, lads?'

The other two youths turned their heads. Their faces had expressions of slavish agreement. In slurred voices they shouted their encouragement, 'Yeah, go it, Lenny. Do it!'

Lenny reached into the buttock pocket of his jeans and produced an object as thick as a thumb and long as a pencil. Then, with a *slitch*, it had a blade. The blade was pointed and thinned by repeated honing, and it winked brightly in the intermittent light.

'Like the man said, no time like the present. So I'll give *you* a present. I'll give you the present of your balls, on a plate. Like that idea, do you?' He leered round at his friends. 'Ere, Chaz, Kobbo. Drop that slag, willya? Give's a hand over here. Pull his fucking trousers off.'

Dan was thinking *Christ, here I am again.* He'd done a lot of stories in the East End of London, of friction between the Bengali, the West Indian and the cockney tribes. There had been much too much nastiness, and always the same questions. Are you a human being who will do something to prevent suffering? Or are you only the reporter, the guy in the birdwatcher's hide who looks for truth, and never messes up the facts? Too often Dan had stood in the shadows as he stood now, and watched brutality unfold, and arranged the words of his story end-to-end in his head.

Chaz and Kobbo heaved the disc jockey up and on to the bar, sweeping the remains of its debris away. By now the man was mewling and squirming. Kicking with his heels he made a few feet on his back along the counter in a bid to escape, but he was checked and hauled back by Kobbo. Kobbo's was a factory-hand's gesture, the securing of an abattoir chicken that almost got loose. A flash of Lenny's knife in front of the disc jockey's eyes made the chicken lie still.

Dan looked up at Jack, questioning again. This time Jack nodded.

Dan groped under the table for a stool and hefted it in both hands. Jack eased himself off the table and touched down silently. He tapped Dan's shoulder and gave a soundless punch to his left palm with his right fist. Dan felt a balloon of excitement swell and solidify in his stomach as Jack counted them down: three fingers . . . two fingers . . . one finger.

'Hey, you!'

They came from the shadows, yelling. Dan hurled the stool at Kobbo. It missed, striking the wall high above the bar and bringing down another cataract of glass. Nudging his foot against an unbroken bottle Dan bent and caught it up. When he raised the bottle above his head he saw the eyes of the one called Chaz pulse with fear. Then a jolt ran through his body. It was, he would realize later, the high voltage of physical violence: the equation *glory = action × risk* running through the viscera. The experience was a new one and he found he liked it. He was no longer the guy in the shadows making notes.

Lenny turned. But before he could raise his knife Jack had poked the Nikon into his face and released the flash. Lenny did not react: the shock of light simply stunned him. Jack released the flash again, and again there was a frozen pause. Then Lenny emitted a long, florid squeal. He doubled over, jamming the balls of his thumbs into his eyes, yelling and swearing and crying. Dan stepped forward. He raised his right hand almost ritualistically and brought the bottle down with an explosion of force. The blow released the sum of all the violence in Dan's body. He thumped the nape of Lenny's neck so hard that the big man went down like a bull crumpling from the snub end of a stun-gun.

Kobbo and Chaz, the followers, took in their situation only slowly. They were now only two, and their line of command was ruptured. The room had cleared by now, but their heads jerked about, seeing in the afterimage of the photoflashes a menacing circle of phantoms surrounding them in the shadows. Their alcoholic glory had soured to nightmare. Dan knew they must do what is always done in nightmares – they must run. It took another few seconds. Then Chaz and Kobbo were blundering towards the door.

Dan and Jack lunched next day in a beach-side *lokanta* with the sea rustling like tissue paper in the fringe of their hearing. Below them, on the sand, oiled bodies turned themselves meticulously, like so many rissoles under the fiery sun.

They ate olives with their *raki* and iced water. Later the waiter brought *pide* bread, chopped tomato salad and a plateful of fried mussels threaded on to wooden skewers. Dan had already drafted his account of the previous night but was not happy with the results. He was not happy with the job. He was not happy at all.

'I mean, this is so *trivial*, Jack. What are we doing here?'

'A good job for our editor. Fetching in the coals that stoke the profits. Not satisfied with that? We got a bit more than we bargained for last night, admittedly.'

What they had bargained for had been spelled out by that editor with brutal simplicity.

'You're to go to some Mediterranean sunspot, and get after the British tribal hooligan on holiday. Get him drinking and drugging himself legless, and doing GBH to foreigners, preferably members of the host nation. I want gory pictures from you, Jack, and I want tight, jagged prose from Dan. This has got to rattle the dentures of the old dears in Cheltenham. I want the law-and-order brigade baying, I want complaints to the Press Council, I want this to really *bite*. Okay?'

Jack had been hired first, and he'd roped Dan in. Jack had convinced Cartwright that he was in the vanguard of the coming generation. After leaving the newspaper office, Jack had given Dan a supplementary briefing in the pub. 'You should know this. The man's got a thing about yobbos abroad. His daughter got arrested in Ibiza last year. Was out partying with a group of Leeds United supporters and broke a bottle over some wop waiter's head. Poor old sod had to fly out there, get a Spanish brief, bail her out, go back and forth for the trial. It nearly killed the old bugger. So this is all about spleen, vindictiveness. He doesn't blame poor little plummy-mouthed Pandora, or whatever her name is. *He* blames the company she kept.'

'What are we supposed to do, hang around the Spanish coast and wait for some aggro?'

'No, we're not going to Spain. I've got a better idea, and I think he'll like it – Turkey, the southern coast. That's the new cheap package Mecca, isn't it – the Costa Kebab? By all accounts they're developing it like they've only just discovered pre-stressed concrete.'

Dan and Jack had chosen one of the most hyped-up new Turkish resorts. The smell of drains, the antlers of rusty steel twisting out of exposed beams and columns, the shipwrecked bulldozers, and litter of unearthed pine trees, all testified to dodgy investors and shortfalling cash-flow. It was still a half-way place, with the remains of its ancient fishing village huddling among the simulated-marble cladding and aluminium fittings of modernity.

Yet the High Street hype had reached the tourists, and they'd signed up in their thousands. By day the beach was choked with grilling flesh. As Jack Bacon had predicted back in London, the place was ripe for an explosion of trouble. All it had needed was a spark.

Dan sighed. 'It's all very well, Jack, but I'm not making any real money, I'm scrabbling around for work. I should never have gone freelance.'

'You can't have your cake and eat it. You don't get rich in journalism, unless you're so famous no editor can afford to say pass. But that's *really* big-time: I'm talking about Hemingway or Schanberg, for Christ's sake.'

'So, *they* did it, which proves it can be done.'

'Only one way, boy. Got to do something shattering. Preferably it should involve almost getting killed.'

'Like last night.'

'That was a sideshow. I mean something where the reporting itself is life-threatening. That's the only thing poxy editors respect, pulling stunts they know they'd never have the nerve to do themselves.'

Dan had become Jack Bacon's friend in the course of the previous winter. They'd worked together on one of the pieces about racial harassment in East London, and subsequently took to meeting at a pub they both liked in Camden Town. Dan found a mentor in the big-framed, chaotic, fast-drinking ex-soldier. But Jack was more than just a highly experienced press cameraman. He had a real eye for the unexpected view. His moody, startling black-and-white shots had lent a touch of class to Dan's spiky, undressed prose.

'So what I need is a war, or something. Go out there and get myself scared shitless.'

Jack inserted a line of mussels between his teeth and drew the stick out. He shook his head as he chewed. 'War's too banal nowadays, and there's too much PR in it. Military dictators are window-dummies in gold braid. Hey, this stuff tastes nice. Try some.'

Jack chewed and swallowed at his leisure, took a mouthful of the milky aniseed liquor, then said, 'No, war lacks plot. But look at this.' He flipped open his wallet and removed a folded press cutting. 'It's an obit from the *UK Press Gazette*. Hong Kong writer poses as a Vietnamese boat person, intending to write up the tragic courage of the refugees as they drift like fallen leaves over the South China Sea. Great idea, yeah? He had his throat slit by pirates in the Gulf of Tonkin, just four days in. I knew him. He was a great writer.'

'But he didn't live to write this, did he?'

'Well, that's not my point. He was actually on the wrong tack. Even if he had lived, the world would've said, "Oh yes, very moving, what's on Page Three?" No sense of guilt, you see. The readers don't identify with the writer's experience, don't see themselves as boat people – they look through the eyes of the writer. That's why you mustn't efface yourself. Be active in the scene you're reporting, parade your ego. The best writing is ego to ego, yours to the reader's.'

Jack sat back and lit a cigarette, inhaling like an asthmatic receiving pure oxygen. 'Want to know what he should have done?' He paused for effect. Dan sat back and waited, but Jack merely helped himself to another skewer of mussels.

'Okay, what should he have done?'

Jack swallowed and wiped his lips with a paper napkin. Then he leaned forward until his chin was almost touching the table top. 'He should've joined the pirates.'

Dan frowned. 'I don't get it. Why?'

'Because it's the dramatic viewpoint. The other is comparatively feeble and sentimental. This has pathos, yes, because it sees the effect of the cruelty of these people, but it's also a torn viewpoint. He's come to know the pirates, see? Knows their point of view, shared it even.'

'But why should I put myself in that position? Isn't it better to stay out of the argument?'

'You can if you like, but it makes for boring copy. Be a faker, a spy. Concealment, deception, pretending to be involved – that's what it's about. It's exciting, it's risky, because if you're rumbled you've got nowhere to hide.'

'Jesus, Jack, I'm too young to die.'

'That's why the story couldn't fail, Dan. Old enough to know better, young enough not to care. We know you can write. Get out there and write something that squeezes the brain so hard the juice comes out of the reader's eyes.'

He reached for a black olive, tilted his head back and dropped it into the hole made by his lips.

Half the stock must have been out in the open air – Iznik tiles, camel-bone boxes, coral necklaces, brass coffee-pots, postcards, fezzes, hookahs, kilims, paperbacks in German and English, leather jackets, Turkish slippers, camel bags, cassettes, embossed posters of Ataturk and tasselled ones of belly-dancers, packets of stamps, bottles of bronzing cream, T-shirts, sandals, sunbathing mats. Dan saw a shadow flicker inside the shop and thought, *Move on! This is all crap.*

But it was too late. Instantly, like a lizard's tongue, the shopkeeper was out of the door and beckoning Dan to his side. Then he was pulling ethnic woollen shoulder bags down from a steepling pile like a man possessed and displaying the variety of their designs. Dan had second thoughts. One of them might do as a gift for Helen, a girl he knew in London. She liked the old hippy stuff. He pointed almost at random at one of the bags. 'How much?'

'Sixty-five thousand *lira*. Is old bag. Very antique.'

'Good God, that's over twenty quid! I'll give you twenty-five thousand for it.'

The man's face dropped. He stepped back as if thunderstruck, as if Dan had called his mother a whore. 'What you saying, mister? You want for me to starve? I pay fifty-nine thousand for this bag.'

'Thirty thousand, then. Look I've seen them in other places for less than that price!'

The Turk's face crumpled. He would like to help. How he would like to! But this would mean penury. 'It is impossible, my friend. Sixty-five thousand is my price. But for you I make special price, sixty-two thousand. Okay? Look very nice, very antique bag, old Anatolian design.'

Dan turned the bag over in his hands, then peered inside as if he might discover additional spending money there. He said, 'Thirty-five?'

At this point an older man, with a pot-belly so inflated that it seemed about to burst, emerged from the shop. Rapidly the two Turks conferred in their own language. Wearily Dan wandered a little way down the street. It was dusty and unkempt, showing everywhere the scars of headlong tourist development. The whimsy of greed ruled this place and Dan, who had not visited Turkey before, could smell it. It was a country very seriously on the make.

The shopkeeper pursued him, holding out the bag. 'I take fifty thousand, okay? Fifty thousand *lira*. Come back with me to my shop, come!'

In the end they agreed on forty-five thousand lira and Dan felt quietly pleased with himself as he reached for his wallet.

'You are being robbed, my friend.'

The voice came from behind him. He swivelled. It was the disc jockey, the one whose masculinity he and Jack had possibly saved the previous night. The man was dressed in a tropical suit and aviator sun glasses.

'The true price should be twenty thousand *lira*. Allow me. I fix it.'

He fired a volley of passionate vernacular at the shopkeeper, gesturing with downward stabs of his stubby fingers as if to say people who charge such prices belong to the devil. The argument lasted several more minutes, until the disc jockey announced, 'He says you can have it for twenty-five thousand. You're giving him five thousand more than you should, but he must have something of his pride. The Turkish man is very proud.'

They walked away together. Dan said, 'Well, thanks. We're quits now.'

'Quits?'

'I mean, we helped you out of a spot of bother, and now you've done the same.'

'Hey, man! That was something else. I pay you back properly for that.'

Dan looked dubiously into the bag he had just

bought. 'You saved me quite a bit of money, anyway. I'm Dan Barry, by the way.'

The disc jockey stuck out his hand and Dan shook it.

'Altan Başkurt. I speak good English, yeah? I work for the Anatolian Airways. It's a –' He shrugged. 'It's a temporary job.'

'Were you really chatting up that girl, or was it all a fantasy?'

'I know her, of course. She's not English but American. She works in Istanbul, like me. But we are not . . . not *together* like that, you know?'

He turned to Dan, suddenly enthusiastic. 'You like her? Hey! I can get her for you, no problem.'

There was a swagger about Altan, the rich local boy which Dan warily admired. He smiled, saying nothing. They were outside Dan's hotel.

'Dan my friend, you will both eat with me tonight. I know a very good fish *lokantası* in a small village away from the town. You will like it. The food here is shit, I should know. My family owns most of this place.'

'Well, that is kind, but there's no need –'

'No need! You saved my balls. I meet you in the bar here, eight o'clock. Okay?'

'Dan, Jack. Please meet Lena Priestley.'

Altan had come into the bar and fetched Dan and Jack out. The girl was in the passenger seat of his black BMW.

Altan opened the rear door and gestured Dan to get in. He slid into the seat and smiled. Lena turned and laid her elbow on the seat-back. 'That was some rescue act last night. I mean, those guys were pretty heavy.'

She opened her eyes wide and looked from Dan to Jack, who had followed Dan inside. Altan stung the engine into life.

'Well, I'm glad to meet the team that saved my honour and Altan's prospects for parenthood. Not that parenthood is a high priority for him right now.'

Altan spun the wheels as he accelerated away. Lena, still turned towards Dan, had buried her chin in the crook of her arm.

Dan spotted the corner of a book poking out of Lena's bag and accurately identified it. 'You're reading Dickens. He's one of my heroes.'

They were alone in the empty restaurant now. Just ten minutes earlier Jack had been telling Altan how he'd hoped to photograph the nesting sites of the loggerhead turtle, and Altan had known a beach not ten miles away where baby turtles were probably hatching at this very moment. Altan and Jack had finished their meals and taken off in high excitement, two boys in search of adventure.

'You take a taxi back to town, okay?' Altan had said, winking to Dan. Dan didn't much like people who winked, but he smiled and nodded. He did like the idea of having time with Lena on her own.

With his reference to her reading he half-expected

an effusion about the quaintness of nineteenth-century England. But Lena's view of Charles Dickens was a surprise.

'It's okay, but you can't believe one word of it. What my grandpa would call a crock of old hokum.'

'Oh, well, I don't know. I mean, Dickens reckoned to know what he was on about. He was a journalist, a reporter.' He was on the point of adding *like me*, when Lena cut in.

'Well anyway, I hate reporters. I loathe and despise them.' She pulled herself up on the edge of an angry outburst, and added more softly, 'My bastard of a dad was one.'

Little pink spots had emerged on her cheekbones, and a flush was beginning to tinge her strong, long neck. Dan could hardly now admit that he worked for newspapers. Yet, inevitably, she asked, putting her forefinger to her carmine-painted lips, 'What do you do, Dan?'

'Why don't you guess?'

She looked hard at his face and frowned in concentration, like someone reading tea-leaves. 'I don't know enough about the British Isles. If you were an American I'd say you were – what, a teacher? Or – I know, an actor. Yes, you'd be a sort of yet-to-be-discovered off-Broadway actor, currently unemployed.'

Dan stretched open his eyes and leaned back in his chair, feigning with concentrated effort. 'Well, I'm stunned. I really *am*. How did you *know*? It was a guess, right? Truth is, I'm a very bad actor, more or less permanently unemployed. *Resting*, it's called. Bloody hard graft, actually, because you have to do all sorts of other things to keep body and soul together.' He was warming to his theme now, the wine stripping out his inhibitions. 'I've played a lot of parts in my time, but not necessarily on stage or screen: hod-carrier, stable-lad. I was once a night-club bouncer until the owner did a runner. The police issued a warrant for his arrest when they found out he'd been screwing fourteen-year-olds.'

The details were true, more or less. Lena's eyes had widened with interest. She said, 'Sounds an exciting life.'

'Once I worked as board-maker to a bookie in the East End of London. You know, chalking up the odds in his shop. Anyway, it turned out the boss was bent as a spiral staircase, and we all ended up two days in the Limehouse nick suspected of conspiracy – the whole shop staff.'

'In *jail*? What was it like in jail?'

'British police cells are very small with very bare walls.'

Sick-green walls, seeming to breathe, in and out, and each time squeezing nearer. Your own chest is tight and feeling like you've got pond creatures wriggling through your guts. Then you think, especially at four in the morning after no sleep, you think that you might never get out.

'How did you get out?'

‘Oh well, it was all a mistake, the police should never have gone in there. Bookies never involve the police in fraud cases if they can possibly help it. Since no one was pressing charges, they let us go.’

The story he wrote had won him the Young Feature Writer’s award, a year ago. It had everything: suspense, pathos, police brutality. He remembered how he walked up through the tuxedo crowd at the Savoy to pick up the award, with everyone applauding. It was the best night of his life. On the strength of it he’d quit his job to go freelance.

‘But don’t you miss the stage? I mean, don’t you long to act?’

‘I’m sorry? Oh! The stage! Oh no,’ he said, confessionally. ‘I don’t miss the stage. It’s a writer I long to be.’

That, at least, was the truth.

‘Dan! For Christ’s sake, Dan, get your head up! I’ve got it, I’ve got the answer for you. On a sodding plate.’

Jack had swept the curtains open and was standing at the foot of Dan’s bed. Dan opened his eyes. Jack was dressed as he had been on the night before, when he’d gone off in pursuit of turtles. His face was animated and glowing with good humour. Dan rolled over, groaned and closed his eyes again.

‘What’s the time?’

‘About half-six.’

‘What? Look, Jack, fuck off and tell me later, will you?’

'No, this is too good to wait. Incidentally, I've been out all night with Altan, got some great shots of baby turtles. The mothers lay the eggs about a metre down, and after the babies hatch and climb out of the sand like escaping prisoners of war. Incredible to watch.'

'You woke me at six thirty to tell me this?'

'No, to tell you about Altan, and what he can do for you. He's been talking a wee bit freely to me tonight. You know how friendly he is – apart from being pissed as a brewery bat. Anyway, it transpires he's into something very interesting. *Very*. It's dangerous, it's criminal and it's international. Perfect for you.'

Dan sat up and fingered the sleep-blindness from his eyes. 'I thought he was an airline steward.'

'He's from a rich family. His father *owns* the fucking airline. Young Altan wanted to be a pilot, apparently, but he was too dissolute to cut the mustard. Dad was so angry he put him into the cabin, where he has to work his passage if he ever wants to come into his inheritance. Dad likes to play King Stork.'

'So?'

'So, Altan gets his revenge by combining obedience with doing very naughty things behind Daddy's back.'

'What things?'

'He's a courier. He *carries* things out of Turkey that oughtn't to be carried. It's well organized and on quite a big scale. There's a contact man in London, also Paris and Amsterdam. They escort antiquities, wanted politicos, peasants with bits of themselves for sale as transplants, drugs, weapons – the lot. Airline staff are very privileged. What they know about getting stuff through customs and security is nobody's business. That's a story in itself.'

'I see. So what do I do?'

'You talk to Altan. You tell him you need a job, and you'd like to live in Istanbul, because you need a lot of money, and you fancy Lena, and –'

'I *do* fancy Lena.'

'So much the better. The main thing is, you've got to let Altan know that you want to get involved. Leave the rest to him. Don't forget, he *owes* you one. That means a lot to him.'

Dan nodded. He leaned back against the bed-head and closed his eyes. He saw Lena's smile, her cheek against his as they'd said goodnight.

*Join the pirates.*

He had no business taking this decision at such an hour of the morning . . . but he took it anyway.

# 2

*Was it a rubbish dump? No, this was on a grander scale: a vast council tip extending in every direction beyond the horizon. It had its hills and valleys, its clusters of rusty and despoiled artefacts, its slow plumes of smoke. You could shoot a film about Armageddon here.*

*Felix Trubshaw, twelve years old again, stood looking around him, bewildered. His bare feet made him reluctant to move, in case of snakes. It was time to go. He called out, 'Blanchard, where are you, you blithering idiot?' The words mocked him, throwing back an echo which died in his ear. Crikey, didn't he have an exam or something? Latin? Or Greek? He couldn't remember. Where was Blanchard? Gone back without him, like he always did. Where were his exercise book and his Osmiroid pen? Sir would get in a raging bate if he forgot his Osmiroid. 'Blanchard!' That was the bell!*

*As he scanned for his classmate he saw Blanchard's bulging form, in a smear of vision, labouring obesely towards him over the brow of a cinder dune. Blanchard looked grotesque in those grey, knee-length flannel shorts, an adult dressed like a child. The shorts so constricted his legs between crotch and knee that they must surely cut off the blood flow to his podgy feet.*

*'Trubshaw! Wait for me, you maniac!'*

*He could hear Blanchard's laboured breathing across the wasteground.*

*'I'm going, Blanchard. We've got afternoon school, remember?'*

*Nevertheless, he did wait. He always waited. Then Blanchard was beside him, his chest heaving and the words struggling out against the panting lungs. 'School? You can forget about school, buddy. I just lit a firework under it. Blew that shit-sucker into the ionosphere. Goodbye school, goodbye everything.'*

*There was the beginning of a whistling noise, like that of a falling body as its velocity increases. It was the wind. Looking upwards, Felix saw that the sky had taken on an unnatural, violet tinge and the landscape had darkened, becoming swept by cold air. Its emptiness suddenly reached inside Felix. He believed for a moment that he was looking at the whole world, and that it was desolate. Blanchard and he were the last two human beings, perhaps the last living things of all. He cocked his head, feeling a pain digging into his neck. Blanchard was still talking, but his voice had changed. It became British and adenoidal. Fuzzy. Said he was the Captain.*

*'. . . like to reassure you that there's nothing to worry about. Just a spot of turbulence. Just relax and in a moment the cabin staff will resume serving drinks . . .'*

*Bump!*

He felt his head topple sideways off the prop of his fist and forearm. Something was happening. He opened his eyes and glanced out of the aircraft's porthole. The plane seemed to be bucking in the air.

God. It could break in half, bits could snap off, like a section of the fuselage: *this* section of the fuselage. He'd read of such things.

He looked at the priest sitting next to him. He sat back and closed his eyes again. It could not go on. He must do something to stop the dreams. The dreams would be the death of him, and he wasn't ready to die.

To control his rising panic Felix had ordered three straight whiskies from the stewardess, and he tumbled them down his throat in quick succession. The drink liberated his tongue, and he had started gabbling to the priest.

'My problem is – what would you call it, aerophobia?' He shrugged. 'Whatever – you probably don't know what it's like. Expect you can fly with a hymn in your heart. But to me, this plane surging through the air at Christ-knows-what speed and at some God-awful height is such a frail little tube. You know, I often think if it broke in two we'd all spill out, like the little balls in a cold-cure capsule.'

He considered the thought while the priest stared at his breviary and held his counsel. Felix went on, brightening. 'There's one good thing about this particular flight, though, father. It'd be so convenient, if we started plunging to earth in flames – for me, I mean.'

The priest looked up at him from the untidy, leather-bound book, a look that said *I'm a priest, I challenge you to shock me.*

'What I'm saying is, you could confess me, couldn't

you? On the way down. Okay, I'd go splat in the Central Croatian Plain, or whatever that is down there, but by that time I'd have made my peace, my soul would be pure as the driven *sheep*, wouldn't it?'

The priest smiled. He flipped the office-book closed, but kept his finger in the place.

'I've done it in some fairly unlikely situations,' he said. 'I do recall a Roscommon sewage-farm one time. Then there was a woman who came up wanting it in the cinema, part way through *The Sound of Music*. But I don't think I've had anyone ask for confession at twenty-seven thousand feet.'

*Twenty-seven thousand feet.* Felix began to tingle with renewed fear. He had flown thousands of miles in his life, dozens of times on this route, and never without a tick of anxiety. But now, inexplicably, the terror was welling up uncontrollably. *I am restrained only by the thin membrane of social inhibition, by the thought: what would the other people think if I started to scream and run about in the cabin?* He shut his eyes but at once he saw himself tumbling through the air. He saw his head impact on a stone pavement, and explode like a faulty light bulb. Then he was at rest, his limbs splayed at impossible angles, his crushed brain void of thought or impression.

'Still, there's nothing *canonical* that says I couldn't confess you here, if you wanted.' The priest took a sip from the whiskey which the stewardess had just provided. Irish, like the priest himself.

In spite of the poofterish ring with the big gemstone

on his finger, he didn't look like a poof. He looked a bit like Rembrandt, in fact: big fleshy face, with a bulbous nose framed by mild grog-blossoms.

For a moment Felix was tempted. The sight of the priest's breviary had given him a rush of sentimental religiosity, as you might get in the street from a whiff of incense or a snatch of Gregorian chant.

*Bless-me-father-for-I-have-sinned-it-is – what? – twenty-five years since my last confession.*

In that time was there any sin he hadn't committed? Well, a few, of course. Sodomy, incest and bigamy had fallen outside his compass. But his conscience was a well-loaded raft. Greed. Deceit. Cowardice. Even murder – indirectly, at least. People had died because of what he did. You could argue they killed themselves, since most of them were already junkies. But he helped.

The priest had left him the option, and he almost took it. But any request for absolution died before he could utter it as the stewardess wheeled her trolley of duty-free goods past their row. When she bent over to Felix he ordered two hundred Rothmans for Sarah, and then said, 'Look, father, I was only joking. I'm rather heavily lapsed, I'm afraid. *Col-lapsed*, in fact. Sorry if it was in bad taste.'

The priest's face seemed to show he took it in good part, and he flipped open the book again to resume his office. Felix took another gulp from his plastic cup.

*

They stood together, Felix and the priest, beside the baggage reclaim conveyor at Yeşilköy airport. As they waited for their own bags to appear they watched a couple of suitcases from an earlier flight going round, unclaimed. They were shabby cases, barely held together with baling twine.

'Like lost souls,' said the priest.

Felix had a desolate thought. *That's how I feel. Unclaimed baggage. An empty suitcase.*

The priest called out with a shout of triumph, 'Ah! Here's mine, first off! Now that doesn't happen often. I must say goodbye then.'

He held out his hand oddly, not quite in the shaking position, but with the palm down and the monumental ring uppermost.

'Thank you, father. I've enjoyed talking to you.'

The man looked straight at him. 'Goodbye then. God be with you.'

He turned and headed off through the green channel of customs, raising a nonchalant, farewell hand. Felix saw the gemstone flashing from his finger under the fluorescent-strip lighting, and he suddenly saw what it must mean. The priest wasn't necessarily gay at all. He was a bishop, and that was his episcopal ring.

In her shabby apartment in Istanbul's old city – it was a slum compared to any place she'd known back home in Australia – Sarah took a sheet of heavy grey paper and laid it on the floor in front of her. She smoothed it out, using her flat hand like an iron. Miss Townshend had done the same, years ago in junior school. She remembered exactly how her teacher had selected a sheet of sugar-paper from the pile in the corner of the classroom and smoothed it down with her wonderful hands.

'A virgin sheet of paper is like a silence,' Miss Townshend had told them once, her mint-green eyes looking around the class. 'You must not think of it only as having an absence of writing or decoration. Blankness is a pleasure in itself. If you can learn the delight of blank paper, life will never be completely miserable.'

Miss Townshend was the one school teacher that Sarah recalled with clarity. She'd had red hair and fair skin and been pretty, though it was her hands that the child had particularly loved. As a ten-year-old she'd stood beside the teacher's desk and watched while Miss Townshend wielded scissors and paste, showing how to make mounts for the magazine-cuttings the children brought in each week to decorate the class. Miss Townshend's long-fingered, shrewd hands were quite unlike Sarah's own, whose stubbiness was compounded by bitten nails.

To this day, more than a decade after she'd last set eyes on Miss Townshend, Sarah used the picture-mounting technique she'd been taught.

The cuttings which Sarah collected were almost all images of defiance. A middle finger in close-up said *Up your arse.* A whale's tail rose dripping from the ocean. Two black athletes on the winners' podium held their gloved fists in the air.

Now Sarah sat cross-legged on the floor and let her hands caress the flat sheet. She had no card or coloured paper, and had to make do with the thick, grey wrapping used by many Istanbul traders. The corner *bakkal* let her have sheets for nothing and, actually, it looked much the same as the grey shades of Miss Townshend's sugar-paper. After a few moments Sarah dotted the centre of the sheet with paste and laid the newest addition to her collection on to it.

It was a reproduction of a British government poster which showed in muted colour a half-naked youth, standing against a brickwork background. His face was like a skull and his body as thin, almost, as a prisoner of Belsen. Yet she saw a beauty in him, and was stirred by his noble insolence towards the bastards who had stood him against that wall and shot him. It was all in aid of their mindless propaganda. They'd forced the young man to extend a forearm, displaying his track-marks. The caption read HEROIN SCREWS YOU UP, and, underneath, the words *Issued by the Department of Health*.

An hour later Felix Trubshaw's bag stood in the middle of her room while he, with legs apart and swaying slightly, stood with head cocked before the newly mounted picture. 'Where did this piece of shit come from?'

Sarah looked up. Felix never talked tough to anyone else, only her. It was one aspect of the role she played in his life. 'From a magazine. I thought he was rather fine.'

'Should be locked up.'

'Well, I'm sure he was.'

Felix turned and walked over to where Sarah sat in a grubby canvas chair. He reached down and took hold of her wrist, turning the arm to bring the inner, veined side uppermost.

The marks were not as obvious as those of the young man in the poster. For performances they could still be disguised under make-up, but she did not try to conceal them from Felix. He said, 'I've never questioned what you do, have I? But do you actually have to advertise it?'

'No one comes here, except you.'

'Well, do you have to remind *me* what you are?'

She said nothing, but turned her eyes towards the Johnnie Walker bottle that stood capless on the table. By Felix's bedtime most of it would be gone.

He let go of her arm and dropped on to the divan. 'All right, that was crass. I'm sorry. You always get me at my worst, you see. Always just before I have to see that bastard over the water at Polonezköy, or just after.'

He drained his glass and heaved himself up. She caught him on his way past her to the bottle, pulled him down and kissed his mouth, tasting the sweet whisky and the cigarette smoke. Then she let him go. 'This chick's got to dance tonight, old man. No time to sit around.'

She walked into the bedroom and opened a small dressing case which lay on the bed. It contained make-up and her costume. He stood replenishing his glass, still feeling the impression of her lips on his mouth.

'Still working the same place?'

'Yeah, still the same. But the manager doesn't like me, I can tell.'

'Look, you don't have to do it at all. I can afford to sub you, you know that.'

'No!' She was leaning into the mirror, teasing mascara on to her eyelashes. 'I'm in hock to you enough for this place. I'll buy my own food and . . . and other stuff. I'll do it with my own money.'

Felix stood in the bedroom doorway, a crumpled figure in his tropical suit. 'I don't really like you wiggling your body around in front of a lot of salivating blokes.'

'Well, it's better than whoring. And anyway, what do you care? You don't ever see me.'

'Would you like me to?'

'A girl would like her nearest and dearest to appreciate her art, yes.'

'No, I couldn't hack it. Sorry.'

Sarah smiled. In fact, she didn't want Felix to see her dance. It would alter their relationship in a way she knew she would not like. But sometimes she wanted to pretend they were a normal couple.

She slammed the tiny brush back into the mascara bottle and twisted the cap. She dropped it into her case with a decisive gesture and shut the lid. The precisely calculated fix she had had just before Felix's arrival was doing its stuff. She felt good, without nerves and without disgust.

'Well, don't wait up for me. Bye, sweetheart.' She kissed him again, almost in passing, touching his hair with her fingers, and then walked out of the flat.

Felix stood and looked at the door she had shut behind her. He raised his glass to it. 'Cheers, Sarah.' Then he turned his face back to the picture of the young junkie she had fixed to the wall. Now why on earth would she make a pin-up out of a wreck like that?

As the ferryboat laboured northwards, against the current of the Bosporus, Felix stood at the rail and sucked in the morning air. The breeze swirled with healthy *élan* down the seaway, and he could find in it no trace of the sulphurous coal smoke which tainted the city's atmosphere everywhere inland.

Sarah had come to the jetty with him. She'd been silent, as she always was in the morning. Sometimes Felix didn't know why he bothered with her. It was only if he caught sight of her face in an unguarded moment, when she didn't think he was looking, that he realized her humanity, and saw it as a reflection of his own.

Yes, she was an ex-whore and a junkie. But his money stabilized her. Without it she would probably be dead by now. Her pinched, abstracted face had looked ghostlike when he'd first met her that day in the Grand Bazaar, outside the money-changer's shop. Now, at least, it resembled living flesh.

He always stayed with her, when he came out to

give Blanchard an account of his stewardship and to get his instructions, but there wasn't much physical contact involved, not with Sarah. She was on a different plane from the physical, most of the time. He smiled. Sarah was his virtue, rather than his vice.

He thought again of Blanchard. Stewardship. He liked the Victorian ring of the word. It had dignity, suggesting a modicum of independent action, the exercise of discretion. But it was at some variance with what was, in fact, the case. What dignity was there in Nathan Blanchard making him hump shit, eat shit, lie down and roll in shit? Pig-shit at that.

Felix felt a phobic tremor. Everything in his life was like this, a train of uncoupled relationships. Yesterday the bishop, last night Sarah and now Blanchard and his pigs.

Felix loathed the whole idea of pigs, anything to do with them. They smelled to him like the septic tanks of hell. Their ramping snouts and niggardly little eyes, always on the look-out for something to bite, were pure evil. Even worse was their skin. The pig's nude skin, here grotesque tumescence, there flapping around in adipose ruches, disgusted and offended him in about equal measure. Pig flesh parodied the flesh-tones of his own race. To touch pig was unthinkable. To live in any proximity to pig would be the rankest horror.

He took a long drink from his hip flask of whisky and looked across the choppy grey-brown water at the Asian coast. Ninety per cent of these people were Muslim and shared his revulsion. How sick, in a nation of fifty-five million pig-haters, to be in business with a pig-fancier.

Not that Felix had to do with these pigs in any business sense. He was an accountant by trade and a carpet dealer by vocation. But carpet dealing is an overcrowded and cut-throat speciality, and Felix had long since given up the idea of making it pay. In practice he earned his living as the London agent of the export company of his old schoolfriend, Nathan Blanchard – Adventure Merchants Incorporated.

Each month, then, he underwent ordeal by pigs. He would fly over to see the boss and would suffer the same test, a stroll past the pig fields, a sty-by-sty guided tour, during which he and Blanchard reviewed the month's profit and loss account. Nathan must have sensed Felix's discomfort, must have enjoyed it. This gross knowledge, of discomfort inflicted and received from childhood till now, lay between the two men. It crushed any warmth between them like a sow overlaying and crushing her babies.

Pigs – *hogs*, he called them in the American way – were Nathan's passion. He loved them as some people love children, with sickly indulgence. He christened them with names out of American kiddies' picture-books, like Mary-Lou and Abner. He gave them all the adoration he had left over from his main obsession, the accumulation of power. It had been his one cavil about Felix's suggestion, a decade ago, that they bring the business out here to Istanbul. That was in the days when Felix's suggestions carried some clout.

'Well, in *my* opinion for what it's worth, Istanbul would be perfect, Nathan. You ought to get a domicile somewhere with a tax system you can manipulate. Now that the killing's stopped, you can really do things in Turkey. There's plenty of merchandise, I mean the kind we're interested in. Believe me, they give a massive welcome to anyone with pocketfuls of dollars. I know the place, I've shifted a lot of carpets out there. There'll be no questions asked. You just go in and start trading.'

'Okay, I believe you. If that was the whole of it, of course I'd be out there. But how the fuck would I get to keep *hogs* in Turkey? Won't gangs of mullah-maddened fundamentalists terrorize me? My hogs would be in danger, Felix.'

'Can't you keep them somewhere else? What about Switzerland?'

Nathan snorted. 'Switzerland? You're kidding. Where my hogs live *I* live. And that will never be in prissy Switzerland. So drop it, I'm not going to no Switzerland and I'm not going to no Turkey.'

It was Polonezköy that changed Nathan's mind. You could keep pigs without let at Polonezköy: in fact you were *expected* to keep pigs there. Polonezköy was a place devoted to the raising of pigs, an enclave of pigs in the land where the pig was virtually proscribed. The news of Polonezköy had made Blanchard mad with zeal. He immediately sold his Pennsylvania farm and bought the place here, moving bag and baggage, pig and piggage, into Turkey.

Felix tried to banish the thought of the pigs from his mind. The more serious matter of what to say to Blanchard was causing his heart to beat strangely. Briefly he saw himself as a cardiac patient, in intensive care, hooked up to bleeping instruments whose digital read-outs provided the only source of light – a cold, dim light. The image switched, and he saw again some of the instruments in his father's laboratory, big tin boxes with old-fashioned analog dials. He couldn't concentrate on anything this morning. He made a supreme effort and focused on his resolution.

He had made it five minutes after waking up this morning. He had lain beside Sarah as she slept and, looking at the ceiling, decided he must take her away. He was only prolonging a kind of living death, going on in this way. He must live with her and he must give everything else up. This was his resolution, but it was going to be hard telling Blanchard. Blanchard was vindictive. He'd known him slice a man's nose off with a kitchen knife, just for cutting a load of grass with sage. *A cut for a cut*, he'd said, laughing.

Felix's mind drifted again as the white and yolk-yellow waterbus zigzagged between Asia and Europe across the thousand-metre width of water. From the mouth of the Golden Horn she churned over to Üsküdar in Asia, and then returned to a jetty beside the palace at Dolmabahçe, the first stage on the European shore. She docked fleetingly higher up at Beşiktaş, and continued on, beneath the Bosporus Bridge, to the trendy village of Bebek with its marina and millionaire yachts. She then steamed past the walls of Rumeli Hisar, the first European stronghold built by Mehmet II, conqueror of Byzantium, before crossing over again to Asia. A few zigzags later she was casting off from the jetty at Emirgan, the tatty, over-developed little village on the European side where young Dan Barry was living with that girl of his.

Felix saw Dan Barry at least once a fortnight. They met in underground car parks, unfrequented cinemas, empty warehouses. But he'd never been to Dan Barry's home, never met his girl. It was another of those meaningless, vacant contacts, a dance with shadows.

From Emirgan the boat returned again to Asia and to Beykoz, where Felix would disembark. With dread Felix watched the wooden landing stage grow larger. Beyond it, he thought with a tingle of self-pitying excitement, lay Polonezköy, Nathan Blanchard and his fate.

'I ever tell you how Polonezköy came to be, Felix boy?'

Felix nodded emphatically. Nathan had told him repeatedly how this tidy, entirely untypical Turkish village had been founded.

'The Sultan of the Ottomans gave the land to a certain Polish prince, a mercenary who helped him kick the shit out of the Russians – I don't know – a hundred-some years ago. In Turkish its name means the *Polish Village*. This is no piece of sentimental historical crap: there's still Polacks living here, right? They never intermixed with the Turks, see? They sent back to Poland for their husbands and wives. That way they went on talking their own tongue, keeping their own traditions. I love that.'

'I know you do, Nathan.'

'You know I do! You know fuck. Was your Mom a goddamn Polack? My mom *was* Polish, right? This place is like coming home to me. I can eat Polish sausage made from hogs raised right here in the village. Here I can even raise hogs myself.'

He raised his eyes to the sky. 'I thank God for this place, Felix. This place is almost too beautiful.'

Felix was wondering when he should try to broach the matter. Not now, anyway. They were setting off towards the big field where several of Nathan's swine could be seen, still distantly but ever nearer. He felt like a missionary among cannibals, trying to gauge the moment for his sermon.

How was he going to say it? *Nathan, I'm handing in my resignation. Nathan, I'm leaving you. Nathan, what you're doing now is unacceptable . . .*

Now between trees which thickly overhung the track, they were passing the pig fields. He caught glimpses of Blanchard's porkers rooting in the ground or plunging their thick nasal cartilage into troughs of swill. He couldn't be expected to argue his case with conviction just now. It would have to be later.

They paused at a field's gate and Blanchard, leaning his three hundred pounds with farmerly leisure against the upper rail, turned to other business. 'How are things cooking in London? You get the last two kidneys okay?'

Felix remembered the pinched, roughly-shaven faces and heavy eyes of the two kidney donors.

'Yes. They were a bit heavily sedated, I thought. Someone's going to get picked up at immigration for drugs or something.'

'Wouldn't'a made a fart's worth of difference if they'd had no medication, Felix.' Nathan laughed in a brief, vicious bark. 'Boy, those two guys were stupid. One of them brought a goddamn sheep's kidney in a polythene bag from his home in the East. Thought that was what we wanted to buy. Jesus. I told him we don't pay six million *lira* for something we can get fresher in a goddamn butcher shop. Then the other guy –' He laughed again. A bubble of saliva had formed round the edge of his blubbery mouth. 'The other guy was so dumb he thought London was a suburb of Istanbul. I mean – Jesus! Did you talk to them?'

Felix's mouth turned down at the thought.

'You should, Felix, you really should talk to these poor bastards. You'd learn a hell of a lot about the Third World and why shit gets done there.'

The saliva bubble burst, leaving a ring of sediment at the corner of his mouth. He took the next item on the agenda. 'How about the last packages of scag?'

'The stuff was delivered. A hundred thousand was paid into Zurich. But Mossman's beginning to act strange, as if he was getting pissed off, as if he might stop taking the stuff off us. Kept talking about the profits he could make out of crack nowadays. Kept going on and on about crack.'

Nathan shook his head, 'Well, fuck him. It's no big hassle, Felix.' He moved to unlatch the gate.

'Well, it could be a hassle, Nathan. It's not easy finding people with that kind of money.'

'Forget it, Felix, we're in a new phase of development now.'

Blanchard's face, under its dead pads of subcutaneous fat, jerked into a grin of grade-A malice. It was time for his fun. 'What say I tell you about it later? Come and meet Trixie, my new gilt. She's a pure-bred Chester White all the way from the States, and the cutest little baby you ever did see.'

Felix swallowed though his mouth was dry, and followed through the gate into the field.

*He was watching with dread.*

*The horizon was a dark cut-out, with this soft illuminated scarf of colours at the back of it. The light seemed more solid along the edge of the land's silhouette, and became progressively diluted to starless nothing above. Needle-pointed minarets pricked upwards from the land. The stillness was pure.*

*Then came the voice, gashing the silence. It was a rasping, crowing, cow-hooting, voice of celebration and triumph.*

*YAAAHOOO! GO-FUCKING-GO YOU BIG FAT BABIES OH MY BABIES GO-GO-GO BLOW THE*

*FUCKERS INSIDE OUT AND TO BLAZES WAAA-HOOO! LIFT OFF! LIFT OFF!*

*The hysteria echoed metallically through the public address system, which he only now noticed. It was an outmoded rig of dented, bell-shaped speakers lashed to telegraph poles and street signs.*

The last words, uttered almost at screaming pitch, woke him. As he came round he was dimly conscious of running feet and panicking crowds and talk of minutemen and warheads. But these impressions immediately came apart in shreds, like wet toilet tissue.

Felix opened his eyes and immediately shut them again. He knew why he had this. It was a simple anxiety dream. Nothing to worry about.

He opened his eyes again and stared at the ceiling. He was in Nathan Blanchard's spare bedroom, the room which he always occupied, though never more than the one night at a time. The evening before, as always, he had briefed Nathan about London street prices, stock exchange movements, money exchange rates, police and political developments. This morning they would have a meeting over breakfast. Felix would receive instructions for the coming month, and would then depart to catch the ten o'clock ferry back to Eminönü. Some time between now and then he would have to deliver his message to the cannibal chief, the message that might end his life with Nathan. Or just his life.

It was a white, sober room, with a few items of Middle Eastern furniture in dark wood: a carved linen-box, a stiff-backed chair, a small chest of drawers with brass handles. The bed was soft and the sheets were crisp. It was decorous and in excellent taste. *Not Nathan's taste then*, thought Felix. Nathan's personality was better reflected in the overall aroma which, as sleep and the memory of his dream waned, Felix's nose recognized: *pig*.

He got out of bed and strode to the open casement window, putting on a swagger and holding his back straight as a guardsman's. This was the way to teach yourself confidence.

The smell was more pronounced by the window. Hurriedly he closed it and turned to the washbasin.

Felix sat down to breakfast alone. There were waffles and maple syrup and Cheerios, but today sweetness disgusted him and he asked for toast and butter. The maid was a raisin-skinned, gypsy-like figure, in a head-scarf, thick woollen cardigan and what seemed to be pyjama trousers under a faded cotton dress. She stood impassively while Felix tried to convey his desire, then shuffled away and brought back Polish sausage, black olives and a chunk of salty cheese.

He would have liked to ask for a drink but didn't dare. He'd hardly nibbled his first crumb of cheese when Blanchard's voice boomed through the house. A curious whizzing sound accompanied him into the breakfast room. He was wearing a shiny boiler suit in maroon nylon and the material gave out this noise as it chafed against itself. It was zipped up so tight under his chin that Nathan seemed nearly throttled, with fat pleats of flesh forced outwards above the collar. The legs of the all-encasing garment were plunged into a pair of gigantic yellow gumboots.

'Been seeing to my sweethearts. Clearing out their shit.'

Jutting unnaturally from his fist like a knife was an eight-inch cigar. He paused to stab it into his mouth before sitting heavily down at the table. Felix realized that Nathan was aiming for the Churchillian effect. The nylon was all wrong, of course, quite apart from the colour of the gumboots.

'That's how they know I love 'em, Felix. I kiss their sweet wet snouts good morning and then I shovel away their shit. You got to do it yourself. They're real clean beasts, hogs. Cleaner'n people. They respect you if you shovel away their poop yourself, not pay some jackass to do it for you. You gotta get their respect – it's all or nothing with them beasts. They like you or they hate you. And the hatred of a hog ain't something you want to have, believe me it ain't.'

Felix did believe him. Nathan Blanchard paused significantly and seemed to reflect. 'Knew one once bit all four fingers off of the guy that was feeding her. One clean take.' Nathan snapped his fingers and sighed. In the few seconds' silence that followed Felix wondered if this was his chance to speak up about the matter, but Nathan's face had glazed over and he would not be attending. Then he seemed to spark again. He put a match to his corona and Felix had missed the chance.

‘Now listen up, Felix son. I got something I gotta inform you of.’ Nathan leaned forward and blew a yellow, bilious draught of smoke. It streamed downwards across the table, deflected off Felix’s plate and spent itself against his face. ‘See, I found out about one of our people, and this is something I don’t like at all.’ Nathan’s small eyes had turned a degree or two colder. He aimed them at Felix like weapons.

‘No, I set a store by loyalty in my people, Felix. Loyalty. You know what that word means?’

Felix placed his hands on his knees. His breakfast lay almost untouched, had done ever since Nathan blasted into the room. Felix was no longer hungry in the slightest. He fixed his eyes on the back of his right hand. He was trying to look as if the definition of loyalty was etched into it.

Meanwhile Nathan’s exposition was gathering pace and verve. ‘Loyalty, my friend, is the same as trust. You got to have trust in the guy on top, the guy who God has placed on top, right? Loyalty is having openness towards that guy. The servant is loyal if he declares with truth whole and pure – whole and pure – everything he is, has been and hopes to be. Now –’

Nathan lowered his huge head and his tone darkened. ‘One of the people I employ is disloyal, Felix. One of the people *ain’t* what he says he is.’ His eyes rested on Felix’s untouched breakfast. ‘I got a *rat* in my barrel of cheese.’

He placed both palms on the table top, jacked himself to his feet and left the room.

He returned in everyday clothes – a worn, off-white suit and a shirt with lumberjack checks. He was holding a rolled magazine which for a moment he weighed in his fist, waggling it up and down. Felix thought he was going to whack him over the head with it. Instead he threw it on to the table. 'Look in that. Tell me what you think.'

It was a colour magazine of the kind put out as weekend supplements by the upmarket British press. Felix picked it up and leafed through. There was nothing remarkable here. Wind-surfers, BMW cars, almost nude models, stately homes. Then he came to a spread of black-and-white pictures which contrasted with the high-definition colour on every other page. In the largest shot a headscarfed woman, who appeared to be Asian, crouched on bare floorboards in a narrow hallway. Her mouth was open in – what? A scream, perhaps, or a yell of hatred? RACE WAR IN EAST LONDON – SCARE OR REALITY? demanded the headline.

Nathan rapped out, 'That's it. That's the one.'

Felix could not see the connection. 'Are we mentioned here or something? What've we got to do with this?' He looked at the cover date. 'Nathan, this magazine is over a year old.'

Blanchard was excited. His breathing came in snuffles and abrupt little snorts. 'Right! A year old. That is significant. Now look at who wrote that piece of shit.'

Felix looked, and saw the point. Photographed by Jack Bacon. Text by Daniel Barry.

*Daniel Barry*. A rat in the cheese? Felix could not quite compute the implications. 'It might not be the same –'

'I checked. The guy is a freelance investigative journalist. I spoke to the paper and they say they haven't heard from him since he turned in this piece. But he's the same age, same build, same hair. He's the *same guy*!'

Felix pushed his chair back and puffed out his cheeks. 'Well, I don't know what to say. I mean, he used to be a journalist, now he's working for us. So what?'

'Don't be stupid, Felix. The creep's an investigative journalist, so who d'you think he's investigating?'

'Well, yes, I do see that possibility –'

'Possibility? The guy's been doing the London run for almost eight months. He can blow away our balls with all this.'

'What are you going to do?'

Blanchard's fists opened and shut, working a pair of invisible grip-springs. His words emerged with difficulty, minced by his grinding teeth. 'Thank Christ he don't know much. And nothing about the new stuff. Thank Christ for that! Now he never will. Son of a *bitch*!'

The new stuff! It was the opening Felix needed. He looked at Blanchard. The fat American had worked himself up into a froth. He tried out some phrases, racing them through his brain like a teleprinter.

*I'm sorry, Nathan, but you're playing with too much*

*horror. I can't live with this. My father – well, let me tell you about my father . . .*

No! Leave dad out of it. Try another tack.

*Nathan, I've had enough. It was okay when it was just antiques, guns, the odd load of Semtex. But this is going too far.*

Going too far. Nathan would never see it that way. Let's face it, back in London people like Mossman knew the score. Blanchard was small potatoes, but he wanted to be a big player. He hadn't gone nearly far enough, yet. Nothing Felix could do would pull him back.

Blanchard was still talking, and Felix hauled his wandering attention back. The American had got on to the consequences of his discovery. 'You can tell Mossman to go and fuck himself, because there'll be just the one delivery and that's next week's, and that's the finish. Same deal with the kidneys. I got one more donor in the pipeline. We'll send the sucker through, but that'll be the last. We'll do it all on next Monday's flight. Then we close down all the operations except for the new one. Nothing is ever gonna jeopardize that baby. The rest, we put up the shutters.'

Felix opened his mouth but no words came out. He must have looked like a fish. He had no notion how to begin. He felt like bursting into tears.

The tight-ass Englishman had just left, thank Christ. Nathan Blanchard sighed, like a monarch tired of all his burdens. He had been thinking about whether the guy should be killed. Little creep.

He was leaning on the yard rail in front of Mary-Bel's sty, enjoying a few minutes' eye contact with his favourite old girl. He raised nearly all the stock in pig-folds over on his large field. But that was some distance away: you couldn't easily take a raincheck on them. For his own consolation, therefore, he kept a breeding sow in a customized cottage-sty beside the house.

Reaching every now and then into the bag of apples in his pocket, he would pitch one low and fast at Mary-Bel, who sat with the alertness of a baseball catcher. Whenever an apple came curving towards her, she moved her mouth with unerring skill into its path before gloving it cleanly in her gullet.

The sow's vigilant, fat-haunched posture in the sty's doorway called to mind one of those mountainous whores in the Galata Kerhane, the street of 'love houses' off the Yuksek Kaldırım. She had the same slovenly magnificence of those public women, to whom Nathan quite frequently had recourse in spite of his wealth. He liked fat whores nearly as much as he liked the company of pigs, and the grosser the better.

Mary-Bel emitted a grunt which seemed almost one of satisfaction, as if she had read his thoughts. Nathan smiled. He glowed inwardly. It was Mary-Bel who loved him best – wasn't that what really counted?

The same could not be said of the humans he employed. They were weak and he was strong, which was why they hated him. So be it. He made his mind up in a single neat skip of thought. When a herd's genetic pool begins to show weakness there's no use in trying to fiddle it back into shape. No, you got to send them to the slaughterhouse and start again with new stock.

So be it. He reached into his pocket for another apple.

# 3

An hour before dawn Lena awoke to the touch of her lover's mouth on her stomach. His tongue tickled around the rim of her navel and slithered inside its tiny, crinkled recess. She stirred and shivered. Dan's hand moved down her thigh, until his fingers fluttered into the hollow behind her flexed knee.

She rolled towards him. Her own fingers hooked into his bent arms and gently guided him up the bed. Her mouth mumbled blindly over his face. Both felt each other's skin as sleep-soft. They held and touched each other with eyes closed, their hands moving gently in rhythm. For a time they lay together somnolently, like two lazy country kids canoodling in the hay.

Then Dan was awake, and the softness compressed itself into tension and urgency. His muscles tensed. He placed his hand against her flank, pushing her to lie flat as his body slid over and across, and he forced himself inside her with spasmodic, gluteal thrusts. She turned her head to one side. 'Go easy. You're hurting me!'

But he seemed not to hear.

In a while the muezzins would begin their ululating dawn chorus. Lena lay in the dark with the upper bedsheet twisted like a hank of rope by her side. She used a corner of sheet to blot dewdrops of sweat from her upper lip and temples. Dan was already up and dressed in uniform. He was padding around the bedroom, collecting things and stuffing them into his overnight bag and briefcase.

In this half-light she saw him as a shadowy blur. She thought, *In a lot of ways this is what he is to me. I don't know the man. He's never quite in focus.*

It wasn't that she had any regrets. But now, whenever she made herself think about it, she wondered if the relationship was working. She liked him all right. But sometimes she was not quite sure what it was that she liked. He was good-enough looking, of course. He was kind to the child, who was taken out, played with, given presents. He maintained he didn't want to be Annabel's substitute father. But in their year together that is what he'd become. Perhaps that was what was wrong. Perhaps she didn't want him to be Annabel's substitute father either.

Making love – well, this morning the man had been selfish. But usually he was okay. He had his own kind of humour which, most of the time, she found childish and unfunny, but just occasionally a crack of his would hit the spot so hard she almost crumpled at the knees. It was then she felt the tug of his attractiveness, a flickering signal which told her he was worth hanging on to.

But the doubts hung about her like cobwebs. They had started to form about eight months ago, at the start of their first winter together. Dan became incommunicative. Lena had even found a bottle of tranquillizers in his sponge-bag. A chemical crutch. That really was bad. Dan had laughed it off. 'Darling, I'm overdrawn on my smiles account, I've just been borrowing from my doctor. No big deal, okay?'

Lena was unnerved by this sense of corners in the man's personality which she had not yet discovered. Oh well. She shut her eyes and watched incandescent images scribbling their atomic diagrams on the inside of her eyelids.

Dan Barry knelt in the hallway to lace up his shoes. In his chest bubbled the sense of power he felt each time he made a run. Sexual release had heightened it this morning. Standing up, he went into the child's bedroom.

Faint dawn rays tested the walls, giving an eerie light. At this hour the silent room seemed to amplify the thudding of his heart, so that it might almost be loud enough to hear. Dan had decided years ago that to be a good journalist you need to be an atheist. But sleeping children, their trustful breathing and sweetly pungent smell, evoked vestiges of a religious emotion in him, some potent incense made of yearning and wonder which he could never quite expunge.

Now he felt it intensely; for a second his vision swam in and out of focus. By mental effort he shook off the momentary weakness.

Her head was lolling over the edge of the bed. Dan bent and kissed it. Then he crouched, his shoes giving out an audible creak. Using only the tips of his fingers, he nudged the hot, damp head back on to its pillow. Annabel had her mother's fair fine hair, and it had slipped down across her face like a veil. He moved a few strands with his forefinger to clear her features. Without warning the child's eyes opened.

It was a blank, defenceless stare, lasting perhaps two seconds. Then her lips moved. 'You tell lies.'

He nearly rocked back on his heels. 'Who's that, darling? Who tells lies?'

But Annabel's eyes were shut once more and her breathing had resumed the regularity of sleep.

Dan backed the crumbling Ford from its space in the garage through wreaths of early morning exhaust. The pollution filled his nostrils and coated his tongue. The tension was growing in him: the fluttering in his abdomen, the powerful sense of gripping steering wheel, doorhandles, overnight-case in strong hands.

Leaving the car at the front of the block, he raced back up the stairs and into the apartment. Lena was waiting in her dressing gown.

'You forgot this again.' She had his shaving tackle. She bent to flick open his case, pulling out the black leather sponge-bag, zipped around the flap. 'New sponge-bag?'

'No! Don't –!'

But he was too late to stop her. She had already unzipped it and was looking inside at a brand-new Smith and Wesson automatic pistol which lay tucked into position, beside a cleaning rod, a spare clip of 9mm ammunition and a silencer extension. He looked at her, smiling, acting as if caught out in some petty deception. She just held the false sponge-bag open, as if she'd found a dead mouse in a biscuit tin. 'What's this? Whose is this?'

'It's a gun, obviously. It's mine.'

'Yours? Yours? Is it loaded?'

Dan took it out and turned it over in his hands. 'Yes. The airline says we all have to carry a gun. New regulation.'

Lena took the gun from him, feeling its weight and the rough-hatched grip of the butt. 'What's it for?'

Dan shrugged. 'Security. You know how aggressively macho these Turks are.'

'But you can't blast away inside a DC-10 in mid-flight.'

'Might have some bluff value, I suppose.'

'I hate this, Dan. It's obscene. Anyway, you've never had even two minutes of weapon training. What on earth are they thinking of, handing out these things?'

Dan knelt and tucked the bag away out of sight again. 'They're thinking of the PLO, the Grey Wolves, the Armenians . . . There's plenty of would-be hijackers. Oh! I nearly forgot. Toothpaste.'

As Dan went back into the bathroom Lena acted by instinct, without forethought. She knelt, nimbly unzipped the case and removed the gun. Gingerly tiptoeing into the bedroom, she slipped the pistol under her pillow, as smartly as a nurse smooths a sheet. Then, just as she was coming out of the room her hand swept up a bust of Beethoven from the top of the bookshelf, a small bronze casting which Dan had picked up as a souvenir during a Vienna stopover. She weighed it in her hands: it would serve.

When Dan came back with a tube of toothpaste and bent to find his real sponge-bag he also checked the small gun case, testing its bulk between finger and thumb.

'Danny, why can't you have a nice safe job?'

He stood and raised his hands to her shoulders. 'It's my vocation.'

'Airline steward? Don't talk crap. I can't see why you wanted this job in the first place. You could do anything.'

'You encouraged me, remember? Anyway it gives me twenty grand tax-free in pounds. And it's safe. Never had an incident yet.'

He kissed her mouth. Her lips still felt dry and corrugated after the night. She ringed him with her arms and pulled him close, enjoying his uniform's crisp contact through the nightdress. The telephone rang.

Dan released her and stepped back. 'I'll go. It's probably the company. Might be a delayed take-off.'

He looked at his watch and went briskly through to the tiny cupboard-like room they called the study, using a heel to nudge the door shut behind him.

She walked into the kitchen to make herself coffee.

As she passed the study door, Lena couldn't hear any words, only a tone of voice: Dan's voice, low and conspiratorial, talking fast from excitement.

Who was he talking to?

'You know what to do today?'

Blanchard's voice was level, but he sounded tense. Dan had never known him call on the morning of a flight.

'Yes, I know. I got the first item, the leather case.'

'Good. That must not go to Orange, I don't even want him to know about it. Remember, it's a special delivery. A guy giving the codename Red'll pick it up in the underground car park, like I already told you.'

'And the other packet –?'

'You will be handed the other package at the airport.'

'Which is for Trubshaw, I know.'

'No names, please. For Orange, okay?'

'Oh, yes, Orange. I forgot, sorry.'

'Have you forgotten who *you* are, too?'

'Oh no, I'm . . . er, this trip I'm . . .' His mind was blank. 'Sorry, I've forgotten.'

'Asshole. You're Green. Remember it. Red'll phone you in your hotel room two hours after touch-down. Be there.'

The phone clicked.

The typewriter on the desk had a sheet of paper in it. Dan rolled it out and read the first lines.

*The courier is the loneliest of criminals: he is appallingly exposed. His crime has always got to be the perfect crime for the penalties of detection are extraordinary. In one country his foot is on the gallows steps; in another his head is quartered by the rifleman's crosshairs . . .*

Lena, he was sure, believed Dan was writing fiction. But there was no point in taking unnecessary risks, and the page was crap anyway. At all costs he wanted to deflect the temptation towards melodrama. Dan crumpled the paper and dropped it in the wastepaper basket.

When he emerged a minute later Dan was hurrying. He was already behind schedule.

'Was it?' she asked.

'Was it what?'

'The airline.'

'Oh, yes, just checking I was on my way.' He looked again at his watch. 'I'm late now. Got to go, bye.'

He leaned forward and pressed her head between his cheek and hand, then almost ran out. Plunging down the stairs, he took two concrete steps at a time, and Lena tracked his hard shoes clattering uneuphonically all the way down to the lobby.

She went through the sitting room to the balcony and saw the Ford take off down towards the Emirgan waterfront. The road disappeared for a moment among houses, then emerged at the T-junction with the main highway. The last she saw of Dan was his shabby car turning south and accelerating along the Bosporus waterside, past the marina with its millionaire yachts, towards the city and its airport.

The sun was up by now, but still low in the sky across the Bosporus. It hung above the Asian hinterland like a sumptuous red fruit: a promise – or a threat – of the day's heat to come. She lingered, looking into the fiery track of light across the water, seeing how it briefly swallowed the ferryboats that crossed its path on their way to Eminönü or Üsküdar. From every direction, near and distant, the raw vibrato of the muezzins began, competing with each other like cocks, as they summoned anyone who'd listen to rise and pray.

Her coffee was ready so Lena went in. Going past the bedroom she remembered the gun. She slipped it from its hiding place and held it as you would a dead rat. The thing was repellent, its barrel a malevolent snout. Lena was possessed by unease. Had she done right in taking it? Her instinct told her it meant danger. But did her taking it increase or decrease his danger? She had no way of knowing. Why had the airline phoned to check up on him? That had never happened before.

She carried the weapon between thumb and index finger through to the kitchen. She wrenched open the fridge and rammed it in among the icy white fur of the freezer compartment, hiding it under a bag of frozen peas.

Dan was driving as fast as he dared. Rust might be

claiming the car's body but its engine was still young at heart. He looked at his watch each minute. At moments of stress he became frantic like this, muttering to himself and swearing aloud at other drivers.

Blanchard had sounded peculiar on the phone this morning. Dan allowed himself a moment of concern and wished he'd been able to see the guy. Nathan Blanchard's body-language was more articulate than his speech. Really, it was terrifying to have such an oaf to answer to.

He was doing it again! He laughed out loud at his thinking like an ambitious young salesman working his way up through the organization. He had to remind himself from time to time that he was an outsider, like a furniture beetle threading its destructive way through a chair leg. He was here not to sustain Blanchard but to destroy him.

All the same he could be branded a criminal. He *was* a criminal.

Dan reached the slip road linking the Bosporus road with Europe-bound traffic coming over the bridge. Even at this hour an incessant stream of juggernaut lorries rolled across the ribbon of concrete which modern engineering had slung so monumentally between Asia and Europe. Dan slipped the Ford behind two girder-carrying flatbeds on the inside lane, then moved out and accelerated past them. As he gathered speed a black Mercedes, which had been parked on the highway's hard shoulder, moved into the traffic stream after him.

The ring road takes traffic in a wide arc across the north and west of the city. At this early hour it was still a fast route, not yet clogged by commuters as it would be in about two hours. The route leaps the upper reaches of the Golden Horn, then sweeps away to the west, alongside the Sea of Marmara where, between the road and the coast, is Yeşilköy Airport.

By the time he joined the airport's approach road Dan's elation had begun to congeal into a hardening lump in his guts. He gripped the driving wheel tighter, but could not prevent his arms from shaking. Sweat trickled inside his shirt. All the time he swung like this, between hyped-up ecstasy and stomach-churning dread.

In the black Mercedes, driver and passenger swivelled their heads as they registered Dan's right-hand drive car stopped by the roadside at a slewed angle some three hundred yards from the terminal. They drove past and then pulled up discreetly in a taxi parking-bay. Both turned in synchrony and saw that the driver's door, on the side near the kerb, was open. The passenger turned to his companion, who shrugged.

Dan was hanging out of the door, retching. He'd eaten no breakfast and little enough last night. Nevertheless bile stung the back of his mouth.

He saw again Annabel's eyes. He saw too her mouth, moving almost imperceptibly to speak her accusation. *You tell lies.*

Gulping the air, still shaking, he pulled himself back

into the driving position. This would not do. He shook his head angrily and restarted the car. Two minutes later he slipped into one of the parking bays reserved for Anadolu Hava Yolları staff. He killed the engine and sat for a few seconds, motionless. That was better. He had himself under control again. He put his right fist on the doorhandle and reached with his left towards the case on the passenger seat. He thought, Never mind Annabel, there was something in Blanchard's tone which said *You Judas*. Or did he imagine it? He filled his lungs and released the air slowly, relaxing every muscle from cheeks to toes. Gradually, the sense of power and certainty possessed him again.

The two Turks from the Mercedes were making their way through the airport crowd. The taller was middle-aged and bald, with cunning eyes and a ballooning stomach that fought against the continence of his nylon shirt. He carried a plastic carrier with the words BUTIK OTOBUS printed on it.

The other, who was carrying a small brown grip, was a slightly built, scruffy individual with a week's growth of dark beard. He was dressed in a dusty, loose suit, collarless shirt and knitted green jumper. His trouser bottoms lapped under his heel in ragged strands. His shoes were cracked and they did not match.

The large man seemed to be mothering the other, pushing him through the dense throng of passengers. They approached the Anadolu Hava Yolları desk, where check-in for the London flight was proceeding.

The pot-bellied Turk stayed beside his charge at check-in and in the slow security line, but he could not go into the departure lounge. He said one last word of reassurance and pushed him gently through the metal-detecting gateway, then turned and walked back into the crowds.

He found Dan waiting for him at the prearranged place, beside the bank of payphones. He opened the carrier slyly, so that Dan could see inside. 'Felix Trubshaw will take these. You telephone, fix the meeting. Okay?'

Dan just nodded, took the carrier and left, disappearing into the crowd towards the airline staff quarters. The Turk did not move.

He remained looking over the heads which bobbed around him, like floats on a sea of bodies. He watched the eddying groups of passengers. A father was loudly arguing, thrusting an open airline ticket into the faces of his wife and daughter for them to read the truth of what he had to say. He saw, too, a couple of western Europeans passionately kissing, mashing their lips together with ferocious energy, standing in the midst of the crowd, but oblivious and alone. A knot of women in their headscarves stood tearful and withdrawn as they parted from a young man, probably their brother, probably off to Germany to disappear in the twilight of illegal work. At last he saw Altan Başkurt.

'I just showed your kidney through security,' said the big Turk. 'You must look after him in London all day. He can't go to the doctor's place until tonight, you know.'

'Yeah, I know. What the fuck am I going to do with him all day, Yakup?'

'How do I know? Take him to the movies. Show him the tourist sights. Find a whorehouse. Anything. He's not complaining. He's from some small village in Anatolia, you know what I'm saying?'

'I know what you're saying. He's a peasant, he was born in a fruit tree, right? And *of course*, he doesn't speak any English.'

'English? You're joking. He hardly speaks Turkish. But he knows what he's got to do. Stay in bed in London one week. Then we bring him home.'

'Minus one kidney, right?'

Yakup smiled.

'Wrong, my friend – *with* one kidney remaining, and rich besides. He goes back to his village and suddenly he is somebody. He owns a few animals now, a field of apricots, maybe. It's a small price for him.'

Yakup turned, waving his arm negligently in farewell. Altan called out to him. 'Yakup! I nearly forgot. What's his name?'

'Same as the other ones: Ali. Same as all the other ones. *Allaha ısmarladık*.' And he was gone.

Yakup walked slowly round the concourse until five minutes later he was back at the payphones. He stopped and dialled. At the second attempt he got a ringing tone and was answered with a grunt. In English the Turk identified himself. 'Hi, boss. Yakup. I'm at Yeşilköy. We all got here okay. Mr Dan seems a little nervous though . . . Yeah, he puked or something on the way here. Maybe he just got a sick stomach. I don't know. Anyway he got the shit okay. Altan's on the same crew, as you fixed it. And Ali went through into Departures. Yeah, no problem. *Tamam*, boss, *tamam*.'

Dan stood in the galley checking everything was there that he would need. Altan wouldn't stop talking about the British package tour courier he'd screwed last night.

'Dan, she was silky blonde, with real blonde pubes, the lot, you know? Just like in a video or something. But my God, she was strong! Her legs, they gripped like a wrestler, you know? I had to fight her to stay on top, fight her. A Turk doesn't like to fuck the wrong way round, it's not so dignified. So I had to fight her. My God! It was the greatest sex I had this year. So far.'

'Look, Altan, you're on a different job now. Bloody concentrate, will you? Have you counted the breakfasts yet?' He turned to the stewardess. 'Nilüfer, how many we got back there?'

'Just about half-full. We're picking up some in Paris, though.'

The captain could be heard in the cockpit, asking the tower if he could move to the end of the runway. He got the okay. As the massive airliner taxied into position, the engines were powered up for their thundering charge down the runway. Altan looked towards the rear of the cabin. 'Ali' was sitting impassively in his seat, showing no emotion. For a guy whose idea of travel had until now been the back of a donkey, he looked incredibly calm.

Dan took a vacant passenger seat and tightened his belt. He loved the excitement of being Nathan Blanchard's courier, but he loathed the servility of the airline cover-job. And yet it was only an act, he had to keep reminding himself. Soon he would have material for a book that would make the shelves at W. H. Smith glow. Dan Barry, international crime buster. He liked it.

The adrenal buzz in his stomach was still there as the DC-10 lurched into flight. Dan looked out of the porthole beside him. In the cloud he saw the image of a little girl with wispy hair covering her face. Then the hair floated away from the face and the sky-blue eyes fixed him accusingly. *You tell lies.*

It was a small child's wild, perhaps random, accusation. But no less true for that.

Lena was in the study. She flipped the pages of the Istanbul telephone directory till she found the page she wanted, and then dialled. She dialled five times before the system found a way to connect her.

'Hello?'

'Is that Alan Peters?'

'Yes, speaking.'

'I'm Lena Priestley, Dan Barry's friend. We met at the airline social at Christmas.'

'Oh yes?'

'I'm sorry to trouble you. You're not flying today?'

'No, grounded with a toothache, I'm afraid. Seeing the molar-minder later this morning. What can I do you for?'

Alan Peters was one of the British fliers, a first officer, working for Anadolu Hava Yolları. They didn't know him particularly well. He mostly flew the Saudi service, and, anyway, she knew Dan didn't much care for him.

'It's just something that puzzled me, something Dan said before he left this morning.'

She wouldn't mention it specifically, but she had to know whether the gun was a possibility, even in general terms.

'Shoot,' said Peters.

Lena frowned. He couldn't know –?

'I'm sorry, what did you say?'

'Shoot away, get it off your chest, your Uncle Alan is all ears.'

She sighed. Peters was the breezy type. It was one of the things about him Dan disliked.

'It's just that he said something about a security alert. That you were all being specially equipped for some kind of, well, attack. Something like that.'

There was a fractional pause. Then Peters came back in the same flippant tones. 'Dunno what the old boy's cracking on about. Attack? What attack?'

'Well, I'm not sure. Terrorist attack, I suppose.'

'Look, don't worry yourself. We've got first-rate

security checks. Nothing gets on those planes that isn't known about.'

'And there's been no warning, no alert?'

'Absolutely zilch, old girl. Just the normal background bitching by the security department. Unattended packages, people acting suspiciously. The usual. Tell Dan to pull the other one next time.'

'Well thanks, Alan. Sorry to bother you.'

She hung up.

As Lena rose and moved round Dan's chair her foot struck against the rattan wastepaper-basket which was tucked between the chair and the wall. The basket bounced over, spilling a small avalanche of discarded manuscript pages and used envelopes, each one compressed by Dan's fist into a tight, secretive knot of paper.

Lena went down on one knee to set the basket upright and scoop the contents back inside. But one screw of paper had been propelled beyond her reach. She collected it on her way to the door, and absentmindedly worked it open as she went through the hall and into the kitchen.

*The courier is the loneliest of criminals: he is appallingly exposed . . .*

Dan had told her he was writing a psychological thriller. He didn't say what it was about, and had positively forbidden her to read anything. 'When I'm ready you can. I hate the thought of you looking over my shoulder while I write.'

Now she felt sufficiently resentful of him to ignore the ban and ran her eyes down the page. There were three paragraphs, two of which described the insecurity of being a courier – a smuggler, she assumed he meant. The last lines were more personal.

*Often the only relief of tension is by laughter. The thought of being commissioned in these acts by a man who styles himself honorary church warden is particularly hilarious.*

So it was in the first person, she had gleaned that much, and it was about smuggling. Once Dan had told her the title – she didn't know if it was *the* title, really. But he said it was a cracking good title – *The Nobody Men.*

She balled the page again, dropped it in the kitchen bin and sighed. She was still no nearer understanding why he'd had a gun in his luggage this morning.

# 4

Mustafa, the hired assassin, had a good view of the aircrew dodging in and out through the short forward passageway, beyond which was the galley and, further back again, the cockpit. With its grubby grey curtain it made a sort of squeezed-together stage.

There were two stewards – one a Turk, the other British. They did not seem to get on too well. The Turk, he knew from Nathan Blanchard's briefing, was a son of the textile tycoon Başkurt, and an utter wastrel. When he'd failed his exams for pilot school the father had made him sign on as a steward, to drill some discipline into the boy. Başkurt Senior owned the airline, so there'd been no problem there. Young Altan knew a hell of a lot of international swingers, the kind whose loose change would finance an Istanbul shanty-dweller for a couple of years. But Blanchard had been smart to recruit this do-nothing to run stuff into western Europe. Altan's father kept him so short of cash he'd take any risk to stop the banks confiscating his plastic. Trouble was that Altan had been a naughty boy: he'd take stuff for his own use, making the weight up by cutting the rest with chalk. You didn't do that, not to a guy like Blanchard.

Blanchard seemed to like the other lad, the British one. 'He's sharp, got balls. I mean the Başkurt boy's got balls, but they're all mixed up in his brain, millions of tiny little tubes sucking at his thoughts, taking his head nowhere. But this English kid was promising. I mean, cool, never did stupid things.'

Blanchard picked up the magazine which lay on the desk between them. 'That's what I thought till I saw this.' He slapped the table with the magazine and threw it down. 'This disappointed me. It really disappointed me, you know?' His eyelids drooped as he relived the emotion. 'I felt betrayed. Kinda like Jackie Kennedy must have when she woke up, married to a president that had been fooling around with a thousand other women, and on top of that was *dead.*'

The hired assassin had laughed, until he caught sight of Nathan Blanchard's eyes. They had clouded over, promising violence.

There were three or four stewardesses, all good-looking girls, but only the slim, rare creature allotted to his section was actually beautiful. When she bent to offer him a drink from the trolley, he jerked up his chin in the gesture of refusal, and noted the tag on her uniform, just an inch above where her delicious left nipple must be. It told him her name was Nilüfer.

He had time to inhale her smell, a provocative compound of sweat and perfume, which put in his mind another Nilüfer, a whore he'd fucked once in Cyprus. He remembered her because he'd never known a woman fake an orgasm with such great ham acting – she jumped and wriggled under him like a hooked fish, so wildly that it got impossible to concentrate.

He'd climbed off her, pulled on his jeans and left. The next day he missed his shot at the Greek hotel-owner he'd been supposed to kill.

Ever since then he'd avoided sex just before a job. It was not a particular deprivation: to kill someone with skill and finesse was an alternative satisfaction.

This Nilüfer, though . . . she had great eyes – luscious, melted-chocolate irises. What had Blanchard said? 'There could be a stewardess or two hanging around. You can kill them too, if you like. You don't have to, just so long as you're secure. It might give credence to the idea of a political hit but –' He shrugged as if too modest to take credit for a clever touch. '– it's as you please. You're the professional.'

*As you please!* He was being given the option. Such a thing had never happened before.

He stretched, relaxed and closed his eyes. If anyone looked at him they would say he was asleep. But to be motionless and alert with eyes closed was a piece of basic tradecraft and he was proud of his mastery of it.

Dan had been disturbed to find Altan drafted on to this morning's crew. Normally Blanchard got Nazım Ali Bey to fix it so they stuck to different routes – Dan to Paris and London, Altan to Benelux. The reason was simply the division of labour. Altan knew the Dutch and Belgian contacts, but he didn't know Trubshaw or Mossman. Dan would be equally handicapped in the Low Countries. Had something gone wrong?

'What the fuck are you doing on this flight anyway?'

They were stacking breakfast trays in the trolley ready for distribution to the passengers.

'I got a job for Harley Street, a live kidney. You can see him down the plane – that peasant who looks like the son of a donkey.'

Dan bent backwards and looked along the row of seats. Among the scatter of passengers there was a scruffy individual of around thirty, in dusty and badly-fitting clothes, with a peaked cap on his head.

'I thought you only flew to Schipol and Brussels. London is *my* beat, you know.'

'Oh don't say it! Your British nose is out of place?'

'Yours will be if it ever smells this.'

Dan showed Altan his fist. It was a sizeable weapon, although Dan could not remember the last time he'd used it. At school, probably. He felt tempted now. The friendship between himself and Altan was flippant and insubstantial. He waved the knuckles past Altan's face, and the nose twitched.

It was a face which, Dan suddenly thought, resembled a hamster's. The eyes were dark and small. They glistened like beads, and his lower lip slightly underhung the upper. This along with his smooth skin gave the face a rueful, juvenile look, which presumably was the secret of the man's success with women. He just didn't look like a serious proposition.

Dan got on with his work, manoeuvring the trolley into the starboard aisle, but Altan had not finished. He reached out and tapped Dan's shoulder. With a sideways feinting jerk Dan evaded a second tap.

'Hey! We've got to get on.'

'What have *you* got for London? I know what you do for Nathan Blanchard, the same like I do. What you carrying today, eh, Dan?'

'That's for me to know.'

'You got a load of shit, yeah?'

Dan gestured through the bulkhead to where the peasant was sitting. 'Well, I won't be holding some peasant's hand across Regent Street, or catching his spit before it hits the hotel carpet, or showing him the function of toilet paper.'

Altan didn't like this. His half-hidden lower lip vibrated slightly. 'He's doing quite a good thing. He's giving up a part of himself.'

'Good? He doesn't know what he's doing, nor do you. You're a butcher's delivery boy. Now *help* me with this, okay?'

Altan jabbed an erect finger to within one centimetre of Dan's nostrils.

'I wish I never get you into this, bastard. I could do things to you. Bad things, know what I mean?'

'Not without the help of Daddy, and you don't want him privy to all your secrets, do you? That you're a gambling, whorechasing, scag-carrying dick-head. Daddy wouldn't love his little boy if he found out about all that, now would he? Now for Christ's sake, are you going to help me with these meals or not?'

Altan paused. His face was choked with anger, his lips rigid. He held the expression for a moment, and then his mouth split sideways into a grin, and he gave Dan a playful rabbit punch.

'All right, but Dan, not for *Christ's* sake.' He jabbed a thumb into his chest. 'This is a good Muslim boy, okay?'

On Mondays, Tuesdays and Wednesdays Annabel went down to Georgette Hamilton's playgroup in Beyoğlu, in a house beside the disused Anglican church.

It stood within the stone wall which surrounded the church and had originally been the vicarage. These days, with the church boarded up, the parish downgraded to the Consul-General's chaplaincy, and the once-fashionable neighbourhood only a little above a slum, the clergyman had abandoned it for a small flat in Cihangir, with sumptuous views of Seraglio Point.

So now the house's ground floor was home to a caretaker, the bull-necked Yakup, and his family. Upstairs were the two large rooms which Georgette had been allowed to take over on payment of a peppercorn rent. Here she had ample space for her small clients to express themselves.

With Annabel, there were just eight of these in attendance today, but the noise seemed disproportionate. Two small boys were wrestling, trying to bite each other's noses, in the home-corner, while a little girl knelt over a swaddled doll yelling a piercing lullaby into its plastic ear. The other children were distributed among various other activities and toys, thumping, banging, whimpering and singing in varying degrees of joy and distress.

Georgette, in dungarees and her hair pinned under a square of printed cotton, looked businesslike. She was perched on a wooden stepladder, fixing a strip of sugar-paper on which was glued a vivid collage of animals to the wall. With the job done she climbed down, very deliberately separated the two wrestlers and settled them to build something out of Sticklebricks. Then she crouched and greeted Annabel. 'Hello, darling. Go and hang your coat up on your hook outside the door, there's a good girl.'

She stood and said to Lena, 'You look peaky. Is that the word? How *are* you, anyway?'

'Dan's gone to London.'

'I asked how you are, you tell me about Dan. That's significant, right?'

'Right. I'm completely pissed off with Dan, actually.'

Georgette's face was suddenly alert. 'My dear, what's he done?'

Annabel returned and leaned coyly against her mother's legs. Lena took a brush from her bag and dragged it through the child's hair several times with strong, determined strokes. Then she patted Annabel on the bottom.

'Go and play, Annie darling. Look, the Playdo's over there. Don't you want to make something with Stephen on the modelling table?'

As Annabel toddled off her mother turned back to Georgette.

'The guy's not levelling with me. I can't put my

finger on it, but he's behaving oddly. You know, originally he was an actor. I guess he's a *compulsive* actor.'

'I thought you were pretty much hooked on the man?'

'I am, I was. Oh, I don't know. He's distant, he's monosyllabic, he's never home. And now he's got a gun.'

'A *gun*?' Georgette spoke distractedly. She'd heard a more-than-usually discordant note emerge from the cacophony behind her. Now she moved as swift as a cat towards the trouble.

'Maisy. Now you know you've got to share. That's how we do things here.'

She picked Maisy up and took her into the home-corner where Maisy started to cry, quietly at first and then with increasing enthusiasm. Lena followed them over.

'Sure. Some kind of automatic, with bullets in the butt. He never told me, of course. I found it in his case as he was going off this morning. He says the airline has issued them to all its staff, as a security precaution. But I phoned one of the pilots who's off-duty today, and he said that was news to him.'

Georgette was drying Maisy's tears and helping her blow her nose.

'Well, that wouldn't surprise me. I mean, the airline wouldn't want people to know if they had issued fire-arms.'

'But is it likely they would issue them? Can you see

the likes of Dan blasting away at a hi-jacker at thirty thousand feet? He's had no training. Jesus.'

'Could be for his own personal protection. I mean he could – well, no, that's not very sensible.'

'He could what? Come on, Georgie! What?'

'I mean he, any of them, could become targets for one of these terrorist groups. You must've seen the graffiti? It's all over town at the moment. They've covered a wall down in the street below us with it. And airline offices sometimes get to be targets. So why not – I'm sorry, Lena, but this just happens to be a likely scenario – why not aircrew, especially while they're on overseas stopovers?' She stood up and put a hand on Lena's shoulder. 'I'm sorry, my dear. That wasn't meant to scare you.'

'Well, I guess it's possible. But I still think Dan Barry's a shit for not sharing this with me – this and about a million other things.'

'Look, he didn't want to frighten you. What'd he say when you found it – the gun?'

'Oh, then he levelled with me. At least he gave me that story, which I'm not sure isn't bullshit, about the gun being airline issue.'

They were interrupted by a voice shouting from the stair head. 'Hello!'

In a reflex, Georgette's hands went up to pat her hair and straighten the kerchief.

'That's Justin Fuller, the new consulate chaplain. He's the playgroup committee chairman. Have you met him? He's quite something!'

Lena shook her head and Georgette shot her a wide-eyed look, as if to say, *Stand by for a surprise.*

The new chaplain came stooping through the doorway, and at once every child in the room piled into him like football players. He began distributing a selection of candied fruits and nuts from a bag which he drew from his pocket.

Lena's idea of a vicar was someone possessing thin, sloping shoulders, a pointed head and smooth, waxy hair. Justin Fuller did not come from this mould. He was huge, at least six foot six, with a bush of tangled red curls, a nose that at some stage had been not so much broken as mashed and a great cleft jaw. He looked, she thought, like a mythical Hibernian giant. She also saw, in his eye, that gleam which denotes either the mischief-maker or the fanatic.

Justin Fuller straightened, squashed the paper bag in his fist, and inclined his body slightly towards Lena and Georgette. 'Good morning, ladies.'

The wall which enclosed the church and house was broached by a heavy wrought-iron gate. Justin Fuller pushed it open and stepped aside to let Lena out first. She glimpsed his eyes, as she passed, tracking down her body as far as the ground and then up again to her face as men do.

'Have you ever seen inside the church?'

'No. No, I haven't.'

'It's fascinating. Designed by Street, you know, who built the Law Courts in the Strand. It's like a little fragment of high Victorian London misplaced: quite ludicrously out of sympathy with anything around it.'

Lena looked up at the sullen, undressed granite of the church's walls. 'Yes, it certainly seems bizarre.'

'Only in this context. That architecture belongs in Lewisham or Pimlico, not Beyoğlu.'

Lena did not know London and could not comment on the justness of this remark. 'Is it ever used for services?'

'Oh no, it's been deconsecrated for years. There are those in the diocese who would like to redevelop it.'

'Oh, I hope they never will.'

'I can't imagine what they'd build here. This isn't exactly a prime site for an office block.'

They looked around at the jostle of neglected houses pressing in on the church on every side, houses whose occupants were, if not at the bottom of the social heap, then perilously close to it.

'No, luckily a useful role has been found for the old place as a warehouse. We let it to a local businessman – a countryman of yours, actually.'

'Oh yes? I don't really know any businessmen.'

'He's only been using it for six months or so, don't know what for, don't inquire. He's done a useful repair job on the roof already, though.'

They looked up to the roof. The twin turrets which flanked the gable end matched in shape the much larger belfry tower which rose above and at one side of the main body of the church. Justin helped Lena over a place where the street had subsided and past the tattered little *cami* which abutted the Anglican churchyard wall. He jerked a thumb at the mosque and chuckled. 'That's a squirt of a place, isn't it? I think of it as the Prophet's guard-post – put there just in case we Christians forget where we are. Oh, and look. There's a different sort of reminder.'

They had reached the junction between the short alley leading to the church gates and a street which rose precipitously to the top of what used to be Pera, the old European quarter. A splash of white painted writing had been daubed across the rendered wall of the house opposite them.

Lena turned to Justin. 'Can you read it?'

'No. But I know what it says. I got someone to translate it the other day. It goes something like *Musa Dağ swears death on the gaolers of Krikorian.*'

'Musa Dağ?'

'It's the name of a mountain – Mount Moses. It was an Armenian centre of resistance during the massacres of 1915, when the Turks tried for the *n*th time to exterminate them. Horrible business. The name's been adopted by this terrorist group, which has sworn to exact a slow and painful revenge: they're supposed to be highly active in the city at the moment. This Krikorian is their leader – a very charismatic chap apparently. He was arrested last year.'

'What do they do?'

'Oh, occasionally they rub out an industrialist or a political baron. Not very nice people. Krikorian's supposed to go on trial next month.'

'And what will happen to him?'

'Oh, I'm told he'll be executed, just like that Kurdish chap last week. They did him for terrorist crimes, they'll do the same for Krikorian.'

'I can't keep up with the various opposition groups. There's so many causes.'

'That's the trouble. All the different ideological hues from Communist to neo-Nazi. The last of the 1930s-style Fascists are here. There's a particularly charming bloke who used to hold Mussolini-like rallies apparently. He always had a leashed wolf by his side. He also had a rabid youth organization, the Grey Wolves, modelled on Hitler's Brownshirts. Then, of course, there's a whole raft of national and religious minorities: Greeks, Kurds, Syriacs.'

'Anglicans?'

Justin laughed. 'Oh, we don't rate very high on the thermometer scale of ethnic hot potatoes. I think my congregation last Sunday was seven souls.'

They turned up the street and Justin pointed out the blue enamel plaque giving the street's name. 'The guy who translated the graffiti also told me the street's name. *Kumbaracı Yokusu* – Bombmaker's Rise. I don't know if there's any necessary connection!'

He gave out a booming laugh.

'Where are you off to now, Lena?'

'The fish market, I've got to buy food for tonight. I'm coming back later to collect Annabel.'

'It's on my way. I'll walk with you.'

They reached Istiklâl Caddesi, the street which was

once La Grande Rue de Pera. Strung along its length were the old embassies – lordly buildings from the days when Istanbul was the capital city of an empire. The Pera district had then been an epicentre for all the plots and counterplots by foreign powers, greedy to manipulate the ramshackle structure of the Ottoman world.

'I thought you were new in Turkey, Justin?'

'I am. Arrived three weeks ago.'

'But you seem so clued up on the scene here.'

'Well, I had a week's briefing at Church House back in London. They filled me in theoretically. I read some books and a fat cuttings-file, and had a crash course in Turkish smalltalk. But of course the theory does nothing to prepare you for the shock of reality, does it? Good lord, what a gorgeous cake shop.'

He had stopped outside the Viennese *pastahane* Markiz. Its window displayed tiered trays, loaded with cream and chocolate cakes, and beyond these could be glimpsed groups of well-heeled Istanbul ladies, with a few suited and elderly gentlemen, tucking in to their mid-morning treats. The walls were tiled from floor to ceiling with giant art-nouveau scenes depicting the seasons. Justin Fuller was captivated. 'I never noticed this place before.'

'Oh, it's notable. It's very what they call Levantine – that means it belonged to the world of European residents of the city, whose common language was French. There's hardly any left now, but the atmosphere of their time still hangs about the place.'

'Well, it's marvellous, and I've got to try it. I collect cake shops. And I wouldn't mind getting a closer look at those amazing tiles. Come in for a coffee. Have you time?'

'It's very expensive.'

'Oh, never mind that. Come on.'

So she did.

From his usual dark corner at the back of the shop, Nathan Blanchard saw them enter. He had in front of him the *Herald Tribune* and a cup of creamy coffee, alongside a wedge of cream gâteau that would have chocked the wheels of a B-52 bomber.

He knew the padre, of course. As church warden he had naturally paid his respects when Fuller arrived. Lena he knew as Dan's girl, the one he had to thank for bringing the creep to the city in the first place.

The worst of it was, he'd *liked* the guy. One day the organization would be big. It would cover the globe like a multinational company: it would *be* a multinational. Then he would need more personnel at the top, dynamic young executives in sharp suits who could make decisions, who he could delegate to. He had already started looking at Dan in this light, as a possible – what did the Mafia call them? – a *consigliere*, a right-hand man for the future. He'd even been on the point of offering him a job organizing outlets for the new merchandise. Thank Christ he hadn't let him in on it yet. But the young man was cute, no getting away from it. Too cute. And now he, Nathan Blanchard, found himself betrayed by him, a sneaking whipper-snapper boy.

A welling of emotion in his breast caught Nathan unprepared. His eyes watered and he had to snatch up a paper napkin to catch the budding tears. He had really settled accounts with the guy, that was something. He wondered briefly whether he should have sent him out with the usual lot of smack. Oh well, he didn't know what he had, and Mustafa would be glad enough of it, in lieu of his fee.

Blanchard looked over to where Lena and Justin were choosing a table. That was one beautiful chick, like some model she was. He preferred them fat, but she was a tasty morsel all right, for a lean one. Was she a part of Dan Barry's betrayal? Well, she'd be suffering when the news came back to her this evening. If she had known what Barry was up to, that would be punishment enough for trying to fuck with Nathan Blanchard.

Mustafa the assassin shuffled with the others from the Anadolu Hava Yolları DC-10 at Heathrow and walked uncertainly along the antiseptic walkways which funnelled a continuous stream of arrivals towards baggage reclaim and customs.

He played the part of the first-time visitor to a western European country. Everything here was bigger and more systematized than anything his character had seen before. So he wore a bewildered look on his face as he stopped from time to time, with other passengers jostling impatiently past him, to thumb through papers drawn from his pocket or check once again in his passport. None of these documents, of course, bore any relation to his real identity.

The real data – the instructions that mattered – were on file only in his brain. From time to time he retrieved them. *Names of those to become corpses . . . location . . . manner of death . . . job to be clearly franked* Musa Dağ. *Collect tools from . . .*

'You collect tools from Dan Barry himself,' Nathan had said. 'He thinks he's delivering a piece for a customer – beautiful, isn't it? If you need any more firepower, you can go to Darren Knight's place at Haggerston. You know him, don't you? Got to go to his place personally, understand? Darren never discusses business arrangements on the phone. Personal calls only. And C.O.D.'

Mustafa was suspicious about this. He knew Darren, of course, a nice enough guy but a dabbler. Blanchard liked him, though.

'Look, he's experienced, and his merchandise is fantastic. I'd trust him with my life.'

But the cockneys were not dependable, were they? Well, he'd spent a lot of time in England, he'd other contacts if Knight turned out wrong.

A collective rustle of clothing, a clank of duty-free bottles, and another surge of arriving businessmen and tourists overtook him. He scuttled nervously to the edge of the corridor to let them go by. Then he ventured onward towards the customs hall.

# 5

Overnight it had rained a little, enough to wash down the summer dustiness and confer a transient gleam on the morning. Dan poked his head out of the DC-10's forward door and filled his lungs. The Heathrow air might be spiked with engine fumes and all sorts of petrochemical smells, but it was damp and cold and felt a hell of a lot better than the reprocessed product he'd been breathing for the past three and a half hours.

He looked around. The last of the passenger transports was half way to the terminal by now, and the cleaning and maintenance crews were already swarming up the steps. Dan waited for the one in baggy overalls who would be first up. His name was Clark, he was black and lifted weights for fun. Dan stepped back, as if to let Clark past. For no more than a second Dan and the massive West Indian stood nose-to-nose in the narrow passageway, walled by aluminium lockers. Then Dan retreated to the first-class seats, where the rest of the crew were waiting for their customs check. Clark, pulling his overall into comfortable shape around him, moved smoothly past without looking down.

Two hours later Dan was standing in a hotel room in

west London, unwrapping two parcels crudely made from pages of *Hürriyet* and *Cumhuriyet* and tightly bound with quantities of sticky tape. There had been no need to bring these through via Clark. The British customs were hardly interested in antiques. They were more occupied with whether crews helped themselves wholesale to the duty-free.

The gun, in its mock sponge-bag, was another matter. That would quickly be revealed by an X-ray check or customs 'rummage'. Even aircrews' baggage was subject to such displays of paranoia, sometimes. Older stewards remembered the days, not so long ago, when airline crew were hardly ever searched at airports. Nowadays, the Clarks of this world were essential relays in a well-greased system. Clark had received the leather case at the top of the aircraft steps, and given it back to Dan on the other side of the barrier exactly sixty minutes later. Dan was not curious about the gun. He let it lie now in his flight bag, the case unopened. Guns did not interest him.

But he did fancy a look at the objects he would later be delivering to Felix Trubshaw. He first cleared a space on the hotel-room's coffee table, ripped the newsprint away from the first figure and placed the piece reverently on the table, then tore at the cocoon of its companion. With both figures revealed, he balled up the mass of paper, stuffed it into the wastepaper basket and stood up to admire the fruits of his smuggling.

After a moment's contemplation he exploded in laughter.

Dan had occasionally tried to find out the provenance of the articles he was carrying. Blanchard's answer was always much the same.

'Statuettes mostly. Bits of fired Hittite clay. Very ancient stuff. The museums and private collectors can't get enough. Demand's bigger'n supply five hundred to one.'

Dan found this imprecision irritating. Like a good reporter he preferred to be answered with clear facts. 'I suppose there are laws restricting export.'

'Restricting? They don't let shit through. The Turks just hate to have these little heritage gizmos pass their borders, for which you can thank the good Lord because if they didn't we wouldn't have a business.'

Blanchard placed a fleshy hand on Dan's shoulder. It was mottled and fish-like. 'You're very valuable to me, young Dan, I want you to know that. Airplane crew were ordained by God Almighty to smuggle, and your old flight-bag is the perfect courier's conveyance. Plus, as you're already making these flights – I mean it's part of your job, right? – I pay no airfares, and there's all the more in the kitty for all of us. It's beautiful.'

Basking in satisfaction, he put the wet end of his cigar to his lips and sucked like a baby.

Dan picked up one of the two pieces in front of him, and shook his head, still laughing. This was the best yet. It showed a man, made of dusky clay, who knelt in a praying monk-like posture, with hands held slightly apart in front of his stomach. Except that he wasn't praying.

He was about ten inches tall, squat, generously paunched and with thick haunches; his black-tinted hair and full beard were sculpted in highly stylized curls, the beard rugging his entire diaphragm down to the navel. But there was nothing stylized about the projection which angled out like a pan-handle from the guy's crotch. It seemed completely realistic – a magnificent, lovingly modelled, fully-extended hampton. Engorged with blood, its glans was aburst like the face of a garrotted criminal. Along its shaft, the complicated anaglyptic route-map of veins was painstakingly modelled. This was a king-size hard-on, and Dan was in no doubt that its owner was actually a king.

Whether the companion piece was queen or harlot he couldn't determine. Also naked, she knelt on all fours to receive her monarch, but Dan didn't know which way round to place her in relation to her mate. The bottom was receptively uptilted, but so, on the other hand, was her face with, as an additional exciting touch, the tongue lolling lasciviously down over her chin.

He placed the pornographic pair in one of their alternative positions on a shelf and stood back to admire the effect. Then he tried them the other way.

Where these items came from, Blanchard never said. Turkish laws against exporting antiquities were not the only reason for his secrecy. Dan had researched this. He'd taken books on the four-thousand-year-old civilization of the Hittites out of the British Council library. He'd visited Istanbul's Museum of the Ancient

Orient near Seraglio Point. So he knew how incredibly rare Anatolian pottery from the Hittite period was. Nathan must have discovered some secret cache like the Dead Sea Scrolls, or those sunk East Indiamen he'd read about whose cargoes of mint Ming porcelain were occasionally recovered and auctioned at Sotheby's.

There was a difference, though. Blanchard had to keep quiet about his find. Apart from what the government in Ankara would do if they caught him, he needed to release this Hittite treasure-trove in patient drips. By flooding the market he'd only sacrifice the chance to make fabulous prices.

Dan sat down by the telephone. Felix had usually rung him by this time, to arrange collection.

A secret Hittite hoard wasn't the story he'd gone after. Dan *knew* Blanchard moved heroin and cannabis out of Turkey, but he'd not yet been invited to take part in the operation. Blanchard's business was strictly segregated, apparently, with the antiques, the weapons and the drugs all being handled by different couriers. It was a matter of trust, he supposed. You proved yourself on the minor trade, and then graduated to the serious stuff.

These figurines were not too serious – not when you remembered that the Turkish penal code specified anything up to death for those caught doing large-scale drug dealing.

A set of knuckles rapped on the door.

'Who is it?'

'Dan, my friend. It's Altan.'

Dan unlocked the door and opened it a crack. Altan pushed and Dan yielded, letting the door swing open. The Turk strolled cockily in.

'I'm sorry, I have to ask a favour, Dan. I hope you didn't mind about the teasing on the flight, by the way. No soft feelings, eh? Look, it's this kidney I got. He's not got to go in Harley Street until this evening, seven-thirty. That's when the doc gets through with his regular work. So I got to mind this guy all day. I mean it really pisses me off, I want to take Nilüfer to a movie this afternoon.'

'You could take him too.'

'He'll be in the way, won't he? He won't understand nothing.'

Altan was looking around the room: only then did Dan remember the two copulative figures.

'Altan, I'm not looking after him for you. I've got things to do too. Now would you mind –'

'Blanchard's gonna kill me if he goes missing. I can't leave him, can I?'

'Don't then. Why can't you just keep out of Nilüfer's knickers till you've got shot of him? We're here till tomorrow afternoon.'

Altan was still moving around. 'You're a shit, Dan. Why won't you do this little thing for your friend? You only go and sit and watch him for maybe two hours or something. You could read a book or – Hey! What are these? Well now, they're quite a beautiful pair of fuckers, aren't they?'

'They'd be bound to appeal to you, I suppose.'

Altan reached out a hand but Dan moved quickly to his side, pressing down the outstretched arm. 'I'd rather you didn't touch. They're valuable.'

'You're telling me. Allah! These are bigger than anything I ever couriered. And much more beautiful. They've really done beautiful work, haven't they? But may I look?'

'No. I'd rather you didn't. These things aren't used to having your lecherous twentieth-century paws on them. I don't suppose you know where Blanchard gets them from? My theory is he's got some sort of secret supply. He's discovered a Hittite tomb or something?'

Altan let out a loud percussive laugh. 'A secret tomb! You mean to tell me you don't know?' He looked at Dan incredulously. 'My God! He really doesn't know!'

He pushed Dan aside, reached out his hand and grasped the tumescent tool of the king. Then he swung round.

Dan was horrified. 'For Christ's sake, Altan, watch what you're –'

With a malleting motion Altan struck the edge of the coffee table with the figurine. A dull crack, then it shivered into pieces. Dan looked at Altan incredulously. He could not look at the heap of crumbly brown potsherds on the table-top.

'You bloody, fucking maniac!'

He jumped towards Altan and pushed him on the chest. The Turk stepped back.

'That thing was probably worth – I don't know, thousands!'

Altan was still laughing. He still had the snapped-off penis, intact, in his fist. He waved it in Dan's face. 'This thing was rubbish, my friend. Rubbish except for being a very clever container.' He pushed the hollow phallus on to his forefinger and waggled it about speculatively. 'Or maybe some kind of, you know, substitute.'

'But it's three-and-a-half-thousand years old.'

'I should doubt if it is that many *hours* old. I know the guy who made it. His name is Mahmut Doğan, and you will find him in the Kapılı Çarşi – the Grand Bazaar – in Istanbul. He is a genius, man! I mean, isn't this the most beautiful work you ever seen?'

By now Dan had looked down at the table and, in a glance, understood how he had been duped. What had seemed to be made of solid clay had been hollow. What had seemed a precious work of art had been nothing but a disposable vessel for a much more precious commodity. Among the broken bits and rubble on the table was a clear plastic bag stuffed full of that commodity. It resembled a bag of salt.

Altan had adopted the tone of a doctor telling his patient to make the best of it. He gestured at the table. 'You can just tell Felix you broke it by chance. It is good at last to let them find out that you know what is inside, right? Well. I go to amuse this fucked-brain peasant for all the day.'

Dan shut his eyes. Altan was becoming cockier than

ever. Now he reached for Dan's wrist, pried the bunched hand open and slapped the Hittite's sundered prick into his palm.

'I don't need this. Maybe you can use it.'

The door slammed.

At last Dan gathered the broken shards together and dropped them in the wastepaper bin. The packet of heroin posed something of a problem. From the bin he retrieved a page of crushed newsprint, wrapped it up, and looked around him. What to do with it? He was still hesitating when the phone rang.

'Hello. Am I speaking to Mr Green? This is Mr Red here.'

All Nathan Blanchard's code names were colours, but the codes changed on every trip. Dan experienced a momentary blank. Christ, who was Red? Was it Felix or the customer for the gun?

This did not sound like Felix, it was more like a foreigner's voice. And then Dan remembered, Felix was Mr Orange today: he'd been Mr Red two or three trips back. This Mr Red was the man to whom Dan owed delivery of a gun. He relaxed a couple of notches.

'Er – Mr Green speaking.' He hated these ridiculous code-names anyway. They made him feel like a character in a children's boardgame. 'Where do we meet?'

'At the place arranged. Fifteen minutes.'

The line went dead.

Dan looked at his watch. He had fixed to meet Jack

Bacon forty-five minutes from now in an Earl's Court pub. He had plenty of time . . .

He entered the hotel lobby with the fake sponge-bag under his arms and saw Nilüfer. She was walking to and fro, looking imperiously about her like a shop floorwalker. She glided towards him excitedly across the marble floor.

'My God, Dan! We have lost the kidney. The peasant has wandered off somewhere, just when we were going to take him to eat lunch.'

'Where's Altan?'

'Looking. Oh, if you see that kidney, you must let us know, please?'

Dan waved a hand amiably, tucked the black leather sponge-bag more firmly into place and took the door which led down into the underground car park. Altan's troubles caused him no grief whatsoever.

Ten minutes earlier Mustafa had paced the distance into the furthest recess of the garage, where the shadows would be blackest. The walk from this furthest parking bay to the pedestrian stairs must be forty yards. He would have adequate warning of Dan Barry's arrival.

What light there was in this vast underground cavern came from flickering phosphorescent strips tacked to the concrete ceiling. He walked into the corner of one of the bays and found a length of copper pipe. Deliberately he smashed the three lights nearest to the bay where Dan would meet him. Then he settled himself to wait behind the metallic ranks of BMW, Jaguar and Mercedes. Occasionally a car-door slammed, a motor started up and accelerated towards the exit, tyres squealing. But this was mostly contract, all-day parking and there was little movement at midday. No one came to claim a vehicle near Mustafa.

He pulled a pen torch out of his pocket and flashed it at his watch. Three minutes. Mustafa especially savoured such moments, holding his excitement in check, waiting for the kill.

Somewhere a swing-door thudded into its jamb. Remembering the pipe in his hand, Mustafa immediately laid it down on the concrete. He held his crouching position. Soon there was a pair of rubber-soled shoes slapping towards him. They stopped. They started again. Then Mustafa heard them crunch into some broken glass and stop once more. At this point he knew exactly where Dan Barry was standing. He slowly rose to his feet.

Dan stood in darkness. Behind him, the pale-violet light hardly penetrated into the parking bay where he knew his customer must be. He waited to hear the voice.

'Mr Green?'

'Yes, I'm here. Show yourself.'

'I am Mr Red. I think you have something for me.'

'I can't see you.'

'It's better that you do not. Have you something for me?'

'Yes.'

'Please would you put it down on the ground, and go and stand by the concrete pillar to your left, the one with the marking J?'

'Show yourself and I'll do it.'

There was some flicker of movement, a shadow marginally paler than the overall coal-hole blackness within the parking bay.

'No. Do it anyway.'

Dan kept his eye on the place where he'd seen the movement, bent his knees and dropped the leather case. It was heavy enough to make an echo as it slapped down on the floor. He moved away towards the pillar.

The grey wraith moved out of the shadow towards where he'd dropped the case. Dan heard the burr of a zip. He called out,

'Found it?'

No answer. A torch flashed. For a brief second the wraith became the face of a man – dark hair, moustache, clean-shaven chin. Then with a click the face was gone.

Mustafa's hands had trembled only slightly, and with hurry rather than nerves, along the outside of the leather case, looking for the opening. There'd be an automatic and silencer. He'd need a few seconds to ram the clip into the box, screw on the silencer, chamber a round and punch three or four fast shots into this English fool. Then he would dump the body in the dark under one of these fancy cars and get upstairs after the Turk and his girlfriend.

His fingers groped inside the bag. Yes, there was the silencer, a smooth gunmetal tube. That was a clip of ammunition. But where the fuck was the gun? And what was this? Not a gun. It felt like a lump of metal.

He squandered a few seconds feeling in the wrong pocket for the torch. He threw a glance towards Dan Barry, who had reached the pillar and turned round. He located the torch.

'Found it?'

Mustafa flashed the torch.

He doubled back to his original station behind the cars and went down on his knees. He moved his outstretched hand over the rough oily concrete like a metal detector. Then he flashed the torch again, and saw what he was looking for.

'Look, have you got it or what?'

What was the man doing? Why had he sprinted back into the darkness? Dan saw the torch flash again from there and in an instant judgement knew that he was not safe. The prickling at the scruff of his neck told him as much.

He turned to get away, but the man was coming towards him. He moved so fast that Dan didn't even have time to put a parked car between them. A thick forearm went round his throat from behind and he was wrenched painfully backwards. Then he was being dragged into the shadows.

He felt a cold circle of metal jab into the soft flesh under his jaw. This was not the barrel of the gun Blanchard had shown him, for sure. The barrel was much longer and its edge pricked him.

The man spoke low, not quite in a whisper. 'Where's the pistol?' He pushed Dan against a wall. A knee went into his back, pinning him in place. 'Where's the gun?'

'I gave it to you. It's in the leather case. There's no need for this.'

'There is no gun there. There was only *this*.'

He let something fall with a brief metallic ring to the concrete and flashed his torch on it. Dan saw the coarse features of Beethoven and recognized the piece instantly – Christ! Lena . . .

'Tell me where's the gun.' The voice was intense and vicious. 'If you do not I will blow your head away.'

As the man's left hand awkwardly tried to frisk him, Dan felt his knee's pressure relax. So, slightly, did the painful jagged metal that had been biting into his mandible.

Out of the chaos of Dan's mind thought came, like a small, clear voice making itself heard in a hurricane. *This is a bluff. This is not a firearm. The aperture against my throat is not a circle, and no gun-barrel ends in a jagged rim.*

With the recklessness of a busted gambler Dan could see no other course than to back his life against the hunch. He snapped his head backwards and made contact with the man's face. The contact was firm but it yielded – the nose, most probably. The man yelped and staggered. Spinning round and grabbing a handful of hair, Dan pulled downwards with all the strength he could muster, and brought his right knee up with an explosive jerk. The knee mashed into the nose a second time, and he heard a small crunch upon impact. Then Dan pushed as hard as he could, and the man pitched away from him, backwards and to one side. Dan broke free and took off, running at the stairs.

Half way to them the little voice in his mind spoke again. *Sawn-off.* The words clanged between his ears like an alarm, and momentarily he broke his stride. *It could've been a sawn-off barrel!* He tried again to accelerate, scrambling round blocks of parked cars and concrete piers in redoubled desperation.

At any moment he was expecting the atrocious explosion that a shotgun would make in this confined space, but kept running, and still it didn't come. Now there was no obstruction between himself and the swing doors which led to the stairs. With a final lunge he crashed through them, and was pelting upwards to safety.

Helpless, Mustafa watched Dan escape. He felt his nose tenderly and took a step. His foot rang against something on the floor. He pointed his torch. The bust of the deaf composer stared sternly up at him and Mustafa bent and picked it up. He turned the object, glinting slightly in the half-light and then, whipping his arm like a World Series pitcher in full spate, hurled it to the nearest parked car. As Beethoven struck, the curved windscreen shivered then disintegrated into three thousand crumbs of glass.

His eyes hunted the dark for a witness to the humiliating scene that had just been played. He longed for there to be someone, anyone.

A filmy curtain descended over his eyes, and motes swam amoeba-like within it. Thoughts would not form in his mind, only impulses. He just wanted to close his fingers on a throat, or bang someone's brains out. He had had attacks like this before, a devil-possession. Once it had ended with a written-off Porsche, twice with designer-decorated rooms being trashed, once in a bystander losing both his eyes.

There was a reverberant thump as the stairwell door mashed into its jamb. Cross-fading with the echo came the crisp pattern of a woman walking on needle heels, coming in his direction. Mustafa dropped to a crouch, then moved without another thought to cut her off. Her car would be one of a trio parked four bays to his right, and of the three he gambled on the hatchback. He was both right and wrong. The woman came to the correct bay, but she slipped into a Mercedes saloon. Well, at least it was the passenger door she'd entered. She would not be leaving at once. There was plenty of time.

Mustafa was breathing heavily, blinking his eyelids. He'd had a good view of her head and shoulders. Smartly dressed, late twenties, blonde hair loose in a bell around her head, beautiful. She had been toting several large paper carriers of the kind issued by expensive clothes shops. She was rich.

He dodged past the tailgate of the hatchback and edged alongside the car. It was only as he did so that he realized the car was carrying foreign plates, and this made him move into position with a rush of panic. It meant a left-hand drive car, and that she was, after all, in the driver's seat. She might fire the engine and take off at any second.

He wrapped his fingers around the handle of the true passenger door and listened. It was thanks to modern technology that he could do what he was about to do, for central locking means also *un*locking. He heard the chink of her keys as she went for the ignition. Then he opened the door and lunged forward, across the stiff, crackling paper that enclosed her purchases. The scent of cologne washed around him as he closed one of his hands over her mouth. He plucked the key away from her fingers with the other.

'I need a car and I need a chauffeur.' He was whispering close to her ear, like a lover. His murmuring lips brushed a simple pearl stud which adorned the lobe. 'Do what I ask and I will try not to hurt you.'

Mustafa leaned further across and slid his arm behind the woman's neck. He pressed the locking button by her left shoulder and with a reassuring thud the locks of all the other doors, as well as the boot, fell into place.

'Look, Jack. Can anything I tell you go no further?'

'No further, I promise. And I'm all agog.'

The pub was beginning to empty after the initial lunchtime rush, and they had found a secluded table. Dan was breathing like a boxer who'd just gone twelve rounds.

'I've been attacked. I mean it, Jack. Some guy tried to fucking *kill* me, just now!'

'Kill you?'

'Yes, kill. Rub me out, top me, blow my lousy head off, kill me.'

'Where?'

'Underground car park. I was supposed to deliver this thing to this guy and I thought I had done, but according to him it wasn't there. Then he jumped me in the dark, jabbed a sawn-off shotgun in my neck. Look.'

He pointed to the angry red mark under his jaw. Around its edge polyps of blood had oozed out and congealed.

'What was it? One of those Hittite thingies?'

'Christ no. It was the first time I've been asked to do this, but I couldn't refuse, exactly.'

'Refuse what, Dan? Come on. Words of one syllable.'

'A gun. A hand gun. It seemed incredible really. Blanchard gave me this gun and told me I'd be contacted by the client in London, when I was to hand it over. The meeting would be in the basement car park under the hotel, the Transnational.'

'That's where you stay, right?'

'Yes. So this geezer rings me up, I go down to meet him, carrying the gun in this small leather case thing. It was like a kit, you know? There was a silencer, ammunition clips, the lot in there, all laid out like a vanity case. Except, when I gave it to him there was no gun.'

'Where was it?'

'That's what he wanted to know. He kept saying over and over "Give me the gun, where's the gun?" . . . It had to be Lena. She saw it this morning, kicked up a fuss. I made up some lame story. She obviously didn't believe it.'

'What did she do? Take it?'

'She switched it for a statue of fucking Beethoven.'

'Jesus!'

'Anyway, I got away. I pulled his nose on to my knee and just ran.'

'What about the shotgun?'

Dan shrugged.

'And who was he?'

'Christ knows. But definitely not the proprietor of your actual friendly neighbourhood gun shop, taking delivery of a new item of stock.'

'But it seems unlikely that you'd be asked to import just a single gun. What was so special about it?'

'Nothing as far as I could see. Ordinary automatic, I didn't really look at it. There must be thousands like it floating around.'

'So what do you think happened to it?'

Dan stared at the head on his Guinness. 'She probably dropped it in the Bosporus.'

Jack lit a cigarette. 'How much does she know about your . . . um, activities?'

'Not a lot. Nothing.'

'You sure?'

'Sure as I can be. She doesn't know I'm a journalist, even. She thinks I'm an actor, for Christ's sake!' He took a long drink. 'I've lied to her about everything, all along the line. Everything, Jack. And now this happens. Jesus! How am I going to explain it?'

Jack Bacon regarded him watchfully. 'How's it going – generally I mean?'

'The writing? Well, that's the other thing. I've suddenly discovered I've been systematically conned for the last six months.'

Jack leaned forward and began rolling a cigarette. 'Tell more, Dan. Tell more.'

'You know those Hittite statues I've been toting into the country, under the impression that because of the Turkish government's embargo they couldn't come over legally?'

'They were priceless, right?'

'Priceless my bum. The paint was hardly dry on them. They were fakes, every one of them.'

'I see.' Jack's eyebrows had a habit of working when he was thinking, squeezing together and stretching out, like some routine of facial callisthenics.

'Sounds like a pretty good scam anyway. Fake antiques. They obviously used you to lend authenticity. No collector wants to buy a piece that's been exported legally. Like Groucho Marx, they'll only join a club if it's closed to them. What's the difference from your point of view?'

'All the difference, because the scam wasn't against the collectors. It was against *me*, Jack. They weren't even trying to make actual, genuine fakes, if you get my drift. Any expert could suss that out at a glance. Those things I was carrying were no more Hittite than a toby jug.'

'So?'

'So, this guy Altan, another steward who Blanchard uses, came into my hotel room this morning just after we arrived and smashed one of my statues. I was horrified, but he knew, you see. I looked at the broken bits only to find about two kilos of finest quality junk had been hidden inside!'

Jack's hand gripped Dan by the forearm and shook it. He laughed. 'You're a dope-smuggler, Dan. You've been one for months without even knowing it. Now you really can write that Pulitzer prizewinner. Lucky, lucky Danny Barry – have another?'

'Lucky? I've been unknowingly committing a capital offence for six months. And now I've been just a finger's itch from having my head blown off, over a gun my girlfriend's stolen from me. I'm friendless, broke and bloody terrified, and you talk about lucky.'

'Yes, but think of what's at the end of the line. Everything we discussed last year, seeds we sowed. They're now coming into fruit. Next thing you know you'll be on first-name terms with Tom Wolfe, George Bush and God himself.'

After another glass of the creamy black beer, Dan left. He meant to seek out Felix and arrange transfer of the smack. He didn't want a repeat of the gun fiasco.

Jack Bacon sat on alone for a minute or two, then rose and went to the payphone. He talked for a very short time, enough perhaps to order a cab or inquire about a train time. Then he, too, hurried away into the street.

As a driver the woman was worse than useless. She was a tourist – she scarcely understood what he was saying, hardly knew her way around London. And all the time she trembled extravagantly and looked at him through rolling, horrified eyes, like a sheep already roped down for slaughter.

Mustafa made her tell her name – Gabriella, Gaby. Mustafa felt sorry for Gaby. The mist had cleared from his eyes now, the amoeba had swum away, but he was still stuck with her. She'd had such a good look at him that he could hardly let her go. Yet she, too, was a foreigner in this metropolis of racial arrogance, and he felt a certain fellowship with her. So it was a pity, really. But he would have to kill her.

After twenty minutes of movement without progress, he made Gaby drive into another underground car park, where he directed her to a bay far from the entrance. He told her to get in the back, and she struggled between the seats before falling awkwardly and lying with her face pressed against the leather upholstery, eyes tight shut. Mustafa ordered her to undress, and patiently took the crisp, fashionable clothes item by item from her hands as she struggled out of them. Gaby was so sweet in her appalled distress, so frantic to oblige him.

He did not, as she expected, join her in the back when at last she sat there naked. He simply twisted his body around and reached for her throat.

# 6

Through the heart of Haggerston runs the Regent's Canal, a now largely unemployed waterway connecting gentrified Camden Town and Islington with the post-modern, hi-tech paradise of London's Dockland.

Haggerston has not shared in the conspicuous prosperity of these places. Forsaken warehouses prop each other up, like drunks tottering on the waterside. Many are in irreversible decay – slates and brickwork have sprouted weeds; windows are starred by children's stones; graffiti scream obscenities from the cracked, shit-coloured rendering that scabs their walls. Inside the weather has taken up residence. The wind weeps into spaces big as ballrooms; its dampness warps the doors, flakes the paintwork, coats metal with verdigris and rust.

Yet even such moribund premises have their uses. Darren Knight, for example, had acquired one four years before as a vehicle repair shop. Darren didn't repair too many vehicles there, but the place was ideal for his mixed variety of interests and most afternoons he could be found there looking after business – choosing the re-spray shades for a motor, testing the small-arms he supplied to a few select customers, fixing for specially-bred dogs to meet and rip bits off each other for the entertainment of Darren's guests. The last was the fastest-growing sport in the East End of London.

Mustafa found Darren in the basement. He was watching two men lash up sections of plywood, blockboard and old doors to form a dog-pit.

'Mustafa! Blimey mate, you look a bit like you come down in the world. Times hard?'

The Londoner presented quite a contrast to Mustafa. He was ever the sharp dresser. Today he wore a spotless camel coat, a big silk tie with diamond pin, and shoes that still had the Italian factory sheen on them. Since they'd met last, he'd grown a thin moustache, no wider than an eyebrow, along the line of his upper lip. By this sinister touch he hoped in vain to compensate for the down-drooping face and bulbous nose. The combination gave him the look of a clown miscast as a pimp.

Darren gestured at the small arena taking shape before them. 'We got a big rumble tonight. You got to be here. The US of A's best twenty-star pit-bull, flown all the way from Oak Ridge, Tennessee, takes on the Pride of Parsloe's Park.'

'Parsloe's Park? What is it?'

'That's where our fucking dog hails from, mate. Come and see.'

With a circular movement of his arm Darren started towards a door at the far end of the room. The cigar belched smoke, creating a slipstream that smelt of sour nuts. Mustafa followed.

'This is one English bull terrier who's so vicious he makes Rambo look like a trainee chiropodist. Wait till you cop an eyeful of him.'

They passed into an office. The exposed brick of the walls was painted in cream gloss. There was a desk, a filing cabinet and, at the far end against the right-hand wall, a massive iron safe. Beyond that, high up, the panes of a window filched some grubby light from what must have been the ground level. Darren held up a hand.

'Hear that? Beautiful music, son, beautiful music.'

From behind the safe Mustafa could clearly hear a murderous, mucous rumbling. Mustafa was nervous. He was no coward, he'd killed fit men twice his weight. But if he had one weakness, it was dogs. The thought of the animal's jaw closing on his flesh, its saliva mixing with his blood, gave him a jolt of pure horror. If you come from a country where a stray dog's bite can mean a convulsive death within ten days, it is not entirely paranoid.

Darren, on the other hand, was unconcerned. He strolled casually into the room and peered through the gloom into the corner behind the safe.

'S'all right. He's asleep.'

Mustafa went hesitantly forward. Lying on a piece of fringed velvet lay a white stumpy-legged dog, the Pride of Parsloe's Park. His snout was resting between his paws, and he was snoring. It seemed about as far as you could get from any idea Mustafa might have had of a canine prizefighter.

Darren threw himself into a chair behind the knee-hole desk and snapped on the desk-lamp.

'It's all hype, of course. That mutt'll be slaughtered;

though I daresn't tell it to the punters. He's a nasty bit of work all right, but American pit-bulls are actually bred to the job right now, today. They know nothing else, like. English bulls've had too many generations of being petted by tweedy old dears at Crufts.'

'And have they sent a dog over especially from the States to fight him?'

Darren's laugh was part snarl. 'Nar. From Sidcup. But there again, I'm not letting on to the punters. They'll come flooding in tonight, panting with patriotism, to cheer on the local hero. There's going to be a lot of ante-post money on Fido here, but only because the mugs want to see him give a hiding to a Yank.'

He straightened up and placed his hands palm downwards on the desk.

'Now, what can I do for you, young man? Or is this just a friendly visit?'

Mustafa didn't much like the 'young man', not from someone to whom he gave a good five years.

'I need a shooter, Darren.'

Darren's eyebrows went up and down.

'Oh? Well, we got some of those. What sort of thing?'

'Handgun. What have you got?'

Darren rose and laboriously unlocked the safe. He brought out a stack of three rectangular cardboard boxes. The script on the topmost said *Van Heusen* and a white square on the leading edge was overprinted *Manhattan*. The boxes had once held shirts. Darren levered one open.

'What have we got? Matter of fact stocks are a little on the low side, but there's a beautiful thing here, a Taurus Magnum. Brazilian. Ever seen one of these?'

He picked the gun out and, placing it on the palm of his hand, proffered it for inspection. The gesture was exactly that of a tie salesman.

Mustafa knew precisely what he was looking at. This piece of fetishistic ordnance had a four-inch barrel, a chunky six-round revolving chamber and a pricked hammer – a clever copy of the American designs he'd seen around most often. But he knew he'd be dead ten times over if he toted such a crude and inaccurate weapon. Darren could see the resistance in Mustafa's eyes.

'It'll do anything a Smith or a Remington can,' he said by way of sales patter. 'It'll blast a guy's head off at six feet. They've only been making them down there in the jungle since the seventies, I believe. But it's a beautiful job. Lovely hardwood butt.'

'Yes, I see. But no, I prefer an automatic.'

Darren seemed disappointed as if the Turk had turned down a star offer in the January sales. He replaced the revolver, restored its box to the safe and unstacked the other two, removing their lids.

'This one's a Browning, the other's a Beretta. Both very similar: 9-millimetre cal, weight just about a kilo, thirteen rounds. But you know all that. I got to say I rate the Browning as the better gun. The Eytie piece has one interesting feature, though, a manual option. You can uncouple the automatic operation here and reload manually. An anti-jamming safeguard, I reckon. Doesn't show much confidence in the engineering, to my mind, but take your pick.'

Mustafa lifted the Beretta. It had an unusually bulky handgrip, but he thought he favoured it over the more old-fashioned Browning.

'May I fire it?'

Opening a drawer Darren picked out a silencer extension and a box of 9-millimetre shells. He stood up and extended his arm. 'Be my guest.'

They went down to Darren's makeshift firing range, rigged up in a cellar below the basement level, which had once been a cold-store. In complete oblivion, the Pride of Parsloe's Park snored on above them.

Later, Darren asked, 'How you going to pay for this, son?'

So Mustafa took him outside and showed him the Mercedes.

'Nice motor. Where you get it?' He stepped back, shoving the air with his palms. 'All right, all right. I shouldn't ask. But it's a foreign reg, right?'

'Yes, a tourist. Should be easy for you, I think.'

It would probably take Darren just a couple of days to have the car resprayed and kitted out with new documents. Then it would be sent off to a customer who had a customer somewhere south of Malta or east of Cyprus. Even at ten per cent of the car's value – the kind of price Darren might consider reasonable – it would cover the cost of the Beretta several times over. Darren pretended to consider, but secretly thought his birthday had come early.

He opened the door and poked his head inside. He smelt the perfume, but it did not mask something else.

'Smells of piss in here, Mustafa. Nice motor, though, very nice.'

He withdrew his head and wiped his palms against each other, the salesman who'd made his sale.

'All right, if she's roadworthy, you got yourself a deal.'

'Do you mind telling me what the fuck is going on?'

Dan's doorstepping technique, which he'd perfected during a stint with a mass-circulation daily, had now come into its own.

'Go in hard, boy,' Truscott, the news editor, had told him on his first day. 'Demand, cajole, and bribe in descending order. Never plead for information. And always pretend to know what you don't know and vice versa. But above all never show weakness, especially to local government officials.'

Come to think of it, Felix Trubshaw looked exactly like a man who had served years in Parking Meters and Permits. His complexion was the colour and consistency of uncooked pastry.

A table which served as Felix's desk stood between himself and Dan. With both his hands resting on top Felix was trembling visibly. He seemed to be any moment about to lower himself out of sight.

'I would remind you you're not supposed to be

here. You're never supposed to come here. I really can't help you, you know.'

He might have been turning down an application for a contingency poll-tax rebate by Al Capone.

'Help me? I'm not asking for help. I'm demanding an explanation. Those . . . figurines, whatever you call them. This morning I broke one.'

He was looking into Felix's eyes and saw the pupils dilate with surprise and concern. It was no more than that, at this stage. Shock, fear, might come later, as the story unfolded. Trubshaw was on his feet, covering the space between his desk and the street door. Dan anticipated him, and barred the way with a hand on the door frame.

Without looking at him Felix reached over the arm and flipped the card which hung in front of the plate glass. To any potential customer it now read CLOSED. He retired to his desk and sat down. He was breathing heavily. He felt for a desk drawer and pulled out a bottle of Bell's. Almost absently, he unscrewed the lid and dropped a few thick gouts of the honey-coloured liquid into a glass. He didn't invite Dan to drink with him.

'Where did this happen?'

'Oh, behind closed doors, don't worry about that. The point is, as you well know, I'm in the picture now. Every week for the last six months I've been cavorting across Europe with a couple of kilos of heroin in my luggage, and no one saw fit to tell me.'

Felix's finger went in a palsied gesture to his lips. 'I'd prefer you not to say that word.'

'What word?'

'That word.' Soundlessly Felix mouthed the three syllables of heroin.

'Oh? What would you prefer – junk, smack, scag? Why wasn't I told?'

'Perhaps if you calmed down. It was not solely with the idea of getting at you, you know. A security measure, that's all. I didn't like it myself, but Mr Blanchard insisted. He said the less you knew, the less guilt or nerves you might betray as you came through. A lot of couriers are caught that way.' He smiled bleakly. 'Body language or something.'

'That sounds fine, but he lumbered me with something else to be guilty about, didn't he? So-called Hittite treasures.'

'You would not, of course, be concerned about those once you have left Turkish soil. They would not matter much at the London end.'

'Unless I was done for bringing in pornography. It's pretty steamy, some of the work of Mr Mahmut Doğan of the Grand Bazaar.'

Felix looked up sharply. 'Who told you about Doğan?'

'It came up in conversation.'

'Başkurt then. It must have been him. You have the contents of the – er – statue?'

'Yes. But you won't see a grain of it unless you tell me the whole story.'

Felix had now regained his composure. He leaned back in his revolving chair and put the tips of his fingers together, the gesture of someone beginning to feel in control. He tipped some more whisky down his throat.

'Yes. Why don't you sit down, Dan? I think you and I had better have a little chat.'

Nilüfer had spent a hellish afternoon. As the hour of the delivery to Harley Street got nearer Altan became reckless with desperation about the still-missing kidney. He talked her into going out with him, convinced the sonofabitch would be hanging out in one of the numerous döner kebab cafés of the area.

'It's his only point of contact with this town – the only thing he can recognize. I guarantee we'll find him arguing about Turkish football teams and playing *tavla.*'

So they trailed off to Güzel Döner, Sultan Mehmet, Boğaziçi Grill, Aksaray Kebab, Döner Palas and back to Güzel Döner again. All in vain.

'Tall stringy man, about thirty. Typical Anadolu peasant, old pair of trousers that don't fit him, knitted sweater, too short and coming unstrung. He probably looks bewildered, he's certainly lost. You sure you haven't seen him? He hasn't been in here at all?'

Their questions were answered by shrugs and concerned faces.

Nilüfer said, 'Does it matter? I mean, he knows he's got to go to Harley Street. Hasn't he got the doctor's name?'

'Of course he hasn't. The man's probably illiterate.

Anyway, the policy is, he knows as little as possible. What we're doing is illegal over here, you know. If the police have him we're fucked, I mean really *fucked*.'

Exhausted, they went back to the Transnational. Altan kept dodging into alleyways, peering behind dustbins. He was confused and fussed, like a bird-dog that's lost the scent. By the time they reached the hotel he was grey and sweating. He kept muttering that Blanchard would kill him, *kill* him, for this.

As they swung through the propelling doors, Altan stopped and let out a yell, a mixture of triumph and hate. The kidney was sitting in the lobby. His forearms were resting on his knees as he leaned forward and stared as if fascinated at the marble floor.

Altan pushed Nilüfer away, ran up to the kidney and jerked him upright by means of his disintegrating knitwear. He spoke a rapid and obscene string of imprecations so close to the guy's face that he could smell his own breath rebounding off it. The kidney quivered. He might have been about to weep. Altan rammed him back into the seat.

'Stay here till I come back.'

He started to rejoin Nilüfer, but halfway towards her he whirled round again and doubled back to where the man sat. As the peasant cringed away Altan took hold of his ear between his fist and his thumb and twisted it hard.

'If you move I'll give your balls to a butcher. Got it?'

The unfortunate nodded his head repeatedly and

hung it down in shame. Altan swung away. Nilüfer could see his irritation had been replaced by elation.

'I told him the score. He won't give us any more trouble. Now look –' He smiled and lowered his voice. He was back on form. 'We still got a couple of hours before we take him to this doctor's place. How about you and me going up –?'

He made a movement upwards with his eyebrows. The fog of anxiety was dispersed. The kidney was stuck firmly in his place. Now he could think of more immediate things. Things like sex.

As soon as the lift doors closed on them Altan pounced. Nilüfer's pleated skirt was wrenched up, she was projected against the wall and pinned there as his body rubbed itself up and down hers.

Altan's attitude to sex was simple: there was no such thing as too much of it. With stewardesses he had often copulated in flight, and once or twice with passengers. To him it did not seem completely impossible that he and Nilüfer could do it while an Otis elevator whisked them upwards through twenty-three floors.

Nilüfer pushed and grappled him. His hands were leeched to her buttocks, his tobacco-flavoured tongue skewering into her mouth, and she could feel the knobble of his prick jerking against her abdomen.

'Altan. No. The lift may ... The door may open. Stop it.'

She was not fighting for her virginity. That had gone long since. In terms of sexual experience Nilüfer did not lag all that far behind Altan. But quasi-public snogging gave her no thrill. She wanted her men slowly, luxuriously and in bed. She liked to tease them until they begged her to let them fuck her, and then go on teasing some more. Then, when she did submit, it would be not to a Heinrich or a Paul or an Altan, but to a being so completely and despairingly possessed by desire that he became, for once, oblivious of himself. Altan's present display was mere exhibitionism, the male's urge to wave his prick around.

Nilüfer's family would, of course, have been scandalized. As an unmarried Turkish girl she was expected to conform to a stereotype – that of submissive maidenhood. Even in the 'westernized' bourgeois background from which she came, the idea of a respectable girl having sexual appetites was itself an affront. To be caught indulging them would result in a swift and punitive marriage, after a sympathetic gynaecologist had been well paid to restore by surgery her ruptured hymen.

But Nilüfer was different. It was why she had chosen this profession – because it left parochial morals behind. Airline people from whatever nation tend to be permissive and it was a job which allowed Nilüfer to indulge her favourite fantasies – whether about foreign cities, foreign men, or exotic opportunities. She knew she was beautiful. She felt in control. And more by luck than judgement she had not yet encountered the shadow-side of sex.

Today they had been too busy going from restaurant to restaurant to think about eating. Nilüfer wondered if this had anything to do with Altan's ferocious rush of passion. Her grandmother had once told her that hunger for food sharpened a man's sexual appetite. She had meant it as a warning: keep your man's stomach well packed and he'll be less bother in bed.

As the doors sprang apart Altan and Nilüfer did likewise. Captain Recep was there, waiting to be conveyed down to the lobby. His two young crew-members collected themselves. As they gave him vacant possession of the lift he smiled, without otherwise changing expression. Nilüfer could not work out if Recep was as remote as he seemed. He knew what was going on all right, though he said and did nothing about it. Perhaps on the quiet he had the odd fiddle of his own in progress.

Once inside her room Nilüfer kicked away her shoes and approached Altan. She forestalled his reaching hands and, grabbing the lapels of his jacket, slipped them upwards and back until his arms slid from the sleeves. She dropped the jacket on the bed. They had two hours, time enough to make a start, at any rate.

'Now, lover, I'm going to take a shower. I want you to get on the phone, order us some sandwiches and something to drink, get yourself undressed and *then* – well, why don't you join me in there?'

He lifted the receiver as she half-closed the bathroom door.

# 7

'Do you know how far Blanchard and I go back?'

Sitting behind his table, Felix Trubshaw was drinking and fiddling with a ballpoint pen. He had grasped it daggerwise and was clicking and releasing the retraction mechanism with his thumb. Dan did not sit down. He moved instead to stand by the side wall, so that his silhouette no longer showed against the bright light.

'A fairly long time, I think he told me.'

'A fairly long time? Is that what he said?'

'Something like it, yes.'

Felix's manner had changed. As the tawny column of liquid relentlessly fell in the bottle, he was no longer the harassed municipal clerk. He had become a schoolmaster or an army officer, relaxing as he patronized a junior colleague.

'A *very* long time would be more accurate. Thirty years is a very long time, wouldn't you say?'

'You both must have been children, thirty years ago. Don't tell me you were bubble-gum barons or something.'

'We were at school together.'

'What? You and Nathan Blanchard?'

'Seems incredible, doesn't it? A private preparatory school in Northamptonshire. His father was in the US Air Force at a nearby base. There was apparently no

American Services School at the base. Or perhaps an inadequate one.'

'I didn't even know you were particularly close. Friends, I mean.'

'Friends? Who said anything about being friends? We were both outsiders. I was the kid sent over from Ireland. They called me Duckweed.'

Felix's laugh was false. It seemed confined to his throat.

'But no, we weren't friends. Between me and Blanchard was something more personal than friendship. He chose me. If there was anything he wanted done, bed made, shoes cleaned, prep copied out, that was down to muggins.'

Now that Felix was coming with these confidences, the patronage had bled out of his tone. He began to wear an expression like a hungry dog eyeing his master at table. Dan was perplexed.

'Felix, why are you telling me this? I only want an explanation of why I was tricked into carrying the heroin. I'd still have been willing to carry the stuff if I'd been told, you know.'

The dog-eyed look vanished as quickly as it had appeared. Felix's voice hardened again. 'Oh, well, that's very simple. He didn't trust you. And he was right, wasn't he?'

'What do you mean?'

'Now he knows who you are, you see. Your credibility is blown away, your goose is cooked.'

He fired a furious burst of clicks from the biro. A

small cloud of doubt appeared in the corner of Dan's brain.

'You're talking in code, Felix.'

Felix dropped the biro and stood up. Placing his hands on the desk, he leant forward. His face was caught in a beam of late afternoon sun, the pasty complexion looking like mortuary flesh.

'He knows that you're a fucking *writer*, Dan. You were going to write us up, I suppose. Make a best-seller out of us, is that it?'

Dan's heart flipped suddenly, like a dying fish. 'Blanchard thinks that?'

Felix had spotted the sudden fear in Dan, the chink of weakness. He moved to consolidate his advantage. 'He *knows* that.'

'Why hasn't he said anything to me?'

Felix inserted a hand into his pocket, reached out an ebony cigarette holder and rammed a filter king-size into the nozzle. His teeth grimaced, gripping the mouthpiece to keep it still as he lit up. Dan spoke again, wishing he could keep the note of panic out of his voice. 'Felix, what's he planning to do? I *can* explain myself, you know.'

'I doubt it.'

'So what's he going to do?'

Felix was enjoying himself. He held the smoke in his lungs for a theatrically long moment, then released it through his nostrils in two thin vapour trails.

'He's going to have you killed, I imagine.'

Reflexively, Dan shut his eyes. *Have me killed?*

'It will probably be quite sudden. A man will lunge at you in some dark place, putting a limited number of bullets into the appropriate segments of your body. Bang, bang, bang. You will fall down.' He shrugged. 'It won't hurt. You'll go without realizing it. That is, unless Blanchard takes it into his head to make you suffer.'

In total recall, Dan now lived again through lunchtime. He saw the darkened far end of the garage, smelled the tyre rubber and spilt engine oil, heard the boom of the foreigner's voice.

He put up a hand and rubbed the place where the circle of metal, the supposed shotgun, had pressed against his neck. *Have me killed!* The phrase was all too credible. That can't have been a shotgun, then, or at least not loaded. Christ! He saw it suddenly as Blanchard had planned it. He'd been intended to import his own murder weapon. Like a condemned man being forced to dig his own grave.

He suddenly felt drenched in stupid gratitude for Lena's impulsive act in taking the gun from his bag, even though – Christ knew – she didn't have an idea what she was doing.

Felix had gone to the window and was watching pedestrians going about their mundane business outside. When he judged Dan might have collected himself he turned back to the room and said in a soft voice, 'If by some chance you should escape death, Dan, I do have a proposition to put to you. You might be quite interested.'

Dan found he was gazing at a carpet hung on the wall. It was a tree-of-life, exquisitely designed. A snake writhed lovingly up the trunk, its mouth poised with sensuous enjoyment beneath something like a ripe red pomegranate. All around were animals and plants in promiscuous abundance.

'I could help you, you see. With the book. Well, I need to get away from that bastard now, and both of us together could really put something together, couldn't we?'

But Dan wasn't listening. He had never faced the thought of his own death. Or not, at least, with this degree of intensity. It numbed his sense of reality. You could have reached into his jacket and removed his wallet quite openly: he'd not have noticed. He was plumbing the bottomless novelty of his fear. He felt it rasping his windpipe, writhing in his stomach, tunnelling through his guts.

On another day, without this parasite of terror hatching and devouring inside him like a nest of maggots, he'd have picked up the uncertainty in Felix's tone. That note of pleading, the hint of a snivel. Felix had sounded cocky and firm when he'd described Dan's likely death. But he knew his own condemnation might not be far behind. Now Felix was grasping at a flimsy chance to blackmail himself out of the pit he'd dug all those years ago. Or rather, the pit Blanchard had made him dig.

'I can give you all the names, at least the ones at this end of the supply chain. Dealers, moneychangers and several high-up users. MPs, peers. I can name one cabinet minister with a habit, and there's even a junkie judge I know.'

For a moment, in Dan's eyes, the tree-of-life came to life. The figures on it seemed to jump and swarm, like flames. The serpent snatched at the fruit, then retracted its neck and snatched again. Dan heard what Felix had said, but the data jammed with the pictures from the magic carpet. He murmured, 'Amazing rug you've got there.'

'I'm sorry?'

Dan felt sick. He needed to be outside.

'Look, I've got to be going. Things to do.'

Dan moved towards the door. Felix half-barred the way.

'No, don't go . . . Well, think about it, at least. You can ring me here. It would be something to do, and you've got to do something.'

Felix's voice was becoming higher pitched as he talked, trying to get the words out before Dan pushed past him. 'And there's another thing, it's the most important thing, really. I've not told anyone, you're the first to know. Blanchard's started something new. He's obsessed with it, says he's discovered the ultimate addictive drug, worth money you wouldn't have dreamed of. Of course it's deadly dangerous. We could go to the government. Or we could sell it as a story, an exclusive. A scoop. Or whatever it is you guys call it.'

But the after-image of the carpet was still in Dan's eyes. Felix let his arm fall from the door-post. He made a last appeal.

'Look, ring me. I won't do anything for twenty-four hours. And for Christ's sake be careful! D'you understand what I'm saying?'

Dan found an extra ration of energy and yanked the door open. The shop-bell clanged with brassy surprise as he lunged through and into the street.

He had been gone ten minutes when Felix realized he'd made no arrangement to pick up the heroin. Now he'd have Mossman on his back, as well as Blanchard.

'Shit,' he said. 'Shit and bollocks!'

He drew down the security grille and locked all the doors.

Mustafa knocked on the door of Dan Barry's room, the firm triple-rap of a chambermaid or bell-hop. He waited for ten seconds. There was no response.

The door had a keyless, card-operated lock. He checked the corridor both ways and crouched down to fish from his bag a bunch of plastic cards, each with its magnetized strip. He tried six or seven in the slot before the catch clicked. He opened the door and slipped inside.

Where was the heroin? He saw the 'Hittite' figures nowhere. He checked in all the drawers, Dan's luggage, the wardrobe. Barry must have them with him.

He sat on the bed with the Beretta resting on his knee, checked and double-checked, the safety-catch off. He waited forty-five minutes.

Nilüfer hardly ever smoked, but now she said, 'I wish

I had some French cigarettes. Gauloises. Tipped Gauloises.'

They were on the bed. She lay belly down, with arms crossed under her face. Her eyelids were slightly lowered and she held her moist lips infinitesimally apart. It was a face voluptuous in repose.

Altan was propped on an elbow alongside her, stroking her back. Both had wet hair from their long, indulgent shower.

Nilüfer raised her head and looked imperiously at Altan. 'I wish I had one right now.'

She was slow and luxurious in her movements, completely in control. Altan, by contrast, was feeling ragged. In spite of the shower his whole body was throbbing and hot, like a car that's been viciously revved over a slipped clutch. All his nerves were tingling with frustrated electricity.

For three months he'd had the itch to screw Nilüfer. He had flown with her on stopover trips only twice before, and both times she had chosen other company. Altan did not easily give up the chase, however, and this time his persistence had paid off. She'd agreed to his invitation to have sex with such facile grace that he might have been suggesting tea in the hotel lounge. Now he was reclining next to her, bobbling his knuckles up and down her naked vertebrae and resting his erection on the back of her thigh.

But why wouldn't she let him get on with it?

'Altan, darling. You'll slip down to the newspaper shop and get me some, won't you? There's a good boy.'

'Nilüfer, this is crazy. We've only got another hour.'

Nilüfer pushed him aside and rolled off the bed. She gathered up a kimono-style silk robe and slipped it on. One delicious breast spilled out as she wrapped the thin garment round herself. She tucked it deliberately away.

'Then, darling, I won't let you have me. It's so simple I think even your dense mind must understand.'

Nilüfer pulled the kimono belt tight and went up to him. She poked the tip of her index finger into his mouth, and wriggled it around. She said, in English, 'You get me Gauloises and me go jig-jig. You get me no Gauloises, and me go right out of here. Got it?'

She snatched her finger back laughing, just before he could trap it between his incisors. Altan grabbed her arms just above the elbows, and pulled. She began to give way, sagging towards him. But she twisted back and laughed. 'I'll cry rape,' she warned. 'And what will your dear papa say then?'

Altan scowled. The muscles near the hinge of his jaw swelled up, hard as pebbles. But it was, he thought, necessary to accept a woman's whimsy, and he forced himself to relax, fetching a deep sigh. Then he rose to get dressed. His prick showed no sign of deflation as he prodded it into place under his pants. He opened the door.

'Fuck knows why I'm doing this. You're a teasing bitch, Nilüfer. I'll be back.'

After he had gone out Nilüfer stood in front of the

mirror. She tongued her gums as far round as she could reach, and then did her facial exercises, a programme of grimaces, pouts, yawns and squints which she had learned from a magazine would keep her face firm and young. If she adhered to the sequence strictly it took her nearly ten minutes to complete.

He heard talking in the corridor, outside the next room. It was in Turkish. Mustafa opened the door a crack to listen. At once a door slammed and someone moved past his own door towards the bank of lifts.

Mustafa swung his head quickly round the architrave to get a look at the departing back.

After five minutes, the telephone in Altan's room trilled.

'It's me. I'm in the lobby. And I don't believe this.'

'What's the matter, Altan?'

'That bastard's gone again.'

'What bastard?'

There was a stilted pause.

'Who did we spend most of the afternoon looking for? The fucking kidney's fucked off somewhere.'

'Did anyone see him go?'

'The doorkeeper says he hasn't been out the front door. I'm waiting around here for a bit in case he's gone off for a crap or something. Can we . . . What we started . . . Can we finish it later on? I mean, by the time I find this bum it'll be time to take him down to Harley Street to be carved up. Why don't you stay in my room, watch some television, whatever – okay?'

'Well, Altan, let's see. If I don't get too bored. See you. Bye now.'

Nilüfer hung up, and sat for a moment in complete stillness, like a posing model. Then she moved across and flipped on the TV. It was a game show and Nilüfer liked game shows. She settled down to watch.

The first knock on the door coincided with a burst of applause from the television audience, and she might have missed it. The second was louder.

'Coming!'

As she swung the door open she prepared an ironic face to greet Altan – Faye Dunaway at her most glacially cool. It was coincidentally just the expression with which to greet the stupid, stubbed face of the Anatolian peasant, Altan's kidney, who was standing there. She looked him up and down and saw he was wearing odd shoes. She could not suppress an aristocratic smirk.

When she looked up again it was into the barrel of the Beretta's silencer, the one he had bought from Darren Knight.

Nilüfer backed into the room and he followed. There was a thumping, sickmaking drumbeat reverberating under her ribcage. She sat down automatically on the bed, forehead hot, breathing reduced to short gasps. The hairs on her neck pricked up individually, which she'd thought happened only metaphorically in books.

The man closed the door softly and stood beside it, against the wall. He looked down on her, but she did not have the will to stare back. He said simply, 'Get your bath robe off.'

So it was like that. She was going to be raped. From a type like this it was not so surprising. At home he probably had sex with sheep. But where had he got the gun from?

She wondered how she would bear it. The question made her – in spite of herself – look at the face of the rapist. She had gone with violent men before. Sometimes they had clawed her skin, or used their teeth hard and drawn blood. Then she had joined in and scratched and bitten them in return. So both had let go all restraint and been satisfied. But what she saw in this man's face promised not abandonment, just pain.

'You look like you want to kill me.'

'You'll find out. Your robe.'

He stretched out his hand as if he might grab the front of her dressing gown and rip it from her body.

'No, wait!' She shrank back and rolled until she was standing on the other side of the bed. Her hand went to the knot at her waist. He watched the robe down to the floor, and said, 'I know you and what you are. You want to be a whore. You don't *have* to be one. You have plenty of money, or your Pa does. But all this is a game, some fantasy you act for your fun. Well, I hate amateurs and game-players. I'm a professional, see? I like other professionals. Give me.'

He held out his hand again, this time palm upward. Naked now, she bent, picked up the bathrobe which lay on the floor and passed it across the bed. The flimsy material made no more than a handful, bunched in his fist. He walked across to the window, opened it and pitched the ball of cloth out into the night. Then he looked around on the floor for the rest of her clothes. They were heaped near the bathroom door. He gathered these and sorted them, glancing up with metronomic regularity in case she made a move towards the door.

He picked out Nilüfer's nylon panties, stockings and suspender belt and lay them over the arm of the easy chair. The rest of the clothes he threw out after the robe. Then he twitched the curtains closed.

She again sat on the bed and watched him as he returned to his sentinel position by the wall. What did he mean, a professional?

It was then that she noticed the scarring around his neck – deep, ploughed-up flesh beneath the mandible. How had she missed it before? He was not tall and in his role as a humble peasant had held his face tilted forward, keeping the area shadowed. Seeing it now she knew it must have been a dramatic injury.

Under normal circumstances she might have moved close to him. She might have traced those scars with a gentle forefinger and asked, in a whisper, if someone had tried to chew him up. She tried to concentrate on not shivering. Verbal foreplay was not on tonight's agenda.

As if realizing that he was exposing his corrugated throat Mustafa moved to the easy chair and sat down. He did not, however, sit at ease but at attention, tense and alert. The chair was covered in an incongruous chintzy material which emphasized his menace.

After half a minute, he placed the pistol on the glass-topped fake-Regency low table. She was aware of his eyes crawling over her. Nilüfer was proud of her body. The skin was almost as silken as the robe she had just seen him crush into a ball. The stomach was flat as a table, the legs were classical, the uptilted breasts – she once had been told – were sublime. She thought, if he keeps me naked and does not touch me, he holds me in contempt. She was not used to her beautiful body being held in contempt. This was a hot night but the thought gave her gooseflesh. Even at gunpoint, someone with clothes keeps a vestige of freedom: without clothes, you are entirely a prisoner.

He read her thoughts and picked up the gun, resting it this time on his knee and keeping hold of its grip loosely in the fingers of his right hand. He said, in a quiet voice, 'Right. I want you to make a call to the desk. You will leave messages for your colleagues Altan Başkurt and Dan Barry, messages to bring the wasps buzzing back to the jam-pot. Then I want to know every detail – where they are right now, how many times you fuck them. Everything.'

It was then that Nilüfer for the first time became afraid of death. Not death in the abstract, the way neurotic people sometimes dwell on it. But on real, imminent death, hers, this night. This man was not a sexual deviant, not a rapist, as she'd thought. He was talking with all the premeditated precision of a killer who detached himself from his victims, a professional psychopath. Like he'd just said to her, *I hate amateurs*.

*I'm a professional.* Out of a suddenly dry mouth she managed to say, 'So this is . . . business?'

'Yes of course, it has all been arranged. It's nothing personal. Now repeat what you're going to say on the telephone.'

Dan came into the lobby of the Transnational, where diners were drifting in and out of the Cromwell Carvery. He had footed it most of the way from Islington and wanted a long hot shower.

His head was clear now. What had been most disturbing was how he'd hallucinated the tree-of-life carpet – his reaction to the threat to his life, rather than the threat itself. Now the visual disturbance had cleared, his danger had come into especially sharp focus. If Blanchard knew he was a writer there was no point now in continuing with his project. He had examined the options, and disappearance seemed the only sensible one. If he stayed around his life and liberty would hardly be worth more than a snap of the fingers. He must phone Lena, get a change of clothes and fuck off out of this. America. *South* America.

At the desk the porter dangled Dan's key, withholding it enticingly while he delivered Nilüfer's message.

'Er, Miss Akyol phoned down a message, sir.' His voice wheedled knowingly. 'She asked you to call by her room on your way up, sir, no matter how late. Said she'd a message to give you, a very important message, she said.' The porter winked.

Dan would ignore Nilüfer's invitation. Christ, what

did she want? He thought he had a fairly shrewd idea, she'd made two or three barely disguised passes at him on previous trips. The girl looked as if butter wouldn't melt, until she landed in a foreign country. Then, according to all the gossip, she turned into the biggest dickchaser since Messalina.

In his room he changed into jeans and a loose shirt, then quickly packed the small case. He found the bottle of Scotch and the Hittite queen and dropped them in between the jacket and trousers of his uniform.

He picked up the phone and punched the six-digit code for Istanbul, and his own apartment number. He heard the long, single-ring tone. He managed to force his voice into a semblance of normality. 'Hi, sweetheart. Me.'

'That you, Dan? How's things?'

'Just getting to bed. All well with you?'

'Of course. I went round to Georgette's and in case you're interested Con wasn't there. So I couldn't make up with him on your behalf.'

'What for?'

'The fight you had Saturday. Don't tell me you've forgotten.'

'Oh, that. The kid all right?'

'Yes. What's the matter? You sound on edge.'

'No. Annabel said something funny to me this morning. I thought it was in her sleep, but maybe it wasn't.'

'What did she say?'

'Called me a liar. "You tell lies."'

'That's odd.'

'Has she said anything?'

'No. She's been a bit quiet, nothing dramatic. I thought she was incubating a cold. I'll ask her, shall I?'

'It's probably nothing. Forget it. She was asleep. Forget it.'

'Will you be back the usual time?'

'Sure, usual time. See you then, okay?'

'Okay. Look, Dan, I –'

'What?'

'Oh, nothing. Just take care, now. I love you.'

'Me too, Lena. You take care. Bye.'

His throat was as dry as hot sand, and there was a lump which hurt like a tumour. *You tell lies*, Annabel had said. And he did. Dan Barry the actor and airline steward had loved Lena all right. What about Dan Barry the writer and heroin courier?

Mustafa and Nilüfer had been waiting twenty minutes when he stooped and picked up Nilüfer's nylons and panties. He pulled one of the stockings through his fingers with enjoyment and then twisted it into an effective length of cord. He told Nilüfer to lie on the bed. Without speaking he rolled her on to her stomach, bound up her wrists and, with the second stocking secured her ankles. Then he caught hold of her nose and pulled her face round to look at him, pinching the nostrils closed. His eyes were contracted and cold. When her mouth fell open to gasp for breath he inserted her panties, pushing them as far back as her tonsils. Nilüfer choked and retched as Mustafa knotted the suspender-belt around her head to keep the gag in place.

He had grown tired of her monotonous pleading whines. They would wait from now on in silence.

After another ten minutes came a knock on the door and the handle rattled.

'Nil! Let me in. I can't find the bastard anywhere. Let me in, Nilüfer.'

Mustafa moved to unlock the door, making sure the catch sounded.

'Nil? Are you still there? It's me.'

The bedroom lights were switched off but Mustafa had left on the light in the bathroom, with the door open a chink. He stood on the far side of the bed, against the dark curtain, and watched the Turk's shape move into the room. Altan closed the door carefully. With the strip of light from the bathroom behind him, he was a clear silhouette, a perfect target.

'Nilüfer, are you in bed?'

Altan approached the bedside. He could hear Nilüfer's body chafing the counterpane as she writhed, trying hopelessly to warn him. He breathed heavily in anticipation of his pleasure, mistaking her gyrations for sexual excitement.

Of the gun, Nilüfer heard only a sound, like a man spitting out the husk of a sunflower seed. Instantaneously a small, punctured noise was released from Altan's chest, and a truncated yip of surprise from his mouth. He pitched forward, his dead weight flopping on to the girl's breasts, as she wrenched back her head in horror. A scream swelled in her throat but was humbled to something more like a cough by the gag.

# 8

Dan showered and packed in a hurry. He didn't have any plan, just the general intention of putting a lot of London between himself and the Transnational Hotel. He entered the corridor furtively, feeling misplaced and exposed, like a chicken on a firing range. Mouthing a curse at the dilatory lift, he took the fire stairs, all seven flights.

The lobby was quiet, with just the ancient hotel porter and a couple of guests on their way upstairs. The porter was speaking on the phone as Dan approached to drop his key. Dan heard him saying in mournful tones, 'Well, I believe he is in the hotel, sir. His key *has* been taken.'

Dan put the key on the desk and the porter cocked his bloodshot, sagging face to one side to read the number. He suddenly became alive, all animated excitement.

'Did you say room number 737, sir? Well, sir, that's a real coincidence. He's here right now, sir. Just dropping off his key.'

Dan was crossing the marbled floor towards the door. The porter's eyebrows shot up and down, signalling. He placed his hand over the mouthpiece and called to Dan, 'Just a minute, sir. Mr Barry, isn't it?'

Then he spoke again into the telephone. 'Who shall

I say wants him?' He listened for a couple of seconds, before holding the receiver away from his face in mock disapproval. 'Hung up. Oh well. That was someone looking for you, Mr Barry. Must have rung your room just as you were on your way down.'

Dan stopped. '*Who* for me?'

'A gentleman. Didn't give his name.'

'From outside or from here?'

'Oh, in the hotel, sir. Gentleman with a pronounced foreign accent. From one of the rooms, but then we got three hundred of those, so I dunno which one. I expect when he heard me say you were here he upped and started down to catch you down here, sir.'

Dan went for the revolving door and straight-armed it with the heel of his hand. It moved a couple of feet and stuck. Dan rammed his shoulder and upper arm hard against the toughened glass. He felt the frame move as his pressure distorted it out of true. But something was making it stick fast.

The porter came out from behind his desk and began shambling towards him.

'Door does like to stick, sir, if you push her too hard. You need to use the right technique. Bit of finesse involved, if you know what I mean.'

Dan calculated how long it would take whoever-it-was to reach the lobby from the stairs. Another minute, at most – assuming he was starting from one of the upper floors.

'Well look, could you unstick it, please?'

'I'll do that with pleasure, sir. All it takes is a prod in

the lock with a screwdriver. Why don't you just take a seat and wait for your friend to catch you up? I'll go and fetch my screwdriver.'

'No. I mean I'm not waiting. I've got a letter to post, I want to catch the –' He glanced at the clock behind the desk. 'The nine o'clock post.'

'Oh, you've missed that I'm afraid, sir. You might as well drop your letter into the box just here. It'll go first thing.'

'Please release this door now, would you? I want a walk.' The panic was rising through him like a column of mercury. The porter, shuffling back to the desk, looked round at Dan with a degree of curiosity.

'All right, sir, no need to adopt a tone. It shall be done in two shakes.'

He had found a long, spindly screwdriver from somewhere behind his desk. Now he shuffled across to the revolving door. For what seemed like an eternity he probed the locking mechanism. Then Dan heard a click. The porter turned back.

'There you are, sir. She'll go round sweet as you like if only you treat her gentle, same as one or two girls I could mention, if you know what I mean.' And he winked. Or was it a nervous tic? He was certainly too old for this job, hovering with geriatric imperviousness in Dan's path. He still did not move out of the way, even when Dan put a hand up to his shoulder warningly. Another thought had struck him.

'And if that gentleman does come down, what shall I say?'

Dan heaved the old man to one side and shouldered past.

'Take down your pants and show him your arse, will you?'

The old porter, staggering sideways, and touching a forefinger to his forehead, didn't hear this clearly.

'Very good, sir. I'll do that, sir.'

By then Dan had spun away out of earshot into the night.

Mustafa was only thirty seconds behind as Barry's shape flitted ahead of him along Lillie Road, continually disappearing behind parked cars or in the shadows between the sodium street lights. But Mustafa was able to keep his quarry more or less in view. He was moving towards Earl's Court, an area which Mustafa knew well. If Barry got to the Earl's Court Road he could probably make it to Kensington police station and safety. He would have to be stopped first.

He saw Barry pause and look back, his face showing orange in the municipal lighting. He had seen or heard something. Mustafa froze. Then Barry took off again, this time running. He disappeared into the deep shadows of the curved portico of the Brompton Cemetery. On rubber shoes Mustafa ran towards the place he'd last seen Barry. A thud and a crunch of gravel told him what had happened. Barry had climbed up the iron railing and was now within the cemetery wall.

So be it. It would be easier in there, among all the

dead. Mustafa adjusted the position of his gun and prepared to make the climb.

Dan looked at his watch. He had been here ten minutes, lurking between ranks of gravestones, peering out from time to time at the central path. Several times he glimpsed his stalker's silhouette moving against the orange-reflecting sky, and then lost it among the huge blot-shapes of the chestnuts bordering the cemetery. The man was going up and down the path, casting about like a spaniel after a wounded duck.

He couldn't understand what had happened to his bag. He'd been sure it had hit the ground near the wall, but he thought now it must have pitched further away and bounced into a patch of tall grass. Whatever, he hadn't been able to find it in the few seconds he could afford to spend searching for it.

Suddenly, several gunshots, muffled by a silencer, coughed into the darkness. Only one round came near Dan. It smashed the face of an angel surmounting the adjacent grave. As the bullet ricocheted away, fragments of the statue's nose and cheek dropped around him, pattering like a shower of stone rain. Had he been seen? Or was the guy blazing away for the hell of it? Dan knew now it had to be the man in the car park. But who was he?

Dan moved off cautiously. Ten minutes later he reached the curved, neo-classical colonnade which encircles the central section of the cemetery. Here the clusters of sepulchres and family vaults, more densely packed than in the outer reaches, made a sort of grand, downtown area for the whole necropolis. It gave plenty of cover under which to move.

Creeping along the rear of the curved monument he found a workman's ladder propped against it. There had been no loose shooting for several minutes, and Dan would give anything to know where his pursuer might be. In the hope of gaining some perspective he tested the bottom rung of the ladder and started up.

The flat roof was lead-covered and its line swept to the right and left in a graceful crescent. From up here the whole extent of the graveyard could be seen, although detail was indistinct. The stones and monuments packed the area in eerie dignity, like silent witnesses at the scene of some unspeakable tragedy. In the moonlight the headstones that were of white marble gave out their sepulchral luminescence, and it was these Dan watched, hoping to see against them the flit of a shadow or a silhouette. But he sensed nothing until he began to inch, belly down, towards the front edge of the roof. Then he smelled cigarette.

The man was standing below and a little to Dan's right, in front of the arcade but shadowed by it from the moonlight. As he smoked he was cupping his cigarette preciously in two hands to hide its glow. He probably had the gun trapped between his arm and body.

Dan crabbed silently right until he was directly above the man. Then, shifting with agonizing care to his haunches, he leaned forward, hung there for a moment over the edge, thinking *This is stupid, I could be killed*, but already it was too late. He leapt, spread out star-fashion like a parachutist, free-falling on to his would-be killer.

He landed on his target with a grunt. The impact flung the man's arms away from his body and in the corner of Dan's eye something black shot out and clinked to earth – the gun. Then the stranger hit the ground, with Dan's body landing on top and bouncing, as on a mattress. The other man's lungs decompressed with a loud crump.

Dan had fallen to one side. He rolled over on to his hands and knees, then got to his feet. He collected the pistol and knelt beside its winded owner, whose mouth gaped and whose eyes popped in the effort to breathe. *The peasant. Of course – the kidney-donating peasant!* Dan's index finger found the trigger and curled round it. Then he placed the business end of the silencer inside the open, gasping mouth and waited.

Mustafa won his fight for breath, only to find his tongue weighed down by a tube of steel. The taste was of burnt cordite. Dan spoke succinctly. 'If you answer my questions I might not blow your head off.'

Mustafa's eyelids and mouth stretched to their limits. He jerked his head up and down. A gurgling sound came from his mouth that might have been *okay! okay!* Dan retracted the gun barrel until it hovered half an inch from the man's lips. 'Your name?'

'Mustafa. Don't kill me! I promise to you I'll –'

Dan thought, *how absurd it is for a killer to beg for his life*. 'You a professional?'

Mustafa looked blank.

'You kill for money?'

The Turk nodded yes.

'Whose money? Blanchard's?'

'*Evet*. Yes! This job is his.'

'And the job was to kill me?'

'And the Turkish steward Başkurt, both of you.'

'Why?'

'I don't know.'

Dan jiggled the gun, chipping a flake from one of Mustafa's teeth.

'You shit. I think I'll kill you now.'

'No, no! I say true, I do not know. Don't kill me. Don't kill me. He said only make it look like a political attack. That's what I know. A terrorist job.'

Mustafa's face was slewed to one side, trying to evade the pitiless attention of the gun barrel. Dan wondered if the professional killer had dreams like this, role reversals where he was menaced by his own victims, so vivid he sometimes would wake up sobbing. He hoped so.

'What happened at the hotel?'

'I kill Başkurt. I wait only for you. I come after you. Okay?'

Suddenly Dan was possessed by the capricious curiosity of the one who points the gun. He had all the leisure, now. The night was all around them, there was no one else, and it didn't matter how long it took.

'So Blanchard conceives the clever idea of making you pose as a peasant with a kidney to spare, right? This keeps you close to us, and gives you plenty of chance to put the bullets in. Have I got it so far?'

Mustafa was staring up at him, immobile.

'Meanwhile, I'm supposed to be the prize mug because I've personally imported the piece with which I am to be killed. Except, unknown to either of us, someone has already stolen the gun from me. Ironic touch. There's just one other small detail. It's not important. Just idle inquisitiveness. How much?'

But Mustafa had stopped listening. He'd begun to shake. Dan stood up, astride him. He gripped the Beretta's chunky stock in both hands and extended rigid arms. Now the gun pointed directly down at the Turk's face from a height of three feet.

'How much did Blanchard offer you? How much is my life worth?'

'Ten thousand.'

'Pounds?'

Mustafa did not understand. Fear had paralysed him. Dan kicked out, contacting the prostrate man's armpit.

'Pounds or dollars?'

'Dollars! Dollars!'

'For both?'

'Yes, yes. For both. And again five thousand if I kill the other man.'

'What other man?'

'The Englishman. Trubshot.'

'Trubshaw! You had to kill him?'

'After I kill you I am to get orders. By the telephone. Oh don't kill me, *effendim*. Don't kill me. I go away, you never see me again.'

'No,' said Dan. 'I can't trust you. And I'm worth more than five grand. I'm going to end your life, you turd. Now.'

He began to squeeze at the trigger. Mustafa cowered back and shut his eyes, shielding his face uselessly with his arms.

The trigger seemed stiff. Dan pulled harder. Nothing. A cat yowled just feet away from them, fractionally disturbing Dan's concentration.

The cat's voice acted like a whiff of ammonia on Mustafa. His head seemed to clear, and he read the situation in one scan. Then he lashed upwards with his foot as hard as he could, burying it in Dan's balls. There was a moment of nothing, then a blazing shock leaping upwards into Dan's groin. As if hurled by a blast, and still gripping the gun, Dan was rammed backwards, his head just missing the white marble coping of a well-tended grave. Like a racing whippet, the Turk was on his feet and running.

For several minutes Dan lay immobilized by starbursts of distilled torture, radiating upwards and downwards, inundating his body. Through it he began to realize miserably why the attempt to execute Mustafa had failed. He managed to thumb the safety-catch forward and sit with the pistol ready, just in case the Turk should return.

*

The Brompton Cemetery had been home to Charlie Maxton for several months already. He had begun by sleeping in one of the mausoleums, his favourite being that of the very hospitable Cartwright family. They offered a hidden location and a fairly spacious room above their vaulted resting place. All he needed to do was wedge the wooden door shut at night and he was safe from all the living world.

Then the contractor's firm of Flynn came to repair masonry and wrought ironwork. It took a while to work out how to get into their huts, but once this was done Charlie really had it made. He only needed to be inside the gate and lying low by six, when the workmen left and the park attendants made their tour. As soon as the gates were locked he was prince of the Portakabins. This was a million times better than the Cartwrights'. It was dry in the huts, and smelt of cigarettes, instant coffee, burnt paint and Swarfega, instead of moss and rotting dead leaves and, perhaps, dead people. He hadn't realized he minded the Cartwrights' smell until he'd known Flynn's. The atmosphere in Flynn's cabin brought rich pictures into his brain, images of his glory days when work up in Glasgow was as plentiful as water in the Clyde. Yes, it was sheer luxury, this. Charlie only needed to clear up after himself and be away and hidden again by seven the next morning, and no one was any the wiser.

This particular night, Charlie had gone off, like one of the dozens of squirrels which lived in the surrounding chestnut trees, to fetch another bottle of British sherry from his hidden store near the Cartwrights' family vault. He was humming under his breath a song from the radio in his childhood:

*Oh I love to go a-wandering*
*Along the mountain track*
*Dee-dum-dum-dum da-dum-dum-da*
*With my knapsack on my back.*

Charlie had just passed by the cemetery's Lillie Road entrance, when a small, soft case came flying over the wall. It landed almost at his feet. At once he heard the scrabble of someone climbing after it. Charlie was chuffed at his self-possession and quick reactions in picking up the case and melting into the shadows.

From his hiding place he heard the whispered curses of the man as he missed the suitcase, and then his running off. He heard, next, another person climb into the cemetery at just the same place, then sprint off in the same direction. Charlie knelt and opened the case. It was clothes he was interested in, warm ones for the coming autumn and winter, and here was what felt like a nice suit. But what was this? A bottle, it felt like. Jesus, Mary and Joseph on a bike! A whole bottle of Teacher's whisky. With trembling fingers he closed the case and headed back to the hut, with bottle and case clasped to his body. Once inside the cabin he put the suit on straight away and it fitted excellently. The clay woman was a puzzle. After turning her over in his hands, he placed the kneeling figure reverently on an upturned tea chest. Then he cracked open the seal of the bottle.

*Valderee, valdera, valderee,*
*valdera-ha-ha-ha, ah-ha-ha-ha-ha.*

Charlie had never had a whole litre of whisky all to himself before. So he celebrated this singular luck by drinking all of it. And, as he half-lay against a stack of high-pressure, propane gas storage-bottles, nodding between sleep and wakefulness, a burning cigarette fell from his filthy, knotted fingers. It rolled off his knee and into a paper bag in which he had saved some scraps of food. The bag ignited, as did the heap of old newspapers beneath.

Eventually Charlie woke up, but it was not to be for long. Within seconds the remaining air in the room was replaced by a raging storm of flame and smoke. As the inferno reached a peak of intensity the gas bottles exploded, launching bits of the Portakabin and its contents fifty feet into the air. There would be no one, anywhere, to miss or mourn Charlie Maxton.

Dan never heard the explosion which disintegrated Flynn's cabin. Long before it happened he made it to the spot where earlier he'd climbed the wall into this ghost city, and began looking again in the bushes and long grass for his flight-bag. But, after many fruitless minutes, he was no longer sure if it *was* the spot. He patrolled the whole length of the wall, looking behind every likely gravestone, every tussock and shrub.

After that he gave up, climbed out of the cemetery and moved north. There was a feeling of hollowness and isolation that is always so much worse in the night in empty city streets. He'd been alone, of course, when he started this, moving out to Istanbul and, with Altan Başkurt's help, approaching Nathan Blanchard. But the fact that no one else, not even Lena, knew his real reason for being there had given him safety. Now there was no safety, and his solitude was that much more real.

He could ring Jack Bacon, couldn't he? Doss down at his place. Dan found a ten pence in his pocket and eventually, beside a scruffy pub near Shepherd's Bush, he came on one of the black-and-yellow booths with which British Telecom had begun uglifying London. He stood inside the minimal plastic arbour and lifted the receiver. The apparatus gave out a purring tone to show it had survived unvandalized since the last repair.

As soon as he checked it out he hung up. How could he phone Jack when he didn't know the number? His address-book was in the missing flight-bag. Then he remembered Directory Enquiries and dialled 142, giving the operator Jack's name and address. There was a pause, before the woman's prim voice came back, 'I'm sorry, sir, the subscriber's number is listed ex-directory.'

'Oh Christ, is it? Look, this is an emergency. Can't you give it me? I need to talk to this man urgently. Very, very urgently.'

'I'm sorry, sir. There are no circumstances which permit me to give out this number.'

Dan hung up again. Anyway, Jack had a family and this mess was nothing to do with them. He walked on.

After a few minutes he came to Shepherd's Bush Green. Here at least the loneliness was muffled by speeding traffic. He must sleep. He crossed over to the Green itself, and looked about for somewhere. He felt dragged down by tiredness.

There was a row of wood-and-iron benches alongside a tarmac path. A huddled human shape was stretched across the nearest of these. Following the line with his eyes, he saw that every one was tenanted by a member of London's vast and ghostly colony of vagrants. Some lay beneath sack and newsprint coverlets while others hugged their knees like clumsily magnified foetuses, abandoned and wrapped in rags.

Finally Dan found a vacancy. He approached the narrow, sloping bench with little expectation of comfort. He lay himself stiffly down, pulling his cotton padded jacket tight round his body and crossing his arms. The gun and silencer lay heavy across his thighs. He slept.

A noise like tearing flesh erupted beneath him. Dan jerked his head from the bench and let it fall with a painful crack. Then he leaned forward cautiously and peered into the shadow below the bench. The sound came again, a long wrenching followed by a splintering climax. He caught a glint of bottleglass and a bunch of grimy fingers curled round its neck. There was somebody sleeping under the bench. He shut his eyes, doing his best to shut out the snoring.

# 9

Mustafa realized what a mistake he'd made about five minutes after legging it. In forgetting to flip the automatic's safety catch Dan had committed the simplest, most suicidal novice's error in gunplay. Then he'd had the Englishman sprawling on the ground, clutching his balls: he'd been easy meat. Mustafa should have fallen on him, smashed his head on a gravestone. He could have shot him at leisure after that.

Why hadn't he even attempted it? His instinct had forsaken him, or else a deeper, more primitive one had asserted itself. He was tired, a draining of strength that was emotional rather than in the body. His fractious, mutinous nerves would entertain nothing except headlong flight.

He reached the wall at the east end of the graveyard and travelled along it, scanning for footholds. He knew the reason why he'd not stayed to kill Barry, but it was more like *un*reason. He admitted it to himself at least, though no other would have extracted it this side of torture. Shame. He'd run for shame, because he'd lost control of his body. He'd lain there, with that vermin poking *his* own gun into *his* mouth, and his mind had gone numb. Then from sheer terror his bladder had emptied itself. Piss-scared. Like the woman, Gaby, this afternoon. He shuddered.

His wet trousers stuck to his thighs and chafed them as he vaulted the wall of the cemetery into someone's back garden. It took him a few minutes to find an alley between these tall, tightly-packed houses. When he did he crept through into the street like a diseased rat.

The car he stole was a modest little number. Unless he intended to sell them, Mustafa never bothered with BMWs or other performance cars – they were too tricked-out with distracting security devices, and too much trouble to hot-wire. This little wedge-shaped hatchback gave him no trouble. He started it up and headed east. The car's dashboard clock showed it was ten-thirty.

As he drove, the smell of his own urine rose to his nostrils and sickened him. To a Turk bravery in a fight is the supreme badge of manhood, far outranking sexual prowess, alcohol consumption or any other yardstick. Cowardice, then, is tantamount to being a nancy-boy, a transvestite. It is the abrogation of virility. And the worst kind is autonomic fear, the kind you cannot control, the kind he showed tonight when, under pressure, he pissed himself.

He hadn't a clear idea where he would go at first. But he found himself driving east, and the rest followed automatically. He knew London pretty well from a time when he had lived here ten years ago. But he had no friends here. The nearest he had to a friend was Darren Knight.

He reached Knight's warehouse in Haggerston

almost an hour later. He left the car three streets away. The entrance was down a cobbled alley, and Mustafa kept to the shadows. He was half-way to the door when it opened and he saw a fellow with a wrestler's build strutting out – the doorkeeper. The door was left open as the bruiser disappeared behind it. Mustafa waited for the sluicing sound of urination, then darted forward and through unchallenged into Darren's premises.

The cellar was palled by thick tobacco smoke under which more than fifty men and women were standing around drinking beer from cans. Most of them were under thirty, the youths in jeans and loose cashmere sweaters, many of them with heavily gelled crew-cut hair and gold earrings. For this occasion their women were obviously perfumed and dressed up in low-cut dresses of satin and silk, or whatever passed for silk. They showed their enticing pale-pink legs all the way up to their thighs.

Faces turned towards Mustafa as he went in. As if they were looking out for someone else their faces showed disappointment, turning to frank distaste when he walked among them.

'Ere, Darren, someone's let a Paki in.'

'Pheeyaw! Dun 'alf pen.'

They were laughing.

'He's pissed in his rounds or sunning, Darren. He a friend of yours?'

Darren Knight came bustling up.

'Come along now, gents. Nearly time for the main event on your programme.'

He pulled Mustafa aside. 'Blimey, son. You been swimming in a karsi or what? These punters are all dressed up for a night out. Couldn't you smarten yourself up a bit – they think you're a bloody Pakistani, in that dosser's clobber.'

A drunken man swayed in their direction and started shouting incoherently in Mustafa's face. Darren pushed the man away. 'Leave it out, Lennie, leave it *out*! Look, Mustafa son. You look terrible. You in trouble or what?'

Mustafa shrugged.

'Yes, I need some help from you, Darren.'

'Then fuck off into my office and keep your head down. I can't do nothing now, we're gonna stage the big fight. When it's over and every sod's gone home, I'll sort you out. Okay? But just keep your boat-race out of here. Sorry you got to miss the action, but these blokes are racist like you'd never believe. Now if you'd turned up in a nice suit . . .'

Mustafa did believe. He'd lived in London, hadn't he? He felt the need to vomit rising in his gorge. His brain palpitated, as if trying to suck the oxygenated blood through a blocked straw. The blood itself seemed to stagnate in his arteries.

He went through to Darren's office, checking gingerly behind the safe in case of any lurking dogs. But the Pride of Parsloe's Park was not there: he was about to meet his Waterloo in the fighting pit.

Mustafa sat down in the desk chair. He shut his eyes. The voice of Darren, as Master of Ceremonies, filtered hoarsely through the door. He was calling the big fight.

'My ladies and gennermen. For the main event on your programme we have an international, inter-breed fight of exceptional quality, *exceptional* quality, ladies and gennermen. And it is between, all the way from the United States of America . . .'

Mustafa roused himself. He wouldn't be disturbed now. A pair of jeans, a shirt and jacket hung behind the door on a wire hanger. Mustafa stripped off his clothes and dressed himself in these. He now turned his attention to Darren's safe. It took him several minutes but this was an old design and the lock yielded in the end. There must have been six or seven grand inside – and two handguns to choose from.

*MUSA DAĞ*. The two words scrawled in lipstick on the dressing-table mirror meant nothing at all to DI Cuffley, of Kensington CID. Had the murderer left his signature on the crime, like a painter or something? He revolved on his heel and faced the bedroom. Some policemen rated murders aesthetically. That was not Cuffley's way, but if pressed he would not call this a particularly elegant crime. It was a journeyman's job, spoiled by gratuitous cruelty to the naked girl.

The killer had also been careless. In his haste he'd not made sure that the sprung latch caught the door as he left. A room-service waiter had found the bodies just twenty-five minutes previously, lying where the killer had left them, the bound girl wedged under the corpse of the man. She was unmarked, but her mouth was gagged with her own clothing, and two plugs of wet toilet tissue had been inserted in her nostrils. The pathologist said she'd died of asphyxiation.

Now they had been separated, and she lay under a sheet under the window. The man's body was spread across the bed, an expression of terminal astonishment on its sideways-twisted face. It lay there, the legs sticking out rigidly over the bed's edge.

Philip Grimshaw came in with the photographer and fingerprint team.

'They're both members of a Turkish air crew on stopover. Anatolian Airways. The bloke was one of the stewards. The girl was a stewardess. I've got the captain and the crew in one of the conference suites – the Brideshead Room. They're practically hysterical.'

'You've got all the rest of them?'

'All bar one. There's another steward missing.'

'Where is he?'

'That's the odd thing, Skip, no one seems to know. Not slept in his room, apparently.'

'Hmm. What do we know about him?'

'Well, he's a Brit. Dan Barry. Now living the expat life in Istanbul, apparently.'

'Well, we'd better find him.'

He nodded towards the corpse. 'Meanwhile we'll get his workmates down the nick and have a chat with them, while the doc gets a t.o.d. and these jokers get on the hunt for pawmarks.'

Cuffley took a last look round, shaping his lips as if

to whistle. He gestured behind him, at the mirror. 'What do you think of the copyline, Grimshaw? Turkish, is it?'

'Don't know, Skip. My languages stop with the pen of my aunt.'

'You disappoint me. Well, we'd better get on. Be on this all night, I should think.'

When Mustafa emerged from the office the dogfight was in full spate. The spectators were themselves yapping and growling like dogs as they encouraged the terriers. 'Go on! Hold 'im. Thass it, break that 'old. Goo on, goo-o on, my son! Easy now. Eeeasy now!'

From below the hubbub he could hear the obstinate mucous snarling of the combatants. He went to the fringe of the crowd and looked between heads. It was not, as predicted, going too well for the Pride. The black and brown brindled pit-bull had him by the lower jaw and was not about to let go. The muzzles of both dogs were blood-caked and their eyes rolled. Painfully, on straddled legs, their heads jerking this way and that, they circled like geriatric dance partners. As they went they streaked the sawdust beneath them with saliva and gore.

Mustafa's stomach flinched with disgust. Cruelty that was human-on-human he understood. He often found it necessary to be cruel and was not averse to it. This, though, was beyond him.

He began to move round the ring of spectators towards the door. He hadn't yet cleared the edge of the crowd when the same drunk who'd accosted him earlier turned and saw him.

'Ere, didn't old Darren tell you to scarper, Gunga Din? You do what you're told, wanker. This is England, right? We are the *English*. And we dun want you 'ere, we want you out. Goddit?'

He was following Mustafa across to the door, jabbing his finger in the air.

'We want all you Paki bastards back in your own shit-hole country, goddit? See, we the English shit on all you Paki bastards.'

Mustafa turned. He edged left so that the door was beside his right shoulder. The drunk was standing ten feet away, in the middle of empty floor. The dog-pit crowd, another twenty feet back, were still engrossed in the contest. Now the drunk was motioning, with both his hands stretched towards Mustafa.

'Come on, say it. I'm a racist, right? What you gonna do then?'

The young man's face was violently distorted, yellow teeth bared, nostrils flared, the flesh on the slope of his nose wrinkled like a snarling animal's – like the dogs over there in the pit. He had turned his palms up and was waggling the fingers in a come-at-me gesture.

'What you gonna do, you brown-arse wanker?'

Mustafa closed his eyes and opened them again. He felt dizzy, and then that strange distancing, the film between himself and his experience, the clogged thought-processes. This was enough. He couldn't talk, argue or fight. He wanted only a simple way out. He reached into his clothes and produced Darren's Browning automatic. It had no silencer. He shot the drunk in the chest.

The shock waves reverberated across a sudden, awed quiet. The spectators turned together with wide eyes and mouths – a uniform pattern of O on every face. Then the expressions crumpled into fear, rage, panic: the instincts that take you over when you see a man deliberately and unexpectedly killed. Without exception they lost control. Some, already inflamed by the violence and blood of the dog-pit, began racing towards him with enraged faces. Some staggered screaming towards the far wall, and the chained-up door of a second stairwell. Others fell for shelter behind the circular wooden paling of the dog-pit.

Mustafa's head was suddenly as clear as a spring morning as he picked his targets. He shot three men dead with carefully placed head-shots. They were at such a distance from him that their faces, when hit, exploded like tomatoes. In horror, the others stopped coming at him and either turned or dropped to the ground. Men are never as brave as they imagine. He took four more of them out with bullets in the back as they scattered in retreat.

He heard Darren's voice coming from behind the dog-pit.

'Mustafa, Jesus, that's enough, drop the gun. We can talk. Oh my Christ, Mustafa, stop it!'

Mustafa waited beside the door until Darren's minder came blundering through from the street-door.

A look of amazement seized his enormous, brutal face. Mustafa stepped up behind him and blew a hole in the back of his shaven head. He fell like a side of bacon.

Mustafa started walking slowly towards the middle of the room, alert in case anyone should produce a gun. None did. A woman was crawling and whimpering between the dog-pit and a wall. Mustafa walked beside her. In one movement he placed his gun-muzzle against her uppermost cervical vertebra and pulled the trigger. Three more of Darren's punters died as they crawled blindly across the concrete floor. It was like target practice on a swarm of terrified, pink-skin cockroaches.

Mustafa knew his magazine was now empty. He leaned against the cellar's side wall and watched the main cluster of people plucking futilely at the chained alternative exit. Now that the flow of shots had stopped one of them turned to look at him, an older, potbellied man. The man detached himself at a run from the others, his stomach bouncing as he stumbled forward. He made it the length of the room and escaped into the night. Realizing the gunman had not killed him, others began to follow in a trickle and then a purposeful flow. Mustafa watched them without emotion. Darren did not look at him as he fled. Within half a minute the room had emptied through the door in a gush of terrified people.

Mustafa was still calm. He walked towards the stairs, passing close by the dog-pit. Incredibly, the two bull terriers were still at it, the American with its jaws clamped into the British dog's mandible, the British struggling stubbornly on, though the pain must have been intense and unremitting. For a second the two animals sensed Mustafa looking at them. Their eyes rolled towards him, and he thought he read an appeal there.

Slamming another clip of thirteen into the butt of the Browning he aimed carefully. He put his first bullet between the pit-bull's shoulder-blades and into its heart. His second penetrated the skull of the English dog. Then he left as quietly as he'd come, picking his way between the corpses.

# 10

The raw recruit to vagrancy wakes early. It was not yet six when Dan unpeeled himself from the bench, his side entirely numb from the shoulder down. He was cold from the inside out.

The taste that lurked in his mouth was metallic. He spat vigorously, with almost the venom of an old dosser, and hugged himself, rubbing up and down his upper arms. Then he hopped and jogged about to get the circulation purling again. As he did so the Beretta banged against the side of his chest and his full bladder rode up and down in his abdomen.

He walked over to a nearby plane tree. When he'd pissed, he tried to reposition the gun. The only way it was both reasonably comfortable and out of sight was rammed into his waistband at the back.

The fear, that seemed a natural, even sensible extension of the long night-time, had receded with the darkness. Now Dan just felt grimy, his skin crying out for hot, soapy water. He remembered he had a bathroom all his own, and a soft bed, and a carpet on the floor, if only he went back to the Transnational Hotel. Somehow, the idea that it might be a place of danger seemed incredible in the crisp light of a Tuesday morning in London, with milk floats whirring and clanking about their business and the first commuters drifting into the tube station.

He would go down there now, at least to wash and breakfast. Then he'd think. For the moment his mind was paralysed, although already lying somewhere in it, like dregs, was the thought of that bag of heroin hidden in the room. If he got to his room he could at least retrieve it. Then call Jack Bacon. He had little money, no credit cards and no passport. He would need Jack's help; Jack was just about the only friend he had in London.

Cuffley had had no sleep. While the uniformed lads were blue-arsing around over some explosion at Brompton Cemetery he was patiently collecting and sifting the statements from the people at the Transnational Hotel. He was also waiting for the missing steward, Daniel Barry, to turn up. Something told him the bloody man wasn't going to, though. Something told him bloody Mr Barry was the murderer. The night porter had some confused story about him leaving the place like a scalded cheetah at midnight.

At six-thirty Grimshaw came in with a tray.

'Coffee, Skip?'

'God, Phil, if I have any more caffeine my eyeballs'll start chucking out sparks. How are our overnight guests bearing up? Comfortable night?'

'The ones who aren't in a state of catatonic shock are getting pretty stroppy, Skip. Shouting the odds about the Turkish consul. We going to let them out this morning?'

'Oh yes. None of them's a suspect – it's the missing

one, the Brit, we want. The captain's a bit of a snake in the grass, though. Wouldn't trust him further than a gob of spit, personally. But I don't think he knows anything.'

'Well, can I go home? The wife'll just be getting up and the bed'll still be warm if I don't hang about.'

'Spare us the cosy domestic details, Phil. I want you to get on to the Turks and tell them what's what – the airline and the Embassy. Do the necessaries, okay? And then get some lads down to the hotel, turn those Turks' bedrooms over. I want complete inventories of their gear by nine-thirty. We'll have to start letting the four of them loose by then.'

'What about the press?'

'Oh well, we're in luck, if you can say that. This lunatic in Haggerston going for the *Guinness Book of Records* is keeping us nicely off the front page. Or any of the pages, come to that. No need to say anything, even if the scribblers should bother to come round. We'll issue a statement in due course, etcetera.'

Cuffley's pile of statements contained little illumination. The night porter's evidence offered a glimmer, but the guy was obviously dealing from less than a full pack of cards. Senile decay, alcohol, what did it matter? Cuffley went through his statement again, but it made almost no sense. Kept blathering on about the revolving doors or some such crap. There had been nothing suspicious about events on the flight, not according to the other crew members. They had been most helpful in forming a picture of the dead man –

vain, witty, rich, Casanova complex. Less on the girl. Some kind of discretion at work here. Oh, and Musa Dağ was apparently pronounced Musa *Dah*, and meant Mount Moses. Apart from that he was none the wiser.

Cuffley's face was convulsed by a yawn. He rubbed his knuckles into his face, his fingers feeling the stubble and accumulated skin grease. It had been just another dirty night.

At eight o'clock he went back to the Transnational and was immediately intercepted by Grimshaw, hurrying across the lobby. There was a flushed look of excitement about his eye and cheek. 'Skip, guess what, they found Barry.'

'Oh yeah? Where exactly?'

'Not *exactly* anywhere. Bits of him everywhere, all over Brompton Cemetery. You know that explosion last night in some workmen's hut, D. S. Matlock was talking about it?'

'Oh, yeah. Bits of him you said? Was he in it?'

'Must have been sitting on top of the bang, sir.'

'Really? So how do they know it was Barry?'

'Well, sir, shreds of his uniform were decorating the trees, like Christmas tinsel.'

It wasn't until he was about to walk into the hotel's slip-road that Dan saw the two police cars parked under the canopy at the entrance, and a young constable stationed beside the swing doors. The policeman was holding himself like a guardsman at ease, staring straight ahead. If he had turned his head he would have had a clear sight of Dan. Dan did not break stride. He went on walking two hundred yards up the road, then crossed and walked back, until he could look again from a more furtive distance. He tried to see through the plate glass of the reception area at what might be going on inside. He could see nothing.

The seductive smell of hot bacon curled out from Kath's Kaff, a workman's café facing the Transnational. Dan had eaten nothing since lunch yesterday. He bought a morning paper from the Indian newsagent next door and pushed through Kath's plate-glass door.

Inside just nine Formica-top tables were ranged together, each one with its cluster of sauce bottles. It was the Greasy Spoon incarnate. On opposite walls hung a Coca-Cola clock and a Pepsi-Cola calendar. At the far end was a counter, with a huge, old-fashioned, embossed till and a stainless-steel tea urn. From the kitchen beyond emanated the even sizzle of breakfasts frying for Kath's only two customers, labourers who sat and sipped from outsize mugs while they read their copies of the *Sun*.

Dan studied the large rectangle of card, pinned above the kitchen door. In Kath's handwriting it detailed the fare: fried eggs, sausage, bacon sandwich, burger, chips, tea/coffee. Kath herself presumably, damp with steam, emerged from the kitchen, wiping her hands on a check cloth.

'Yes, love?'

'I'd love a bacon sandwich, no, *two* bacon sandwiches please. And a mug of tea.'

With a sigh the woman drew off his tea and turned back into the tiny, crammed kitchen. Dan took up his station beside the window. From here he could keep an eye on the hotel entrance.

He opened the paper. The headline over the lead story was explicit: *GUNMAN SLAYS 13 AT EAST END DOGFIGHT.*

Dan read the brief story.

*Police are this morning investigating a gangland connection in the murders late last night of 13 people at an illegal dogfight in north-east London. Witnesses said the shootings took place at around eleven-thirty, when a man of Asian appearance fired at random into the crowd of about fifty at the event, which was held at a Haggerston warehouse. Most of the victims were in their twenties, and are believed to include at least two women. Police say they are still trying to identify the dead, and cannot release a full list of victims until all relatives have been contacted.*

*In a report published as recently as last Christmas the RSPCA warned about the spread of dogfighting in London, which is described as 'a cruel and callous activity, well organized by racketeers keen to cash in on a section of the public's fascination with canine aggression'. A spokesman for the society said last night, 'It looks as if some kind of vendetta or power struggle may have started. Our officers know this so-called sport is run by criminals, so such a thing is quite likely . . .'*

Dan riffled through the rest of the Home News pages. He found no reference to events at the Transnational Hotel, Fulham. Whatever Blanchard's thug had done there last night it had not yet impinged on the media. Perhaps the Haggerston murders had overshadowed it.

'You can't sleep in your bed these days for fear of being murdered.' It was straggle-haired Kath, wading round from behind the counter to bring the labourers their plates. 'I mean it's everywhere. You hear what went on in that hotel over there last night, then?'

One of the men grunted. It could have meant he had heard, or that he hadn't. The ambiguity did not stop the woman.

'Bloke shot a girl right in her room. Sex killing. Milkman told me s'morning. Shocking, really.'

Dan looked away again, through the window. A *girl* shot? It didn't make sense. He thought that it was Altan who'd got it.

There was activity outside the hotel. Two more police cars drew up, disgorging five uniformed men, one woman and two suits. Without waiting they swept inside.

Dan's breakfast came. Each sandwich was made from two slices of factory-baked bread. The bacon inside was crisply grilled, curled and lumpy. As he picked up the top one in both hands and bit into it, hot bacon grease spurted on to his chin. He shut his eyes and chewed.

He swallowed slowly and luxuriously and opened his eyes. A coachload of Japanese tourists were filing out of their transport in front of the canopy, and through the hotel doors, looking with curiosity at the immobile constable posted beside it. One or two of the men photographed their wives posing next to him. Three minutes after the empty coach had gone, another car turned up, an official black car – nothing very stretched, just one of the lesser Rovers, but driven none the less by a uniformed chauffeur.

Two passengers were together in the back seat. They stayed talking for thirty seconds. When they got out, Dan had a clear view of the one on the side near him. He was probably forty, lean and fit-looking, with close-curled grey hair and a brisk military manner. He had Intelligence Services written all over him. He walked up to the uniformed copper on the door, flashing an I.D. His companion joined him. There was something familiar about the second man. He was in cords and a baggy cotton jacket. Still keeping his back to the road, he hovered like an assistant while the army type spoke to the policeman. Then for a brief moment the sidekick turned to survey the scene behind him. His eyes seemed to linger on the café window and Dan got a direct view of his face. He resembled the earlier Japanese arrivals in just one respect: an expensive-looking single-lens reflex camera slung round his neck.

A towel-service van passed between them. But Dan had already seen who the man was. Quickly he put his face into his palms. Had he himself been spotted through the window? And what the hell was Jack Bacon doing arriving on an assignment in a government motor?

*

Cuffley stood tapping his foot in the centre of Dan Barry's room, a few doors down the corridor from where the bodies had been found. He was watching the team of forensic men crawling around the carpet with tweezers, collecting hairs and any other human detritus that might lie among the tufts. Grimshaw was on the phone. He cradled the receiver and glanced towards his chief, who was looking dangerously close to eruption.

'Well? Any news of the fucking bow-wow?'

'On its way, Skip.'

'On its way? Should have been here forty-five minutes ago.'

It had been one of the forensics who'd found a grain of white dust on the coffee table. It might of course be anything – sugar, salt – and he'd sent it down to be analysed.

'Sod the lab, Grimshaw. A canine's quicker than a chemist. Or it would be if they'd shift their arses and get the mutt here.'

'The desk says there's a bloke called Craike downstairs looking for you.'

'Craike? Never heard of him. Copper?'

'Well, he's a Major, Skip, so I reckon not.'

'Major Craike? And what does the good Major want with us?'

Grimshaw shrugged.

'I don't know. Talk to you, I suppose. Something to do with this lot.'

There was a knock at the door. Grimshaw opened a

crack, and then wider to admit a golden Labrador with his handler. Cuffley rubbed his hands in anticipation. He was certain there were drugs at the bottom of this murder. Everything, the fact that these guys were flight crew, the country they came from, everything pointed to drugs. The grain of whatever-it-was had merely been the first clue. Now this pooch would give him the clincher.

'What about Major Craike, Skip?'

'Tell you what, you go and see him, Grimshaw. Find out what he wants, tell him I'm too busy.'

He bent and fondled the sniffer dog's ears, two perfect triangles of folded velvet.

'Come on, Fido. Let's get on with it.'

By eight, with Dan on his third cup of tea and Kath's business a little brisker, the Press had started to turn up in force. Dan recognized some of them: Ian Petrie from the *Standard*; Freddie Stubbs; Crawford Dalziel, doyen of crime correspondents, always immaculately dressed, always kitted out with the utmost up-to-date equipment. The reporters were swarming together near the hotel entrance, the photographers moving back to get shots of the tall, concrete building in which the murders had taken place.

A minute later he saw Stubbs and Petrie crossing the road towards Kath's Kaff. Quickly Dan raised his newspaper. The two newsmen clanged through the door and took up positions at the window table on the other side of the door, just a few feet from him.

'Well now, thank God for a haven of no-nonsense cuisine,' said Petrie. 'I'll have a cholesterol sandwich please, love – er – bacon sandwich, that is. Freddie? *Two* bacon sandwiches please.'

'And coffee – two coffees,' chipped in Freddie.

They lit cigarettes and began to talk in lowered tones, their sharp, lean faces inclined towards each other. If Dan could eavesdrop he might glean what had taken place over there last night – and more to the point how much the police knew about it. It was quite likely, with his disappearance, that they'd consider Dan a suspect – especially if they found the drugs in his room. As the conversation went on, the two hacks began raising their voices. Dan caught a few fragments.

'... four measly per cent ... I told him ... offer was as much as he could afford ... that's not including the car ... I mean it's derisory, that fuck-wit Peter Benson's getting twice as much ... I mean where, where actually, do they *get* these figures from? ... So I told him, no bloody editor's going to put a ceiling on *my* expenses! And he said, right ...'

Jesus, thought Dan. He got up, in full view of his two colleagues. Their vulpine faces never looked up, as he knew they wouldn't. Back and forth they traded their views on RPI and VAT, collective bargaining and sweetheart deals, portable pensions and the mileage allowance.

Dan found enough money in his pocket, dropped it on the table and slipped away. He smiled, almost laughed out loud. Through sheer bloody blind cupidity, they'd missed out on the day's best exclusive. Him.

Grimshaw had found his boss sitting on the bed looking smug, as only he knew how.

'Skip, I think I ought to warn you, this looks like a Special Branch job.'

'Oh? What makes you say that, son?'

'Well, I been talking to this major downstairs. It turns out he's M.o.D. or something, from the Empress State down the road anyway.'

'They're mostly Ministry of Defence, Grimshaw, yes. And what was the Major's interest in this thing?'

'Said they'd been trying to catch someone who's been using this hotel for signal intercept. Something like that. Wondered if the murder had any bearing.'

Cuffley looked even more disgusted than usual.

'Bloody brass neck. When do they ever let us poor bluebottles in on their exciting world of spook-busting? Yet they come flexing their bureaucratic muscles in on us when it suits them. What's this about Special Branch?'

'Well, I was filling him in, and this other bloke he had with him – no name supplied – with the details, and I happened to mention the Musa Dah thing, on the mirror. Well, he says, I suppose you know what that is? And of course I says it means Moses' Mountain. And he looks at me like I'm some arsehole, and he says, no, it's an Armenian terrorist group which goes round knocking off Turks around the world. So that's why it's a Special Branch job.'

'Is this Major still downstairs?'

'Yes, Skip. Said he'd still like a word.'

'Well, he can't have a word. I want you to go down there and tell him something from me. It could be a Special Branch job, and it could be something else. It could be a Drugs Squad job. And until I'm absolutely certain which it is, it's going to remain a Brian Cuffley job. Take a look in that.'

He indicated a manila evidence-envelope which lay on the floor near his feet. Grimshaw crouched and pried it open. What it contained was unmistakable – the shibboleth of modern police work. Cuffley's I-told-you-so expression said it all.

'Behind the bath. He unscrewed the panel and tucked it in on the other side. Good concealment, but it took our Fido just a couple of tail wags to find it. So this Daniel Barry may have been a terrorist, yeah. But that's speculation. What's certain is that he was moving a great deal of H. Enough, I'd say, to send him down for twelve years.'

*'The train now standing at Platform 3 is the nine-thirty-six Intercity service to Oxford, calling at Reading, Didcot and Oxford. Platform 3, the nine-thirty-six to Oxford. The nine-forty-two Cornishman Service to Penzance will leave from Platform 6. . .'*

Under the soaring span of Brunel's roof Dan walked past the Paddington Station war memorial, with its gigantic infantryman, putteed, greatcoated and bandoliered. This figure had always made him uncomfortable. The bronze, despairing face under the soup-plate tin hat seemed to glare down at the passengers as if at a plague of trench rats. Rat-like, then, he scrambled against the tide of commuters and scuttered down the stair with its brass handrail into the men's lavatory. At Paddington this is below ground – functional rather than comfortable. However, from one slot machine he acquired a disposable razor, from another a ready-pasted toothbrush, and during the ten minutes spent in that dripping, white-tiled chamber he crapped, washed, shaved and brushed, feeling afterwards more like a member of the human race.

He did not want to hang around the station. If, as he guessed, he was now a wanted man, the mainline railway terminus for Oxford, Wales and the West of England would not be a smart address. But he had to do something with the Beretta first. In the lavatory stall he sat and studied the gun. He remembered from his teenage reading that Ian Fleming had made this Bond's choice. He smiled at the thought: how uncool to prize a gun because James Bond used the same one. Like eating spinach because of Popeye.

He seemed to be looking at a run-of-the-mill automatic weapon – at least judging from what he'd seen displayed sometimes at police press conferences, and in films. He'd never handled one before, let alone shot with it.

He began to teach himself the rudiments. He screwed the silencer into place. That presented no problem, and he took it off again. By fiddling at the base of the butt he learned how to slide out the magazine. He found it contained two columns of bullets, one of six, the other of seven rounds. He filled his palm with these menacing, snub little objects. He might have been handling a set of dragon's teeth. He refilled the magazine slowly.

Before sliding the clip back into place he operated the safety catch and pulled the trigger. Nothing happened. He turned the gun round and round, until he realized it wasn't cocked. The way you cock an automatic pistol is by firing a round. This jerks the slide mechanism which cocks the hammer and chambers a round. But for most guns a manual method is required to cock the hammer before the first shot. Dan discovered this, pulling back the slide and seeing the hammer rise and click into readiness. He squeezed the trigger, trying to get used to the necessary pressure. Drily, the firing pin snapped down.

When – short of actually firing the thing – he'd learned as much as he could about the Beretta, he began wrapping it, with the silencer, in a cocoon of toilet paper. He went on wrapping until it was an unrecognizable lump, which he pushed into his jacket pocket. He returned to the station concourse. At the bookstall he bought a sheet of brown paper and a small roll of tape. He made a tightly-wrapped parcel and stood in the queue at the left-luggage counter. He exchanged the package for a ticket. Then he prised off one of his shoes, lifted the insole and slipped the ticket underneath.

*

He was walking west, along the towpath of the Grand Union. A few joggers and dogwalkers were around, but otherwise the canal was quiet. Dan had happened on it, but he had seen at once that it was the perfect escape route – a secret footpath that led all the way out of London and on for hundreds of miles. A path which surely no one would think of watching, not for him.

He couldn't understand about Jack Bacon. Suppose he put a charitable construction on the events: Jack was concerned for Dan's safety. He had contacted the police with his worries yesterday, following their meeting at the pub, and in no time found himself talking to Customs and Excise, say, or the Drugs Squad. After the sequel of last night he had been picked up by this government type and whisked over to the hotel to see whom and what he could identify.

But what, in fact, *had* happened last night? Had that ape really killed Altan? And where was the ape now – stalking him? Looking for Felix? And how much had Jack told the authorities? Jack, after all, knew every detail about Dan's projected book. For Christ's sake, what was he playing at? The charitable construction looked more and more unsafe. At this stage of the game, Dan appeared simply to be no more than a criminal, a hard-up journalist who turned to drug-carrying to pay his debts. His only hope of credibility was to deliver the book to a publisher and the evidence to the police simultaneously. It would be disastrous if he were arrested and put on trial now.

So what was Jack up to? He must know he'd be

dropping his friend right in it if he started whispering in policemen's ears. The revelations had to come from himself, not from Jack. Officially, Jack Bacon knew nothing. Unofficially he'd had updates on Dan's progress, but that was social, it was pub talk. As far as writing the book was concerned, Jack Bacon was supposed to be in the back seat.

No. The more he thought about this, the less charitable he felt. As soon as Jack knew for certain that Dan had carried drugs from Turkey to Britain, he had contacted the authorities. It was a deliberate betrayal. The only explanation that made sense was that Jack had become afraid of being charged with conspiracy or as an accessory – in other words he'd done it to save his own skin.

Which was why, while Jack had official transport, Dan was on the run, with hardly any money and no more than the clothes he was wearing. Dan put his head down and walked on.

'Come here, Runcie, you bastard! Wait till I ... Runcie! Come back!'

The shouts were chasing a dog, a curly-haired stubby-legged mongrel terrier, which was haring along the towpath towards Dan with something pink – apparently its tongue – flapping from its mouth. Looking past the animal he saw a moored narrowboat, the cabin brightly painted in reds, yellows and blues, with a woman standing on the deck and pointing.

'Hey, you! Can't you stop that dog? The little bugger's pinched my lunch.'

With feet apart Dan straddled the towpath and waited. Runcie would not have much room to side-step, since the path was bounded by the water on one side and a stone wall on the other. The mutt didn't even check when it saw Dan. It lengthened its stride and from a distance of three feet tried to leap past him.

Dan took the dog with a simple expedient. He bent sideways, closing his hands to make a hoop around the space through which Runcie was already committed to jump. At the halfway point in the dog's trajectory Dan snatched him upwards and in a single movement swung round. In surreal surprise the dog's tongue seemed to fly away as the animal's jaws opened in a biting reflex, only to snap shut on the empty air. For Dan had already let Runcie go. He continued through the air, twisting clumsily, until he exploded into the water about seven feet out from the bank.

The woman stood looking on, shading her eyes with a hand. Then she was clapping.

'Bravo! Bra-vo! You deserve a trial with the New York Mets.'

Dan retrieved Runcie's detachable tongue, which proved to be a raw lamb chop. He brushed off the worst of the cinder crumbs and carried it towards the narrowboat. The dog was swimming along beside him yelping. He reached out for his collar and yanked him out of the water, depositing him immediately on the ground to avoid getting wet. He needn't have bothered. A few steps further on and there came from behind him a sound like lashing rain. He turned and was hit by a cascade of cold canal-water centrifuging from Runcie's coat. There was a scream of laughter from the woman.

Reaching the narrow boat, he extended his hand, with the cinder-coated meat hanging from it. 'Yours, I presume.'

The woman was still laughing frankly as she took her chop from Dan's fingers. 'Your face when the water hit you. God, it was a scream.'

She inspected the meat, as one might look at goods in a January sale. 'Jesus, I can't eat that now, can I?'

With a gesture of unselfconscious freedom she pitched it over her shoulder, over the side of the narrowboat and into the water.

'Then that bastard dog shan't have it either. It's all his fault, little tyke.'

She was thirty, maybe. She wore a royal blue jump-suit and canvas shoes. A multicoloured scarf contained her boiling mass of red curls. She had suppressed her laughter now, but was smiling still. As he looked at her, some of the knot inside him began to come loose.

'Why do you call him Runcie?'

'Ah well. The poor little fellow may not know what he is, but he so wants to please, you know?'

'Even by making off with your lunch?'

'Well, even the Archbishop of Canterbury must have his moments of frivolity, or so I imagine.'

She looked at him now, a disturbing, searching appraisal. 'Are you walking somewhere or just strolling?'

Dan shrugged. He wasn't walking anywhere in particular, but on the other hand he wasn't strolling. She went on, 'Just that if you've no more pressing engagement, can I offer you a glass of something? Or a spot of lunch?'

He looked over her shoulder at the canal.

'But your lunch has gone to the dace and the tench, or whatever coarse fishes are down there.'

She shrugged. 'I have a couple of eggs and some bread. Fancy a boiled egg buttie and a glass of wine?'

He did. 'That'd be lovely. No, I have no more pressing engagement.'

'I'm Marilyn Mills. You've met my dog. And this, the *Pumblechook*, is my boat. That just about completes the family introductions, from this side.'

She stood in his way and looked at him steadily. There was still laughter in her mouth but her eyes were serious now.

'You'll have to tell me your name before I let you aboard. It's an old canal custom.'

'Oh, yes, of course.'

He looked around. Water, cinder path, brown brick canal wall, hump bridge about thirty yards ahead.

'It's Bridges. Jeff. Jeffrey Bridges.'

Like a prat he'd said the name of a film star. But she did not seem to register. She stood aside.

'Then come aboard, Jeff Bridges.'

It was a coincidence that Edward Craike's office was just five minutes' walk from the Transnational Hotel.

Set back from Lillie Road, the Empress State is a decayed, Orwellian government building whose three wings sprout outwards from a central core like a monstrous concrete-and-glass parody of a tricorn hat. It is largely the preserve of the Ministry of Defence, of which Craike's department, although in practice autonomous, was nominally an offshoot.

He and Jack Bacon chose their moment to walk back there just as the press men, many of whom might have recognized their colleague Jack, were in conference with Cuffley. The two men had quite failed in their mission to obtain even a degree of cooperation from Chief Inspector Cuffley. But perhaps it didn't matter.

'Nothing will convince Cuffley that he's not dealing with the greatest drugs bust since the French Connection.'

'Yes, but I notice he's keeping Drugs Squad at arm's length.'

'He's keeping everyone at arm's length. God preserve us from police inspectors with the delusion that they're Heinrich Himmler.'

Bacon laughed. 'That's a bit strong. I'd do the same if I was him. He doesn't know what we know.'

Traffic crawled at slower than walking pace along Lillie Road, exhaust pipes juddering, the trucks' gears changing ratio impatiently in thuds and growls. Jack Bacon had to raise his voice to be heard. 'What difference will the death of Barry make to everything, by the way?'

'None whatever. He might have been useful ultimately, Jack, but quite frankly he wasn't much good to us so far, was he?'

Bacon looked rueful. 'We got some quite good stuff, didn't we?'

'What, all that garbage about Hittite treasures, and the supposed site of the Tower of Babel?'

'No, I mean we got a pretty good picture of Blanchard's movements, when he was leaving Turkey, where he went, things like that.'

'Granted, though I could've got that by a less circuitous route. The thing that bugged me about Dan Barry was that the bloody man was a journalist. We could never have got him to work for us consciously, like Başkurt, because we'd never have been sure of his loyalties.'

'I'm a journalist, Ed.'

Craike stopped walking. They were alongside the car park barrier of the Empress State building. He looked up at the extraordinarily belittling architecture of the block. It was utterly out of sympathy with anything else in the area, yet he found it oddly inspiring.

'But you were army first, Jack. Barry didn't even know he was working for us. Unwitting agents can be useful at the right time and place, but they can also be a bloody liability when they suss you out. And Barry was intelligent. It was only a matter of time, I always thought, before he'd work it all out.'

'And what about the loss of Casanova?'

'Well, he'd outlived his uses, hadn't he? Becoming a bit of a dodgy number too, I thought. Not to be trusted.'

'Christ, you're hard, Ed. I mean, don't you feel you used these men? Don't you feel at all responsible?'

'No time for that sort of thing. I serve the crown, I'm responsible to *it*. No, I see these killings as a setback, because they could mean we lose our line to Blanchard. But the man's such an idiot I don't think it'll be hard to keep tabs on him.'

'And meanwhile, there's a killer about.'

'Blanchard's contract man, not dangerous.' He laughed. 'I mean not of any general danger. Trubshaw on the loose could prove much more of a problem, I fancy. We need him collared pretty fast.' Craike looked down at his shoes, paused a moment, then said, 'Look, I'd better go in, and you'd better not hang about – might be seen by one of your deadline-chasing friends. Cheerio.'

Jack Bacon hurried away. Craike passed through the vehicles' security barrier and across the car park into the vast building from where, in three small caged rooms, he operated his network.

Craike showed his pass as he went through the glass doors. He had already rough-hatched the next move in the Blanchard operation. He just had to fill in the precise details.

# II

A triple sneeze racked the squat frame of Nazım Ali Bey, General Manager of Anadolu Hava Yolları, as he sat before the spotless expanse of his desk. Nazım Ali was superstitious, and – since in his office there was nowhere for dust to accumulate, no papers even – he had the uneasy feeling that this fit of sneezing must betoken something unpleasant in the offing.

'*Geçmiş olsun*, Nazım Ali Bey. May it pass.' His secretary Ayşe came in with a thin sheaf of correspondence for his signature.

'Can't understand it, Ayşe Hanım,' he complained, unscrewing the cap of his fountain pen. 'I don't think I have a cold coming on.' She stood behind his left shoulder and positioned the first letter in range of his nib. He steadied it with a blunt, well-manicured left hand, fashioned his autograph in a series of loops, dives and dots, and reached for the see-saw blotter. Ayşe placed the next letter on top of the first.

'There's been a man hanging on the phone for the last ten minutes, says he must speak to the General Manager in person. He got very agitated when I told him you were holding important meetings.'

'What does he sound like?'

'By the voice, an Armenian. But he doesn't give his name.'

‘And what does he want?’

‘Won’t say. Just that it’s very important and can’t wait. But to me he sounds like just another irate passenger. Shall I tell him to write in?’

Nazım Ali stroked his ramrod military moustache. ‘No. Put him through. One should try to keep in touch with the public mood.’

Deliberately he screwed the pen together as Ayşe retrieved the last of the signed letters and withdrew. Apart from the blotter and fountain pen, the only objects on his desk were two telephones, a black and a white. He picked up the black phone and put it to his ear.

‘Is this Nazım Ali Karabaş?’

‘Speaking.’

‘The General Manager of Anadolu Hava Yolları?’

‘Yes.’

‘And is flight AH586 your service to Paris and London?’

‘Of course, who else’s service to Paris and London could it be?’ He glanced at the huge timetable which hung framed on his wall, and added with a certain pride, ‘It is our premier route. They are presently on the ground at Heathrow and fly back this afternoon.’

‘Then I have this message for you. We have sent an operative to hunt down members of your crew. By now they will have died. This will add another droplet to the ocean of the Armenian people’s vengeance against the Turkish butchers of 1896, 1915 and 1922. That is all.’

As if unaware that a buzzing noise meant the other party had hung up, Nazım Ali went on holding the phone to his ear. His face was frozen in a mask of perplexity. He held the position for two, three, four seconds. He blinked. Then he threw the phone down and leaped up, sending his chair crashing backwards into the wall.

'AYŞE!'

His roar could be heard two floors beneath.

Breakfast had been the usual struggle. Annabel asked for porridge, and changed her mind as soon as it was made. Then she would not get dressed. Holding the saucepan in one hand Lena used the other to drag her into her bedroom, and she'd retaliated by throwing a toy concrete-mixer into the porridge because she said the porridge was concrete.

Lena had arranged for Georgette to run the child downtown for nursery this morning, as she did about once a week. So, at seven twenty-five, she stood ready with her daughter in the open air outside their block.

In his usual frenetic style, the *kapıcı* was using his mop and bucket on the apron of concrete around the door. He would slap the water down, slop out some gouts of bleach, and rhythmically worry at the mixture with the rag mop. He had a grotesque disfigurement: a flabby horn of flesh which grew out of his cheek and hung down to his jaw. As he agitated his mophead across the wet slick in that way he had, this projection, as thick as a frankfurter sausage, would waggle up and down, and then wave airily from side to side, like a tapir's nose sniffing the wind. On occasion, when he was working more than usually hard, the thing would go into a centrifugal revolve on his face. The blemish fascinated Annabel. To keep the child from staring, Lena had firmly walked her into the middle of the small, dry lot which was faced by the entrance to the flats.

'Here's your lunch – sandwiches, boiled egg, fruit cake and an apple. It'll probably be much too much for you. I've put in some money for an *ayran*. Got your reader?'

Then there came a moment of pure calm. The two of them stood as if entranced in the morning air, the child tilting her scrubbed face up towards the sun, her mother looking downhill at a porter, just beginning the painful climb up from the Bosporus shore. He had a small dining table and four chairs lashed precariously to his saddle, and they lurched from side to side of his bent back with each step. A human donkey.

Lena put her hand palm down on Annabel's head. She suddenly had an intense experience of her child as a trusting, vulnerable dependant. Such moments were rare and Lena felt simply grateful. It gave the only possible meaning to all that washing, cleaning, shopping, driving; the endurance of tantrums and bickering, the daily erosions of the life of a parent.

For someone who was not a parent, or at least only an honorary one, Dan was very keen on how parenthood changed you. It had been the cause of the rift between himself and Conrad Hamilton at the restaurant the other night. Dan had become drunk and argumentative.

'Okay, you're talking about the sixties. Lena and I were only just born in the sixties. The world was up for grabs and we missed it, just our luck. But you two are classic gussies, right?'

Georgette had screwed up her face interrogatively. 'Gussies – what are gussies?'

'Grown-up sixties swingers, that's you two, right? You were the people who could've really grabbed the world by the balls. You had the chance. How did you fuck up?'

'How d'you mean, fuck up? I'd like you to know –' began Conrad.

But Dan was unstoppable. 'No, you fucked *up* because the world was grabbed back by the same guys who were throttling the life out of it before – industrialists, big unions, crime syndicates, dynastic politicians. It was their system. And they sure as hell weren't going to let go without a bust-up.'

Conrad was smiling, reminiscently.

'There *was* a fight, if I recall. Quite a few fights. Kent State University, Chicago Democratic Convention.'

'Yeah, and you *lost*.' Dan laughed. 'The hippies marched on Washington and all they did was link hands, thousands of them, in a giant circle around the Pentagon, trying to levitate the fucking thing! They thought you could float anything away you didn't like on a cloud of cannabis resin.'

'Yes, but wasn't it *funny*?' said Conrad. 'That's what you serious young property-freaks of the nineteen-eighties can't understand. You're too hung up on money and position to see that it's much nicer to laugh and have fun. That was the real meaning of Karl Marx, by the way. Make furniture in the morning, garden in the afternoon and philosophize after dark. Or, put it another way, play all day and fuck all night.'

Conrad Hamilton was an archaeologist at the American College. His left-wing credentials were impeccable, including having sat out the Vietnam war in Sweden.

'That's *shit*! Marx has nothing to do with the case, he was a sponger who lived off his wife and rich benefactors and never made a joke in his life. But you hippies, Con, you lived in the present, which was fine while the trip lasted. But you came down eventually, didn't you? You came down, especially, with kids.'

Georgette made a face. 'You make it sound like a dose of something, Dan.'

'So it is, Georgie. A dose of reality.' Dan's face was flushed with excitement. 'The system has us hooked. If we wriggle, it hurts; if we try to tear away, we leave essential bits of ourselves behind. And then we die. So we have to teach our children to survive as long as they can on the hook.'

'I don't much like what you're implying. How do we do our children any favours by simply endorsing the military industrial monster?'

Dan took a long pull at his glass of wine. 'I'll tell you how for free. Because it's honest. Face it, Conrad. Having kids has turned you into a materialist, same as me, same as everybody. We're all opportunists, even Conrad draft-dodger Hamilton.'

Conrad turned to Dan fiercely, pointing a stringy finger at his chest. 'I don't like the sneer in your voice. I was not aware of you ever putting on a uniform.'

'Ah, I'm too young, Conrad. And I'm British. We have the sense only to send the willing to war. No, Con, you should've gone out there and zapped the gooks, like a good old American boy. But you went out on a limb. You'd never go out on a limb now, would you? Else what the fuck are you doing peddling the American dream to the Yankee-doodle junkie kids of the Turkish ruling class? Dope, coke, fragmentation bombs, *Newsweek* – it's all the same! We all do it.'

Conrad's face was a study of restrained fury. He stood up. 'It's late, Georgie. We should go now – the babysitter.'

But Dan wouldn't let it go.

'Or maybe I've got the sequence the wrong way round. Maybe you only had kids because you *wanted* to become like this, as an alibi. A cast-iron excuse.'

Conrad had already dropped his share of the bill on the tablecloth and was walking towards the door. Hurriedly Georgette picked up her bag and said good night. Dan raised his glass and smiled in triumph at the Hamiltons' backs. 'Good night, hypocrites.'

He had insulted her friends, and yet Lena felt a tug

of compassion for him. In his cups he was invariably tactless, just as, sober, he was quiet and reserved. It meant the man had few, if any, real friends.

Georgette's car crunched to a stop beside them. As Lena stood and waved Annabel away she thought, *I don't remember now why she came into existence. But as soon as she did, Annabel's needs completely took over my life, superseding any other needs.* Men find it so hard to accept that shift – women, of course, have no choice. But men are babies. Underneath that self-contained exterior Dan was a baby.

She turned and climbed the stairs back to the flat. This morning the library was closed and Lena was going to make jam. That's how much Annabel had changed her. A jam-maker. The only times she'd felt in any way her old self was when she'd got away and left Annabel behind. Like when she'd gone off to the coast last year, when she'd met Dan. Christ, how they'd behaved – like teenagers in the first flush.

She got out the various pans she'd be needing and switched on the radio for company. It was tuned, as ever, to the short-wave frequency of the BBC World Service. She began washing the fruit.

The tear ducts of Nazım Ali's eyes had been primed all morning, and a bubble of self-pity had lodged itself just beneath his breastbone. Bar the loss of an aeroplane there could be few things more disgraceful for a general manager than to have his expensively trained personnel getting themselves killed abroad. Let one of those individuals be the son of the owner and you were really in trouble.

Bearing up as best he could, Nazım Ali buzzed Ayşe. 'Did the two relief crew get off okay?'

'Yes, Nazım Ali Bey. On the British Airways flight at noon.'

'Good. Now I want our people out of the hands of Scotland Yard and back home on our own flight this evening. Fax the London office to hire a good lawyer.'

'They want to know should they be telling the British police about the terrorists' phone call to you?'

'No. Nothing. Tell them nothing. Get everyone home, and then, maybe. You can fax that to the London office too, but make it cryptic.'

'Oh, and Nazım Ali Bey –'

'Leave me, Ayşe. No more for now!'

'Forgive me, but you've got to go and see the families. Dan Barry was . . . er . . . living with someone – Lena Priestley. She's got a little one, but calls herself Miss. The story will reach the radio and TV any time now, plus the evening papers. The entire press corps is camped outside. They want a statement and I can't go on stalling them forever. You don't want Miss Priestley and the Başkurt family to find out about this from the news, do you?'

The general manager groaned. 'Can't Murat do it?'

Ayşe spoke with gentle insistence, like a patient mother. 'No, Nazım Ali Bey. It must be you, you are the chief. That is protocol.'

'If I must, I must. Thank you, Ayşe Hanım.'

First Miss Priestley, then. He looked up the address. He could drive round by Emirgan and then sweep on and around to the Başkurt place. He buzzed Ayşe and told her to bring him Barry's and Başkurt's service files and get his driver to bring the car to the rear entrance.

Ten minutes later they were bouncing along the Bosporus road, with Mehmet chattering about a load of pyjamas he'd bought cheap over in Üsküdar, and was hoping to sell at a great profit in the Grand Bazaar. Curtly Nazım Ali told him to shut his noise.

Nazım Ali tried to visualize Dan Barry, but could not get a clear image: these lean-faced, fair-skinned north Europeans all looked much the same. Barry's employment by the airline had been the result of the phenomenal growth in Turkey's tourism in recent years, so that it became company policy to recruit native speakers of the passengers' languages. He remembered chatting to Barry and his girlfriend at the staff's New Year party. It had been an excellent chance to practise his English, but he hadn't liked the man excessively: too much the supercilious Englishman.

The girl had been another matter, of course. Blonde and tall, with blue eyes so intense. *Brigand eyes*, as the Ottoman poet had it. Yes, brigand eyes, and a delicious blush to the skin. He remembered he had toyed with the notion of propositioning her: it was clear she could hardly be satisfied by this starched-shirt of a lover. But in the end, and with regret, he'd done nothing about it. His sexual life was in enough of a tangle as it was. He settled to think up a few words of comfort.

It was two-thirteen when he rang the doorbell. He should allow perhaps twenty minutes for this. It would be painful, but, after all, it was his duty. The lock turned.

As soon as she opened the door, Nazım Ali could tell that Lena already knew; had just, in fact, found out.

Miss Priestley's fetching blush was gone. Her face was grey and rigid with shock as she stared uncomprehendingly at him for a few moments. Then she seemed to understand his arrival, and motioned him into the narrow lobby, where they both stood awkwardly and said nothing. Nazım Ali cleared his throat but, strangely, not one of the fine phrases he'd thought up in the car seemed in the least suitable now.

Abruptly Lena walked through into the sitting room, and Nazım Ali followed. There was a pervasive smell of cooked fruit. No children around the place at least, that was a blessing.

A service hatch opened into the kitchen, and from within the Turk could hear the funerary tones of the BBC World Service winding up its news. Allah! She must have only found out this very minute! What a fool he was not to think of it. You can make the local TV and radio shut up about a thing like this, at least for a few hours. But, of course, you can't gag the foreign stations, and he should have known she'd be listening: the English never quite leave their England behind, do they?

He nodded towards the open hatch. 'Miss Priestley, you know then?'

'I know.'

There was a pause, in which Nazım Ali traced the pattern in the carpet with his eyes and then counted the legs on the sideboard. At last he raised his head and looked at her.

'A terrorist attack, Miss Priestley, random. Not a personal thing at all. More like an ... like an accident.'

Lena Priestley spoke, suddenly ferocious. 'Couldn't you have stopped this?' She was staring hard, forcing the words out like single interjections. 'He told me he was warned. Couldn't you have *stopped* this?'

'Warned? Warned by whom?'

'By you. By the company.'

'By us? Miss Priestley, I don't think I understand.'

'But you must, Nazım Ali Bey. You must understand. Isn't that why you gave him this?'

She walked through the kitchen, wrenched open the fridge door and pulled out the pistol, now furred with frost. She thrust it out towards him, grasping the butt so that its barrel pointed at Nazım Ali's stomach. Seeing her white knuckles and shaking arm, he was for a moment afraid that she was threatening to shoot him. He stepped back in dismay. Then Lena's arm dropped and the gun hung at her side. She looked exhausted.

'He forgot it yesterday morning, I suppose it might have saved him if he hadn't . . .'

'Look, Miss Priestley, I don't know where Dan has got this gun from, but I assure you it was not from ourselves, not from the company. Is that what he has told you?'

'Yes. All the staff were issued with them – for anti-terrorist purposes, he said.'

Nazım Ali frowned and shook his head.

'Well, I'm most glad that you have told me this, Miss Priestley, because I can take the opportunity of denying that my firm ever issued its personnel with firearms. Absolutely not. We never would do that.'

This was not going well. This business of the gun had rattled him, he was too much on the defensive, which was the wrong tone to use at this time. She ought to have words of consolation. He cleared his throat again.

'Of course airlines *are* at a certain risk from terrorists, and what I *can* tell you is that Dan put up a hell of one fight, Miss Priestley, and he certainly did save the rest of his crew from death, yes, a certain death. So you can be assured of one thing, if it can be of any comfort. Your – ah – friend died a hero. Yes, a hero, Miss Priestley.'

Her eyes were very eloquent. They said, *so what? He's a dead hero.* Then they said, *please go, please leave me alone.*

He began to move backwards towards the door.

'I regret, now I must find the family of the other dead man. I wish I could adequately . . . I wish there was more I could do right away. Is there a friend who could be with you? The company will talk to you about – well, if it can be of any financial assistance, money and things like that. But that time will be later, of course.'

He had reached the door. She stood, not even looking at him, with the gun still dangling from her right hand. There was really nothing more he could say to her – just the conventional condolence blessing. She would not even know it, perhaps. But with a little bow of the head and neck he said it anyway, '*Başınız sağ olsun*, Miss Priestley.'

Then he let himself out. Soon the expatriates would be rallying round. She would be all right.

As his car drove on towards the Bosphorus bridge, the Anadolu Hava Yolları General Manager felt reasonably satisfied with his performance. That stuff about Barry being a hero wasn't bad. Of course, he hadn't the faintest idea of the circumstances of Barry's death, as yet. But you had to bolster up the poor woman's morale with something.

Then he was seized by a paralysing thought: the gun! Where did Barry get it from, and what had he been up to? More to the point, was it wise to leave it in the hands of his grieving girlfriend?

He almost ordered Mehmet to turn around and drive back to Emirgan, so that he could take the weapon into safe keeping. But truly the gun had nothing to do with the Company or with him. It would hardly be politic to meddle in this; his action might be misconstrued. Besides, she had a child and was not the foolish type: she would wear the stiff upper lip well. Moreover, he had yet to face the formidable

Başkurt family. He said nothing and let Mehmet drive on.

Lena sat in a folding chair on the balcony. She could not dwell on anything in particular. Her thoughts drifted with the aimlessness of someone drugged. From a nearby house a radio spooled out a nasal female vocalist, being tortured apparently by a harsh and relentless musical backing. The heat was intense.

Lena felt utterly limp. She tilted back the chair until her head touched the wall behind, and shut her eyes. With the sunlight on them, her lids were translucent and pulsing red. She thought of Dan's blood. The news had mentioned an explosion, so he must have shed blood. She wished she had more details.

She found the sun too hot and went back inside.

There were so many questions she had to face. How would she meet her friends, with their pity? How could she explain to Annabel? And where would they go, the two of them – what would they *do*, for Christ's sake? It was as if her brief life with Dan had been a break with the past, a new start in a new world. Now she was adrift back in the old one again, and it was a world she hardly thought she knew any more.

She stood in the centre of the sitting room and revolved slowly, noting the everyday objects, the detritus of family living, around her. The gun lay on the sideboard where she had put it earlier, after Nazım Ali Bey had gone. But now it was no longer significant, no more than another item from a household inventory, like that plastic calculator, the stack of cassettes, the can of fly-spray, Annabel's Postman Pat books, the hand-painted fruit bowl they'd bought at Easter in Iznik.

She moved through into the little room off the hall which doubled as study and spare bedroom. Its slatted shutters were closed against the brightness, and the room was stuffy with that naphthalene smell of rarely used blankets. The semi-darkness welcomed her now, after the glare and heat of the balcony.

The room contained little except a single divan bed, a bookcase, Dan's rickety writing desk and a cane chair. She sat down at the desk. It had been salvaged from a heap of discarded furniture which had appeared one morning on the waste ground beside the block of flats. Dan had wire-brushed it and applied a few coats of Prussian blue paint. He'd said, 'I'll use it to write my novel on. You just wait. One day I'll find a formula, and then I'll be off. I'll jack in this job sooner than you can say *Finnegans Wake*.'

The desk had a knee-hole and, to one side, four drawers of varying depth. She opened the top one. It revealed a scramble of paper clips, stamps, india rubbers, pencil stubs and drawing pins. She stirred them around with her fingers and pushed the drawer shut. She slid the second drawer open. There were only envelopes, blank postcards and a scatter of used cheque stubs. The third drawer contained several spiral-bound notebooks and two or three bundles of letters and postcards held together by rubber bands.

She picked out one of the notebooks. It seemed to be some kind of dream diary, but she couldn't bear to look at it now and pushed it back in the drawer.

The last of the desk drawers appeared empty. She put her hand right inside, feeling as far as the back. Her fingers met a smooth surface, whose edge she found with her fingernails. It was a photograph. She picked it out.

The black-and-white print was unmounted. It showed two rows of eight boys, each in grey flannel shorts and white shirts. They were probably about eleven years old. Their ties were variously askew, and most of their faces looked unnaturally tense, as if their noses or bottoms itched. It was the common expression of children in snapshots. Behind the boys was a brick building with ivy and part of a mullioned window. In front of them was a card, propped up on the grass, which read 'Class 3B' in juvenile script.

It was no professional school photograph. The focus was not all it might have been, and the composition was slightly askew, giving the class an uncomfortable list to port. She examined their faces.

Dan was probably the skinny, knobble-kneed kid second from the right in the front row. He looked slightly dazed, with his mouth twisted into a grimace. It was strange how she could see a picture of Dan aged eleven and feel no emotion: she was sure a more recent shot would be insupportable. Yet this was the same person she was looking at now.

Or was it? This was a Dan she had never known,

whose head was filled with quite alien details: stamp collecting and football statistics, Latin declensions and anxiety about bullying or a cricket fixture. It was not a Dan she could grieve for.

She glanced on the reverse side, but there were no names written there. The other faces were just faces, forgotten classmates of a murdered airline steward. Once these freckled, button-nosed, spike-haired urchins had defined the world for him. They had as much reality for Lena as a set of chessmen. Yet how many of class 3B, she wondered, had died, like Dan, in the intervening three decades?

Lena carried the photograph through to the sitting room. She tried to visualize her lover's face as she had last seen it, to chart the ways in which his face had changed into adulthood. But she couldn't. She went to the bookshelves and pulled out all the photograph albums she possessed. But Dan had always been behind the lens. Lena realized she had no photograph anywhere of the adult Dan. The juvenile school group contained possibly the only image of him she possessed.

The doorbell rang. She opened the door to her friend Georgette.

They embraced, hugging each other tight.

'Conrad heard the Turkish news. He rang me at once. Oh God, Lena, you poor, poor darling!'

Georgette held Lena for a full minute, and then drew away. There were some arrangements to make, and she ought to be brisk about them. 'Look, I've got the kids in the back of the car. I've already asked Annabel to come back to us for tea and stay the night and she wants to. Do you want to come too?'

Lena did not even consider it. 'No, I'll stay here. There might be more news, and I'll be better on my own. I will.'

'If you're sure. But you'd better come over tomorrow. I can keep her with me if you like. She'll have to be told, Lena. If not, she'll find out on her own.'

'Not yet. I don't want her to know yet. Okay?'

Georgette's face for a second showed a spasm of sympathetic pain. Then she said, 'All right. We'll talk tomorrow anyway. But in the meantime you know how to use the phone. If there's anything, you ring. *Anything*, at any time. Right?'

Lena managed a twist of a smile. 'If there's anything, I ring.'

# 12

Marilyn Mills held up the bottle.

'Well, are you going to take the risk?'

Dan was perched on the cabin roof, looking down at her. He laughed, cautiously. He said, 'Look, sitcom writers make jokes about this. Like, haven't you tried my home-made nettle wine – I always boil it up with a pair of dirty tights to give it body? It's slightly on a par with you must see our collection of naff holiday souvenirs.'

'It may be deadly, but it's not deadly boring.'

Marilyn up-ended the bottle into Dan's glass and the straw-coloured liquid glugged down.

'Really it can be pretty good stuff when I've made it right.' She poured for herself, took a long swallow and wiped her lips. 'Well, what I mean is, bugger the taste, just so long as it makes you pissed. What d'you think?'

Dan took an experimental sip, holding the stem of the glass between thumb and index finger. He spat into the canal.

'Hey! Don't waste it!'

'I'm just tasting. That's how it's done.'

'So, what's the verdict?'

Instead of replying he tipped the whole glassful down his throat in one slug.

They ate scrambled eggs and drank the home-made wine. Marilyn talked and Dan drank recklessly until, in time, Blanchard, and the airline, and Istanbul itself became veiled from his memory in the muzz of Marilyn's conversation and her acidic brew. He drifted. He forgot his grudge against Jack Bacon, his fear for his own life, his love for Lena. He drifted across a flood of fatigue and alcohol. He spun and drifted like a man falling asleep in a rubber raft.

A sound-system hung on brackets inside the cabin door. She slipped a tape into the slot: Sibelius. Dan was following Marilyn's hand as she talked, gestures flowing from her slim arm and wrist, beating time. She told fluent, cynical, amusing stories about her life on the canal. But if you didn't listen to the words, only her voice against the music, and watched her hand as it gestured, it was sensuous, a mesmerizing experience. Dan leaned back against the door of the cabin. He closed his eyes as the ice-bright violins cut the air.

Time passed. There was a noise from somewhere underneath him, like a large animal clearing its throat, then a deep and comfortable pulse mixed in his head with the smutty perfume of diesel exhaust. As he opened his eyes, Marilyn was on the bank casting off. She must have been matching him nearly drink for drink, but she seemed not in the slightest the worse for it. Dan was having trouble focusing his eyes.

'Which way are we going?'

'Away from London. I want to make Bull's Bridge. Then we'll tie up for the night.'

Dan tried to sit up. The music was finished. 'What, you tie me up? Or me you?'

'Don't be cheeky. Look, do you have to be anywhere at this moment in time?'

'What is this moment in time?'

'It's three o'clock. You've been asleep, nice company you turned out to be. I'm asking you, do you have to be anywhere, go anywhere?'

'Not that I'm aware of, no.'

'Then for Christ's sake get down there and finish your kip on one of the bunks. You look terrible.'

She settled herself on the stern rail beside the tiller, reached for the throttle and bumped the engine into gear. The *Pumblechook* at once began to nuzzle gently forward through the water. Dan grunted and rubbed his eyes. The aft deck was a tiny space, with barely enough room for the two of them. The bank was moving past his eyes with, so it seemed, unnerving acceleration. His feet felt a long way from his brain.

From nowhere the dog, Runcie, appeared, racing along the tow path. His yelps bounced between the water and the cut's brick walls. Marilyn held in, edging the boat nearer, and the dog took a running jump to land, four paws together, on the cabin roof. He sat on his haunches and panted, tongue dangling. The look in his eyes was not the usual indiscriminate adoration. Runcie had a message for Dan: *I haven't forgotten, pal, I'll get even.*

Dan struggled to his feet, hanging on to the cabin roof. The sickening effect of a vertical plane was decisive. Without another word he plunged down through the door and into the cabin.

The general effect of lying down in a throbbing wooden chamber is to give a childish excitement. Dan enjoyed this womb-visit for a while, but then began to speculate lightly about Marilyn, whose living quarters these were. She was older than him, just about thirty maybe. Her ring finger carried a wedding band, but there was no husband about, no sign of one in the cabin. The man was gone, then.

Marilyn was not quite beautiful like Lena. But she was vital and funny, the essential sexual qualities. When she talked, the tip of her small, pointed nose wobbled in a way which he found erotic. So was her body in that jumpsuit, cinched tight at the waist. A smile crept over his face. He slept again.

For most of the day Mustafa slept too. When he awoke his brain felt airy, clear, as if an electric storm had just lifted.

He lay on an old sofa. The upholstery was thinned like an old man's shanks, and several springs projected into his ribs. Around him it was quiet, just the ticking of a clock and distant traffic. The clock, which stood among a heap of tourist souvenirs on a grey marble mantelpiece, told him it was two in the afternoon.

He rolled off and crawled to the window. The street had bushy green trees growing at intervals along it. He had seen it last night in the dark, but then the surroundings had seemed obscure and disorderly. Now, as he saw, it was actually a model urban environment, the pavements brushed clean, the cars of recent make – a middle-class area.

He'd taken a risk, of course, but Mustafa had not acted completely without calculation. He was now a mass murderer, and the British police would be going crazy trying to collar him. What's more, they would know whom they were looking for. He had to have shelter, indoors and inconspicuous.

He'd used the British burglar's tradecraft taught to him by a cellmate in Gartree. He'd been caught at Heathrow with a pair of unlicensed automatic pistols in his luggage and he'd got two years. His instructor in stir had been a compulsive burglar named Kelvin. You learn a lot about a foreign society from talking to its burglars.

'It's summer, Mus, right? So stands to reason some residents in any street have got to be off on their annual fortnight's holiday. But how do you know which ones? Well, it's simple – look in the dustbins. If most of the bins in the street are full, the empty ones must belong to those who are off on the Costa del Package Tour, see? Easy, ain't it?'

Entry had been easy too: laughably easy. Even in Turkey, where there's not much housebreaking, they use better locks and catches. Padding through this musty house Mustafa saw first a pile of mail on the mat, under the letter-slot.

'It's only a question of reading the signs,' said Kelvin. 'Where there's a heap of letters on the floor then nobody's coming in the daytime, like to clean or whatever. Even if it was a neighbour drawing curtains or turning lights on and off, they always, I mean *always*, pick up the letters. Just can't resist having a good look through them, see?'

Just to be sure Mustafa had gone round looking for signs of recent cleaning. He found the opposite – a plate in the sink with mould growing on it. Even better, in the living room was a video recorder. He remembered Kelvin, swinging his legs as he perched on the upper bunk in their cell, telling him just what to do with this.

'Now, that video's the first thing you'll have away, of course. But before you do, here's a tip: press the programme display button. If there's still a load of recordings programmed in there, you know the people are not about to come back. Then you can really relax, take your time, spend the night and all next day, if you want.'

Mustafa had found last night that a programme several days ahead was entered for recording. He knew then that it was safe for him to sleep here.

When he looked at the place in the wider scope of daylight, he saw it was occupied by a single man. There were no female things anywhere, except for some odd make-up items, three loose tampons in the bathroom, a bunched up pair of tights in the bottom of the laundry basket – things left by overnighting girlfriends.

In the bathroom he switched on the water heater,

then went through to the bedroom and picked out some clean clothes. The owner was near enough to Mustafa's size, and he helped himself to a pair of jeans and a clean shirt. The shoes were all too small. He stripped off his own rags and put on a bathrobe, pushing his own clothing into a plastic bag which he left by the front door. They would have to go with him.

Back in the bathroom he found nail scissors and a razor. He used the scissors on his scalp, hacking until he had made his cranium a patch of scrub and tuft. He trimmed the moustache to the same stubble that already flourished on his cheeks and chin, then soaped his face and head, picked up the razor and shaved until his face was smooth as an apple, and his forehead extended as far back as the crown of his skull. When he had finished he had created himself anew – a bald, clean-shaven, worried, *older* man.

He sat on the bed and lifted the phone. It hummed.

'I'll be in London the next day. Call me,' Blanchard had told him. Blanchard would not be too happy with what had occurred in Haggerston, and Mustafa could not think why he would help him out. Yet Nathan Blanchard was his one hope. Deliberately, he dialled the number which he had been made to memorize.

Dan woke up hungry. At lunchtime he'd drunk far more than he'd eaten but, surprisingly, the homebrew left no hangover. The smell of a rich tomato sauce simmering in the narrowboat's gallery made his stomach fizz.

Ten minutes later he and Marilyn were sitting on opposite sides of the table in the main cabin. After making several miles during Dan's impenetrable nap, Marilyn had moored at Bull's Bridge, the junction of the Paddington Arm with the main line of the Grand Union Canal. The dinner, like all food on canal boats, was simple: pasta washed down with a Bulgarian Merlot.

'It's like the marriage at Cana,' she explained. 'As the day progresses, I progress to better booze. Some nights I end up in bed with a *Brut*.'

'Like the bride at Cana?'

Marilyn's eyes opened wide, as she popped a forkful of vermicelli into her mouth. When she'd swallowed she said, 'Now I've told you all about me, I want –'

'Have you?'

'Course I have. You had the whole dismal story this afternoon.'

'Give me the headlines again.'

'Just because you were too pissed! I told you! It was a saga about the ideal husband married to a woman of no importance.'

Dan stopped chewing.

'I don't get it.'

'The bastard I was married to for five years has decided he's gay. Can't live without this hairdresser he met. So he's left.'

'So what's ideal about him?'

'He just *seemed* ideal at the time. Clever, well qualified. He's a five-star accountant but a grade-A pillock.

So he sold the house from under me, threw the boat keys in my general direction and told me I could live in it till I found somewhere. Then he sodded off to sunny Yorkshire. Now lives in Scarborough. He never even faced me, not properly. He hasn't been near the boat. I mean, the things he had on board are still here.' She gestured her incomprehension.

Dan growled like Humphrey Bogart.

'Sounds like the story might have a wild ending.'

They both laughed. Marilyn said, 'We won't know till the final curtain, will we? Anyway, shut up. I'm trying to ask about you. Why were you palely loitering by the canal today? Why are you still here with me now?'

He raised his eyebrows, as if her question needed no answer.

'I meant, why haven't you anywhere to go, or the need to go anywhere? Most people, most of the time, are expected somewhere, aren't they?' She leaned forward confidentially. 'I get it. You're in trouble. You escaped from the maximum-security wing of Salford University. You double-parked your roller skates. Oh my God, you didn't commit an unnatural act with the Royal Albert Hall?'

She was looking at him steadily, deadpan. Dan began to see that the jokes were a feint. This was a hard woman and she'd want to know lots about him. He was already calculating odds on his chances with her. He wanted those slim arms wrapped around him, locking him tight. He was getting drunk again. Alcohol and sex: the most irresistible places to hide.

Besides, what could be a better hidey-hole than this boat? Who would ever look here? He lifted his glass. The challenge was to make her, and still give nothing away. He found himself falling back on the old lie he'd worked out for Lena.

'I'm an actor. No, you've never heard of me, I play in rep, the Fringe. Bit parts, no major roles. Not until now.'

The canal water moved audibly against the side of the boat, trickling and slopping behind his back.

'And now?'

'Now I've got a great part.'

'Which is?'

'Don't laugh.'

'I won't.'

'Promise you won't laugh?'

'I promise. Now tell.'

'I'm playing the Grand Union Canal.'

She laughed.

'No, that's what I'm doing here. I'm travelling the whole length on foot. Well, that was the idea. To get to know my character. It's research.'

'For God's sake. Whoever heard of anyone playing a canal?'

'It's a radio play. It's quite normal on the radio, you get to play lots of non-human characters – a malignant tumour, the North Wind, the rivalry between two kings. Quite normal.'

'I don't believe you. Speak some of the lines.'

'Can't. I haven't even seen the script yet. Producer

only cast me last week. Told me it wouldn't be ready for a fortnight, and I was to prepare as best I could.'

'Walking the length of the Grand Union? The vicious sod! Does he have any idea how long it is?'

'Oh no! That's all my own idea. I'm not working just now, so it seemed a good idea. My old acting tutor was very keen on Stanislavsky – you know, he's the one who said it's no good playing a part, you must discover the character inside yourself.'

'A canal?' she spluttered. 'You're priceless, you are! And where's your kit? If you want to know what I think, Mr Jeff Bridges, you're either an inspired fraud or a bit simple.'

His face went blank. *Jeff Bridges?* Christ, for a moment he'd forgotten the name he'd told her. Time for a diversion. He slammed his fists on the table between them and half rose, contorting his face with anger. 'DON'T EVER CALL ME SIMPLE, RIGHT?'

She shrank back in a mock flinch. 'Okay, okay!'

Then they both laughed a little. In the silence that followed, she looked at him, dabbing with the back of her crooked hand where the mascara was minutely smudged. Now was the moment. Now he must make his move.

But the table was between them.

He reached out and put his hand on her cheek. He said, 'You've been kind and I've not been very forthcoming, have I?'

She put her hand over his, and gently pulled it away

from her face. She looked at his hand, still holding on to it, as if examining an unexpected find. She shook her head. 'No, I can't say you have.'

She put his hand down on the table and looked at him. He couldn't tell if she was calculating too. He said, 'Obviously people on narrowboats don't have narrow minds.'

'But they do have narrow beds. I know what you're asking with those eyes, and the answer's no.'

'Really no?'

'Really no.'

Dan opened his eyes to dancing freckles of sunlight reflected up to the cabin ceiling. He swung off the bed, padded forward in T-shirt and pants and leaned out of the double doors which opened on to the tiny triangular foredeck. The *Pumblechook* was berthed at a boatyard wharf, with several river cruisers and a few narrowboats moored nearby. One of these was being sluiced down by a paunchy man in Bermuda shorts, hauling up buckets of canal water and whistling as he worked. From others came hollow bumps and low voices, as their occupants made breakfast. Marilyn was not in sight.

Her note lay on the galley counter, written in a confident, spiked hand. *Gone for grub to early-opening supermarket. See ya by half eight.*

Dan checked the fridge. His mouth and brain felt desiccated and he yearned for cold liquid, preferably fruit juice. There was only milk, and he poured himself a glass. As he drank he drifted around the boat, opening units and drawers.

Marilyn did not keep a tidy ship and she had certainly not tidied away her marriage. Perhaps she hadn't accepted it as over yet. So, although superficially there was no obvious sign of him, traces of husband Mills were found in almost every container and cupboard. There was an electric razor, a packet of condoms, a framed wedding photo, a passport in the name of E. A. Mills, a bundle of unopened mail addressed to him, books with *Ted Mills* on the flyleaf, a cupboard full of male clothing.

Dan looked at his watch. Nearly eight. An idea began forming in his mind. At first it was sluggish and semi-opaque, like a chrysalis. But the idea gained form and life rapidly, wriggling in its pupa-case, demanding to come out and be noticed.

He opened the passport. The photograph was in monochrome and showed a plump self-satisfied face, with an eyebrow-style moustache, straight fair hair and glasses. The description of the bearer told him that Edward Albert Mills was a company director, born in Goole, Humberside. Since then he had attained 1.8 metres in height, and was twenty-eight years old.

Dan snapped open the door of the closet containing Ted Mills's clothes. At the bottom he'd noticed a small canvas holdall, which he now pulled out. It was dusty and he blew on it before setting it down agape on the floor. Then he ripped off his T-shirt and collected his other garments, dropping them one by one into the bag. When he had done this and was naked except for his briefs a shadow of doubt flickered. He flipped open the passport again and checked the expiry. It was valid for another six years.

Then, methodically, Dan began to dress himself in Ted Mills's clothes. 1.8 metres is six foot. It was his own height and Ted Mills's clothes fitted well, if loosely, for Ted was on the plump side. The shirt collar was a size too large, but the blazer jacket felt okay around the shoulders, and the belt looped through the waist of the grey flannels needed tightening only one notch more tightly than Ted's usual. He bent and slipped into his own shoes, checking first under the insole for the left-luggage ticket. It was safely in place. He then chose, from the accountant's ample supply, a club tie and tightened it so as to close up the oversize shirt at his neck. Lastly, he wet his hair and combed it straight back, in something like the style worn by Mills in his mug-shot.

In the mirror Dan saw he needed to shave. He returned to a drawer he had rummaged through earlier and picked out the cordless shaver, which whirred sufficiently at a press of the switch. He ran it over his chin, cheeks and jowls – but left the upper lip – before throwing it back among the junk. As he closed the drawer a glint caught his eye. His fingers groped among the tangle of oddments and hooked out some spectacles. One of the shafts was broken, but when he compared the glasses to the passport photograph he saw they were the same.

He balanced them on his nose and went back to the mirror. With the marginally fuzzed vision conferred by the glasses he found himself looking at a slimmed-down, almost moustache-less, passably convincing simulacrum of Ted Mills.

He turned this way and that, admiring himself. He smiled, thinking of the real E. A. Mills up in Scarborough, waking, yawning, playing with his hairdresser friend's cock. He laughed aloud.

There was a thump behind him as a foot landed on the deck. The door latch snapped immediately, the hinge squeaked and then she screamed. The air at his back seemed to part, like a sheet tearing.

'Ted! What in Christ's name –?'

He spun round as she dropped her shopping. Oranges bounced out and rolled towards him.

Her hand had gone to her mouth in consternation.

'It's not . . . It's you. But why are you –?'

Dan walked round her to the door, stepping over tins of baked beans and a jar of coffee. He closed the door, turned the key and slipped it into his pocket.

'For a moment I thought it actually was him. What are you doing?'

'Sit down, Marilyn.'

She backed away. Her face changed slowly from surprise to anger, her rounded mouth crumpling.

'This is – oh, this is repulsive, despicable. I mean, what do you think I felt like, seeing you dressed in his things, wearing those glasses? I don't like your sense of humour, Jeff.'

'It's no joke, believe me. Sit down, Marilyn.'

'What are you, some kind of pervert? This is creepy. You're trying to scare me, are you? Well, you've succeeded, okay? Does that bring you the right kind of frisson?'

She bent and picked up a large can of fruit and held it in front of her stomach with both hands.

'Marilyn, will you please sit *down.* Then I'll tell you.'

She sat on the upholstered settee. The fight had bled from her face, and now it showed only fright. But Dan knew he couldn't afford to lighten up.

'Marilyn. I'm grateful to you for your hospitality, but I'm afraid I'm going to impose some more.'

He picked up the passport and put it in his pocket.

'I need to become someone else, for a while. I need an identity. It's nothing personal. Just that me and . . . er, Ted are about the same size, and all his clobber happens to be to hand. Even more handily,' he tapped the breast pocket, 'almost providentially you could say, he happened to forget his passport when he scarpered out of your life. Though he's not out of your life yet, is he?'

She did not speak, just stared at him. Dan moved the pile of her husband's mail until he found one envelope he'd noticed before. It was unopened and bore the logo of the American Express company. Marilyn had written the forwarding address in Scarborough, but had apparently not got round to posting it. This, too, he slipped into his pocket.

'Well, if it's any consolation, pretty soon I'm going to be out of your life.'

A tabloid newspaper lay on the floor with the dropped shopping. He bent and retrieved it, tucking it into the holdall, which he zipped up. She was still open-mouthed and unable to speak. As he edged back to the door he found the key in his trouser pocket. He said, 'You could call the police, I know. Or even your husband. I hope you won't. Please? I don't think I've taken anything of yours that wasn't freely given.'

Now he had unlocked the door and swung it open. He watched Marilyn intently, as if she might spring on him like a cat, but she seemed rooted and paralysed.

From just outside the door, he said, 'I'll come back when I'm myself again.'

And he was gone.

Dan caught a commuter train for Paddington Station from Hayes and Harlington. As soon as he'd settled in his seat he slit open the Amex letter, hoping it was not a piece of junk mail. He wanted to find Mills's credit statement, or at least some mention of his card number. Armed with this he could visit the American Express office and con a new card out of them. He badly needed resources.

When he extracted the envelope's contents he found something better. It was a brand new rectangular piece of plastic, attached to a card which told him *THIS IS YOUR NEW AMERICAN EXPRESS CARD*. All he had to do was copy Mills's signature from the passport on to the card and he was in funds.

He sat back and breathed deeply. Then he reached into the holdall, and pulled out the newspaper. An enormous headline blazed under the masthead: THE FACE OF EVIL. Taking up most of the rest of the page was a six-column police photograph of Mr Red.

Carefully, he read the account of the Haggerston bloodbath. Then, on an inside page, he learned of his own demise, in an explosion at the Brompton Cemetery.

Nathan Blanchard wanted to take Mustafa by both his ears and slam the back of his skull against the wall.

'You stupid, stupid asshole. What did you do it for?'

'I don't know, boss. My mind went boom, you know?'

Mustafa had refused to meet Nathan indoors, so they were at a public garden nearby. The place showed up on the *A–Z Streetfinder* as Memorial Gardens and the wall upon which Mustafa's head might have been pulped supported the names of members of the civil service killed in the London Blitz. But on Blanchard's mind was another, more recent mass murder.

'But Christ! Thirteen people. Your mind went boom so you blew away thirteen? Thirteen who got zilch to do with any of this? Jesus.'

A pause. Mustafa's head was fractionally shaking, like Parkinson's disease, side to side. Nerves were firing at random all over his body. But his eyes still had that cold vacancy.

'Boss, the English police got my description, they know my name. You know I've done time in this country. I need to get out. You help me, boss. Please, you help me.'

'I'll help you. I'll help you to get fucking crucified.'

Blanchard could do without this. The greatest coup of his life was about to come off, and instead he had to deal with this no-brain.

'Do you know how they're painting you in the media? I mean you're part way between the Terminator and Adolf fucking Hitler.'

He knew he had maybe three options. He could cut Mustafa loose, let the Brit police take him. If he did that the guy would bounce them straight back to him. So, instead he could kill him, but that wouldn't be easy. Mustafa was jumpy. If he knew anything at all it was supposed to be how to kill and not *be* killed. And anyway, maybe, if the creep was frightened, he could still be useful. There was, after all, Felix. All the references said Mustafa was good at what he did. So what was this going berserk – some kind of nerve storm?

Blanchard did not dwell on the horror. He thought only of maintaining control. The dead were multiplying around him, and he had to keep his grip. He said, 'Look, Mustafa, you killed Başkurt and Barry, right?'

The Turk looked at him warily. He'd last seen Dan Barry breathing.

'I kill them, yes, that was before I was at the dogfight.'

'I read it in today's paper that Barry was killed by a bomb.'

It was the first Mustafa had heard of this. But if the papers said Dan Barry was dead, who was he to contradict them?

'Sure. I blow him away, I fix it. Easy.' He grinned, a humourless baring of the teeth.

Blanchard sighed. 'Right, I'm giving you a chance.' He held up a rigid finger. 'Just one chance, Mustafa. If you fuck up I'll let you rot, so help me. Understand?'

Mustafa nodded warily. Those empty eyes might have been looking through Blanchard's face, right through to the Wall of Remembrance behind him. Blanchard went on, 'Okay. If you do this one more thing for me, and do it right, I'll pay you the money we shook hands on for Barry and Başkurt. I'll get you papers and safe passage to any location in the world. You just name it.'

'What is the job, boss?'

'Find Felix Trubshaw, like you were supposed to do before you started greasing the sidewalks of London with fresh blood. Find him, okay? And take him out. I'll tell you where to go in a minute. You do it quietly and unobtrusively. I don't want him found, ever. Is that straight? It should be easy enough, as a matter of fact.'

Mustafa made a show of considering the offer. Then he nodded his head. '*Tamam*, boss. Just tell me where I find him and I can do it just like you say.'

# 13

Felix lay and looked at the sky. In cloud, the city night-sky glows with a thrilling, lolly-orange incandescence. It reflects the city's size and power, the concentration of human will, the great hum of the place. A city is a massive, humming generator of passions and hopes.

But Cork City is only half a city. In Cork people go up to a tourist in Patrick Street and ask would they happen to be lost. In Cork, everybody knows the notable figures – the clergy, the bank managers, the keepers of the specialized shops, the bus conductors, *gardai*, schoolteachers. Cork is part city and part overgrown market town.

Felix lay flat on his back in the Corporation Park like any poor tinker, with a flask-bottle of whiskey beside him. How easy it had been. A train, a ferry, a bus and he'd come home to his native place.

He'd come to Cork because here was the sense of safety. Here he could do anything, go anywhere, bathe in the hot springs of his family's name.

'You're Lou Trubshaw's boy? Grand man, your da, so he was. What'll ye have?'

He rose and kicked the empty bottle. He had a hotel, he could be going to bed. His room overlooked the quays of the River Lee. He laughed when he thought of it. In the hall was a sign saying FAMOUS MURDERER JAMES HANRATTY STAYED HERE ON THE RUN. Some advert for a place.

Opposite the quay a pub was open. Byrne's Saloon Bar. Select Beers and Stouts. He heard the comfortable rumble of conversation topped by arpeggios of laughter. No harm in a nightcap. He'd not exactly any pressing business in the morning. He went into the alley beside the pub and, leaning against a rubbish bin, took off his shoe. He felt around inside the shoe until his fingers prodded a flattened wad of notes, which he removed. He peeled off a tenner and stuffed the rest back.

'All right?'

A pair of feet crunched past him along the alley. Felix hurriedly returned his foot to its shoe, laced it clumsily and went back to the pub door. He pushed into the happiness of a crowded bar.

'And yure not listening to me when I'm talking. The greatest Corkman was Christy Ring, and second to him MacCurtain. I'm telling you.'

'Ah well. You cannot settle an argument like that one. It's a matter of opinion. My wife would say 't was Father Matthew, the Temperance Apostle himself.'

Felix ordered a large Paddy and stood at the bar.

'Would you settle a small spat we got going here, mister?' He looked up. He was being spoken to by a tall, gaunt man in a black suit.

'Who'd you say was the indisputable greatest

Corkman of all time, now? My colleague Mr O'Rourke here says it was John Wayne.'

The other man, tubby and red-faced, broke in. 'Marion Michael Morrison, alias John Wayne, d'you see?'

Felix looked over the bar at the ranged whiskey and gin bottles, up-ended into their optics. Their labels were reversed for the purpose, and he could clearly read the distiller's signature on the bottle from which his own measure had been drawn. He raised his glass. 'No question about it. I would nominate James Murphy, who guarantees the excellence of this in his own hand.'

Mr O'Rourke's laugh was like a machine-gun. Slower to let go of his opinion, his tall friend pounded the bar with his fist. 'By Christ, he's the *third* greatest, so he is! After Ring and MacCurtain, he's next. Have another?'

A younger, ginger-haired man was drinking at the end of the bar. He wore a frayed blue jacket over a stained vest, and had the tattoos, bulging deltoids and dusty eyelashes of a construction worker. He was watching with close attention the small drinking party of three as they argued and laughed. Slowly he sidled around the bar until, imperceptibly, he had joined them, standing a round and having his share of another. By now the time had drawn past closing. As the landlord meaningfully polished the bar under their elbows the conversation veered towards the perfectibility of man.

It proved a subject in which the newcomer took especial interest.

'Amn't I after doing a coupla years stir on Spike Island? We'd a lot of perfectionism in there that time.'

'Ah!' said the adherent of the hurling player Christy Ring. He looked reflectively into the depths of his empty glass, as into a crystal ball. 'The penal institution will aim to clear away imperfections, right enough. Rehabilitation, now. Spot removal. The soul's dry-cleaner.'

'I learned how to blow every type of safe in the Allied Irish Banks,' said Ginger. 'From experts. Infallible.'

Mr O' Rourke heaved a sigh.

'Well, I must be trudging to the homestead. You coming, Donal?'

His friend nodded and the two men backed reluctantly from the bar. Felix drained his whiskey glass and followed them out.

Outside he found himself joined by the former convict. The other two had melted into the night. Ginger tapped Felix on the shoulder.

'How does a woman grab you?'

'Sorry? I didn't quite –?'

'I'm saying, a woman. Get your leg over. I can fix it all right, just around the corner, a couple of streets from this place.'

'Oh, I don't think –'

'Come on, pal. She's a sweet little teenager, tasty as lemon tart. Cost you twenty pound for the best shag of your life.'

Felix paused in befuddled hesitation. He saw the man's grin twinkling in the darkness, and beyond him the water twinkled, as it does at night in any city built by the water – Venice, Hong Kong, Istanbul. Felix swayed on his feet and said nothing. Ginger took his arm.

'Will I tell you all about her as we walk? Well now, her name's Kathleen and she's only after leaving school last year and she's – what can I tell you about her? She's got a thick bush black as a pint of stout and such beautiful big bubbies that if you put your face between them sure you'd be smothered in a coupla minutes, you would. And cherry-red nipples to the pair of them, fat and luscious as you please. Come this way, we're going along there. The lovely little whoor is waiting down here now. Panting for you, she is. Panting.'

Felix let himself be led along. He was entranced by the music of the man's voice, and by the images he was calling up. It was longer than he could remember since he'd had a woman, but it was not the tug of desire that took him along in the man's wake. He didn't want the evening to end. He didn't want to close the door on himself at Hanratty's refuge.

They were stumbling down an empty, barely lit street, with Ginger quickening his pace. Now that Felix was hooked, Ginger walked slightly ahead, with more urgency in his step. Felix felt himself wanting to laugh. In Ireland nothing was ever what it seemed. The public bar was a forum for the discussion of philosophy and history. The man who looked like a brickie was a ponce.

'She's waiting for ye, all right. Nothing she likes more than a good hard fook, does young Kathleen. And ye're the feller to give it her. In here now, in you go.'

They had reached a stone archway, with a padlocked, iron-bound gate. Let into it was a subsidiary door, which squeaked open when Ginger pushed it. Drifting through as if on a ghostly, alcoholic dolly, Felix tripped on a capsized paving stone. He staggered a few paces forward into what seemed to be a garbage dump.

He was in a cobbled courtyard, surrounded by disused stone warehousing. Looking up he saw the projecting beam of a hoist against the sky. Around him were strewn broken furniture, burst mattresses and eviscerated bags of rubbish. The place was a rat-run.

Ginger walked past where Felix was standing. The door swung back as he let it go, crashing against the frame. For a moment his shape was traced by silver as the moonlight caught it. The scrape of a shoe followed with Ginger's silhouette suddenly now looming larger again as he came back towards Felix. At this point Felix would actually have had time to get back through the door and stumble away, but he didn't even try. He was immobilized by a fog in his brain made of whiskey and fatalism. He was empty of fear and of feeling.

The vacancy lasted just as long as it took Ginger to hit him. First something hard and brassy seared his lip, and from the contrary direction a second, knuckled mass jolted his temple. Ginger followed the combination with a mashing, eye-watering ding on Felix's nose and Felix went down floundering, his head a mass of pain, into the heaps of rubbish.

Felix's head lay against something, but he wasn't conscious of an edge, hardness or sharpness. A pillow? It was still dark. The pillow, whatever it was, was warm and wet and clung stickily to his face.

He moved his head and pain wrenched coherent thought out of his mind. It seared down his shoulder and left arm, and ended throbbing in a puffy, inflated hand. The same swollen sensation affected his skull. He lay still and re-thought his position. Under the weight of his head the cheek was rucked back from his teeth and gum, and spit was dribbling out of his mouth. On his tongue was the rank, yeasty taste of almost-fresh blood.

He opened the eye that wasn't lying crushed under the weight of his head. Something wet and white, some piece of food smelling of decay, touched his nostril. Then, in the corner of his vision, he noticed a flick of movement. Fighting the pain he lifted his head. A grey rat was poised just above his face, as if deciding whether to touch down on a rich new source of putrid food. Its tail twitched and Felix felt the cold end of it brush his eyelid. The rat darted away into the unfocused darkness as Felix's yelp of fear echoed upwards into the shaft of decay above.

Ginger had done a comprehensive job. Apart from the shoulder and arm, Felix's ribcage felt mangled, pain stabbing his side with each breath. He remembered taking a volley of kicks from a blunt, hard shoe after going down. His nose, mouth and hand had bled over the pile of plastic rubbish bags on which he'd landed.

He inched himself over and upwards into something resembling a sitting posture. His skin tore away from the adhesion of dried blood with the sound of sticky tape coming off its roll.

There would be pain involved in bending the neck, so he eased his good hand blindly towards his feet. The groping fingers only confirmed what he already knew. Looking around, he saw his shoes a few yards away, laceless and splayed out like fallen blackbirds in a cold pool of moonlight.

He lapsed back against the lumpy bin-bag. He had no money and no strength. He would just have to lie here. There was nothing left to do. He closed his eyes.

*'Nature is a woman, my dear boys. A savage, untrained, uncivilized, unscrupulous female.'*

*Looking down he sees a science lecture room. You can tell it isn't a modern set-up because the place is so gloomy. The wood-stain is dark. The water and gas fittings on the demonstration table are of brass, but it has blackened. The north light entering through the high sash windows is compromised by encrusted dirt and green lichen.*

*A lecture is in progress. This seems like a university and yet, when Felix looks around, all the class is dressed as schoolboys, in serge shorts. The heavy, heavily-bearded professor struts around like a turkey cock, shouting scientific assertions.*

*'Well, that's not a new idea, it's been a commonplace since the beginning of human thought. But d'you know what? I have made a discovery. Yes, the bitch is holding out on me. She's got a secret – a dirty, dirty secret.'*

*He pauses, bending slightly forward. He has a bush of frizzled hair exploding out of his head, as if electrified. He searches the faces of his students, his face beneath the wire-rim glasses leering. His forehead sprouts beads of sweat. He slaps the flat of his palm into his forehead and sweat scatters through the air.*

*'I am a virile, inquiring thinker, am I not? So how am I going to get this horrid secret out of her, eh? Any ideas?'*

*A scattering of hands goes up.*

*'Sir! Sir! Me, sir!'*

*The professor holds up his own hand like a traffic cop.*

*'Bradshaw. I hope you're not going to tell me to reason with her. Not anything namby-pamby like that.'*

*'No, sir, course not, sir,' says Bradshaw, with a snigger. Bradshaw is the class smart-alec. 'You got to squeeze it out of her, haven't you, sir? Apply a bit of pressure.'*

*'Right, boy! That's the manly way. And that, dear boys, is how science began. With the discovery that the*

*whoor has a whole string of dirty little secrets, and our job, our job as scientists, mind, is to squeeze out the truth. She won't volunteer it, y'know. But how do I squeeze her? Can anyone tell me that?'*

*More hands shoot up.*

*'Sir! Sir!'*

'Dad! Dad!'

*This time the professor ignores them all. He is walking round the demonstration table. A woman lies on it. She is naked and bound. He picks up a wooden pointer and slaps it into his palm as he speaks.*

*'I'll tell you how. I'm going to challenge her. I'm going to be ruthless, use interrogation techniques. I'll lock her up in my laboratory, deprive her of everything she knows, strip her naked, tie her down. And, if I have to, I'll not shrink from torturing the witch until she tells me. Right?'*

'Dad! Dad!'

*The lecturer is possessed now by evangelical fervour.*

*Flecks of saliva have caught on his beard like thistle down, as the pitch of his excitement rises.*

*Felix calls out, and continues to call out, unheeded by his father.*

Felix called so loud he woke himself up.

He was shuddering. His body hurt everywhere. He felt nauseous, too sick to form intentions in his mind, certainly not of walking to his hotel, wherever it was. He dragged himself to one of the doorways, grouped like sentry boxes around the ruined courtyard, and dossed down to await daylight. He lay like a dying animal, willing to accept any development so long as it didn't mean moving.

But he could no longer sleep. He was cold, and anyway he was afraid of the dreams. His brain lay stagnant.

But after a while his thoughts stirred, like a sheet of water shifted by a breath of wind. He wasn't ready to bloody die. He was thirsty. He concentrated on the thought of a drink. The little sting on his tastebuds, the trickle of it round and down past the epiglottis, cold in the recesses of his mouth. Gradually he marshalled himself and with just the hint of light in the sky he limped out of the courtyard.

It was properly dawn when Felix got back to the hotel which plugged itself as a murderer's retreat. Before venturing in he tried to smooth his clothes into something like normality. But the gaudily blood-caked shirt, the torn-off buttons, made this a remote hope. He went forward and pushed on the door. To his surprise it was open.

The only light in the hotel entrance was a failing fluorescent tube, by which the tiny lobby and lower stairs flickered in and out of darkness. Somewhere in the rear there was a smell of frying onions. He nearly threw up.

There was no one to see him as he took his key and quietly mounted to his room.

He stood for a moment beside the bed. Then he buckled in complete exhaustion across it. Blindly his head found the nylon-covered pillow and he slept again. This time he didn't dream.

*

Felix awoke in a tight foetal curl. It was dark already. Christ, he must have been lying here all day.

Gradually he spread his limbs and pressed both hands over his face. It was greased with sweat.

He twisted himself over on the bed, enduring new pains, from stiffness rather than punches or kicks, and fumbled the packet of Pall Mall from his jacket pocket. In a series of painful jerks and contortions he got one out and between his lips. Shit! He'd left his matches in the pub. God, that was a long time ago.

He lay and thought about a drink instead for a while. Later he got up and paced an aimless path around the brown room. There was no future in imagining it, only the thing itself would do. But of course he had no money now. Then suddenly he remembered. His hip-flask! He'd filled it from the last of his duty-free bottle. It was somewhere in the room.

He got up and fumbled around. He could not locate it on the table, and he could find no light switch. He crawled on the floor, sweeping his outstretched hand across the ancient linoleum like a metal detector, hoping the flask was lying there. It was not.

He emptied his bag by inverting and shaking it. There was no deep thump as the weighty flask hit the floor. He sat back on the bed with a sigh and stuck his hand in his trouser pocket. Well, at least the bastard hadn't gone through that. He had seventy-seven pence. Later he slept again, with the coins clasped tight in his fist.

*

Early was the market's happiest hour. It teemed with customers and rang with the percussion of jingling cash. Pushing through the crowd Felix smelt fruit, and then roast coffee beans, and toasted nuts. He heard the sizzle of cooking from somewhere, a breakfast café. The sound and smell stirred memories of home, and of his mother singing as she turned the French toast in the pan. He had watched her then in hunger and fascination, just as his mouth dropped open now as he saw a waitress through the café window glide between customers with a plate spilling over with fried breakfast. Felix had not eaten since he was on the ferry. All of a sudden he was ambushed by ravenous hunger.

But seventy-seven pence! He wanted to save some for a beer or something. He couldn't afford to pay for a meal.

He sauntered along the market, and came to a stall heaped with bananas. A loose one lay just under his hand as he passed by and, without thinking, he grabbed it. He hid it in his hand until he reached a safe distance, then slipped it into his pocket.

Years ago Felix had done this kind of thing, as a student, or was it a schoolboy? It was mostly for dares. Now he remembered the terrifying exhilaration of it. He strolled on trying to look casual, a balloon of fear expanding in his chest. Ahead of him was a table displaying wholefood – herbal teas, organic honeys, muesli. The bearded hippy who minded it was talking animatedly to another longhair. Felix sidled through the narrow gap between this table and a barrow of green vegetables, as if making for the middle of the street. He had come this far, he might as well go on. He helped himself to a square of carrot cake, slipping it in beside the banana.

He glanced around. Sweat was pricking his temples and he had the awareness of eyes watching him, the neurosis of all sneak-thieves and pickpockets. This paranoia goes along with the desire to run and keep running. And the urge to urinate. Felix felt all these. But there was one more desire in sharp and impetuous conflict with them. Something sweet. He must have something sweet. He would *kill* for something sweet.

He headed back, looking for a sweet stall he'd seen further back. He forced himself to walk slow.

The stall was held by a red-faced, obese woman who undoubtedly ate much of her own produce. Her main trade was confectionery sold from jars by weight. There were sugared almonds, mint balls, chocolate-coated nuts, sugar-frosted candies, jellied fruits, Turkish delight. Felix was glad to see a supply of loose Turkish delight on a display tray at the end of the stall. A sign was stabbed into it: HAJI BEY'S RAHAT LOUKUM – *Authentic Turkish Delight made exclusively in Cork since 1906.* He edged his way past a customer until he was alongside the *loukum*, then he plunged both his hands among the squashy cubes of gelatinous sugar. His fingers closed over a dozen or more of them and he walked swiftly on, head down, trying to force them into the side pockets of his jacket. But he was in too much of a hurry now, and the pockets had flaps. He couldn't use his fingers to get purchase on his pocket flaps, without dropping the *loukum*. His crammed hand stabbed ineffectually at the side of the jacket, streaking it with the sugar-powder with which the confection was dusted.

Then a shadow froze in front of him. He raised his eyes to a row of polished buttons, a polished black cap-peak, a pair of brown leather gloves and the sarcastic face of a *garda* constable about to make an arrest. Felix opened his fingers, and the *loukum* cascaded to the ground. It was instantly kicked in all directions and then trodden flat by feet hurrying by.

In the holding cells at the *gardai* barracks Felix fought constantly against sleep. Sometimes in the following hours his body and brain screamed for unconsciousness but his soul was afraid. If he slept he thought his soul would shrivel in the glare of his dreams, and curl like a sun-dried fish from which even the shape and memory of water had evaporated.

But he could not prevent fits of sleep, and then the ferocious dreaming . . .

*Cold in the lecture theatre, like a trapped pocket of the winter. His hands were mottled blue-pink as they gripped the pen, trying to transcribe the Professor's words.*

*His father was bent over the demonstration table. On it was stretched the experimental apparatus: test-tubes, connecting tubes, glass retorts and flasks; brightly col-*

*oured powders and liquids. It was all held by steel clamps and stands, and heated by murmuring burners. And lying through it like a scarf of smoke was the wraith of the naked woman.*

*'All we have to do is add a little . . . then apply a small amount more of heat . . . and then add a little more . . . No, she is not persuaded. Then I must turn up the heat.'*

*A glow in the centre of the glass victim, in her belly, began to incandesce, pulsating and spinning and growing larger. Felix stopped writing. He found he was alone in the audience. The ball of light at the centre of the experiment was the size of a pumpkin now. His father scratched his beard with delight and rubbed his hands.*

*'Good, good. At last she responds!'*

*He made no move to get himself away, in spite of the manifest danger. The vortex of light was accompanied by a mounting roar, a sound like a wind tunnel. Then the apparatus began to twist and buckle and break loose from its fetters. The spinning light was still growing. Felix stood up. He knew he should run. Yet he watched as the fire consumed the Professor. His father's outline was leaping frantically, at first merely because it was lit by the leaping flame, and then because it was within the fire, leaping and dancing until it frazzled and disappeared.*

*Then the glare ballooned to an incredible size and intensity, and seemed to advance purposefully on Felix himself. He stood rooted as it ate up the floor, exploded into the benches in front of him. He saw it now in the shape of a raging hellhag. Her mouth opened and shut and he seemed to see down her throat, and his own figure within her now, spinning away to eternity.*

His scream met the air like a cutler's grindstone. He screamed until his noise brought the duty sergeant, running to him in a jingle of keys. And, still when he was fully awake, and with a ring of police around him, he went on screaming for a long time.

# 14

'After today I won't be seeing you children again until next week,' said Justin. 'I've got my suitcase all packed. I'm off to Greece, to the island of Patmos, for a holiday. It's a holiday for all, of course, this week, isn't it? But you don't want to know why there's a holiday, do you?'

Twenty-four flawless eyes, in a dozen fresh faces, gazed up in expectation. A shaft of sunlight glittered in their hair as some of them nodded, while others shook their heads.

Perched massively on a child-size chair, he watched the collective wriggle as the children found more comfortable positions on the floor, nudged each other and exchanged whispers.

'It's the same reason there's a lot of sheep around the city at the moment. But you haven't seen any of the sheep, have you?'

Slowly, and then with increasing urgency, their eyes opened wider in protest. Yes they had! They *had* seen the sheep. Justin's gaze surveyed the faces and then settled on one of them – Lena's daughter, little Annabel in the pigtails.

'Oh well, excuse me! But does anyone know *why* there's all these sheep in the streets?'

It was understandable she was here this morning.

Dan hadn't been her father, though he'd been with the family almost a year, nearly half a lifetime to Annabel. Lena would want to keep her grief from the child. Better Annabel attended nursery as usual, as if nothing had happened.

'Then I suppose I've got to tell you, have I? It's called the *Kurban Bayramı* and that's when people in Turkey remember something that happened a long time ago. It's a story in the Bible.'

He cleared his throat and the children shifted their bottoms, settling anew for the story. Justin was good at Bible stories.

'It was like this. There was an old man called Abraham, and his old wife Sarah, and they had no children, and they were sad about it. They were really much too old to have children, Abraham was a hundred years old, and Sarah was ninety years old.'

How was Lena feeling now? Torn apart, furious, bitter, betrayed? Listening to her when they'd had coffee two days ago, Justin had not found her brimming over with love for Dan Barry. So how would she be feeling?

'But suddenly God said never mind that, you can still have a child, if you want.'

It was him that was brimming over. He saw Lena's face ghosting behind the daughter's features, and looked hurriedly away.

'But Sarah thought it was a huge joke. "What, me? Have a baby? At my age?" she said. And she laughed and laughed. But you know, Sarah *did* have a child, a baby son. So they called him Isaac, because that means joke in their language.'

Now and then Justin was taken aback as his brain presented him with an image of the woman, the almond-shaped face regarding him over her coffee cup in *Markiz*, the cadences of her Virginian voice. A tantalizing, fugitive image. Clumsily he would grab for it and always close on emptiness.

'Now, you can understand how much they loved that boy. They were brimming over with love for him. So, of course, they taught him to say please and thank you and not pick his nose, because they didn't want to be disgraced when Granny came to stay. And he learned well.'

Would he see her today? Would she come and collect her child? He longed for her to come. The emotion was barely two days old, it was fresh as a spring flower. *She must come!*

'But when Isaac was nearly a teenager, God decided Abraham must be tested. God wanted to see if Abraham loved him even more than he loved Isaac. So he ordered Abraham to take his beloved boy to a mountain top, and give him back to God. And do you know how he had to give Isaac back to God?'

He paused. He let the question sink in, watching the children begin to formulate answers, and then he broke in. 'He was told to sacrifice his boy, the one he loved most in the whole world. He was to put a knife in him so that he would die and then burn his body so that the smoke would carry Isaac back to God.'

The children looked at him in wonder and shock. Justin blinked rapidly and swallowed. He leaned forward and went on. He brought the story to its end more quickly than usual. '. . . and they found a ram with its horns tangled in a bramble bush, and they sacrificed that instead. And on the way home Abraham said to Isaac, Didn't I tell you God would give us a sheep for the sacrifice?'

He leaned back to ease his spine.

'And *that's* what everyone is remembering. Turkish families all sacrifice a sheep during this holiday. And that's why the streets are full of sheep.'

Playgroup ended and the mothers drifted in to pick up their little ones. But *she* never came.

He asked, 'Is little Annabel's mum not coming, Georgette?'

'No, Annabel's staying with us, until Lena gets over this. She's still in shock, you know.'

It sounded like a reproof.

'Of course, of course. She must be, poor thing. Well, I'll be off. Have a good break, Georgette.'

Justin left his suitcase with Yakup the *kapıcı* and stepped through the Memorial Church gate. He started down towards Tophane, the waterside district from where the *dolmuş* would take him north to Emirgan. His heart was thudding in time with his downhill tread.

He deliberately hadn't told Georgette where he was going. Given that they had just been talking about

Lena, to mention it would have been quite natural, but Justin's secrecy was instinctive – the hoarding away of powerful emotions.

At intervals down the hill knots of muddy-fleeced sheep were gathered with their shepherds. He watched as one was bought by a respectable, clerkly man in a blue suit. He led the beast away awkwardly on the end of a length of baling twine, as she bleated what might have been a pitiful farewell to her sisters. He thought about the sheep's fate: the patriarch of the household driving the knife into her throat, slicing it across her jugular and windpipe, the blood flowing on to the earth, the menfolk of the family clapping each other on the back. *Kurban Bayramı* was like Christmas, the occasion of familial excess. Except here the intoxicating liquor was not alcohol. It was blood.

The posting to Turkey had been quite a shock to the urban Midlands curate that Justin had been. He realized he was a fish in the wrong water, an English tench or dace blundering through a tank of feather-finned exotics. For Istanbul is also Constantinople, the New Rome, headquarters to several orthodox churches, as well as the fourth most holy city of Islam. The bearded, long-robed ecclesiarchs who surrounded him here bore more resemblance to Biblical prophets than to the Marks-and-Spencer-clad clergy of home. More like Abraham than the vicar of St Mildred's.

But Justin had determined to do his best to be the pastor to his flock, creating as nearly as possible a normal Anglican parish. So, where there is a death, there should be a visit to the family. That was his rationale for the business remaining before he flew out on his holiday to Greece.

The *dolmuş* was one of the very finest, a black Chevrolet Bel Air, whose grille, closely related to a Rock-ola jukebox, sported a fine convolution of chromed organ-pipes bent into place. The Bayram traffic was already beginning to clot the city arteries, and progress along the Bosporus road was hot and slow. By the time Justin got down at the Emirgan stop, he was sweating freely.

The road which rose from the Bosporus shore was steep and ragged at the edges where its thin macadamized crust had crumbled. As he toiled the three hundred yards to Lena's apartment he asked himself again what state she would be in.

Images of profane aestheticism flashed. Lena as a figure in anguish, tortured by the cut-off tail of her love, lashing reflexively as the residual nerve stimulus dies. He knew these pictures for what they were, sexual images, pornographic imaginings. He shut his eyes, squeezing as if to eject them.

He continued doggedly up the hill.

All morning Lena had been absorbed in a frenzy of activity. She'd hardly slept in the night and, at six-thirty, had been out to the corner *bakkal* for cardboard boxes.

She'd filled nine of these with clothes and shoes,

papers and books, household objects and carpets – all his stuff. Now she stood with an errant shoe in her hand, wondering into which box she had tucked its mate.

Her first impulse was to ignore the doorbell. But perhaps it was Georgette with Annabel. She tiptoed to the spyhole and put her eye to it.

It was not Georgette. It was someone who had turned away from the door. She saw dark trousers, short-sleeved grey shirt – a man. But a tall man. She could not see far enough up to judge the colour or shape of his hair.

She unlatched the door.

The large priest turned on his pink, sandalled foot and made a nervous circular gesture of greeting with his right hand.

'Lena. I . . . er, I hope this isn't an intrusion.'

Lena felt at a sudden social disadvantage. Even though she'd had coffee with this man only two days ago, she'd completely forgotten his name. For some reason her inability to remember made her feel it was impossible to turn him away. She stepped aside. 'No, no. Please come in.'

The visitor ducked as he went through, as though to avoid butting the lintel, although this was well clear even of his considerable height. What *was* his name? It was something fairly silly. Dunstan?

'It was . . . er . . . so nice talking to you on Monday, Lena. It was a nice place, that cake shop you introduced me to.'

'Yes.'

She'd forgotten almost everything that had happened on Monday. She'd forgotten what they'd talked about; she'd forgotten how she'd acted. And though she did know he wasn't called Dunstan the silly name kept getting in the way of her remembering his right name.

They were in the sitting room. She stood looking down at his feet while she groped for a loose strand of hair at her temple.

'You're packing,' he said, looking round.

'Yes, it's not my stuff.'

She showed him the shoe, and gave out a fragmentary laugh. 'Men's shoes are so ridiculous. Like great barges.'

She found she was still looking at his feet. The toes stuck massively out of the sandal-ends. They were globular and pink, and crowned with thick, misshapen, yellowish nails. How can anyone pretend to find a man's feet anything but laughable?

The vicar shifted, aware of what she was looking at.

'Well, I came because I wondered – I hoped I might be able to be of some use.'

Lena heard but didn't know how to answer him. It sounded so strange, so like an appeal. It should be she who sounded that note.

'I don't even know who his next-of-kin are. I suddenly find I know nothing about him.' She threw a fragile gesture at the nine stacked boxes. 'Just what's here.'

'Are you going away?'

'Where to? No, I don't think I'm going any place. I'm staying right here.'

Lena walked to the balcony window, and parting the curtains which were drawn against the sun, she looked across the wide strip of water at Asia beyond. He didn't speak.

'I wish I'd never come here now, you know,' she said.

'You must not blame yourself for what's happened. It's nothing to do with your being in the city. Just a freak thing.'

'But I brought him here. Anyway, that's not what I meant. I meant, I wish I had never come down here to Emirgan. It's so isolating.'

'Well, perhaps you could move –'

She suddenly lost her grip on herself. She swung round fiercely.

'I wanted to be in the *centre* of things. In Cihangir or somewhere. I didn't want to be in this beautiful fucking suburban outpost! It was supposed to be temporary. Now it's too late to move.'

'I don't see –'

'Well you should, damn you! It's too late, because now it doesn't matter where I live. I mean I might just as well be – like this here as any place else.'

The priest cleared his throat. His face and neck had blushed to a deep strawberry. His nose had winking beads of sweat in its fractured crevice.

'Look, I'd better go. I'm off abroad this afternoon.

But I just wanted you to know that there was somebody who . . . well, that you could turn to me if you need to. I'll be back after the weekend. This has my phone number on it.'

He dropped a rectangular card on the low table in the centre of the room and began backing towards the door.

She saw him out. She had regained control, and she nodded her head with a tight, formal smile. As soon as she had banged the door she remembered. Justin. Justin Fuller. *That* was his name!

She laid her forehead against the door and began to shake with laughter and then with sobs.

On the way back to the city Justin dwelt on his failure. He had made no impression. He had been tongue-tied and foolish, like an adolescent. Yet still he felt in his chest that slight sense of uplift, of pockets of helium. He had been with her.

In simple catechism terms this was temptation for, in her grief and fury, he loved Lena even more. He shut his eyes and suppressed the sudden lust he felt wash over him. He bared his teeth, biting hard, tightening the muscles of his face to get rid of the feeling. What is more foolish than a clergyman in love?

He willed to mind the opening words of the 63rd psalm, one of his favourites: *Oh God, thou art my God; early will I seek thee . . .*

Before he could suppress it, the words had come out in loud ejaculation. He looked sideways at his neighbour in the car. All the passengers in the *dolmuş* were looking curiously at him. He covered his face and, with eyes shut, he silently continued to recite the psalm.

*My soul thirsteth for thee,*
*My flesh longeth for thee*
*In a dry and thirsty land where no water is.*

But even the words of scripture carried alternative profane meaning. They could make religious and sexual longing interchangeable. He loved her. He loved God.

He looked at his hand, so large and pink, with the russet hairs sprouting along the fingers as far as the knuckle. She had taken this – not shaken but *taken* it – when they said goodbye after that coffee. She'd been so warm, she'd made it seem almost possible that – He shook his head.

*And my soul shall be satisfied as with marrow and fatness*
*And my mouth shall praise thee with joyful lips . . .*

The *dolmuş* set him down at the Tophane Fountain below Beyoğlu, and he began another steep climb in this vertiginous city. As he climbed, the grip of disturbance began inexplicably to leave him and he remembered his purpose in going back to the Memorial Church: his suitcase.

He was escaping Kurban Bayramı for a long weekend, and had booked on the three-thirty flight to

Athens. He must go straight to the airport, after picking up his suitcase from Yakup, caretaker of the redundant church. Otherwise he'd be late.

Justin could see the church tower up ahead of him now. He regretted the church's redundancy, in a way. Of course the building was a millstone really, a regrettable anachronism. To hold regular Anglican services in it would be a Theatre of the Absurd. They were much better performed in the more modest consulate chapel, half a mile away at Galatasaray. And yet the church testified to a more confident Christianity of a century ago. These days the Christian religion seemed so etiolated. One had to accommodate oneself to so much – to uncertainty, doubt, redundancy of buildings, shrinking congregations, not to mention militant Islam. Yes, the old Christian muscle had been taken over now by Islam. There had already been Iran and Pakistan. And perhaps one day Turkey, too, would fall into the grip of fundamentalism.

He thought of Yakup, the very opposite of a fundamentalist. Yakup seemed entirely pragmatic – not very clever, perhaps, but cheerfully willing to serve any master for just as long as it made him and his family comfortable. Yakup was a kind of secondment, servant of the American businessman who acted as honorary church warden. Since deconsecration two years earlier such a post hadn't formally existed. But the American had seemed besotted by the idea of the warden's title, and what harm had there been in indulging his fantasy? In return he'd rented the place and provided a caretaker. He had even paid personally for essential works to the roof. Thank the Lord for rich Americans!

And, depressing though every secularized church must be, Yakup's tenure in the vicarage was symbolic of a kind of continuity. But the fellow's pragmatism was like a marker in once-sacred ground – a beacon winking above the muddy tide of militant Islam.

When Justin turned in at the church gate he found half a dozen chickens scratching about in the churchyard dust, marshalled by a fine gaudy cock. A puppy dog jumped around in its loose-fitting skin, worrying a punctured ball and squeaking like a rusty pulley. This was Claudius. He had been given to Yakup with the idea that he would develop as a guard dog. He tumbled towards Justin and tried to gnaw his shins.

Justin called out, 'Yakup! *Nerdesim*?' There was no reply. He walked up the steps to the porch of the house. The door, behind its mosquito screen, was locked.

He looked at his watch. If Yakup wasn't here then he must have left the suitcase somewhere. Justin had specifically asked the man to have the case at the vicarage so he could pick it up and make the short walk from there to *Şişhane* and the airport bus.

He looked into the church porch. There was no suitcase. He rattled the weighty iron handle of the church's oak door. The nursery had long since packed up for the day, and the house was locked. He called again and looked around.

A brick-dust path made a circuit of the church, and,

trailed by the panting Claudius, Justin set off along the west side. He passed Yakup's vegetable plot and the base of the tower, coming at last to the southern end of the churchyard, between the chancel and the high yard wall. Here the place had a gross, untended look, with waist-high clumps of yellow grass. There were several massive, tangled rose bushes and quite a few mature cacti. Claudius cocked his leg against one of these. Here, too, was a tin dustbin, used by Yakup as an incinerator. The place had a sweet-and-sour smell.

Justin remembered the door next to the base of the tower, the old vestry door. Perhaps Yakup had parked his case in there, though God knows why he should. He walked back to it and tried the handle. Then he produced a key which slotted into the spring lock.

Through a square room at the base of the tower he entered the vestry. The sun slanted in from the south, back-lighting the dust-caked glass of the mullioned windows, and the thick protective wire mesh on the outside. Opposite the windows were the two great mahogany cupboards which had once housed the vestments and vessels. He opened one. Lying in thick dust on a shelf was an unstrung tennis racket and a copy of *Hymns Ancient and Modern*. He picked up the book and flipped through the pages.

*Cover my defenceless head*
*With the shadow of thy wing . . .*

Justin shut the book, making a puff of dust. Still

holding it he stepped back and looked around at the floor. Like the body of the church, it was made up of coloured rhomboid tiles, many of which had been displaced or broken. Most of the damage was concealed, however, by a litter of broken-backed books and old magazines. There was no sign of his suitcase.

He opened the door which gave on to the church's south transept. Claudius darted forward and his squeaks could be heard echoing weirdly inside. Justin followed, brushing his hands palm against palm to loosen the dust. He hadn't been inside the church since he'd first arrived here, several weeks ago.

He looked first, as a matter of reflex, towards the altar. It was in pretty good order, a marble table raised above granite steps, with a low, not too fussy, wood-panelled reredos behind. Above it, though, was the church's chief glory, the soaring south window showing a mounted St George thrusting his lance down the throat of a serpentine, fire-belching dragon, with two admiring saints looking on from flanking panes. One of the supporting saints was St John the Evangelist. He had an intelligent, slightly smug look, like a young bond-dealer posing beside his first BMW. John's opposite number was Mary Magdalene, her hair flowing and tumbling almost in the style of Botticelli's *Venus*. Justin found he was staring at her, as if for the first time. He saw the figure's beauty, the pale ellipse of the face, the gracefully executed folds of the dress, the delicacy of the hands as they proffered a jar of ointment. Outside the church, behind the section of the glass on which the face was painted, a tree's branch must have moved, catching the sun. The movement made the Magdalene's eyes seem to flicker, like ship's riding lights across a mile of desolate water, like a spark of life in a flint-strewn wasteland. What was this? A shiver zig-zagged through Justin's body, as quick as a bead of mercury. Then a light, teasing voice broke against his thoughts.

*All right, Juss?*

It was an ordinary voice, a working-class accent. But Justin did not look around or behind him. He stood his ground. He knew where the voice came from.

He looked at the Evangelist. John's face displayed the confident, calculating languor of the privileged. After all, he was the favourite. He had a direct line to the boss.

*She's lovely, ain't she, Juss? Pretty as a plate of salad.*

John's arm seemed to gesture across towards the reformed whore who stood in balance with him on the other side of the window.

*She ain't for you, though, Juss. Give up the thought. He's got something else in mind. Something more momentous lined up.*

Justin frowned, puzzled. He looked back at the Magdalene. Beneath her feet was a ribbon inscribed in gothic script *Maria Magdalena.* Suddenly he was all attention. He smiled. He nodded his head, as if agreeing that John was right. He turned his eyes back to the

Magdalene. *Magdalena.* Yes. John was right. Something more momentous. It must be so.

Justin looked into the centre of the window. The dragon's eye flashed pain and vengeance, while St George, high above it, curled his lip in disdain. He moved his eyes to the right until they rested on Mary Magdalene once more. He lost himself in her strong, sorrowful face.

Claudius was snuffling around the marble pulpit and yipping with excitement. Probably after a rat. Justin roused himself. With effort he turned from the altar towards the nave and was so startled that the hymn book, which was still cinched beneath his arm, dropped to the floor making a resounding plop.

It was odd that this object had not registered instantly, but had somehow managed to escape his attention.

'What the heck –?'

The chairs, or pews, had been sold off long ago and the nave was an open, empty area. Except that now it was not empty. Standing in the centre of the space was a huge bell. It seemed to be that shape at least, although it was covered in green tarpaulin. The bell was probably ten foot high and as wide as a car, with a bump at the top as if there was a ring to hang it by. In the gloom of the church he could make out no more details. He squinted his eye and stepped forward, bringing himself alongside the pulpit. He was just going to advance another step when he heard the muffled shout of Yakup somewhere outside. Justin stopped and looked at his watch. The time! He was meant to be going on his holiday.

Justin hurried outside. He had just closed the door of the tower and made his way half-way along the side of the church when Yakup came scurrying round the building with his suitcase.

Before the two men closed on each other, the voice came again. Justin was not sure whether John was issuing a warning or a threat.

*I'm sticking around, Juss. I'll be having words again. T'rah for now.*

# 15

'What you, some kind of private ice?'

'No, a friend of his. I was here with him on Monday, doing business.'

Felix's shop had the closed sign showing. An old fellow, trailing a long-handled broom, had answered Dan's ring with suspicion cross-hatched into his grey, grooved features. A handmade cigarette drooped soggily like a bent twig from his lips.

'I Brizscinski. I clean here. I clean all this row shops.' He showed the broom, as evidence. 'He's gone, Mr Trubleshaw. He goes much away.' Brizscinski shrugged. 'Don't tell where.'

Dan said, 'Why did you ask if I was an investigator?'

'Many fish things go on round here. You are my second private ice come looking today.'

'I'm not a private eye, I told you. But you mean there *was* an investigator here?'

'Yeah, like a Greek or maybe a Paki, I could not tell.'

'And he said he was a detective?'

'Course he say it. If not, how do I know?'

'Look, could I possibly come inside? I ought to write a note or something. Maybe his desk diary will say where he is. It really is most urgent that I contact Mr Trubshaw at once.'

Brizscinski opened a little wider and hung between door and jamb, considering. He shrugged again, stepped back and picked up his broom. 'Just don't take away nothing you don't bring with you.'

When Dan walked into the shop Brizscinski walked out. He began sweeping the pavement.

Dan looked at the tree-of-life carpet which had frightened him on his last visit. It seemed so innocuous now. The snake had a rather rueful expression, its forked tongue projecting between a semi-human smile.

He remembered, or half-remembered, Felix's confusing behaviour when he was here on Monday, first threatening, then pleading. There had been something precarious about him, a sense of the mind teetering on some edge. But hadn't he claimed to have things to tell about Nathan Blanchard?

Dan sat in the swivel-chair behind Felix's desk. There was not much on it: phone, stapler, ashtray, card-index, mug crammed with pens and pencils, wire letter-tray. He fingered through the card-index, but it had only the names of antique dealers. The in-tray was equally unproductive – invoices, a list of forthcoming auctions, a monograph on Isfahan designs, a travel agent's brochure and a note from Felix's bank manager. Felix, Dan saw, was more than £6,000 overdrawn.

The desk drawers contained stationery, a few document wallets with records of carpet sales and purchases, three old diaries, a letter balance, an almost empty bottle of whisky. He did not find a current diary. Nor did he uncover any sign of the drugs for which Felix acted as a conduit. These were the plain appurtenances of a business for buying and selling antique rugs.

He swung the chair around and examined the bookshelf on the rear wall of the shop. On the left were the expected reference works and price guides. He smiled at the odder titles – *How to Date an Oriental Carpet*, *Buzzacott's Guide to Pile*, *A Prayer-Mat Primer*.

It was only when he shifted his eyes to the right that a false note pinged in his mind. Here was a comprehensive collection of very different works – *Nuclear Winter*, *Nostradamus and the Bomb*, *Facts on Nuclear Proliferation*, *Defended to Death*, *The Curve of Binding Energy*, *The Liquid Metal Fast-Breeder*, sets of magazines with names like *Atom* and *Nuclear News*.

He went back to the door and leaned out. Brizscinski was sweeping three doors down, and Dan showed him an issue of *Nucleonics Week*. It happened to be the bumper Christmas double-issue showing reindeer with molecule-models in place of their antlers.

'Do you know why Mr Trubshaw read all these magazines?'

The man stopped sweeping and squinted at the magazine cover, forward round the doorway where he was working, leaning on his broomhandle.

'Dunno. Whassit?' He looked the complete gawpus, mouth open, chin slack.

Dan said, 'It's a magazine about nuclear science. You know, nuclear weapons, bombs? Did he ever talk to you about it?'

The gawp slowly cleared. 'Ah! Yes, he do talk to me. The bomb is very bad. He was crazy about that. Crazy, crazy, crazy.' He shook his head, pityingly. 'Talk about it all day, think all night he said, he gets no sleep sometime like it's going out of date, you know? We all get blown up or we die with X-rays, thing like that.' He grinned, still shaking his head. 'Crazy man. Normal, well, he drink too much. But he's crazy man about the nuclear.'

He recommenced sweeping and Dan went back inside. He was half-way back to the bookcase when the phone on the desk sounded. He stood indecisively while it completed six double trills, then pre-empted the seventh by snatching up the receiver.

'Is this London 226 3434?'

Dan looked at the number on the phone. 'That is correct, yes.'

'Who'm I speaking to, please?'

Dan took a lungful of air. The voice was breathy, female, Irish. She said *London* before the number. That meant someone calling from abroad. He said, 'This is Mr Trubshaw's assistant. Can I help you?'

'Yes, I'm speaking from the Irish Republic, from Central Barracks of the *Garda Siochana* in Cork. This is Sergeant Marie Keane. Now you say you're Mr Trubshaw's assistant. Would that be Mr Felix Trubshaw?'

'Yes.'

'Ah, well look, we have Mr Trubshaw in custody, I'm afraid. He is not being very cooperative so I've had to resort to the London telephone directory.'

'You've arrested Mr Trubshaw? In *Ireland*?'

'Yes, Cork City Barracks.' Sergeant Keane was a patient woman.

'On what charge?'

'Oh, it'd be nothing at all but a petty theft charge, if we ever *did* charge him, like. He was picked up in the market, nicking some bits of food.'

'Food? Are you sure?'

'Sure I'm sure. Now what would your name be, sir?'

'Mills . . . erm, Edward Mills. Look, what sort of state is Mr Trubshaw in right now?'

'Oh, he's very troubled, sir. We'll likely be having the police psychiatrist to him. Very confused, he is.'

'Well, I'd better come over right away. You'll be keeping him in, will you?'

'You can be sure of that. We'll take good care of him, sir, until you come. Sure, we know who his father was so he'll come to no harm here with us.'

She made it sound like cosy farmhouse bed-and-breakfast hospitality of the kind that exists only in tourism commercials.

'Right, give me twenty-four hours – thirty-six at most.'

The sergeant gave him the address and telephone number and the conversation ended. *We know who his father was.* Dan shut his eyes and tried to remember if Felix had ever mentioned his parents.

'And what sort of fuckin' mess *is* Mr Trubshaw in?'

The voice had come from near the door, but Dan could not see who was standing there. The midday sunlight outside Felix's shop window blazed so bright that he saw only a bulky silhouette haloed by glare. Light is sometimes as blinding as darkness.

'Who wants to know?'

He hadn't recognized the voice. He should have, but the atmosphere in the shop, the presence of so many carpets soaking up the soundwaves maybe, turned voices dead and characterless. But when it was heard again, advancing into the centre of the space between Dan and the door, he immediately picked up its peculiar resonance and knew the intruder. 'You!' he said.

'Yes.'

Now the whole man came into focus, the fat figure standing with legs slightly splayed, the tired tropical suit, the straw hat, balanced on both hands inside up, like a platter of rich food.

'You're supposed to be dead.' The voice was matter-of-fact and Dan tried to match it although a cold nail of dread was working its way into his chest.

'Am I?'

'I sent a man to make you die.'

'But as you see . . .'

'He blew you away is what he told me.'

'No, he blew *it*.'

Blanchard looked into his hat which he began slowly revolving, passing the brim through his hands, first one and then the other. 'Sit down, Mr Barry. I want to talk.'

With his throat dry and feeling the weakness behind his knees, Dan took the revolving chair. Seated he managed to appear more composed.

'You're a writer, right?'

'I have been.'

'So what you doing pretending to be a steward?'

'It's a job. It was, until you tried to have me zapped. Writing isn't all that profitable. There's too much of it about.'

'But you worked for me. You couriered stuff for me.'

'Profit, Nathan. You understand that, don't you?'

Blanchard shook his head slowly. 'I liked you, you spied on me. We were like this small family, all of us. You were going to sell us out. Loyalty and family mean so much to me, son. Know where I learned those values? At one of your English schools. And you were going to split us apart like some atom.'

Dan heard a menacing, unmistakable *slitch*. Blanchard had picked a switch-blade out of the crown of his panama and released the spring.

'I need to know where Trubshaw is.'

Dan fought his shaking. 'I don't know.'

'Like fuck you don't.'

He turned the knife in the air. It was thin: the point came to a very acute angle. The well-kept blade flashed.

'Hey, mister, you not finish yet?'

The splintered English of Brizscinski cut through Dan's fear.

'Hey! Who we got visit? You know this guy? You better not stay longtime more, I gotta lock.'

Blanchard covered his head, ramming the hat into

place and making his jowls shake seismically. He said in a low voice for Dan's ears. 'I'm going to let you live for now. Just for now. Your life is on loan.'

He pushed past Brizscinski and got into the street. Dan followed him to the door, and leaned on it gratefully. He looked at Brizscinski. 'Do you know him?'

Brizscinski shook his head. 'Never seen that one. But he got the private ice with him, the one came early today.'

'What?'

Brizscinski was pointing outside. Dan plucked open the door and was in time to see Blanchard disappearing round the corner with Mister Red, the man from the cemetery.

He tore back to the desk and snatched the telephone, pressing 999. A cool female voice answered him. 'Which service do you want?'

'Police, police.'

He was connected quickly with another switchboard. He spoke rapidly. 'I want to report that I've just seen the guy who murdered all those people in Haggerston. He's wearing blue jeans and a tan zipper jacket. And he's in Islington, in the –' He tried to think of the name of the area they were in. 'Camden Passage, the Angel. Round there. Walking with a fat man in a panama hat. I've just seen him.'

'How do you know it's the wanted man, sir?' said the police operator, coolly. He sounded like he handled six hoaxes a minute.

'From the paper, the picture in the paper this morning.'

'What number are you calling from, sir?'

Dan hung up. Brizscinski looked at him like he was insane. 'What you call police for?'

'Look, um, Brizscinski – is that your name? Mr Trubshaw is in a bit of trouble. *I'm* in a bit of trouble. But I'm going to try and do something about it. It would be best if you didn't talk to anyone about this, okay? Not anyone. Good man.'

He touched the bewildered Pole on the arm, slipped through the door and into the open air. He made his way down the passage and into the High Street, where he immediately hopped on a number 38 bus for Piccadilly. As the bus pulled away Dan saw the flashing blue lights of police cars come flooding into the area. That should keep Blanchard and his hitman busy, he thought, pulling himself up the stairs to the upper deck.

But, as Dan's bus waited at the lights by the congested Angel intersection, a swarthy, bald man in jeans and a lightweight cotton jacket jumped aboard and took his place on one of the lateral seats beside the conductor's station. From here he could carefully watch every passenger off the bus. His overweight companion stood in a recessed doorway and observed the bus accelerating away from the lights.

The sun was shining and Edward Craike had forsworn lunch and cleared his desk, hoping to catch a few hours of decent cricket at Lord's in the afternoon. Just as he was leaving, his phone shrilled. He answered with curt impatience.

'Sir, it's Jenkinson.'

'Fire away, Jenkinson.'

'Thought you'd better hear this a.s.a.p. The Yard have just been on to me. You know I asked them to keep us up to date on any relevant action while Blanchard's in London. Well, apparently they've picked up an American in Islington. He's heavily built, in a light-coloured suit, and a panama. No I.D. on him, and he's kicking up merry hell.'

'Oh bugger. That sounds like him all right. Look, I was just on my way up to watch some cricket, but I'll hang on here for a bit. Find out what happened and ring me back in ten minutes max.'

Craike sat and gnawed his lower lip as he waited for the return call. Middlesex must be half-way through their innings by now and he was going to be extremely pissed off if the only players left to bat when he got there were a bunch of tailenders flailing away like hysterical girls.

Jenkinson called again seven minutes later. 'They had an anonymous tip-off that the Haggerston killer was walking round the Angel Islington with a fat Yank. They found the Yank and hoiked him up to the nick for questioning. He was alone, though. They're thinking of charging him with possession of an offensive weapon, an eight-inch flick-knife.'

'Have they confirmed identity?'

'Well, I have. They faxed me through a Polaroid. It's Blanchard all right.'

Craike hung up and dialled the Assistant Commissioner.

'George, Eddie here, Empress State. Your blokes in Islington have a feller in their bang-up, an American called Nathan Blanchard. Now we're extremely interested in this chappie over at this end . . . Yes. And you see the last thing we want is him up before the beak or anything like that. Can you get them to let him out without charge? Well – let's say in an hour from now. Great. Thanks, George old man. I'll remember it.'

He punched some more numbers.

'Jenkinson? Get someone up to Islington. They'll let him out in an hour. We'd better keep tabs on him from now on.'

'D'you think there's any connection with the Haggerston killer?'

'Could be. The man who did it was a Turk, wasn't he? Of course the flatfoots won't make that connection, they'll treat it like a hoax, right?'

'Right – they're not interested in Blanchard, they think it's a mislead.'

'Good. So get a tail on Blanchard, will you? I don't care about the Haggerston business one way or the other, I just want to know what he's up to. Got it?'

He dropped the receiver into place. Before the phone could ring again he was out in the corridor and on his way to Lord's.

# 16

Mustafa pushed his shades back to the bridge of his nose and hung over the rail.

Out here, between wind and granite-grey sea, he was particularly naked and exposed without the head of hair, moustache and stubble. His face felt like a snail dispossessed of its shell.

He looked queasily down the side of the ship. All around the sea palpitated massively. It swelled up to him, up and back, as if moved by gigantic lungs that inflated and deflated somewhere in the deep. Across the surface skeetered patches of foam which bunched and stretched, broke apart and merged together in a hectic kaleidoscope. A porthole opened in the side of the ship below where he was standing, and a fling of potato peel swished into the sea. With cackles of delight, the rabble of seabirds that inevitably hang over a ship's wake swooped to their supper.

Mustafa, too, was very skilled at maintaining a tail over long distances. He'd once followed a Lebanese businessman from Cyprus to Santiago. But even he was tired now. Barry had taken him first to Paddington Station ticket office. Then he'd collected a package from the left-luggage and disappeared into the toilets, emerging after five minutes with the package no longer in his hands. He'd boarded a train for south Wales.

Mustafa had ridden in the adjoining car, scanning the platform at every stop in case Barry got off. It wasn't until Swansea Harbour that he did.

Movement between Britain and Ireland is casual, and it had been no problem boarding the boat, paying for his ticket with cash from Darren Knight's safe. If the police were watching, there was no sign – they missed him, anyway. Then, after sailing, he had watched from the deck beside the window as Dan sat in the bar. But Dan could not escape him now, and in the meantime Mustafa's innards had begun to shrink and expand in counterpoint rhythm to the rolling of the ship. He moved away and threw up beside a life-boat.

At the other end of the ship, Mustafa stumbled across a miniature casino. A couple of one-armed bandits stood beside a blackjack machine near the bulkhead, but the main attraction was a roulette table, presided over by a female croupier calling the numbers with all the passion of a telephone operator. Mustafa bought some chips. It took him twenty-five minutes to lose them, then he bought some more.

Some three hours later Mustafa had been efficiently parted from all but his loose change. He returned gloomily to the deck.

The gambling losses had not purged his weary, congested mind. He could not be rid of that night at the cemetery in London, when Barry had stood over him and aimed the pistol at his chest. He'd pissed himself. It was his index of fear, a calibrator of shame.

He thought then of Can, his father's friend, the barber's son from their village. Can had fought alongside his father with the Turkish contingent in Korea. One afternoon in Mustafa's twelfth year, he and his father had stood together at the place where apricots dried in the sun while his father had told him Can's story.

'There had been hand-to-hand fighting, the two of us were side by side. We fought well. Our uniform tunics were soaked in blood. All of our unit had run out of bullets, so we unclipped the bayonets from our rifles and went close up to the Communists. You could smell their breath, that was how close we were as we killed them.'

His father had looked out over the field whose carpet of fruit turned black where it lay. His voice was flat, but Mustafa, young as he was, had recognized emotions deeper than a catch in the throat.

'I was busy with this Communist soldier, sticking my bayonet into his ribs. So I lost sight of Can. Then I saw him again. He had gone down, lying next to a burnt-out jeep. A Chinese was straddling him, lifting his bayonet. Next moment he would stab it down into Can's chest and twist it before dragging it out. I just watched. I was so appalled I forgot everything. I was too far away to do anything, I could only witness the moment of his death.

'He was saved by a stray shell. It hit the jeep and lifted the Chinese soldier up and clipped him sideways. It was like his ankles had been chopped through by a scythe stroke. Being on the ground the blast missed Can completely. He got up and walked away.'

Mustafa had looked at his father in awe that he had seen, and himself done, such deeds. His dad's eyes were dry and narrow, the deep lines pointing inwards at them like arrowheads as he squinted into the low sun.

'Can never recovered. He knew, if a man lies at the point of the enemy's sword, he is already dead in spirit. If he happens to be saved by a fluke, without deserving it, he looks forward to nothing but a life of hatred for himself. He will be alive but dead. And Can knew that I saw what happened; it was because of this we could never be the same friends again. After the war he went away to Ankara and I heard he died, oh, three or four years later. Cancer. But as I said, he was already dead. It made no difference.'

Can's snapshot had been taped to the mirror in the father's shop, where it could be studied as one sat beneath the barber's scissors. Mustafa remembered it clearly, a yellowing image in neat uniform, the cap tucked into the epaulettes. He would sit and stare, trying to figure out how it must feel to be alive and yet dead. The idea made him shudder and then he'd be told to keep still or risk an earlobe.

Stars were spattered around the sky. Each of them was like a life. And how many more lives would he have to waste before his own would gutter out from shame?

He lay full stretch on a seat, wrapped his arms around him and tried to sleep.

*

The cell-door's peephole revealed a hollow space painted cream, with a narrow wood-frame bed and a concrete floor. Felix sat dejectedly on the bed, his elbows on his knees and the palms of his hands massaging his face.

Sergeant Keane removed a painted fingernail and the flap swung back down over the hole. She said to Dan in a low voice, 'Come in here with me and meet Dr Doherty.'

She preceded him back through the station. Dan found himself watching her rounded hips as she walked. Their swing seemed exaggerated by the fitted blue serge of the uniform skirt and the severe black stockings.

Dr John Doherty, official psychiatrist to the Cork police force, was a careworn man with thin, overlong hair and an extraordinary suit, so tight at the shoulders and thighs that, overall, he appeared shrink-wrapped. He took off his half-moon glasses as Dan and the sergeant came in.

'Dr Doherty, this is Mr Mills, Mr Trubshaw's associate.'

Dan said, 'Well, Dr Doherty. I hope you can shed some light on Felix's extraordinary behaviour. I've never known him do anything like this.'

Sergeant Keane was called away to take a telephone call, as Doherty scratched his nose consideringly with a skeletal little finger. He looked appraisingly at Dan, the kind of glance which says: how much of the truth can this person be told?

'You know he's an alcoholic?'

Dan nodded. The doctor was staring at him. Did he suspect Dan in some way? He seemed suspicious of his clothes. The grey flannels and blazer were beginning to look a little travel-worn, but they were not bad. Doherty continued. 'But that is not, I feel, at the root of Felix's problem. It's more a question, I'd say, of delayed mourning for his father, manifesting itself in prolonged depression and fear of nuclear war.'

'Nuclear war?'

'Yes. His dreams are very graphic, full of balls of fire, mushroom clouds, nuclear physicists.'

'But where does his father come in?'

'His father *was* a nuclear physicist, here at University College Cork. I knew him, you know. Died four or five years back. Very distinguished man, a pioneer of Ireland's nuclear programme. Very well known in Cork, he was.'

Dan drew out a chair and sat down. 'I didn't know Ireland *had* a nuclear programme.'

Doherty continued, as if he hadn't heard. 'This is obviously the reason Felix has come over here so suddenly and so unprepared. A return to the scene of the crime, so to speak.'

'What crime? I'm sorry, I don't understand.'

'The Oedipal crime, the killing of your father. Of course Felix never killed his old man. But he has come to believe that he has. Hence all these dreams of his father being consumed by fire while the son looks on. Guilt. Pure, unresolved Oedipal guilt.'

He spread his hands, opened his eyes wide and spoke like a Grand Master executing checkmate. 'Classical!'

Sergeant Keane came back into the room.

'You know he had hardly a penny on him? And he has a number of bruises and cuts, but he tells us nothing, poor man. We can't for the life of us find out what happened to him. Won't talk to us at all.'

'So how,' asked Dan, 'do you know about his dreams?'

Doherty seemed to have turned his attention back to Dan's clothing. He snapped rather impatiently, 'Oh, he tells us all about *those*.' But he seemed to regret the sharp tone, and added, 'I'm something of a hypnotherapist, you know.'

Dan was by now thoroughly confused, and he attempted to clear his way to some simple explanation.

'So what does all this mean, actually? He's – he's going mad, is he?'

'Mad? We don't use that word at all. Dear me, no. He's very disturbed. He has a mass of unresolved problems. He will need constant, prolonged care.'

'Well, may I take him away then, back to England I mean?'

He looked from Doherty back to Keane.

'Who would there be to look to him?'

'Well, myself and my – my wife, Marilyn. We have a second home in Scarborough, you see. It's very quiet and salubrious. I'll take him there as soon as we get back to England.'

'Sounds just the ticket,' said Doherty, rising. 'I'll leave you now in the capable hands of Sergeant Keane. The final decision is hers – whether or not to prefer charges. But as far as my recommendation goes, the son of Professor Louis Trubshaw ought to be free to recuperate in his own sweet time.'

He stretched and strolled to the door, and turned with his hand on the knob.

'Oh, by the way – your tie. I've been looking at it. Would that be, by any chance, the insignia of the Skibbereen Oddfellows? It's a defunct club now, of course, but my father was a member and I think they'd an almost identical – No? Ah well. Be seeing you.'

He wandered from the room.

'Was your father really in charge of the Irish nuclear programme?'

They were driving west in a stolen car. Dan had never stolen a car before, but it had seemed the only thing to do. He had Ted Mills's Amex card, of course, but no driving licence, so hiring one was out.

'He was. It wasn't much. A little research lab at U.C.C. with a couple of part-time assistants. Very small potatoes.'

'That shrink says you're suffering from nuclear anxiety neurosis.'

'It's true. I have hellish dreams.'

'He also says it's all bound up with your old man.'

'Crap, there's a much nearer cause. Couldn't we stop for another drink?'

He trained both his index fingers on a wayside pub ahead, but Dan did not ease the gas pedal. Felix's fingers swung round, like a swivelling ack-ack gun, as the car sped past.

It was a Ford estate and suitably, given Dan's adopted persona, a representative's car, with a number of cardboard boxes, crammed with presumed samples, in the rear. The theft had been quite spontaneous. They'd been walking towards the Cork suburb of Douglas and wondering what to do, when the car had drawn their attention to itself by screeching up to a tobacconist's a few yards ahead. Its driver had jumped out and run into the shop, leaving his engine ticking over. Dan and Felix exchanged a glance, moved to their respective sides of the car, opened the doors in a synchronized movement and slipped inside.

'Falling off a log,' murmured Dan to himself, as he accelerated away and he had felt again that fleeting sense of his own power. It was as if the torque which shifted those wheels around at seventy mph was coming not from the 1750 cc engine, but from his own hands and feet, hard on the controls.

But by now, some fifteen minutes later, he was worried again. It was really a stupid thing to have done, because it put them back on the wrong side of the law. How long would it take the police to pick up their trail? He certainly wasn't going to stop at a pub which was in plain view of the main road, just to supply Felix's addiction. They'd stopped briefly in several bars during their stroll through Cork, and

Felix would have to regard himself as, for the time being, tanked up. It was the reason he was in so much better shape than when Dan had seen him earlier this morning.

At one of these pubs Felix had sprung a surprise. 'You know I've got a girl?'

'No. No, I didn't.'

'Don't sound so surprised. She's a little thing in Istanbul, Australian originally. Got into drugs, then prostitution. I set her up in a flat, gave her a small income, nothing much because I haven't got much. Blanchard may have made his fortune out of other people's misery, but he never shared it very much, not with myself, at least.'

'What's her name, this girl?'

'Sarah. Lives in the old city, up the hill above the Yeni Cami. I feel badly about her, really. Haven't sent her any money this week. Hope the poor thing's okay.'

'You should worry about yourself for the moment, Felix. Your own problems are enough to be getting along with.'

'You can say that again. Cheers.'

And he drained his stout, loudly rapping the base of the glass on the bar as he replaced it.

They'd been driving for half an hour before Dan broached the subject that had brought him over the Irish Sea in the first place. 'When we talked at your shop you said we could collaborate.'

'Did I?'

'You did. You said you had stuff I should know for my book.'

'Did I?'

'Don't you remember?'

'I need a drink.'

'Look, we can't stop at the moment. In a little while I'll get off the main road. We'll look for somewhere to stay. Just another thirty miles or so.'

Felix looked over his shoulder. 'You'd think they'd be haring after us by now.' He lapsed into a self-absorbed silence.

They entered a straight stretch of road and Dan looked in his mirror. A dark blue saloon with a pimple of blue plastic surmounting its roof was eating up the road behind them. Dan's stomach tightened.

'Here goes,' he said. In spite of himself he pressed his foot harder down. This made not a scrap of difference, as the other guy must have been doing a hundred. The Ford seemed to flinch in the squad car's turbulence as it passed, so fast that Dan couldn't tell if the driver had noticed them at all before streaking on his way, regardless.

'Didn't seem overconcerned.'

'Who didn't?' Felix hadn't even noticed the police car.

'We'd better get off this road.'

After another two miles, Dan turned off, following a sign which directed them to 'Cappuns Hall quality Guest House. B 'n B. Bar. Anglers Welcome. 8 miles'.

'Good,' said Felix. 'A bar at last.'

Dan said, 'Well, it's off the beaten track if it's eight miles down here.'

The road was narrow and overloaded with hedges in which bramble and white bryony tangled with the fuchsia. It took them twenty-five twisty minutes to reach Cappuns Hall which turned out to be a small converted farmhouse, smothered in ivy. A narrow ribbon of concrete, divided into parking bays, separated the house from an arched bridge. This took the road on across a decent, middle-sized trout stream.

'We'll be having trout for dinner,' said Felix.

But as they drew abreast of the place, Dan knew they would not. The blue squad car was the only tenant of the parking spaces, standing smug and empty beside the trellis porch of the guest house. Dan simply drove on, across the stone bridge.

This time Felix did not miss the police car. He said, 'Shit! Where am I going to get a drink? I'd like to know why we had to steal this car? If we hadn't we could be perched on a decent pair of bar stools by now.'

Dan was possessed by a despairing sense of futility. This was like crawling through an unending steel sewer pipe. He thought of how it had all started, those long pub discussions with Jack Bacon. How to get rich, for fuck's sake! You would have thought that after a year of unrelieved tension and deception in Istanbul, flying that route week by week, carrying Blanchard's merchandise and waiting for the breaks, you'd think *that* was bad enough. But he remembered the sense of inner strength he possessed then, the sense that only he knew the secret of himself. It had borne him along through all that time. Now the secret was blown and the inner strength seemed to have drained away.

The serpentine by-road continued alongside the river. There were no turnings or intersections, just an occasional farm or house. Each time he passed a driveway Dan checked the distance clock. When they'd left the last farm a mile behind he slowed down. 'We're going to find somewhere for the night.'

'What – sleep out here? For Christ's sake, I can't sleep out here.'

'Need a bed, do you?'

'I need a *drink*, pal!'

Dan nearly missed the stone barn, hidden so tidily between road and river. But catching just a corner of grey roof-slate he braked and backed up, telling Felix to open the gate. He parked the Ford tight under the fuchsia hedge, where it couldn't be seen from the road. From behind the barn the river's liquid purr was audible.

Felix lapsed once more into self-absorption. He stumped this way and that, sometimes stopping and looking at the sky, as if to judge the upcoming weather. Then he'd kick at a stone, mutter a curse and resume his prowling.

Dan looked into the barn. It was derelict. There was no hay, as he had hoped, just a floor of corrugated mud and a few rusted farm implements – a tractor-drawn harrow, a plough.

'I'm going to the river to get a drink,' he said. As he went Felix's bitter laugh followed him.

'Mills,' Craike was saying. 'Edward Mills. Name mean anything?'

Jack Bacon shook his head and looked at Jenkinson. 'Not to me. Is there nothing on file?'

Jenkinson compressed his lips, as if it were hard for him to admit the lack of such a file. 'We've never heard of him. All we have is a description from the Irish police, but it's skimpy.'

Craike's office was no wider than a corridor – metal-frame window at one end, and a plain, unpanelled door at the other. The walls were tightly packed with books and files. In this confined space, big-boned men like Jenkinson and Bacon invariably felt ill at ease. Now, nervously, Jenkinson referred to a sheet of A4 paper.

'There was one thing. Actually, it's not much. He was apparently wearing some sort of club tie, similar to that of the –' Jenkinson squinted at the paper '– the Skibbereen Oddfellows, it says here. We've been trying to find out who they are. The insignia is a heraldic device of some kind. Shall I check with the – ?'

Craike shut his eyes and cut in briskly. 'For God's sake, forget the Skibbereen Oddfellows, it's a red herring. The point is, we know now that Trubshaw's gone to ground in Ireland, and this man Mills is with him. Trubshaw may be pathetic but that doesn't mean he's not dangerous. If he's sharing information with Mills, that makes Mills dangerous too. We've got to find them both.'

Craike dismissed Jenkinson curtly, telling him to start by tracking down any of Trubshaw's Irish relations. Then he slid open a drawer and flipped a small, thin book on to his desk. It spun for a few seconds before coming to rest. Jack Bacon saw it was a diplomatic passport, bearing Craike's name.

'Jack, I'm going to Istanbul. Tomorrow.'

'Tomorrow? Bit soon, isn't it?'

'I think it's best to be on the spot. I won't be needing you out there yet, you can join me later. I want to see Dan Barry's girlfriend. She may give us a line on Mills, but it'll need careful handling, which is why I'm going myself. Also, Trubshaw had a girl out there – you didn't know that, did you? Australian bit, junkie, probably of no significance. But I want to check her out anyway.'

Craike sighed. 'Things are looking a mite rocky just at the moment, Jack. Got to steady the ship.'

'There's no going back now, is there, Ed?'

'Exactly. There's no going back.'

Later, Dan sat on a breeze-block beside the barn wall. 'Where d'you want to go? Apart from a pub?'

'I've got an aunt in Kenmare. That'd do, for a bit. Keep my head down.'

'Right, we'll go tomorrow.'

'Don't think the old bitch will be too pleased to see me, but still.'

There was a pause. Dan studied his feet. The town

shoes, the flannels and blazer, looked odd in this bucolic setting. But no one was looking.

'Felix, why won't you tell me about Blanchard?'

'Get me a drink and I'll tell you.'

'For God's sake, can't you forget about that? What do you need a drink for?'

'I'm a drunk, okay? I'll be happy to tell you when I'm happy – not before.'

'Oh, fuck it. I'm going to sleep.'

He sloped over to the Ford. It wasn't quite dark. He looked in the back of the traveller's cardboard boxes. They'd have to come out to make room.

He leaned in through the hatch and, bracing himself on one hand, pulled the nearest carton towards him. The flaps were loose and he had hold of one of them. He heard a chink of glass from inside, and parted the flaps to see what the samples were.

'Oh, no! Oh, Jesus, no!' He started laughing, lowering his upper body until his forehead rested on the edge of the box. Fatigue and hunger made the whole thing seem much funnier. Laughter flowed out of him like water out of a punctured rain butt.

Felix came over, curious. 'What's so sodding amusing? What's to laugh at?'

Dan indicated the box of samples by slapping it with his hand. Felix gingerly separated the cardboard flaps, which had sprung back over the contents.

He saw four rows of miniature screw-down bottle tops, nine to each row. At first he thought they were pharmaceuticals. Then he picked one out.

Dan had stopped laughing. He was watching Felix's expression as it changed from curiosity to incredulity.

'Whiskey? I don't believe it. Not the whole lot of them?'

His fingers began scrabbling among the miniature bottles. His face looked likely to explode from shock and pleasure.

'Oh my God. Oh – my – Go-od, it's whiskey, all of it.'

Feverishly he reached for the other boxes, fumbling them over on their sides, spilling their contents with a joyous rattle of glass.

'All of it's whiskey, that is, except for the – the gin, rum, vodka and – what's this? What's this? Ha! Irish Cream liqueur!'

He hurled a miniature of Irish Cream high into the air. It spun up, then down in parabolic flight, before crashing against the barn roof.

'Alleluia, Danny boy. My prayers are answered. It's a miracle from heaven. We've stolen a high-performance, four-door cocktail cabinet. Have a drink.'

Felix drained his third miniature and placed it carefully on the ground in front of him, in chevron formation with the other two empties.

'It was this way. Blanchard liked you, I always felt it. He'd tried you out over time, now he was on the point of making you a full partner, y'know? You were in. Then you blew it.'

He selected another bottle, examining the label in

the moonlight. Dan said, 'But you said he was winding up the smack dealing anyway.'

'So he was – well, he'd decided to. You see he's seen the way it's going, straws in the wind.'

With a twist of his grip he cracked the seal and delicately unscrewed the bottle top.

'The Colombians are moving into London. The guys who were buying from us, Mossman and Co., were getting nervous, afraid to miss the crack 'n coke gravy-train. They were beginning to tighten the screws on Blanchard, telling him they'd not pay so much for the stuff, wanting different quantities all the time. It was getting like they were softening him up.'

'Seems an odd way to go about it. Why not just dump him, if they wanted to?'

'Well, you can't act that way with a guy like Nathan. He's like an animal, like one of his own pigs or something.'

Felix shuddered to think of the pigs, and crossed himself.

'You've got to get him used to an idea, never make a sudden move. If you do he'll bite off some part of you before you've had a chance to sidestep. No, to get him to accept a new idea you have to make it come out of him, y'see? Make him feel he thought of it himself.'

'And did he?'

'Yes, of course. He's not stupid. He said to me not long ago, "Felix, the time is coming when junk is going to be just that. I got to find something that isn't going so fast out of fashion."'

'And?'

'That's exactly what he did. As from this week Nathan Blanchard has stopped dealing in heroin. He's stopped dealing in guns and human kidneys and Hittite treasures – oh yes, there were some genuine ones, although you didn't touch them. But he's stopped all of that. He's concentrating his resources – undiversifying, you might say, which is why he was busy retiring all of us this week.'

Felix drained yet another miniature. But he was beginning to plateau now, and took his time selecting its successor from the box at his side.

'You know what he said to me? "Those little operations, they're only making pissholes in the snow. Watch me. I'm going to get me a fucking Niagara Falls."'

'What did he mean? He'd never get into the cocaine market, he's working from the wrong end of the world.'

'And don't I know it. Wasn't I the one who persuaded him to go East? He thinks if instead of Istanbul we'd gone to Bogotá or Medellín in 1980 he'd be one of the fifty richest men in the world. That's shit, of course. He'd be dead. But you can't tell him that.'

'So come on, Felix, tell me. What is it he's getting into?'

'I *will* tell you. I'll tell you now.'

He paused, swaying slightly, his chin tucked in as if on the edge of a burp. He looked at Dan through watery eyes that caught the moonlight, and held up his finger.

'He's dealing in the most addictive, most dangerous, most expensive fucking drug in the world. You know what it is? I'll bet you fifty pounds to sixpence you can't guess.'

Another ruminative pause: the drunk, thinking he's pacing himself for maximum dramatic effect.

'Trivial pursuit. I'll give you a clue or two. You don't sniff it. You don't drink or smoke it, you don't even inject it, at least not into your *self*. And it's made in Britain. You'll never guess what it is, because it's on a completely different scale to everything else. And pricewise, compared to the purest most expensive coke, it's the difference between fish paste and Beluga caviar. I mean it costs, now wait for this, it costs – '

Felix leaned forward. He was enjoying this to the full. Dan was not.

'Come on, Felix, what?'

'It costs two million dollars a kilo on the black market.'

'For fuck's sake, Felix, tell me!'

'All right. It's plutonium, Danny boy. The very finest, weapons-grade, five-fucking-star plutonium oxide. And Nathan Blanchard has got himself ten million dollars' worth.'

# 17

Mustafa's troubles had begun once Dan and Felix walked out of the *Gardai* barracks together. He followed them on foot for hours through the neglected streets, waiting outside pubs and shops, scuffing his shoes, picking his nose, trying to bring to mind lines of poetry learned at school. Their progress seemed aimless. Sometimes he walked ahead of them, with a swagger, daring Barry to see through his disguise. Other times he lagged back, afraid they had already recognized him. This was why he nearly missed witnessing the theft of the Ford. He came up only as they were driving away.

He had, however, an excellent view of the Ford's dispossessed owner rushing out to find that nothing remained of his car but a shake of exhaust-smoke settling over the kerbstone. The man's face was screwed up, not so much in anger as hurt, as he chased twenty yards up the road waving his arms and uttering incoherent shouts. He returned to the shop and Mustafa heard him calling almost plaintively for a telephone. In due course a blue police saloon, driven by a single young officer, answered the telephone summons. The policeman, too, parked outside the shop.

Mustafa had been unsure what to do. He needed transport and quickly if he was going to catch up with

Dan and Felix. But it wasn't until now that a complete programme of action flashed into his head.

At the newsagent's counter, his notebook poised, the young policeman took the details of the stolen car. Then he stepped back to his own vehicle and reached through the lowered window for his radio handset. As he did so he found himself looking down the barrel of the Browning handgun which Mustafa had stolen on his second visit to Darren Knight.

Mustafa whispered, 'Drive first, then you radio.' He pointed in the direction Barry and Trubshaw had gone. 'That way.'

The officer took off like a Formula One racer from the grid, leaving the salesman looking out with a puzzled expression through the newsagent's window.

Mustafa rose up from the floor into the passenger seat. 'Now radio. Tell them all is okay about the young man's car, the stolen one. It was just a joke, not stolen. Then say over and out.'

The young policeman obeyed his instructions implicitly. He could not even, in his panic, think of a way to code-signal his distress. When he finished, Mustafa took the handset, lowered the window and threw it out. 'Now drive fast. We will catch those bloody thieves.'

So quickly did they drive that after twenty minutes they came up behind the Ford unexpectedly and Mustafa told the constable to overtake, as if they were chasing some quite different emergency. After they had outdistanced their quarry by a few miles he ordered a left turn, into a narrow lane.

The lane went into a dip and up a higher, steeper hill on the further side, twisting to the left as it levelled off. From the brow of the hill Mustafa could see forward for quite a distance, as well as back to a stretch of the main road and the place where they had turned off it. Here he told the policeman to pull up and get out.

Mustafa got out simultaneously and ordered the *garda* to the rear of the car. The young policeman – he looked about nineteen or twenty – was visibly terrified. His face twitched as he obeyed Mustafa's instruction to open the boot. Then he straightened and turned, as if in some kind of indecision, as if on the brink of a fearful action that he couldn't quite bring himself to do. Mustafa didn't hesitate. He shot the boy once through the chest, heart and lungs. The jolt pushed the kid backwards and he folded, his spine bumping on the rim of the boot. Mustafa laid down the gun and moved forward. He had only to grip the body behind both knees to pitch it into the open cavity. His victim was not quite dead as the lid slammed. Crouching to retrieve his weapon Mustafa heard the boy's life being choked away under the smooth steel.

Rising, Mustafa checked the road in both directions. He was just in time to glimpse the Ford down on the highway approaching the intersection with the lane. Expecting to see it continue on its way along the main road, he intended to turn around and follow it discreetly. But when, instead, it turned into the lane and came towards him, he jumped like a rabbit.

Seconds later he was driving, looking for a halt which Dan and Felix would pass without spotting him. There was nothing for miles, until he came upon Cappuns Hall Guest House. The parking area was entirely vacant when Mustafa pulled in. It was alongside the barn-end wall of the house with no downstairs window, so no one would see him duck his head down, waiting to hear the passing swish of Dan and Felix in the Ford. This would be all right. They would imagine the policeman was inside the bar enjoying a pint. They would drive past with no particular sense of danger.

Mustafa checked a police road map which he found in the glove compartment. He located the side-road and followed it with his finger, coming to a dead end after about twelve map-miles upon the lower contours of a small hill. Perfect.

He drove slowly on, scanning gateways and breaks in the hedgerow's abundance, and stopping every quarter of a mile to listen. The lushness of the vegetation, and the generous, green perspectives which it lent to the landscape, unnerved him. Mustafa was accustomed to the more grudging earth of his own country.

He never saw the stone barn on his right because he had just glimpsed a fox, zigzagging warily up the field on the opposite side, its vivid red coat standing out against the green. Mustafa slowed down. Every now and then the animal would freeze and prick its ears, just as Mustafa was doing along this road.

After several miles he reached a five-barred gate and

a sign warning against trespass. The gate was chained and padlocked. Mustafa cursed and started back. He must have missed them, they must have turned into one of the farmhouses he had seen in the first few miles after the guest house. He began to feel depressed about his chances of finding them now. He could hardly bring this car out on to the main road again. They would be looking for it. What was more it was getting late. He banged the steering wheel with the heel of his hand in frustration.

Then his luck changed. He saw the smoke first and increased his speed, in order not to be noticed passing. There was a thin blur of flame visible through the gateway. He stopped the car twenty-five yards further on, walked back.

Felix was there; he couldn't see Dan. Felix was walking up and down, talking to himself.

Mustafa doubled back to the car and drove on until he found a wide enough scallop of verge. He deposited the police car there and began moving cautiously across the field towards the source of the smoke. He thought again of the fox.

Once he started talking, Felix's feelings burst out as if a bag had been opened. 'I didn't ever feel really guilty about importing heroin or guns. I needed the money and anyway I was kind of helpless. I do know I'm an alcoholic, you know.' He pushed this out a shade defiantly.

Dan looked at him. 'Were you really helpless?'

'Nathan Blanchard always had this hold on me. I was dependent on him, as much as on booze, although the difference is I hated him. Any bad name you care to put on Blanchard will hang there comfortably. He's a shifty, calculating, double-dyed psycho. You know, it wasn't till I knew he was going in for nuclear garbage that I really accepted that? I always excused him. But spreading the bomb everywhere, that changed me. I became his enemy and a traitor within the ranks. You want to know why?'

'Why?'

'You don't *really* want to know why, do you?'

'Yes I do. I'm a writer, Felix. I have this insatiable curiosity. I want to know why.'

'Okay. My dad – yeah yeah, the shrink in Cork had this sussed out – my dad was one of the biggest shits of all time – and I mean *biggest*. But the Cork people all loved him. He was a walking contradiction and knew it. He used to quote a riddle – see if you can guess it:

> *Dark caused by bright light.*
> *Weightless caused by great weight.*
> *What is it?'*

It was not a particularly cold evening – they had built the fire as much for something to do as for warmth. In its light Dan saw Felix take a slug from a newly-opened miniature bottle. By this time he'd started on the vodka.

'Dark coming from light, weightlessness coming from weight. So? What is it?'

Dan shrugged. 'Don't know. Give up.'

'I'll tell you then?'

'Go on.'

'A fat man's shadow.'

Felix chuckled and chafed his hands together in pleasure. 'My dad weighed twenty-four stone. When I realized what his work was, that he was a nuclear physicist, privy to masses of secret, top secret and mega-secret secrets, I was right up to my neck in his shadow, right? It chilled me, it was *heavy*! I was sure he made bombs. Bombs! For Ireland! God, it seems so laughable now. But I was a kid, and anyway real nuclear fear doesn't work logically. I remember the Cuban missile crisis. Jesus, we used to go to bed at my school telling each other we'd wake up dead. Anyway, I developed this rabid kind of phobia about my dad. I wouldn't speak to him, unless it was to accuse him of terrible crimes, such as the murder of my mother. This was later on, though. In my teens.'

He had started to look morose. The flamelight threw itself around him, as if trying to erase his face.

'My mother died of cancer, and my dad had a lot to do with it. I mean he broke her down. He didn't like women. Used to read *Arabian Nights* to me as a cautionary tale, saying the story of Scheherazade proved you must never listen to females, they sap your strength. Well, that's normal Catholic misogyny. But he also thought science was a virile activity which cuts out fuzzy-minded women. My poor fuzzy-minded mother never amounted to much in his eyes.

'When she died I blamed him. I turned against everything he stood for. After *he* died I sort of generalized it into this thing about nuclear weapons.'

'I know. I've seen your bookshelf.'

'You think it's unhealthy, an obsession? Well, I can see you do. And it is obsessive. But we are talking about the annihilation of the world.'

Dan wanted to draw Felix back to Blanchard and plutonium. 'Tell me about how Blanchard gets this stuff. Where does it come from, and how do you find a buyer?'

Felix ignored him. He hunched his shoulders and took another drink.

'It's bad enough with the five nuclear big-boys having the bomb. But hand it out to a bunch of designer dictators in South America, scatter it among the unassimilated tribesmen of the Middle East, and then what have you?'

He shuddered visibly and hurled a newly emptied miniature at the wall of the barn. With deliberation he chose another.

'Nuclear anxiety is a very personal thing, Daniel, a very personal thing. You know what? Politicians can make speeches against the bomb, CND people can write pamphlets. But is their concern felt, or is it just up here?' He tapped his temple. 'Maybe they never felt it, never lay in bed sweating, imagining annihilation until they thought they might go mad. Not just their own annihilation, but the whole thing, everything which they came from, every bugger that nurtured them – the houses, the schools, the factories, farms, churches, shops, libraries, the printing works, the music studios, the theatres – everything blown away to nothing. Even the genes that made them twisted out of recognition, like the bent girders of the blown-away buildings. Everything reduced to shapeless rubble and nothing recognizable continuing. Terrible fear, terrible, and it's nothing to do with the brain, by which I mean the intellect.'

He made a screwing movement with a finger to his forehead. Then with his other hand he clouted his chest. 'It's *in here*. In the heart, lungs, liver. In the – whass they called? – the viscera. Thass where it matters. The viscera.'

Felix was becoming enormously drunk and Dan did not want him to keel over before some basic information had been passed.

'Felix, I need to know a little bit more about what Blanchard's doing. I mean, who's going to buy this plutonium from him?'

'Oh shit, no problems getting a *buyer*. They're queuing up. Chile, Argentina, Israel, South Africa, Pakistan, Iraq, Egypt, Libya – plenty of customers.'

'Where does it come from?'

'It's got a Made in Britain tag on it. They make it in Sellafield, that's what reprocessing means. They turn the spent fuel from nuclear power stations into the ingredients for bombs. One-and-a-half tons of it every bloody year. And they have this amazing accounting system which allows for a one or two per cent play in either direction – you know, one or two per cent of the stuff can either be surplus or unaccounted for at the end of a day, and nobody gives a shite or a shoe-shine.'

'But who delivered it to Blanchard?'

'How should I know? Can't know everything. A bloke in Madrid supplied him, shipped it through Morocco or somewhere.'

'Where is it now?'

'In Istanbul, of course. Or soon will be.'

'That's quite incredibly dangerous, Felix. Are you *sure* –?'

'Course I'm sure. Course it's incredibly dangerous. It's one thing to sell a little misery-dust to people whose own poor fault it is they got bloody hooked. The harm stops in their veins, doesn't it? This is dealing in global insanity. A few addicted politicians putting the survival of the world into a dice cup! Crazy. Crack's another drug that makes people crazy, a bit. But this is crack to the power of a thousand million – grade-A, gold medal, paranoid powder, with added apocalypse.'

'How will Blanchard sell it?'

'Oh Christ, plutonium is just like any desirable item. You don't usually see more than a few kilos at any one time. So these governments become compulsive collectors, they buy as and when, and build up their stocks any way they can.'

'But how do they actually buy it? I mean you can't just go on the streets with a pocketful of plutonium dust in twists of silver paper. You can't open a stall or advertise.'

'Collectors collect competitively. They're looking for opportunities to bid their own prices. So if you're a seller, you use that to bump up your price. It's the same with a Van Gogh painting.'

'But you can auction a painting.'

'Exactly. You got it in one. Except you don't send a flask of plutonium 239 to Sotheby's, things have to be a smidgin less formal than that.'

'You mean Blanchard's going to *auction* this stuff?'

'That's how it's done. To the highest bidder.'

Dan began to laugh. 'This is sensational. Inside a black-market plutonium auction! It's mind-numbing, Felix. But how do I get inside?'

'It's a bit late. Blanchard is ready to feed your balls to those pigs of his.'

'But if I knew when and where this auction's taking place I might get to the bidders. Talk to them. Get their angle.'

Felix shook his head.

'It's crazy. You'll be dead.'

But for Dan at this moment, talking with this weird combination of drunk, drug dealer and nuclear paranoiac, the present moment seemed pregnant with all manner of possibilities. Yes, the book would be written. Blanchard's extraordinary career would be the portrait of a modern, multinational Fagin. He suddenly found himself filling up with a new hilarity. Mr Red would do as Bill Sykes. Felix here was a middle-aged Artful Dodger. He sank his face into his arms and his sides pulsed with laughter.

Mustafa looked out from inside the barn, peering round the doorway like a boy filching a few minutes out of bedtime. Actually he didn't know how long he'd been squatting in here – but it was long enough to put an ache into his knees from holding the one position. From time to time he fingered his gun. It would not be a difficult couple of shots. The two men had built the fire more or less squarely in front of the building, and were hunched together with their backs to him, the firelight showing between them. Trubshaw was plainly drunk, swaying as he helped himself to small bottles from a cardboard box by his side. Dan Barry was laughing, he must be drunk too.

Mustafa was waiting patiently for the right moment to kill. Sometimes there is a necessary rhythm to such things, as he knew from seeing bullfights in Spain.

He felt again the warmth of his own moral decay, like a sudden quickening of panic, heat in his neck and face. Little enough was left to him, if his courage collapsed, if he began to fear death. And he remembered again Dan Barry poised above him, raising the gun – his, Mustafa's, gun – in the London cemetery. He had been able to read Dan's mind in his face, to read the resolution of a man deciding to kill. And for an instant Mustafa had perceived the terror of death. In that moment he was damned. If it hadn't been for the safety catch, the cat yowling, he would now be in hell. In any case, he was on his way there.

There was maybe a way out. Maybe you could reverse the flow of destiny, turn it back on itself. Dan Barry had been the agent of his humiliation. If he could be manoeuvred into suffering Mustafa's fate, if Mustafa could stand over him and watch him wet himself as bullets pumped into his body, then, maybe, hell would recede from Mustafa's brain and he would become comfortable with himself again. He gripped the Browning tightly and waited.

'I need a piss.'

Felix meandered across to the barn wall, just beside the open doorway. Bending his knees, he foraged in his fly as if unable to locate his penis. He finally stood upright and let fly a purling rope of water against the stones, singing to himself gently.

Dan was thinking about Lena. He had made up his mind now to return to Istanbul, and try to crack open the plutonium auction. But could he approach her? How would she have reacted to his disappearance, and to his reported death?

Dan had heard of people reading their own obituaries, and felt as if he had done the same. It gave a certain macabre satisfaction. But if she loved him it would be a very different matter for Lena. And now, having adjusted to his death, she would have to readjust to his resurrection. He thought of her impulsiveness and volatility – the outcome could not be predicted.

Suddenly he was aware that Felix's singing had stopped. He turned and could not see him. 'Felix? Where are you?'

He got up and went towards the barn. 'Felix? You in there?'

One moment Felix had been relieving himself beside the barn doorway, the next moment he was lost to sight. He must be in the barn. Bloody man had sunk ten or eleven of those miniatures. If he tripped over something in the dark he could easily gash himself or break a bone and the last thing Dan wanted was an injured Felix Trubshaw on his hands. He walked up to the barn doorway. He could clearly see the darkened scallop of stone where Felix's piss had flowed. He stopped and listened, then entered the barn, groping round the stone jamb as if for safety.

For several moments the darkness was total. He heard a rustle somewhere within the blackness and a mumble, like someone trying to laugh through a mouthful of bread.

'Don't fart-arse around, Felix. Come out. There's a lot of rusty old equipment in here. I'm sure you'd rather not – Christ!'

A deafening percussion split the air. To be in the same room as that noise caused snapping, shuddering disorientation, so loud and reverberant that Dan's head cracked back in shock against the stone wall. For a moment there was no feeling, then pain from the impact began pumping up his brain in short, rapid strokes. In five seconds he thought his skull was going to burst.

He flattened himself against that wall and began a series of jerky sideways movements, instinctively towards the smear of moonlight at the entrance of the barn. The pungency of cordite drifted across to him as his eardrums blared.

He reached the edge of the door, wondering how many more seconds he had to live. Only then did he realize how his silhouette would be exposed if he tried to move into the doorway. Whoever fired that shot would be waiting for him to do just that, but he wasn't about to give him the satisfaction. Instead Dan dropped to a crouch and tried to listen, as the ringing in his ears slowly died.

There was something like a rusty scrape, followed by a thud. Dan pictured Felix's limp body sagging to the ground. So they had been shadowed and Felix was dead. Now it was his turn. Yet still he waited, motionless.

Mustafa, too, stood frozen in the darkness. He had been hustled into this. When Felix had finished his piss he'd blundered into the barn's entrance and stood and stared into the darkness as he fiddled his flies together, all the time murmuring his tuneless song. Then he'd seemed to lose balance. He staggered sideways towards the rotten remains of the barn door, beside which Mustafa was posted. As he lurched, Felix's arm had shot out to steady himself, but it missed its aim and met the cloth of Mustafa's jacket. The Turk did not allow Felix's astonishment to turn into alarm. He moved first, spinning round and crushing Felix's mouth into the palm of his hand, before dragging him backwards into the heart of the darkness. He was already looking to see if Dan turned. He did. He glanced towards the barn, called out and rose to his feet.

Dan's shape was outlined just for a moment against the night sky as he called again. 'Felix? You in there?'

Then he entered, disappearing in the blackness to the left of the door.

Felix wriggled and almost slithered from Mustafa's grip. There was only one thing for it. Mustafa lifted the piece, removed his hand from Felix's mouth and simultaneously rammed the barrel of the gun between the Irishman's teeth. Then he used the rigidity of the pistol against Felix's palate to heave him round, bringing them face to face. In this position, with Felix practically dangling on the end of the handgun, Mustafa raised his left hand to cover his right on the gun-butt and pulled the trigger.

Many times had he fired unsilenced guns, but in that hollow, confined space, the noise seemed cataclysmic, even to him. There was no scream from Felix, no gurgle or death rattle. Only the after-echo and then the ringing in the ears.

He dragged himself together and pushed the lifeless weight down. Then he stood still.

Hearing a movement he levelled his gun, but lowered it again. Dan's voice came spitting at him out of the dark.

'You bastard. Who the fuck *are* you?'

The movement came again faintly, like cloth on stone.

Mustafa estimated where it might be and fired. Again the sound shock roared in his ears. He'd hardly recovered from the recoil when he saw a shadow flickering round the doorpost. Dan Barry had fled into the open air.

Mustafa lurched forward, but planted his foot in the slick of Felix's blood. As momentum slid the legs ahead of him his body floundered backwards towards the ground. He did not even have time to cry out before he struck the sharp, metal protuberances which he had not known were there.

Dan remembered that he too had a gun. He crouched in the shelter of the car, wrenching the door open and fumbling the Beretta out of the glove compartment. Then he was away again. He crossed the road, put several fields between himself and the barn, and sank down under a blackthorn hedge to listen for sounds of pursuit. There were none. The night was quiet and still.

He waited a quarter of an hour, then moved back to the road gripping the automatic handgun tightly. This time he had not forgotten the safety catch. Dan assumed the gunman did not know where he was at this moment, but took care to move slowly and make no noise. He found the blue police car in the lane, with no key in the ignition. So where the hell was the gunman?

Then he drew back and climbed into the field between the car and the river. In the dark he saw a place where the ground hollowed, and there were bushes. He dropped into the hollow, twisting so as to land on his hands and knees, and he felt soggy turf give way beneath his weight. Slowly the water began to seep into his shoes and through his trousers. He crawled to above the mud line under the edge of the hollow and prepared to wait till it was light.

The dawn, grey and damp, slid his eyelids open. Dan's face was lying sideways on his forearm, and the dank smell of earth filled his nostrils. The gun rested on the ground, his fingers wrapped around it.

He lifted his head and shook it to clear the sleep away. He looked round. It was a long, riverside field with the barn at the far end, now far removed from the welcoming refuge that Dan and Felix had found the night before. Now that barn contained horror.

He began walking towards it. He was empty now of the adrenalized fear which had driven him a few hours earlier. Whatever happened would happen, it was simple. But he must, he *must*, go back to the barn and see for himself what had happened there.

He climbed a crude wooden fence and crossed the area of bare earth in front of the barn. He passed the Ford and stopped to disturb the blackened, still-warm remains of the fire with his foot before taking the dozen further steps to the barn door. He paused a second, then he stepped decisively inside.

He found Felix lying on his back, the body sprawled, the head twisted sideways. Dan could see that the back of the skull, from crown to nape, presented a jagged hole, partially plugged by an accumulation of caked and blackened blood. Tufts of hair hung round it to make a bloody and irregular fringe. Most of his brains had been blown out through the hole, and bits of yellow-red debris lay on the ground along the bullet's path. It looked like vomit.

This was horrifying enough to see. But the matching corpse was worse. In death, Dan did not at first recognize the hitman he had last met in the Brompton Cemetery and, before that, in the Transnational Hotel car park. The body was propped backwards in an ungainly posture, the legs a stiff bridge between the ground and a wooden pole that seemed to support it. The heels were planted at the end of two skidmarks and the face was stretched in a rictus, the teeth grinning as if at the sick joke of a lifetime.

Dan bent to look underneath. Blood had dripped copiously down the wood. Even though the light was dim, Dan could see what had happened. His would-be killer, whatever his name was, had been fatally impaled upon a projecting pitchfork, whose shaft was firmly buried in a heap of rusty farm spares and implements.

He walked out into the air and took a series of heaving breaths. Then he went to the river and knelt down in the stream, bathing his face. When he returned to the barn, he collected an old pick-axe and a shovel which he'd seen there and took them into the field. Deliberately he began to dig.

Later he would remove the cars to another spot. With a bit of luck, no one would know what butchery had happened here.

# 18

Justin Fuller stood in the evening on an outcrop of rock and looked across the sea towards Asia Minor. The sun, coloured like a blood orange, was floating on the horizon-line, between the smudges of two distant islands. Its light seeped on to the sea and stained it red, and the red was flowing towards him, straight to him, running like wine spilled on a glass table. And then familiar words came to him, offering him a gift of new meaning.

*And I saw as it were a sea of glass mingled with fire.*

Patmos was the place of the Apostle John's exile, the place of Revelation. It seemed so ordinary, when you saw the land in plain day. It had all the furnishing of any Aegean island: the baked earth, olives, vines, carobs, figs, thistles, donkeys.

And yet here John had seen blood run from the winepress, and the rivers turn to wormwood, and stars fall like unripe figs shaken from the tree by a storm.

He revolved on his rock through three hundred and sixty degrees, eyes boring into the landscape. He saw where the glistening insects crouched, where the lizard's throat pulsed. Justin had always been afraid of looking too closely at things. At school his biology marks had been abysmal, because he could never bring himself to look into a microscope, not even a magnifying glass. The detail of creation repelled him. But now he faced it without effort, as if for the first and last time – fluids swimming with particles, baby creatures naked and stringy as old men, the segments of worms, the ooze of the gut.

He completed his revolving and stared, as before, at the sun. He thought now he could make out the churning flames on its surface, and feel the annihilating force of the heat. Then his eyes followed down the track of fire which ran across the water. It raced towards him, a lit fuse. He was standing directly in its path. He could not avoid it.

He shut his eyes and for the first time asked what he must do.

Lena sat on a towel, a thick novel beside her. She stared at the sea. On this coast the waves never amounted to much, just gentle laps of a wide, wide tongue, endlessly repeated. Lena found it desolate.

Annabel came running from the water's edge swinging her red beach-bucket. A thick mud-pack of sand pasted the backs of her legs and her bottom. She skidded up to her mother and poised on one leg like a flamingo, the other foot slung in her hand.

'Mommy, what language does the sea talk in?'

'I don't know, darling. Different languages, I expect, in different places.'

'Well, what language does it talk in in this place? Does it talk in Turkish or English?'

'Turkish, I think. Its own kind of Turkish maybe. Why?'

'Well, I was trying to tell it a story.'

'What story?'

'A story about my Daddy.'

'Tell me the story instead.'

She reached out to cuddle Annabel, but her daughter wriggled free.

'No. It's not the kind of story you tell to people. It's the kind of story you tell to the sea, stupid.'

'Well, I'm sure the sea can understand story-English. Why don't you try again?'

The child wandered back to the water. She had never known her real father, of course, but Lena had done her best to explain about him: a one-night stand whom she'd met at a party in New York. Lena recalled hardly anything else about him, so the information she'd been able to give Annabel was minimal. She could no longer even remember his face or his conversation during their encounter. He'd hinted, as he pulled on his pants the next morning, of a job on Wall Street. But that could easily have been a lie. She had not expected him to call her again and it didn't matter anyway. He'd had *married* written all over him.

Lena looked along the beach to her right, towards the promontory. She remembered how deserted it had been last year. Now that most of the new hotels were properly open for business the tour operators had begun flying in their weekly pleasure-seeking planeloads. So the once-empty sand had been transformed into a plantation of parasols, and from beneath each pool of shade protruded the slicked flesh of British and Germans at various stages of skin-burn.

Given that it was *bayram*, Georgette had been lucky to get Lena and Annabel on a flight from Istanbul and into the *pansiyon*. She'd taken it on herself to organize this 'break with everything' and was due to join them in two days' time.

'It'll be the best thing for you, a week by the sea with your daughter. You rest, you relax, you forget – the month, the year, the state of the Union, the name of the President. Just lie in the sun and learn you can feel good again. I only wish I could go down there with you. Conrad's got this Boston bigshot flying in tomorrow and he says I've got to stick around to cook for the bastard. Con says he just might be our ticket back to the States. Exciting – at least he thinks so, I'll believe it when I see it. Anyway I got you these tickets, they were the only ones left. Have you been down there before? There's some impressive remains. Anyway, you just go and forget.'

Had she been here before? Jesus. If forgetting Dan was what this was all about, Georgette couldn't have happened on a worse booking. But really she was better off here, better at least than in the apartment. Back there she would only dwell on the negative stuff, his secrecy and morose selfishness – the things that had come forward in the last six months.

She was anxious for Georgette to join them. She looked forward to her friend's tactful reserve, her toleration of silence. As things were, Lena was suffering from the predatory attentions of every English-speaking male on the beach. First there were the boys, ludicrous lobster-pink British youths in sunhats and Bondi Beach bermudas. Their T-shirts and tattoos featured mostly Union Jacks and football teams, and their fists were invariably wrapped around cans of beer.

‘ ’Ullo, darling. Fancy a bit of wossname? Best offer you’ll get today.’

It was Annabel who’d get rid of these bozos. They wouldn’t fancy a bird with a kid in tow, however tasty she might look. However, though her daughter saw off the younger element, she acted like a powerful magnet on the older men, the slack-paunched ones in their thirties and forties. First they’d kid around, give the child a piggyback ride and mock-box her. But in no time they’d be dropping casually down on the sand beside the young mother to discuss hotels, climate, the exchange rate, all the time making with the eyeball telegraph. This morning Lena had already been optically raped by a systems analyst from Rickmansworth, a research chemist who lived between Bath and Bristol and the manager of a Basingstoke shopping mall. She was feeling she’d filled her quota for the day. Then a man’s figure was blocking her sun.

‘Is this bit of sand taken?’

She glanced up. From his accent this was another Brit. He was gesturing to the ground on one side of her. She looked about, meaningfully. The beach might be well populated but it was not overcrowded – there were plenty of open patches. Still, she shrugged. 'Go ahead.'

He was, admittedly, a bit different from the usual. He wore a plain T-shirt, white cotton shorts and deck shoes. His body was slight but toughened by a shell of muscle, and he was older – a lean fifty-year-old with eyes hard and pale like shards of rock crystal. He sat down no more than two yards from her. Lena opened her bulky paperback and turned the pages at random, trying to select a line of print to focus on. Perhaps if she ignored him . . .

The words on the page hardly penetrated her understanding. Her eyes followed a line which read '. . . she had kissed and caressed him, draped herself round his naked body . . .'

The guy was making her feel hot and uncomfortable. Why? Was this harassment or what? She knew he was looking at her, but not with the wet-tongue lewdness of the other men. This felt more like a curiosity that could easily become cruelty. Other lines from the novel suddenly appeared, as if highlighted. 'Driving behind him she felt the tension drying the membranes of her throat.'

The man spoke. 'There is a book *I* rather admire. It's the handbook of a retired Japanese samurai called Yamamoto. He warns the young samurai in his care they must never drop in on someone uninvited, as this may lead to slips of the tongue and errors of judgement. In which case, I fear I am at fault.'

Lena still did not lower the book. She found herself

reading '. . . Marcia's body opened to him like the petals of a flower.' Lena's face flushed – she couldn't help it, as if she had read out the words for him to hear.

She glanced up fractionally to locate Annabel, then took refuge again in the novel. This time she turned the page.

The man shifted his position, crossing his legs to achieve the half-lotus position. 'On the other hand, Yamamoto does tell us, whatever trouble or madness we have at home, we must never, ever turn a caller away. Which I'm afraid puts you in the wrong too, Lena my dear.'

Lena straightened in alarm. 'How do you know my name?'

The man met her eyes with a perfectly level, unblinking look. It was the response of someone utterly in control, someone without shame. 'It's my business to know your name. My work.'

'Your work?'

'I work in government.'

Lena looked up, then stared out to sea.

'This is something to do with Dan.'

Still he did not look away, his eyeballs did not move. She thought of those other men on the beach whose popping gazes wandered so impertinently about her body. She could not quite understand it, but this one seemed to see all over and around her, although he gazed only at her face.

'Yes it is. I'm afraid it is.'

'Have you come to ask me questions?'

'Yes, I have a few questions. And some information to trade, some – some things you might care to know.'

'Trade? What things?'

'Things about Dan, his death.'

Now she threw down her book. Anger rose in her, a choking defiance. 'That he died a hero, I suppose. Yes, I heard about that. Did he die gung-ho, my Dan, like Nazım Ali Bey told me? Went down like a real man, did he, whirling a battleaxe? Jesus, you men. He's *dead*, you know? You guys think if you go to die prick forwards it makes it better.'

She was shouting. People were looking at her over their Dick Francis thrillers, their sex-and-shopping romances. The man did not visibly react. He simply said, 'There was nothing heroic about it, not as far as I know. But I can tell you how he died. And more to the point, why – if you want.'

'I don't want. I don't want to know anything about it. It's sick. I hate it and I hate him and I'm getting ready to hate you. Just leave me alone, will you?'

She got up and strode to the water's edge, where Annabel was still in communion with the monotonous sea. Lena crouched and hugged her daughter. Later she turned round again, in the hope that the unwelcome visitor might be gone. Yet she could not immediately believe it, finding that he had.

By noon the heat was intense enough, even in June, to make it a relief to return to the *pansiyon*. Yet walking back along the dusty, pitted track Lena felt her inside fizzing, as if she had taken amphetamine. She was possessed by frustration at what she ought to have said to the Englishman, and how.

She should have told him that Dan Barry's death was Dan Barry's affair; it might conceivably be the British government's affair; but it was none of hers. She had finished with him. She should have left it there. She should not have lost her cool.

The frustrated energy of these thoughts dammed up within Lena. She had spoken already, and said too much, and the moment was gone now.

She turned to call to Annabel, who was dawdling behind. After lunch the child would have her siesta and, with the prospect of ninety minutes to herself, Lena decided to walk to the ruins at the end of the beach. She hadn't yet been there, and longed to be on her own.

The main glory of this tiny ancient Greek port had been the theatre. Its semi-circle of tiered seats made a gigantic, stone dent in the hillside which rose above the stage area. Lena sat for a while on the highest row. She looked down and tried to imagine what the performances had been like. Were they always packed out, like big-league baseball? Or did the plays sometimes flop and close inside a week?

None of the tourists were in sight. It was not for Hellenic ruins that they came to Turkey, after all. Lena imagined the men from the beach as they would be now, sprawled in their hot, concrete cells, drunk from heat and lunchtime wine, viscidly snoring.

Lena looked beyond the theatre towards what had been the centre of this town. Columns were the chief glories of the site; from the beach they were its most clearly visible features, bristling up into the sky like missiles. Some, she saw now, were toppled, their stones littering the ground. But many, though chipped and lichen-stained, remained intact. She rose, thinking she would walk around among them, and began to descend the steep terracing in a series of jumps.

As she came nearer the bottom her leaps became more rhythmical and confident, so that she was almost flying when, just five tiers from the stage level, her concentration was broken. It was the green-brown flicker of a lizard, exactly at the spot where her foot was about to land, that did it. Too late she tried to avoid treading there, missed the step altogether and tumbled, first cracking her ankle against a lower step and then, with plenty of downward momentum, somersaulting. On the way down she struck her head between forehead and crown and finally crashed on to a stretch of sand at the edge of the stage area.

Lying curled around, not yet trying to move, Lena computed the damage. Her head throbbed and it seemed as if someone had been using a chisel on parts of her shoulder and spine. Her ankle felt pulpy, with squibs of pain darting into it. She test-wriggled the foot and instantly the pain dug in its teeth, wrenching a cry from her mouth.

*'Shit!'*

She knew she'd not be able to walk on it. Should she shout for help, try to crawl back to the beach? No, someone would come soon, someone would have to come soon . . .

After no more than a minute someone did.

'Are you alive?'

She opened her eyes. She had begun to feel a strange and dangerous sense of comfort, lying there in the heat of the sun.

'Good. Not much use to me dead.'

She could not see him from where she lay, but she recognized the voice.

'Can you get up?'

He didn't sound compassionate. She twisted her head and squinted. 'I think I've done something to my ankle.'

'Oh dear.'

This was not the Good Samaritan.

'For fuck's sake. I'm hurting down here. Aren't you going to help me?'

'Righto. I'll help you to a seat, shall I?'

He stood, hooked his hands under her armpits and jerked upwards. The movement jarred her foot and she yelped as he hauled her a few feet towards a stone block. The drag on her ankle was excruciating. Finally, she was propped with her back, sore as it was, against the corroded stone. He stood back as if admiring a flower arrangement.

'Hm. There's no blood so far as I can tell. How many of me can you see?'

'One is one too many, if you hurt me like that again.'

'You're a lovely girl, Lena. But I expect you know that already.'

'Look, I need help to get to where I'm staying. I think my ankle is sprained.'

He ignored her, squatting down and doodling in the sand with his forefinger.

'The child's a pretty little thing, too. Dan Barry wasn't the father, I take it?'

'Who are you?'

'Name's Craike, Edward Craike. I'm part of a team looking at what happened to Dan and his colleague . . . er, what was his name?'

'Are you a cop?'

'Ah, yes, Altan Başkurt. I believe you knew him. No, I'm not police. Security service.'

'Security! New word for fascism, isn't it?'

'I didn't know you were political, Lena. Now, there've been some later developments since Dan's, um – and we thought you might be able to help, you see? It's a matter of a few friends of his, people you might have run into.'

'I didn't know his friends.'

Suddenly, as the pain in Lena's ankle receded, she found she wanted to know the things which this man could tell her. Who was Dan Barry, really? Who were his friends? What was his purpose in life? She knew him even less than ever, and now he was dead. But she said, 'Look, I can't help you, okay?'

Craike looked up from his doodling. His face had a cunning look. 'But I can help you, can't I? Now, let's see that foot of yours.' He reached for her injured foot and jerked it from side to side.

The pain was like an iron bar skewering Lena's ankle. She screamed, 'You bastard!' and tried to shrink back from him, but with the stone block against her back and no chance of standing up, it was hopeless. 'You going to torture me, are you?'

'Calm yourself. I'm just testing the injury. Let me try this.' He pressed against the ankle with his thumb, pushing in just at the most tender spot. Lena writhed and tried to pull her foot away, but the pain grew remorselessly as Craike increased the pressure. 'We need to know about a man called Mills, Ted Mills. He may have known Dan. Have you ever met this man? Heard about him?'

Lena's face was set in a tight grimace as she tried to manage the pain. She shook her head. 'Stop – doing – this!'

He relaxed his grip and said, 'Now, will you please talk to me?' He sounded aggrieved, like a husband whose wife has been throwing crockery. 'This is better than what I could do if I got really vindictive, you know. I could have you picked up by the Turkish police, on a charge of accessory to drug trafficking. I could have your flat planted with enough heroin to put you in gaol for forty years. Would it be worth it to you, then?' He opened his eyes wide, to convey his candour. 'You see? I'm simply trying to persuade you to act in your own interest.'

Lena thought for a moment, then seemed to make up her mind. 'I don't know much about Dan Barry. He was a bit of a loser, he wanted to be some type of a writer, though I could never figure out what – novelist or whatever. He was a closed book to me anyway. I never heard of any Mills. The only friend he ever talked about from England was a guy called Jack. No one else. Not even family.'

'But you lived with him for a year.'

'So? That means shit. Do you live with someone?'

'All right, forget about Mills. We also need to find a girl. She lives in Istanbul, so you may know her anyway. She was apparently kept by Felix Trubshaw. Do you know Felix Trubshaw?'

Lena did not react to the name.

'Well, this girl is quite a pathetic little thing by all accounts. Takes drugs, no real job. Lives somewhere in Istanbul, used to entertain Trubshaw during his business trips to this country. Two of a kind, really. Her name is Sarah McAskey, Australian.'

Lena shook her head. 'I never came across anybody by that name, no.'

'Are you sure?'

His hand hovered over her ankle, and she flinched. Then he seemed to give up. 'I don't understand. Whatever happened to the honest open-plan relationships we used to idealize in the sixties? You young people are so repressed. You tell each other nothing.'

He rose, bent and picked her up, almost tenderly cradling her. 'You're not very heavy, are you? Come on then, I'll convey you back to the guest house where I expect they will minister to you with tribal possets and ancient potions.'

Lena lay stiffly in his arms as he picked his way between the stones of the ruin before striking down the path which led back to the beach. She was careful to hold her head in such a way that it did not touch his shirt.

Craike flew back to Istanbul later that afternoon, angry at having wasted a whole day on a misconception. Jack Bacon had warned him, but he hadn't listened.

'Look, Ed, we know this Mills guy, whoever he is, was helping Trubshaw. But that doesn't prove he had anything to do with Dan. And, even if he had, it's going to be the devil's own job finding the connection.'

'Lena will tell us that.'

'Christ no, not necessarily. I knew Dan Barry. Mills could have been his greatest mate, an old school chum even, and his other friends would probably not even have heard of him. Dan was like that – he ran his social life like the IRA, in isolated cells. The members never knew who the others were or, come to that, if there *were* any others. It's ten to one on Lena's just the same.'

'When I get to Turkey I'm going to see her anyhow. We've got to find out who Mills is, and how involved he is. Anyway, she might know where Trubshaw is.'

He had booked into the Pera Palas, between the

British and US consulates. The unique atmosphere of what had been the plush rail-head hotel for the Orient Express admirably suited his taste for faded grandeur.

Craike had left Jack in London, to rejoin him when the Blanchard operation reached its climax. Jack would have his own particular role to play in that. In the meantime, an office was commandeered at the Consulate-General and Craike spent a couple of days organizing his communications. He met with Schultz, the local CIA man, and informed him of a major British surveillance exercise. He liaised too with the Istanbul authorities. They were not told too much: it would be insane to alarm them. He merely informed them that the Ministry of Defence believed the city was being used as a meeting place by some arms dealers the British were interested in. He wanted the Turks – as NATO allies – to clear his presence, without providing an excuse for them to interfere.

He knew he wouldn't quite relax until he found Felix Trubshaw. The news from Ireland, of his arrest and release, had not been reassuring. *Trubshaw is trouble* was the graffiti scrawled across Craike's mind whenever he thought of him. Even Blanchard did not trust him. As a complete dipso, he might fly off at any tangent, commit any indiscretion.

Yes, he ought to be under lock and key, as the Irish had had him before they lost him, blast their cross-eyes. Better still, he ought to be under six feet of earth. Locating Sarah McAskey would be an essential step towards achieving one of those two objectives.

This man Mills was another question. Was he a part of the Blanchard organization, or some sort of accomplice of Dan Barry's book-writing project? Either way, Mills's existence showed a disturbing hole in Craike's own intelligence net. He was anxious to patch this up, and quickly.

Then he could concentrate on making sure Blanchard jumped through all the right hoops.

# 19

The London office of Earth First was in a recycled Victorian shop, between a newsagent and a sandwich bar. With the kind of impertinence for which the organization was already world famous, the site had been deliberately chosen. It stood directly opposite the Department of the Environment.

Brian Harrison balanced a cup of coffee on the palm of his hand and looked out at Marsham Street. The entire field of his vision was absorbed by a vast screen of concrete and glass, the hideous, crushing elevation of the hated government offices.

'No wonder they can't think straight, working out of that place. I may go mad, just looking at it.' He turned away and rejoined Dan Barry at the circular table which stood in the centre of his office. There was no desk. He nodded towards the Earth First pamphlet, *The Truth about Nuclear Proliferation.* He had been waiting for Dan to finish reading.

'What d'you think of it?'

'Scary.'

'Does it confirm what your friend told you?'

'There certainly seems to be a hell of a lot of plutonium blowing loose around the world. And no one seems to care much.'

Harrison bit into a Kit Kat and chewed reflectively.

'Don't get the idea that it's only a question of negligence. I mean, a good part of this is deliberate.'

'But how *can* it be? I mean, this stuff is really –' Dan couldn't find a word to match his thought. Harrison supplied one of his own.

'It's malignant. Plutonium's like a tumour in the biosphere. It seems to be part of nature, but it's not, it's false or perverted nature. But plutonium's very plausible, Dan. It can be made to seem exactly fitted to our civilization's needs at this juncture. It can masquerade in green – can give a convincing performance as a lean, clean fuel. That's how its supporters present it. Our conviction, of course, is different: what we have here is a cancer, growing out of control, invading normal tissue, contaminating vital organs, preparing to kill the planet, and us along with it.' He shrugged. 'That's why we can't simply agree to differ. The future of life depends on this.'

Dan had come to Harrison straight from the airport. He needed to confirm, at least in outline, Felix Trubshaw's story. It had been told compellingly enough, but spun out of a brain poisoned by alcohol and neurosis. Dan remembered Dr Doherty's opinion – nuclear fear syndrome, plutonium paranoia. The whole thing could have been a paranoid fantasy.

Dan had met Harrison three years ago while following a story about river pollution, and they'd kept sporadically in touch in the meantime. Harrison was a fanatic, of course, but he knew his stuff, and he was honest. If Harrison said Trubshaw's story would stand up, that was good enough for Dan.

'Can you just explain that, though? How do you equate what seems to many people just another source of energy – how do you equate *that* with cancer? Leaving bombs out of it, I mean – let's just assume we're talking about power generation.'

'Big assumption, but all right. It's the nature of the material. Of course, coal, when it's burnt, pollutes the air, oil is nasty if it gets into the food chain, but both are relatively easy to clean up. Plutonium's different. Suppose a handful of plutonium dust has been spilled six miles upwind of you, and it blows towards you. Okay, the particles get dispersed, only minute amounts would reach your lungs. Let's say as little as thirty infinitesimal particles get inside your body. Within a matter of hours, with those specks inside you, you will have received as much radiation exposure as you normally get in a lifetime.'

'So, you get them out.'

'But how? You can't cough them out, they're too small. They're lodged in your lungs. But you really *do* have to get them out, because unlike oil, nothing breaks this pollutant down. You have to wait for it to decay naturally.'

'But aren't you assuming –?'

Harrison held up his hand.

'No, this is important. You have to wait for it to decay naturally, okay? The half-life is the time it takes for fifty per cent of an atom's radioactivity to do this. Now, what do you think plutonium's half-life is? A month? A year? Ten years? Wrong! It's twenty-four *thousand* years.'

Harrison savoured the moment of revelation. He threw his weight backwards, canting his chair on to its back legs.

'So quite frankly, if you breathe in even one grain of that stuff you're in the deep shit.'

Dan was beginning to comprehend the depth of Felix's neurosis. 'Cancer. Real, actual *cancer*.'

'Exactly. Plutonium is just about the most carcinogenic substance ever discovered. Spill a few kilos of this dust in the air and you've got an emergency far worse than a Richter 8 quake hitting San Francisco.'

'Okay, what I was going to say was, why do you have to assume that plutonium is going to be spilled?'

'It's inevitable – if not by accident then deliberately, by blackmailers, lunatics, pariah governments, subnational terrorist groups. And all the time our nuclear industry is in expansion. Right now the world contains almost 1,000 tonnes of civilian plutonium – five times more than the amount stockpiled in nuclear weapons – and that's growing, because we're breeding it at a rate of 100 tonnes a year. And all the time small quantities are being siphoned off, diverted, stolen.'

'Can't that be stopped? I heard something about a rather lax accounting system – can't it be tightened up?'

'They're trying, they can do a little. But even using the best technology that anyone can foresee, a steady one to two per cent of the plutonium coming out of plants like Sellafield will be unaccounted for – lost in the works or stolen. You just can't get close enough to control it effectively, the material is too lethal.'

'So there's a black market?'

'Too right. A thriving one, from what we hear.'

'How does it work?'

'How does any black market work? It's just like anything from crack to Exocets: there's demand, there's supply. The two will always find a way to get together. It's the birds and the bees, except the motive is money instead of sex.'

'I heard something about auctions.'

'Yes, there are auctions. Centre of it used to be Sudan, they'd flog the stuff off the block in some hangar at the Khartoum airport. The presidential family was supposed to be involved, some way. Sick, isn't it? Like a parody. Capitalism frantic to sow the seeds of its ultimate destruction.'

Dan knew now he had a story. A story that pushed his original ideas into a cocked hat and jumped on them with hobnail boots.

'If it's time for the Marxist homily, I think I'll pass, thanks all the same. I've heard that bit.'

He got up and showed Harrison the pamphlet. 'May I keep this?'

'That's what it's for. What exactly are you working on, Dan? We haven't seen anything under your byline for some time, have we?'

'Oh, this is a long investigative thing – taking much longer than I'd meant.' He moved towards the door. 'You'll see the upshot eventually, Brian, you can count on it. And I should think you might be happy.'

'Let's hope so. Precious little to be happy about

these days. Have you seen the latest data on the ozone layer?'

'Look, thanks for everything, Brian. I'll be in touch.'

He started down the stairs with a feeling of lightness that hadn't been with him for weeks. He had a story, and it was *good.*

'You're not paying me enough, Hakim Bey. I need more.'

The young girl stood in front of his desk and fingered the envelope he had just handed her. She was insolent, when you would expect a tone of supplication. Hakim Öztürk clicked his tongue. He was probably the youngest hotel manager in Istanbul, and he'd done it by stringent efficiency. In business it is necessary to separate what cannot wait from what is dispensable. He looked at the girl.

'Now, Sarah, you are from where? Australia, isn't it? I have never been there. Maybe in Sydney workers come to their managers and ask for more pay, just like that. But here in Turkey it is not so. Here the workers wait until they are granted higher wages. And they are granted them when they earn them.'

'But I haven't enough to live on.'

'You have been working here for, what? Six months, isn't it? You have never complained except now.'

Her mouth turned down sulkily. She looked at her feet, mumbling. 'Things have changed. I need more now.'

Öztürk seemed to consider. Then he went on the attack. 'I've started to have complaints, Sarah. Some guests have been concerned. They say you are looking too thin for dancing. Are you ill?'

'No, I'm not ill. I don't get enough to eat, that's all. Pay me more.'

'I'm sorry. I will fix it so you can eat here in the hotel, with the staff, on the nights when you are performing.'

'But look, I have rent to pay.'

'You are in debt, it is not my concern. I'm sorry. You must get fatter and you will please the guests better. There are many dancers in this town.'

He threw in the threat mildly, as a gentle reminder of her position. Actually it wasn't quite true, there weren't many like her, and he didn't particularly want to lose her. It would be a nuisance. It wasn't that she was all that good – the tourists didn't know the difference anyway. It was the fact that she wasn't a Turk. An Australian belly dancer was a gimmick, like an American bullfighter in Spain. Good for publicity.

Nevertheless, he would have to sack her if she did not improve her appearance. The girl was beginning to look a mess which even her make-up could not disguise. He sighed. She could hang on a little longer, but in the end she *was* dispensable.

'I can do one more thing for you. You will see the hotel doctor, he will check you up. Okay? I fix a time and let you know.'

'I don't want to see your bloody doctor. I'm fine, really. I'm sorry I asked.'

'I think I must insist that you –'

'Forget it, okay? I'd better go now.' She was already on her way out.

Öztürk called after her, 'Don't forget to eat with us, Sarah. Every night you dance, okay?'

He sighed again and scribbled a note to himself on his desk diary. He must ask Dr Süleyman to drop in one night when Sarah was dancing and look her over. These days one could not be too careful.

Standing beside the bishop, Justin Fuller looked out across a miniature giant's causeway of black pillar-box hats.

Beneath these headdresses flowed a grey sea of beards, as the phalanx of Orthodox priests advanced towards them. Their crow-black robes billowed, their heavy crosses flashed silver at their chests.

By Justin's side the suffragan Bishop of Chichester was becoming impatient. 'Why does everything they do have to take such an age, Justin? How long have we been out here, twenty minutes?'

They were waiting for the retinue to dispose itself around the entrance of the Patriarchate, where the bishop was due to exchange gifts with the Patriarch himself. The presentations were scheduled to be followed by an ecumenical meeting to discuss Sacramentality. Justin shrugged. 'I'm a new boy here myself, Bishop. This is my first high-level ecumenical.'

'Well, I only wish they'd move it along. And don't call me Bishop – it's Ron, okay?'

At last His All Holiness the Patriarch Athanasius emerged, a barrel-like figure whose eyes flashed from beneath a tangled shrubbery of eyebrows. After they had swapped pleasantries, Ron received an icon in a jewelled frame, and in turn handed over an illuminated manuscript. Then Orthodox hosts and Anglican guests shook hands and filed into the building for lunch.

After food they repaired to a high-ceilinged conference room. Long opening statements by each side were followed by an exchange about the Eucharist. Bishop Ron was fidgety and impatient, while the Patriarch folded his podgy hands across his belly, lowered his head with the air of a ruminant and, for all anyone could see beneath those hirsute brows, may have slept the conference away. Justin did not even try to concentrate on the proceedings. His body was fizzing all over with frustrated energy. He stared out of the window, thinking about Lena, listening to what John had to tell him.

That morning a letter had come, the envelope written in a hand he did not recognize. He flipped it over and read the return address: 5/34 Balikci Yok. Emirgan. It was hers.

Hastily he ripped the envelope open.

*Dear Justin*

The sight of his name, *Justin*, written like that in her own hand, sent a jolt through his stomach, half-erotic, half-fearful. He thought of her long fingers holding the pen as she wrote it, and of her brain forming pictures as she did it. What image did she have of him? If only he knew.

*But you do know! You know perfectly well. She sees you as a clergyman, she'll always see you as a clergyman. But it's you, isn't it? You make the difference, because you don't see her as a clergyman would see her. That's the difference.*

He read the letter.

Look, I'm sorry if this is presumptuous. You did offer your help. I tried to phone you, but you were out. I am going away for three weeks to the S. coast but I desperately want to get Dan's things out of the apartment. I have boxed them all up, but (as I think I mentioned to you) I don't even know who his next-of-kin are. Can you help with this, at least? Maybe Anadolu Hava Yolları know who to send them to? If no luck, is there anywhere I can store them – the Consulate? I really will be shattered if I have to face that stuff again when I get back. My friend Georgette Hamilton has my house-key. She's joining me here in a day or two and I've asked her to deliver the key to you before she leaves. I would be *eternally* grateful if you could do anything to help in moving all that stuff out of there. Thanks.

The letter was signed, simply, *Lena*.

It was when he read her name that he realized, with the utter integrity of revelation, what he'd got himself into. His eyes traced her handwriting lovingly. He loved her writing, he loved her notepaper, he loved the back of the stamp which she had licked.

Foolishly, he had pressed the letter-paper to his lips, seeking the taste, or the smell of her.

*You find that exciting, don't you? It's like an animal, that is, sniffing out the smell of her like that.*

And it *was* like John said. Justin's love was not some sentimental construct: it was urgent and physical. It required action.

He acted immediately on her request, telephoning the office of AHY and receiving an invitation to come in and see Nazım Ali Bey, General Manager, at ten-thirty the next morning. That was all right: Bishop Ron was due to fly out before breakfast. He would have to be seen off at the airport, but Justin would be back in the city by ten at the latest. He could scarcely wait. He was on fire to serve his love.

Now, as the cracked academic voices picked their way through the minefield of comparative theology, Justin was asking himself all the terrifying questions that madden lovers. What did this love of his imply? What sort of future for himself would it yield? What of his work, his religious faith? The voice of John, for the moment anyway, would give him no answers.

Suddenly the Patriarch stirred, raising his eyes. The ascetic-looking Archimandrite to his left was well launched into a long speech about the penitential Rite. He was rudely cut into by a loud, commanding laugh from his spiritual boss. The Archimandrite faltered and fell silent. In curt, chortling phrases, old Athanasius delivered himself of a brief speech. When he had finished he signalled to the interpreter with a fractional inclination of the head.

'His All Holiness says he was almost converted to the idea of personal confession the other day, when talking to a bishop of the Roman church. Evidently this bishop's neighbour on a plane from London requested to have his confession heard at ten thousand metres up in the sky. His All Holiness thinks there must be few sacraments that have been celebrated more than one mile high.'

Everybody smiled. The Patriarch's chair screeched on the tiled floor as he pushed it back and rose. As he spoke again Justin thought he could see the relief behind his eyes. His interpreter, on the other hand, wore a mask of profound regret.

'His All Holiness regrets he must leave us now. He prays that the Holy Wisdom will inhabit the rest of these discussions.'

The centre of Sarah McAskey's Istanbul was the teeming commercial quarter between the Grand Bazaar and the Golden Horn. The great *Yeni Postahane*, a civic post office on the grand scale, was just a few streets away from her apartment, and she was on her way there.

Sarah hugged a shawl about herself as she walked. There was the usual, choking heat, but she felt cold. It just wasn't fair. She'd got her habit managed. She knew just how much she needed in a week, and she could live within the budget. There were no luxuries, what did she expect? But with the job and the rent money provided by Felix, she used to have enough. Now she had no rent money. She was in the shit.

The stuff she'd bought two weeks ago had run out late last week. Kipper Kevin, the dealer she knew best, had let her have a little extra on account on Saturday and this she had used up by yesterday. This morning, though she'd pleaded with him, offered herself to him, even promised to pay double when some money did come through, Kevin had slammed the door in her face. There would be no more free samples, no more tick, he shouted viciously. Who did she think he was, some kind of Save The Junkies Fund? She knew no other dealers well enough to try the same again.

She drifted along the street keeping well in under the buildings. Despite the sunshine the world seemed shadowed and threatening. She might have to do sex for money again. Not with the landlord, he was a poofter. He was also a sadistic swine. If she didn't pay him tomorrow . . .

Sarah climbed the wide steps of the *Yeni Postahane*, and entered its high, domed hall. At the poste restante counter she recognized some of the junkies and travellers ahead of her in the line, from the Pudding Shop and other hangouts. She didn't go to the Pudding Shop now, anyway. You went there when you first arrived in town, and Sarah had used it later to look for clients. She didn't like all that optimistic, New Age talk. Astrology really pissed her off.

She came to the front of the queue and gave her name to the clerk. Her face must have looked ready to break, because when he returned and told her '*Yok*', he said it with a wide gesture of the hands to express his regret.

Sarah left the post office. What had happened to

Felix? Why didn't he write? On the steps she sat down and buried her head in her crossed arms.

'Hi, Sarah.' It was Donna Lubomir, a big redhead from Philadelphia. She sat down beside her. 'How's it going?'

Sarah raised her head and stared down at the street. 'It isn't. I'm broke.'

'What happened? We heard you got yourself a real sugar-shaker.'

'Not exactly that. He kept me going though. Anyway, he's pissed off. Hey Donna, you can't help me with some smack? I'm desperate.'

Donna Lubomir shook her fat mass of ginger curls.

'I don't do smack now. I'm into crack. You should try it. Wow.'

'I will if you give me a free hit.'

'You're kidding! Every milligram that I get comes from Raffi. You know Raffi? He's my new boyfriend. He's Iranian or something. Anyway, he's really like jealous and he makes me smoke it right there in front of him. Why don't you let me introduce you?'

Sarah considered. 'No thanks. I think I have enough problems as it is. What can I do, Donna? I need money.'

'You quit whoring, right?'

'Yes. I don't know if I can go back.'

'Why don't you try the priest? Back home in Philadelphia, when the junkies got real sick and didn't have nowhere else to go they always showed up at the church. What are you, Catholic?'

'No. I don't know. Episcopalian, I guess.'

'That's tough. I guess there's no Episcopalian priest here.'

Donna was wrong. Sarah remembered reading about him in the *Turkish Daily News*, the English language paper. He was new or something. It showed his picture under the unlikely headline ISTANBUL GETS NEW ANGLICAN VICAR. Sarah remembered thinking he was surprisingly young and good looking.

Back at her place Sarah went through the pile of old newspapers. It hadn't been so long ago, she might still have that number. But she couldn't find it.

Now Donna's idea had fired Sarah up. She decided to walk across to the British Consulate-General at Galatasary. They would tell her where to find this vicar, and though it meant a painful trudge up the Galata hill, the guy might – just might – have some charity fund for people like her. It was not unheard of.

Justin reached the cool haven of his flat with unspeakable relief. Dear God, it had been a long day. Nor was it yet over. Justin would have just ninety minutes to himself, then he was taking Bishop Ron out to dine.

He poured a glass of orange juice from the fridge, sank it in a single, grateful draught and went into the sitting room. Like all the apartments in the steeply sloping Cihangir district, his room looked over to the tip of the seraglio where the Ottoman sultans had their palace and kept their harems. Normally the sight of all that sparkling water was a refreshment after the stuffy, polluted working day. But now the enchantment was not working. His heightened emotional state had stretched his nerves to the point of exhaustion.

He threw his jacket at a chair, snapped the popper behind his neck to release the dog collar and grey dickey, levered off his shoes and dropped his black trousers to the floor. He slumped on to the sofa in vest, shorts and socks, knowing he must soon raise the energy to get up again and shower. Then the doorbell rang.

Bugger.

It was probably one of his ladies with some footling problem about the gala fête or the bridge tournament. He sat rigid, hoping for the sound of retreating feet on the stairs.

Instead the bell shrilled again, longer and more insistent. He groaned. He couldn't face the ingratiating posture and dog-like eyes of those women. Several of them were attracted to him, he suspected, and one or two were not above making a pass.

For the third time the bell sent out its note of hysteria. Only then did John make his wishes known.

*I want you to go, Juss. I want you to open that door. Don't be paranoid. Do it. Open the door.*

He sighed, threw on a robe, went into the hall.

The tiny young woman who stood there was a surprise. She was not dirty, but she had a rubbed look, like a worn carpet. She stood and looked up at Justin, through narrowed eyes, jutting out her bony chin. The face wore a resentful, angry expression which immediately put Justin in a combative mood.

'You the vicar?'

'Yes.'

'I want a word.'

She was demanding, not asking. Justin had met the type back in his inner-city days: prickling with hostility, hating to ask for help. It didn't mean they didn't need help, but it was intensely irritating, and Justin was in no mood to put up with it now.

He looked at her and thought again of Lena. He couldn't stop thinking about her. And what a contrast. Lena was tall, had clean features and a healthy bloom on her skin. This little chit was pinched, with a prominent bone in her nose and lank, greasy hair. She probably didn't think of her appearance from one week to the next. Not that it mattered, but she was different from Lena, that was all.

'Sorry, it's a bit difficult right now. I'm just dressing, got to go out in a minute.'

'You sending me away then?'

'Well, no, not exactly. I'm just suggesting you might pick a better time, that's all.'

'Look, this won't take long. I need a bit of advice, you know what I mean?'

'Yes, I know what you mean. I'm wondering if you could come over and see me in my office . . . um . . . tomorrow afternoon? Or better still on Thursday. Do you know where my office is?'

The girl's face was still for a moment, as if his words were only slowly penetrating her brain. Then her features twisted in scorn. 'Oh, all right then, stuff it. I don't need this.'

The girl turned from the threshold, hunching her shoulders. She walked towards the stairs which rose two flights to the street, then turned at the stairfoot. 'You're all the same – snobby self-regarding bastards.'

'Look, if it's *that* vital, of course I'll –'

But by now she had started up the stairs. She turned again, a shade theatrically, half-way up the flight and looked back at Justin. Then she continued up the marble stairs.

Justin shut the door and leaned against it, closing his eyes. Snobby? Self-regarding? It was so unjust.

'It's unfair! Tell her! It's quite unfair, John.' He had spoken aloud. Just as loud, filling the cavity of his head, came the voice of his mentor.

*Look on the floor, Juss. Look! The keys!*

He did as John was telling him, and he found the keys right away. They were near the wall, where the door must have pushed them as it opened, which was why he hadn't noticed them right away.

The keys were on a ring, just three keys, with a paper luggage tag attached. Georgette Hamilton must have posted them in the letter slot while he'd been out. On the tag she had written: *Lena will pick these up herself some time when she returns. In case of problems I've written our address at the coast on the reverse of this. Thanks. G.H.*

Justin realized he could go to her flat now, any time he liked. He closed his fist possessively over the keys. His fist was shaking.

*

The administrative offices of Anatolian Airways were in the mid-section of a high-rise block whose reflecting windows looked down over Taksim Square. As he sat waiting, Justin leafed through an in-flight magazine printed in English. He paused over a shot of some members of an aircrew, standing on the tarmac with an aircraft in the background. The caption read: *One of our senior pilots, Captain Recep, enjoys a joke with his air crew prior to take-off.* Of the men and women standing around, one did not look like a Turk. He was a tall, blond young man without the obligatory moustache. Was this Dan Barry?

Justin shut his eyes. Somehow it had been more hopeful loving Lena when he knew nothing much about the late boyfriend. Now he was about to know his dead competitor a good deal better.

A capable-looking woman appeared and brought Justin, still clutching the magazine, into the presence of Nazım Ali Bey, who rose from behind the desk and extended a beautifully manicured hand. Justin saw that the General Manager was only about five foot five, though he maximized himself with a posture so rigid he might have been wearing a back-brace. His double-breasted suit was immaculate, his hair and moustache were minutely trimmed and had an almost moulded appearance. He exuded a powerful whiff of cologne.

'Won't you have a seat, Mr Fuller? You wish to consult me about poor young Dan Barry? A very tragic affair.'

He shook his head. Justin looked for signs of sincerity, and found none.

'Yes, Nazım Ali Bey. Miss Priestley, with whom, you know, Dan Barry lived, has asked me to dispose of his personal effects. They were not married and so she is not his next-of-kin, and I am wondering if you can tell me who is.'

Without breaking eye contact Nazım Ali Bey flipped up his left hand and received from the capable secretary a manila file. He smiled. 'Let us see what his file says, shall we?'

He opened the file and picked through the documents contained in it like a diner perusing the menu. He hummed gently to himself. 'Ah yes. Oh dear. Hmm.' He looked up. 'Well, I'm afraid when he filled in our personnel form he omitted the details of his nearest family. You see?'

He turned the file around and jabbed it with a stubby finger. Justin leaned forward and saw he was indicating three blank lines.

'I see. You can't help me, then?'

Nazım Ali shrugged and stretched his face fractionally backwards. It was out of his hands, beyond even his circumference of power.

'Did he not have any friends among the other air crew who might know something about him?'

'Well, his friend – the one who introduced him to us actually – was Altan Başkurt. Sadly, he too was assassinated in the incident. But surely Miss Priestley must know something? I would say if she did not know, then who?' He shrugged again in bafflement. Justin saw he was right. A man who lived with a woman and told her nothing about his family would be unlikely to confide in anyone else.

He had got up and begun to apologize for taking up Nazım Ali Bey's time when he was motioned back into his seat.

'There is something I should perhaps tell you. Dan Barry had a pistol at his apartment. I know about this because I went to inform Miss Priestley of the death, and then she showed it to me. He said to her, untruly, that it was issued by the airline for security reasons. I do not know why he had it. Miss Priestley keeps it in the ice box. I was worried about this.'

'Have you told anyone else about it? The police?'

'What have our police got to do with all this? It happened in London. That gun was Dan Barry's affair, and he's dead.'

'But the papers have said that Armenian separatists killed him. They may have been based here in Istanbul. He may have had the gun because he was warned.'

'Well, I don't know about it. There are Armenians everywhere. Anyway, this seems like London gangster fighting to me. But all this – I stay out of it, as much as I can. I told you about the gun because perhaps you are concerned with Miss Priestley's welfare. I do not know if it is wise for her to have this weapon after what has happened.'

'Nazım Ali Bey, thank you for telling me. I am grateful. I won't take up any more of your time. *Allaha ısmarldık*.'

'*Güle, güle*, Mr Fuller. I shall be coming to your British fête. I do come every year, you know.'

Justin left the offices in haste. A gun. Lena had a gun at her flat. But was it still there? He would go there today.

Sarah had been unconscious, but it did not feel like sleep. In her dreams she had been chased by a mixed pack of zoo animals for hours. Her final refuge had been an oil drum, where she lay as in the womb while gorillas, pandas, giraffes, warthogs, gemsbok, tigers and bears rubbed promiscuously against the steel cylinder.

Her waking was no better. She craved chocolate, sugar, anything sweet, but had no money. She searched her flat uselessly, finding only a little tea at the bottom of the caddy-tin. When she brewed up the tea tasted bitter.

She walked two blocks to the *bakkal*'s shop. The doorway was hung with mops and brushes, and cluttered with washing powders and plastic containers of liquid fuel. The fat grocer was serving a customer ahead of her. Sarah waited, demurely.

Sarah knew, if she asked for cheese, the grocer would go into the back-store to scoop a chunk from one of the tubs of brine that were visible through a bead curtain. If, on the other hand, she asked for the high-price white cheese, he would follow the same procedure, but come back with something else. She waited, twitching inside, the excitement rising like an ocean roller. The other customer gathered her packages and left. Sarah stepped forward.

*'De lüks beyaz peynir, var mı?'*

*'De lüks?'*

To show he understood, the *bakkal* gave her a knowing look, and wiped his hands on his apron.

*'Kac gram istiyorsun?'*

*'Elli gram, lütfen.'*

The shopkeeper waddled away into the dark store, and after a minute returned with a slim, square package wrapped in paper. Fifty grams of cheese was not very much.

Sarah held the package flat in her open palm and eased the paper half open. The sliver of cheese was there, and sitting on top of it was a plastic envelope, about the size of a tea-bag, or a sachet of airline sugar.

She closed up the package and handed the *bakkal* almost all her money. Sod the rent, this was more urgent. She turned and hurried home.

# 20

In the week after *Kurban Bayramı* the Istanbul weather continued hot and dry. Dogs slumped in any shade they could discover. Men clustered round faded baize tables in tea-houses, tossing their cards down with more than the usual resignation. Such heat sapped even the *simit* vendors' energy. Only flies liked it. The mounds of street garbage made treasuries of sticky corruption in which to lay eggs.

The air-conditioning freshened Dan's skin like a smear of witch-hazel as he pushed into the American Institute Library. Briefly he hung around the notice-board near the door, reading a few 'Items of Cultural Interest to English Speakers'. The place was almost deserted. The tables were occupied by a sprinkling of readers, who disturbed the atmosphere to the extent of an odd page being turned. There was the clack of heels on parquet from somewhere behind the book stacks. At the issue desk, a middle-aged woman was rattling a computer keyboard.

He inhaled the compound smell of dust, floor polish and bookbinding gum. It reminded him of his first stint as a trainee reporter on the Salford *Evening Echo*. His editor used to send him down to the public library to look up one useless fact after another – more as a form of harmless employment than out of the need to know. He remembered the teasing he had received from the young women librarians – harmless enough, but personal, the kind to make a self-conscious seventeen-year-old blush to his hair-roots.

'You shouldn't spend so much time in this old place, Daniel, you'll lose that nice complexion of yours. How d'you get those eyelashes to grow so long? God, I'm envious – what I wouldn't give!'

And he'd flee through the heavy swing doors, hearing them laugh together the way women sometimes do in the presence of an adolescent boy.

The set-up at Lena's workplace was different. Formality and academicism were the essences here. He had only rarely been into the library. Spectacled now, and with a new moustache, there seemed little chance of the purse-lipped woman at the issue desk knowing him. She was Miss Brooks. Often Lena had talked about Miss Brooks, her chief – 'intolerant old harpy' were three of the many disrespectful words she used – but Dan had never actually spoken to the woman. He would have to now, though. He checked that no one else was in the vicinity and stepped up to the desk.

'Is Miss Lena Priestley anywhere around, please?'

Involuntarily, he had slipped into an uneasy Teutonic accent, as if trying to reinforce his disguise. Miss Brooks, however, did not look up from the VDU she was studying.

'Not in today.'

'Will she be coming tomorrow?

'Nor tomorrow.'

Miss Brooks looked up for a fractional moment, and then returned her gaze to the computer screen.

'Miss Priestley is on indefinite furlough.'

'Do you know where she is? Can I contact her?'

'We do not give out the addresses of our staff, for security reasons.' Miss Brooks sat back and looked at Dan firmly, over her glasses. There was not a glimmer of recognition in her steel-rimmed eyes.

'We've had bomb threats, you know. We are classified by Washington as a Most-Likely Target Grade Two in terrorist scenarios.'

'Well, I'm not a terrorist. Just a friend of Miss Priestley.'

'That's exactly what a terrorist *would* say, isn't it? Anyway, I can put your mind at rest, Miss Priestley is not even in Istanbul. She's gone away, somewhere south, to the coast.'

So Lena was out of town. But where? Wherever it was, that would probably be a safer place than here. The American Library was not the place to be seen hanging round.

Dan was aware of a figure approaching the desk from behind him, and he moved rapidly back to the door. In the street a hot breeze was beginning to disturb the air. Dan crossed between speeding traffic to reach the *kyosk* opposite.

Ordering *ayran*, a tart mixture of yoghurt and spring water which soothes the dusty throat like a lotion, he took a stool and watched old American limousines, painted in taxi livery, nosing through the traffic like marauding sharks. Dan had arrived that morning. He'd got to Paris at the weekend and flown on yesterday to Ankara. He was tired.

Rest, though, was impossible. Ever since he had been told about the plutonium by Felix, he had been on that particular high which came only when he knew a story was right. He'd felt it on just two other occasions: once in Angola, when he'd learned of a SWAPO raid into the northern province of Namibia, and was told he might go along; again in East London, when he knew he had finally got that racist bastard Bradley to commit himself to an interview.

He had been near it on this story, when Altan Başkurt had first shown him how he could infiltrate the Blanchard organization. But it had faded through the long year in which he had waited and patiently worked his way in. There had been excitement, of course, but until now he'd never felt the buzz that told him he'd cracked it.

But Dan had a lot of work to do. He still had no fix on any of the possible buyers of this plutonium. And he wasn't absolutely sure where Blanchard was storing the stuff, though he had a fair idea. His mind returned to a conversation he had had with Blanchard at a party given by some consular official the previous Christmas.

The room had been full of diplomats and their wives getting pissed, as they did most nights of the week, but even more at that time of year. Blanchard, breathing heavily, had literally cornered Dan between the end of a bookcase and the wall, leaning towards him and emitting clouds of acrid cigar smoke.

'I guess you never thought you'd be talking to an Episcopalian church warden here in Istanbul.'

'No, I didn't, that's true,' agreed Dan.

'Well you are, because I am. Ain't that great? You probably didn't know that this was part of the great Anglican diocese of Gibraltar and Malta?' He waited for Dan's reaction.

'No, Nathan, I don't think I'd ever copped that fact.'

'Well, it is. And right here in Istanbul is a parish, with a church and a vicar and now a church warden. Me.'

'I don't get it. What do you want to do something like that for?'

'I'm very religious. Didn't I ever tell you my dad was a TV evangelist after he left the army? We were very God-fearing.'

He dragged on his cigar and sank the remains of his glass of brandy. Nathan could drink vast quantities of alcohol, and he never seemed affected by it.

'Anyway, I was talking to the vicar and he told me he had a problem. This church of his is disused and deconsecrated, and it's falling down. But it's a historic memorial, right? He can't just pull it down, and he don't have shit to put it to rights with. Well, I told him he was looking at the man who had. I'd lease the property, plug the holes in the roof, smarten the place up gradually. I could make good use of it as a storehouse meanwhile, just a few things, no big deal. And would he kindly make me church warden, since I would be warding the church, see?' Blanchard laughed complacently. 'Only a courtesy title, of course. It's good for business, right? The goodwill factor is extraordinary.'

At the time Dan had seen in Blanchard's face that there was something more to it than goodwill. And now he was pretty sure what it was.

He approached the church from below, climbing the narrow street warily. From every cast-iron balcony washing hung or was being taken in. Doleful *arabesk* pop music wailed out of a window somewhere above him and the smoke of burning trash, rekindled by the slight breeze, caught his nostrils.

The church gates were a few feet up a side turning, on the corner of which stood the small, guardian mosque. Dan was just about to turn the corner when he heard a voice.

'. . . now you seen it, ain't you? Ain't that enough?'

'No, my friend, it's not. You're new at this and I tell you . . .'

He flattened himself behind the stone gatepost of the little mosque. The first speaker had been Nathan. If they turned right down the hill they couldn't fail to see him as they passed.

A passer-by, poorly dressed and carrying a plastic water bottle, saw Dan take shelter and stopped to stare. Dan motioned him on, but he would not budge.

The two voices were nearer, with the man who wasn't Blanchard speaking.

'. . . sorry to hold things up, but Pretoria says I still got to do the test . . .'

Dan beckoned to the passer-by and whispered, '*Bey efendi, gelin, bakin bu nedır*.'

The man stepped forward and taking his lapels Dan drew him close. He bent and pulled the man down with him, so that they were both crouching, with backs to the street. The smell of garlic bounced with the man's breath off the cobblestones. Dan pointed at something non-existent on the ground, gabbling a string of Turkish words in no particular order. But by the time the man had stood up again, concluding he had run into a madman, Blanchard and his companion were on their way up the street towards Istiklâl.

Dan went in pursuit, leaving his impromptu ally bemused. Seen from behind, Blanchard was his usual shabby self, so that the other man made quite a contrast. He was perfectly bald, with a shiny pink pate. From behind Dan noticed the wrinkled nape, the laundered sports shirt and slacks, the moccasin shoes.

Keeping his distance, Dan saw them pause at the brow of the hill, which was also the junction with the main drag. Then a massive taxi, one of the sharks, began to bounce down the street towards Dan, hiding the two men for a moment. He flattened himself against the wall, and by the time the car had passed they were no longer in view.

Dan raced to the top and looked left and right.

Across the road he spotted the bald head, moving towards Galatasaray. Of Blanchard there was no trace. Dan followed Baldie.

Dan had not seen him before, but there was no doubt why he was meeting Blanchard. Dan's pulse quickened. Even if the guy hadn't mentioned Pretoria, the heavily clipped accent would have been unmistakable.

Baldie left Istiklâl and strode through side streets, stopping occasionally to glance into a shop window. He might have been looking for souvenirs for his children, or checking to see if anyone was following him. Dan took a risk. He turned off the street along which the man was walking and into one that ran parallel. He glimpsed his quarry as they passed a second connecting alley. By now Dan didn't think he could lose Baldie, because he was sure where they were going.

They reached Tarlabaşı Caddesi, which runs along the northern side of the Pera district and commands to its right a view of the upper reaches of the Golden Horn. Here stood the concrete tower of the Etap Hotel, and facing it across the road the more traditional style of the Pera Palas, built solidly in the Grand Hotel mould. It was into the latter that Baldie disappeared.

Dan did not follow. He would be conspicuous in the small hotel lobby. And anyway, there might be another way to find out what he wanted to know.

*

It took him twenty-four hours to find the address of Felix Trubshaw's girlfriend. He went to the Pudding Shop restaurant, where the successors of the hippies and the ashram trekkers still left messages on the free noticeboard. He had walked the length of Divan Yolu, once the main street of the Byzantine Empire, now an untidy, traffic-choked thoroughfare where tourists dodged hawkers and hasslers as they swung between the Blue Mosque and the Grand Bazaar. Every hustler and western-looking drifter he came across he asked. Marooned by destitution or addiction, many of these people openly beg and prostitute themselves, right in the eye of the tourist whirlpool, just as they do in Piccadilly Circus, the Beaubourg and the Spanish Steps. They are a changeable, fickle population, and, for a long time, Dan had nothing that could be described as luck.

Then in the gardens of Sultanahmet Square he approached a thin Dutch kid with gappy teeth. At first the boy thought it was a pick-up, and jumped to his feet, ready to claim Dan and whisk him away to whichever crummy hotel was convenient for relieving the mugs of their fluids and their dollars. Dan curtly motioned him back down to the bench where he'd been sitting. 'I just want to find someone. A girl called Sarah. Used to be a dancer, maybe still is. Know her?'

The youth looked puzzled. 'Please?'

Dan opened his wallet and took out a five thousand lira note. 'Sarah McAskey, Australian girl, dancer. Used to be around here a lot. Do you know where she is?'

The rent-boy's eyes rested on the bank note. Dan could tell not only that he knew Sarah, but was trying to calculate how much the information was worth. He didn't care who Dan was – police, ponce, pusher. It was only a question of price.

'Yes, I know her. And I know where she lives, also.'

Dan took another note from his wallet and showed them both to the Dutchman. 'Where, then?'

'I don't know the address. Also I don't know the name of the street. I can show you, but that' – he nodded his head at the money – 'isn't enough, you know.'

Dan took two more notes out, and then two more. The young man nodded and got up. 'Fine. Follow me.'

Once they reached the house, Dan didn't want the Dutch kid with him anymore. 'Here's your money. Now fuck off. I'll come back and kill you if this information is wrong. Which floor is hers?'

'But it's right, really. I mean, she lived here last week, anyway. Second floor.'

Dan waved the Dutchman away and pushed open the street door.

Once all but the most sumptuous buildings in the city were made of wood, their elevations built up from lapped horizontal planks, stained rather than painted, and hung with carved balconies. Fire had long since disposed of most of these dwellings, but in the Old City a few survive still, supported askew by flanking breeze-block buildings, whose straight steel railings and window frames only emphasize the rule-of-thumb approximations of the old Ottoman builders.

It was to one of these crumbling wooden houses, near to the *Rüstem Paşa* mosque, that the Dutch youth had led Dan. The passageway which he now entered was mean and dirty, the stairs were weakened by rot. He moved up them carefully. The stairwell had a little more light as Dan passed the first floor landing. Some thin illumination struggled in through a dirt-caked window in the outside wall. He stopped and listened. Somewhere a marital row was going on, pans were being banged, a baby cried. But these sounds were from neighbouring houses.

He climbed to the second, where the only door – Sarah's, presumably – swung slightly away from the jamb. It had not been properly shut, or perhaps the catch was busted. Dan only had to push and it swung open.

He was in a short passage, with a door to his left, another to his right and a third directly facing him at the end. He moved towards these doors, past yellow plaster walls which were dirty and unadorned.

'Hello. Anyone home?'

He was beside the left hand door now. He tried it and found a tiny, filthy kitchen, windowless except for a closed skylight so fouled that hardly any light penetrated. When he flipped on the light, the kitchen became the scene of panic evacuation by dozens of cockroaches. He could hear their insect legs rattling across the floor as they scurried in every direction. He flipped off the light and shut the door.

The end door was a lavatory and shower, while the third gave on to a sitting room, with two windows looking over narrow balconies at the street. The room was deserted, with minimal furniture – low coffee table, a couple of bentwood chairs, divan bed, ancient card table. The floor boards were meagrely covered with rag rugs.

Dan walked to and fro, restlessly. On the table was a large pewter bowl, which had been used as an ashtray. A bunch of dried grasses and flowers stood in a jug next to it. There was an iron ration of books lined up on the floor: *The Prophet*, *Europe on $5 a Day*, Emily Dickinson poems, *The Little Prince*, *The Naked Lunch*.

More interesting were the pictures. Each one was a magazine cutting, carefully pasted to thick grey paper, used by the *bakkal* to wrap purchases. Each one was fixed low down near to the floor, with more dried flowers stuck into jars on the floor beneath them. Each one contained a unitary image, the blue whale's dripping tail-fins, the leather gloves of the Black Power athletes, the carnation in the barrel of the soldier's rifle. These were icons, images to give courage, yard-sticks of hope in a desperate time.

Only now did Dan notice that there was a further room, behind a door that was covered by an ancient and tattered curtain. He found it closed, but not locked. He knocked gently. 'Hello. Anyone about?' He eased the door open and walked in.

It was a bedroom, heavily shaded. She sat propped

against the wall on her bed and he could just make out her face. It registered his presence, but showed no change of expression as, gently, her head nodded up and down like a mascot in a car's rear window.

'Sarah? Sarah, can you hear me?'

The girl muttered something.

'What was that? Say it again.'

Her voice was tiny and expressionless. The lips hardly moved. 'I'm not here. Went away. Didn't want to come back. Not yet.'

He looked down at the bed beside her. He picked up the syringe that lay on the counterpane and went into the other room to wait.

'I'm in big trouble with my job, on top of everything else.'

They were sitting on the floor, and it was evening. She lit a cigarette, leaning her face into the match flame. Dan saw the bones so close to the surface of her face.

'I've been warned. I've got to pull myself together or the hotel manager says I can't dance there any more.'

'Does he know you do smack?'

Sarah shrugged. 'Could be. Either way he doesn't care. He's just a bastard. He only hires me because I'm cheap.'

Initially Dan had waited an hour and tried to talk to her again. But all she could do was repeat that she'd gone away, a little holiday. She said it over and over, like a mantra. Sixty minutes later she was coming out of it. It had taken another two hours to get her to trust him.

In the end Dan had come right out with it – Felix was dead. He wasn't sure, even so, if she had taken it in. Then he had gone into the roach-infested kitchen and made some tea. He gave her a glass with three heaped spoons of sugar. It was then she began to talk about her job.

'Look, Sarah, you know I said I was Felix's friend? Well, I've come back here to make the people who killed him pay for it. Do you understand me? It's important that you do, because I think you can help. We shall punish them, together.'

'Together? Me and you? How do you mean?'

'It's because of where you work. Now are you really going to get the sack, or can you go on still dancing there? What's the man warned you for?'

'Crap like there've been complaints from the tourists about what I look like. He says I'm maybe too skinny for a belly dancer. It's just the fucking tourists. The Turks go a bundle. What do you think? Am I too skinny?'

'I really don't know. But I do know I want you to keep that job, and that means easing up on the smack.'

She laughed. 'Oh, I don't do it like this every day. Can't afford it, it's only when I'm flush, you know? I call it having a little holiday.'

'You mean you don't have a habit?'

'Oh, Christ yes, of course. I don't go over the top, that's all, except once in a while. Like today.'

'Well, I think the manager's right. You can't belly dance on an empty belly. I'm going out to buy some food, then I'm coming back to cook it. I'm going to build up your strength, Sarah.'

He left her and walked the few blocks to the Egyptian Bazaar, Mısır Pazarı.

The ancient food and spice market would soon close for the night. There was a throng of last-minute shoppers inside and Dan moved through it, intoxicated by the heady compound of smells – roots and resins, pastes and powders, seeds, musks, mastic, all displayed in jars or open sacks that bulged and spilled enticingly across the ground.

He bought bread and yoghurt, dried figs, a melon, eggs, fish, vegetables and rice, a carton of orange juice and six bottles of beer. Then he returned to Sarah's house.

He was hot by the time he had climbed the stairs. His head was flushed and dizzy, and sweat began to evaporate from his forehead. He dumped the food in Sarah's kitchen, scattering another starburst of roaches, and called her name.

He went through to the sitting room. The cigarette haze was fresh, but Sarah was gone. He returned to the kitchen, cracked open a bottle of beer and began to cook.

Every week Conrad Hamilton hired himself out to the

private sector by taking a party of tourists around Istanbul. Conrad's were discerning groups – professional people and academics from the Ivy League towns and similar places. They were familiar with the basics. They had seen the Sultan's jewels and knew them to be mostly paste. They didn't want to shuffle round the harem and be told another crock of lies by the half-educated official guide. They'd been there, they'd done all that. So his Istanbul was a circuit of lesser-known gems: the church of SS Sergius and Bacchus, the Calligraphy Museum and the extraordinary prefabricated iron church of the Bulgars, whose sections were cast in Vienna over a century ago and shipped down the Danube on a hundred barges. One of the favourite spots on the tour, however, was the *Rüstem Paşa* mosque – a small masterpiece of the architect Sinan, the Ottomans' own Christopher Wren.

It was a small group today, and he had given them, he thought, a bravura rendering of his lecture on the Iznik faience – letting their breath be caught by the majesty of the soaring tilework on the mosque's interior, then deflating them with the news that this – even this – was not quite the best period of Iznik. And, finally, bringing them up again by revealing those few sections where the mosque *does* display some of the very deepest blue colour-work, the most flawless glazing, from the greatest Iznik period – which occurred, as they must know, in the two decades before the middle of the sixteenth century.

Now, as his party was making its way down the steps and back into the street, Professor Rochester from Berkeley – or was he in fact Professor Berkeley from Rochester? – was making some technical quibble about the Iznik kilns, something to do with their superiority over the original models, at Tabriz in Persia.

'Because, Dr Hamilton, this, as you said in your talk, was where the Iznik craftsmen came from, and my point is that the air-intakes used by the Tabriz people were markedly inferior in design to those found at Iznik in the classical period . . .'

But Conrad was no longer listening. He was looking with a puzzled frown over the professor's head and along the street. A man in his twenties was walking towards them, carrying a load of shopping from the Egyptian Bazaar. The man was familiar, but at first Conrad couldn't place him. The way of walking, the set of the head on the shoulders, were familiar, but something seemed wrong. And then he realized. The glasses and the moustache – without them, there was no doubt. But that only deepened Conrad's sense of shock. This guy was supposed to have been killed last week, and in London.

It wasn't until he got home that Conrad did anything. God, he wished Georgette were there to ask about it. But she was away at the coast, and her dependable counsel not available to him. Conrad poured himself a bourbon and looked up a reference in his personal address book. Then he picked up the receiver and dialled.

# 21

It didn't at first occur to Conrad Hamilton that the Armenians would be interested in Dan Barry's resurrection. It was Pete Schultz who planted the thought in his head.

Pete was the CIA chief at the US Consulate – officially he was Deputy Trade attaché, but everyone knew differently. Pete had his hooks into practically every member of the US community in the city, everyone who counted, at least. He knew their credit status, who they were having affairs with, what they were embezzling, what kind of recreational drugs they took. It was an abuse, of course. After all, the CIA is supposed to attend to America's enemies, not target her own citizens. But Pete's system of indirect blackmail gave him one of the best networks of informal intelligence in the Near East – so good, he boasted, that the Mayor of Istanbul's wife's poodle didn't take a shit without he knew about it.

Officially, Conrad was on his books as a useful informer, a draft-evader whose wife desperately wanted to get back to the States. Of course the Carter pardon had helped men like that back in the seventies, but in recent more conservative years it had been difficult for expatriate Americans with a history of radicalism to get University jobs back home. A good word from the Agency, however, and he could stroll into a decent mid-West Chair, if not quite the Ivy League or Berkeley.

In fact, over the years Conrad had evolved into something more than a small-time stoolie, and when he had phoned in last evening with 'an interesting anomaly', Schultz had arranged a meeting in his office the next morning, early.

'Con, I hope this is good. I got to go see a guy who claims to have heisted the Libyan diplomatic bag. Says he wants a million bucks – Jesus, it would have to contain Gadaffi's balls to be worth that much! Okay, shoot.'

'Well, you remember that Brit, one of the Anatolian Airways staff who was shot in London last week? Musa Dağ were supposed to have done it, yeah?'

Pete Schultz nodded. 'I remember. His name was Dan Barry.'

'Yes. Anyway, I knew Dan Barry quite well. His girlfriend is a good friend to Georgette, sends her kid to the nursery. Well, here's the weird part. Dan Barry is not dead. I saw him yesterday near the Egyptian Bazaar. He's wearing a moustache and glasses and I saw him carrying groceries. He's living down there!'

'He used to live in Emirgan, right?'

'Right. Shit, Pete, your data-recall is phenomenal. Anyway the point is nobody, not even his girlfriend, knows he isn't dead. Don't you think that's peculiar? I mean, what's going on?'

'Conrad, this could be useful, thanks. I don't know

why, but there's something weird going on connected with London. Ed Craike's in town, and that only happens when something extraordinary is about to blow.'

'Who's Ed Craike?'

'Oh, forget it. Look, I got to go now. Thanks again. I tell you one thing, I wonder what the Armenians would think of this. If they did try to rub this guy out, they'd like to know where he is right now, wouldn't they? On the other hand, if they didn't, I guess they'd be very anxious to know more about who's been taking their name in vain. Still! That's for them to sort out. Bye, Con. And thanks once again.'

Conrad hesitated. 'Just one thing, Pete. I know you're in a hurry. I'm applying for a Chair at Sacramento. You know how much Georgie wants to get back Stateside. Anything you can do, much appreciated. Okay?'

'Well, of course my influence is limited, Con. But, yes. I'll put in a good word, of course. Quote my name to the good guys back in Sacramento.'

'I was thinking more of the Office putting in a good word, for my security clearance.'

Pete Schultz tried not to look too encouraging. But maybe the Hamiltons had served out their time now, maybe they deserved to get back home. He'd better sleep on it. It might make sense if he let this depend on the strength of the Dan Barry information. Yes, he would let it lie a few days.

'See what I can do, Con. See what I can do. Catch

you around, okay?' He rammed out his hand, shook Conrad's and smiled.

Back in the street, Conrad was puzzled. Why had Pete mentioned the Armenians like that? And why had he let slip that name – what was it, Ed Craike? Pete never did anything casually. It meant something.

Dan awoke, sure that someone had walked through the room. But perhaps it was a dream. There was a lump between him and the mattress. He shifted his weight, to get at whatever was wedged there and pulled out a paperback: *The Naked Lunch* by William S. Burroughs. Ten seconds later he realized a night had passed and he was still at Sarah's place, lying on her divan. Six empty bottles of *Efes* beer stood in a huddle in the middle of the room.

He shied the book across the room and, with the help of his right hand, brought his left wrist in line with his eyes. Eight o'clock. He rolled on to the floor and looked around feeling stiff and stupid. Sarah. She'd gone off and not reappeared. He'd cooked, waited, eaten the food, started reading. Must have dropped off after that.

Dan gave himself up to a powerful yawn, after which he started at last to think more clearly. He pulled himself to his feet and went into Sarah's bedroom.

The room was empty, but the bedclothes were pulled back. He leaned forward and put his hand down. The sheet was warm to the touch.

'You were sleeping like a tiny tot, so I just left you.'

Dan swung round. Sarah was standing in the doorway dressed in a clean cotton dress. Her hair was washed and she looked fresh as the bottle of milk in her hand.

'What time did you come back? Where did you go?'

'Oh, I had some things to do.'

'Were you in a fit state to do them?'

'Hardly, but I'm fine now. Let's have some breakfast.'

Sarah's new-found self-possession was impressive. While she made tea, he asked her again where she'd been.

'Had to see the owner of this place. He's a complete bastard – a ponce, actually. If I don't pay him every week on the nail he sends round gorillas to throw me out. It happened once before when Felix sent my money a day late. I had to spend the night at Sirkeci station.'

'So you've just been to pay him.'

'I told you, I can't. Got no money. I was trying to get him to give me time. He won't though, thinks it's a sign of weakness.' She sighed. 'So, it'll be the station again tonight, I reckon.'

'No, I'll pay your rent.'

In truth, Dan's money was running a little short and he would have to risk a visit to the bank today.

Sarah's eyes softened. 'With Felix gone I – I don't quite know where I am.'

'I wasn't sure you had taken it in about Felix.'

'Oh, I took it in. But you don't react to things, you see? It'll be, well, difficult without him. But I expect I'll survive.'

'Sarah, are you going to help me?'

'What? Get the people who killed him? That is what you said, isn't it?'

'Something like that, yes.'

'I don't know, Dan. I'd be afraid.'

'It's not dangerous, Sarah. Look, come on. I'll pay your rent, and then you pay me back with this. It's straight business. I want you to get talking to someone, get some information, that's all. It's very easy, I'd do it myself but it needs a girl, needs to look like a pick-up.'

'I have to sleep with the guy?'

Dan thought for a moment. 'Yes, I suppose you might have to – to go through the motions with him. What I want to know is more likely to come out as pillow talk. But you've done that sort of thing before.' It was a statement, not a question.

Sarah sipped her tea, then straightened her back. 'All right. Now kindly tell me all about *it*.'

When Justin used the key which Georgette had given him his heart seemed to throw itself about, wrenching at its moorings like a buoy in a storm.

He stood in her living room and tried to imagine Lena's presence. Here is where he had last seen her. The pile of cardboard boxes filled with Dan Barry's things stood where she had stacked them, but at first

Justin ignored these. He was looking for things that told of her. He found a bunch of knitting with needles thrust into it, a sweat-shirt draped over the back of a chair, a large, sprung hair-clip.

The blood was banging in his temples. He walked through to the bedroom and stood for a long time looking down at the bed. Tenderly he turned back the covers, felt the sheets, picked up a pillow and pushed it into his face. He could smell her. He was like an animal, tracking her scent. He had an overpowering urge to lie down then, to curl up in the place where her smell was strongest.

*Come on, son. You've got work to do. You're nothing but an effing layabout, we all know that. No need to prove it. Pull your finger out, okay?*

He went back to the living room and began humping boxes down the stairs, sliding them into the hatchback of his car. When he had taken them all out he returned to the flat and, suddenly, he felt arid, a dried-fish sensation which began in his throat, but seemed to extend down inside him, as far as his stomach and his guts. He opened the refrigerator, reached for the bottle of mineral water that was racked in the door, filled a glass and drained it in one continuous movement. Then he filled it again. This he drank at more leisure, wandering out on to the balcony. A huge Russian tanker was churning southwards, spewing out bilge-water. Justin looked for sailors, but he saw none. He was always uneasy when he could see no life on the ships in the waterway. These vessels were monster robots, pursuing their ends independently of man. But controlled from where?

Back in the kitchen he replaced the bottle in the fridge. Then his hand hung in front of the ice compartment. He had been putting this moment off. Now he had to face it.

He pulled the flimsy door open and felt inside. There were some frozen vegetables in their plastic envelopes which, when he moved them aside, he found to be covering up the gun. It was half-sunk in the white fur of ice, and took a minute to dislodge. By the time he had done this his fingers were chilled through. He put the cold hand to his face and then the iced steel of the pistol. It did something to cool the fever.

Now he wanted to be gone. He quickly wrapped the gun in a towel and, slamming Lena's door behind him, took the stairs two at a time. He knew what he should do, conventionally. He should stop the car at some convenient place on the banks of the Bosporus and shy the gun, high and far, out into the water. But he wasn't going to do it.

*Can't do that, Jus. Might need it. Never waste a good shooter.*

Yes, some part of his personality, the small-boy part, the Billy-the-Kid part, was pleased at the thought. He had a gun now. He was armed.

Conrad had a faculty committee and then had to take a postgraduate seminar on the Cappadocian potsherd record this morning, so it wasn't until lunchtime that he could think things through. Pete Schultz had always especially valued Conrad's tie-up with the Armenians, even using him as a conduit for CIA money a couple of times. Perhaps he was now asking him, in his roundabout way, to make contact with the Armenians and tip them off about Dan's return. They would be glad to get a lead on who had been killing in their name over in London.

Conrad had first become involved with the Armenians because of his naïvety over the Armenian question. He'd only just arrived in Istanbul, he didn't even appreciate that there was such a thing as an Armenian question, and he'd gone off to the East one summer to measure up some ruined churches around Kars, on the Russian border. One day he found himself surrounded by a platoon of the Turkish army's meanest, each pointing their AK47s at his heart.

Later he had been told he was excavating without a permit. No, he said. Where was his digging equipment, his team? He was only drawing, hoping he might be able to dig next year – he'd apply for a permit then.

The permit was, of course, refused, and Conrad barely escaped prosecution and expulsion from the country. At this point he got the bit between his teeth. He became a bore on Armenian medieval architecture. He went to the Armenian church authorities for details about monasteries long since deserted. He filed for dozens of permits to work on Armenian sites, in the hope that some might get through. All were refused without explanation.

What was curious was the silence of his colleagues. Whenever he raised the matter in the Common Room, people inspected their shoes, started to read or chatted conspicuously among themselves. No one wanted to talk about why Conrad's Armenian enthusiasms were being met by an official brick wall.

'Don't they like my face or something? I don't get it!'

There was one Armenian member of staff, old Kervork, whom the Americans on the staff knew as George. He was a political economist well into his sixties. Nowadays George had retired to grow tomatoes in Bebek. Back then it had been he who had taken it on himself to explain the Armenian question to the young archaeologist.

'Armenia doesn't exist to the official mind here. We are a non-people. Why do you think our young ones have started to talk seriously about fighting against the government? We are not a violent people, we only want our history and our culture to be returned to us. Do you know, in the East, around Lake Van and Erzurum, there were hundreds, *hundreds*, of our churches, still standing in perfect order even a few years ago, beautiful, unique medieval churches. Some of them were as big as English cathedrals. Well, my boy, you've been out there, what can you find? Most of them are gone, aren't they? Wiped off the map, or just heaps of rubble. The official story is, they were knocked over by earthquakes – heavily *selective* earthquakes, which left every Ottoman mosque and every

Syriac church in the area intact. In reality, the army uses our old churches for target practice. Field guns, rocket launchers.'

Old George had shaken his head. 'It's a bad world, Conrad. They have tried to wipe us out so many times. They are still trying.'

After his talk with George, Conrad gave up applying to work on Armenian sites. Later his head of department had told him, 'Con, we just wanted to see how long you'd go on trying! *No one* works on Armenia out here. You can't get any permits. I mean, Armenia's not even in any of the history books, it's been written out of the Turkish edition of *Encyclopaedia Britannica*, for Christ's sake. You were pretty persistent, I'll give you that. But even you dropped it.'

But Conrad hadn't dropped it. Through old George he met younger Armenians, was invited to their houses, their weddings and christenings. He got to know the gentle, intelligent Armenian subculture, and fell in love with its extraordinary religious music and liturgy, and its complex symbolic mysticism. Then, gradually, he had become aware of the parallel Armenian political movement, the secret movement which in part had now crystallized around the condemned prisoner Krikorian, alleged leader of the Musa Dağ organization.

And all the time, Conrad was reporting on these contacts to Pete Schultz – feeding him names, addresses, house purchases, holiday destinations, business travel. Schultz, of course, stressed how sympathetic America was to the Armenian cause, and how all this stuff was merely good background to help channel that sympathy. But each time he spoke to Schultz about the Armenian community, it was with increasing dread, and then he had gradually begun withdrawing from those he betrayed. It had suddenly occurred to him just how dangerous these people could be. And if they found out what he was doing . . .

It would be even worse now, with Krikorian's execution near. The atmosphere of suspicion was thickening and Conrad hadn't spoken to any of his Armenian contacts for weeks. But Schultz's hint this morning had been clear enough – get back in.

The welcome seemed genuinely effusive. 'Dr Hamilton! How wonderful. Some tea? Or a glass of *raki*?' Conrad knew the young man as Hagop. He spoke English with a lordly ease that the American found obscurely intimidating. Hagop he knew only a little, though he had clearly risen to somewhere near the top of Musa Dağ since his brother's death.

The room in which he was received was dark, the windows shaded from the light or from prying eyes. Two or three other young men sat around on divans, dressed, like Hagop, in cotton sports shirts and jeans, with trainers on their feet.

Hagop sat in one of two armchairs, and invited Conrad to take the other. A boy of about twelve brought them glasses of tea.

After they had exchanged pleasantries, silence fell. Hagop looked at Conrad inquisitively. He had a commanding presence, like a young warlord receiving an embassy. Conrad was intimidated.

'Look, I thought you might be interested. It's about the shooting in London, which someone tried to attribute to Musa Dağ, and which I know you – which I know Musa Dağ didn't do.'

Hagop leaned forward, lacing his fingers together over his knee. 'Yes? It sounds *most* interesting.' He said something to the others, and they all nodded their heads, in polite agreement.

Conrad cleared his throat. 'Well, one of the supposed victims of the shooting isn't dead at all. His name is Dan Barry.'

There was an itch in the crook of his right knee. He worked a finger into it and rubbed. Hagop's eyes bored into him, it was like being trapped in two beams of light. *Keep talking, just keep talking.*

'He's an Englishman, who was working for the airline as a cabin steward. I saw him in Istanbul, yesterday, near the Egyptian Bazaar. He's disguised himself, and he's not told anyone apparently that he has returned. I don't know what he's doing, but I imagine you – Musa Dağ, I mean – would be interested in finding out who used their name for those murders. Maybe this information might help them do so.'

He dried up. Hagop nodded his head several times, as a parent listens to his child retailing events at school.

'Yes, well, it's most interesting, Dr Hamilton, most interesting. Should they get hold of that piece of information, Musa Dağ would be most grateful, I am sure of it. Tell me, did you go to the game last Sunday, Galatasaray against Fenerbahçe? A terrible fiasco. Maybe you read about it?'

He shook his head in disbelief, talking about scandals of poor sportsmanship in football and basketball, until he could decently rise and indicate that the interview was over. As Conrad was being handed by one elbow towards the door, Hagop stopped him and said, 'Oh, Dr Hamilton, that piece of information about the Englishman. Did it come from your own observation, or from your friend Mr Peter Schultz?'

Conrad went suddenly cold. All he could do was stumble out his assurances. 'I saw him myself, Hagop, I saw him myself, at the Egyptian Bazaar. Now look, you don't think I would –?'

He looked from face to face. Every pair of eyes was fixed on him, like pistols. Hagop spoke soothingly. 'I think nothing, Dr Hamilton, nothing whatsoever. Please!'

'I've always been a good friend to you guys. You know I have. I wouldn't do anything to harm you.'

'We are all tools of American policy, Dr Hamilton, isn't that so? All tools! Well, goodbye. It was good to see you again. Keep in touch, okay?'

Conrad shook hands numbly and left. So Musa Dağ knew of his connection with Schultz. In spite of the heat, he felt chilled.

Hagop, meanwhile, had returned to his companions

in the darkened salon. They debated urgently together. Then their chief issued a string of orders and the meeting broke up.

# 22

A plaque on the door, which he passed on the way to his room, informed Jerry Dorp that the neighbouring suite had once been occupied by Dame Agatha Christie. The South African was not particularly impressed.

Dorp considered himself a cultured man, which was why he'd booked into the 'elegant, old-school hotel'. But, as he'd quickly realized, the elegance had been supplanted by a sort of inverted vulgarity. The place was monopolized by groups of heritage tourists, eager to rub the relics of a time when a Sultan was on his throne, and the old Orient Express was on the rails. Dorp regarded such people as carrion-pickers. They would no more be seen at the Turkish National Opera or an exhibition by modern Istanbul artists than eat a sheep's eye or give to a beggar in the street. They did not want this to be a living city.

On the other hand, they seemed to relish revolting displays of belly-dancing in the dining room. On the previous evening Dorp had been half-way through an overdone tournedos when harsh music had abruptly burst out through speakers in the corner of the dining room. A slim, unskilled dancing girl began to oscillate her abdomen and flap her arms, in what looked like an ungainly attempt to fly. All the while, as she circulated between the tables, her lips made lewd kissing movements.

Trying to look in another direction Dorp had fixed his eyes on a wonderful brass samovar which sat grandly on a dresser at the end of the room – probably a treasure pawned by some Russian Imperial family fleeing the revolution. But the samovar could not hold his attention long enough. Over the skirling gypsy music he picked up the approach of the girl's bare feet on the wooden floor. Behind his left ear he could hear the tinkle of the tiny cymbals she wore on her finger ends.

Dorp, in spite of himself, looked round. With a tug of unwilling eroticism, he saw her navel, and the undulating flesh of her stomach. Then, raising his eyes to her face, he almost jumped. God, she might have been his daughter! Young and fair-skinned, she had a woman's body and an adolescent face. The girl's clear, hard eyes seemed to be making an examination, tracking over his own body as if approving it. Then they widened emphatically, her lips pushed outwards in a moue and she danced away. Dorp tried to put together the reason why he had found her so disturbing. It took him a few minutes to realize that her eyes were not Turkish eyes. They were as blue as the sky.

Belly dancing during dinner may have been necessary to keep the hotel in business. But the strategy was not, apparently, successful enough to allow fresh decoration and new fittings. Dorp's was a large but dingy room. It reminded him of a commercial hotel in some boring hole back home, such as Kimberley. On the floor he noted a once-precious, now mangy, rug. The drapes were faded and worn, and though the brass bedstead was of gracious design it needed shining up. The bathroom was a stately, blue-and-white-tiled space with a gigantic tub and great brass fittings. But many of the tiles were cracked and the bath was stained. The top of the wardrobe was thick with dust, as Dorp verified with his forefinger.

This evening Dorp thankfully had an appointment for dinner at an outside restaurant, and would avoid the dancer's attentions. He showered, scrubbing his white skin astringently with a rough cloth. Then he dressed in light blue slacks and a Fred Perry sports shirt, which his flesh filled tautly. Dorp's body was large, smooth and well cared-for from the hairless pate down to the doeskin shoes.

He left the shade of the hotel canopy and crossed the narrow road. Soon he was striding uphill through a network of streets with a plan of the city folded open in his hand. He was on his way to meet Blanchard.

The restaurant had subdued dignity. It was carpeted thickly to soak up the diners' conversation, and the linen was fresh and crisp. Blanchard was sitting alone beside the window which had a view on to the garden of the Swedish Consulate. The royal-blue jacket was stretched into corrugations across the expanse of his back. It was frayed at the cuffs and grubby at the collar. Seeing Dorp enter he stood clumsily, with legs wedged between table and chair and waved the South African over. His voice exploded across the restaurant. 'Jerry. Great to see you. Get your ass over here.'

Blanchard shook Dorp's hand purposefully, like an angler waggling a fly-fishing rod, and gestured towards his guest's chair. 'Order now, then we'll talk. Great food in this place.'

He motioned to the waiter and flipped open the padded cover of the menu. 'I'll take the scallops and the baked swordfish with *patates* and a haricot salad on the side. And I guess a bottle of Chablis – that wine okay for you, Jerry? Well now, this is fine, just fine.'

He slumped back in his chair with a sigh and seized a breadstick, while Dorp ordered steak rare, with a green salad and a bottle of mineral water.

'So. How d'you like the town, Jerry?'

'Full of bloody tourists.'

'Aw, you don't notice them after a while.'

'You have been here long?'

'Seven years, give or take. Seven good, happy years. Happy business, good takes.'

Dorp leaned forward. 'Business in what, exactly?'

Blanchard opened his hands wide. 'You name it, Jerry. I traded cotton T-shirts, dried apricots, red wine, bauxite, cement for school books, tomato catsup, Japanese whisky, Polish vodka, personal stereos, army boots.'

As Blanchard talked of money-making opportunities – shipping deals, unsuspected mineral deposits in the Turkish hinterland, the slipshod accounting systems of the army – his face became long with applied sincerity.

'But all of them were legitimate business situations, Jerry. Apple-pie legitimate. Glass of wine?'

Dorp refused by extending his hand over the top of the wineglass, and reached for his mineral water which fizzed as he poured. The waiter brought food, and Blanchard began to eat his scallops dogwise, in greedy gulps. His head was tilted towards the plate, and his eyes rolled in time with the movements of his jaw. Dorp said, 'Not everything you do is that way, is it, Mr Blanchard? For example, I'm not here to buy slices of apple pie. How d'you get into this line of trading? I've bought pluto for my government all over the world – Sudan, Nigeria, West Indies. I never heard of you till now.'

Blanchard swallowed his mouthful and waited a second for it to soft-land in his stomach before speaking.

'It's a natural extension, right? I've done arms deals – Blowpipe and Stinger missiles were a speciality a couple or three years back. I have a great delivery record. I'm expanding, I'm a good capitalist.'

'You deal drugs?'

'You make me sound like some punk on the streets.'

'Oh well, forget it. It makes no difference.'

Blanchard was feeling for something in his pocket.

'No, I want you to understand, Jerry. Yeah, I shipped smack and hashish in my time. I gave it up, though. Drugs are just another merchandise, people take them out of free choice. This was how the free world was made, right?'

He was having difficulty extricating his hand, but when he did it held a gold-edged business card. He passed it across the table.

Telefon 150 3366

*Nathan Blanchard*, MBA

Adventure Merchants Inc.
Camhuriyet Caddesi, 1486
Istanbul

'See, I like to think of myself as in the tradition of Columbus, Vespucci, Marco Polo. I don't give two shits about national boundaries and laws. I make my own frontiers and laws.'

Dorp handed back the card.

'Well, Mr Blanchard, you've shown me your yellow flask. But of course you can't show me what is inside it.'

'Pure plutonium, weapons grade. Ten kilos.'

'Would you mind explaining just where it came from? My government expects to know the – how shall I put it – the *provenance* of this kind of merchandise.'

'I bought it in Spain. I got a scientist to check it out.'

'Can I talk to him?'

'No, he's dead.'

'I see. Well, I have my own testing equipment on the way. Where was this stuff made, is it British or French?'

The main course arrived and with the waiter gone

Blanchard talked and ate simultaneously. 'The guy who supplied it said it came out of Sellafield in Britain. It was lifted by a group of workers there. You know, they produce so much of this stuff, and I mean tons of it, that they seemingly never quite know how much they *do* produce, not exactly, not down to the last few sugar-bags. But it's good stuff, the very best. I only sell the very best of anything, and I just know when you test it you'll find it Grade-A. Do you have one of those remote-control drill gizmos for taking out a sample?'

'Arriving tomorrow with a technician. Now, I don't mean to be discourteous, Mr Blanchard, but there's still one or two matters I'd like to get clear. Is anyone else in the market for this merchandise?'

He fed the last of the breadsticks into his mouth before replying. 'Yeah, you'll meet them on the day.'

'You won't tell me how many?'

'I guess it does no harm. Just two other governments.'

'Have you told them about me?'

'Shit, no. I mean, I'm very discreet, Jerry. There will be no names, no national flags. Very, very discreet. Okay?'

'That sounds good to me, Mr Blanchard. Very good indeed.'

Dorp didn't wish to linger in Nathan Blanchard's company. He declined a dessert, but was forced to watch as his host devoured a glistening semicircle of cheesecake, followed by raspberries and whipped cream. At the same time he received a detailed lecture on the difference between the sexual parts of domestic pigs and wild hogs.

It was ten o'clock by the time the two men went their separate ways. Dorp thankfully made the five-minute walk back to the hotel and entered the bar, feeling warm and dry. He ordered fresh orange juice on ice and sat down with Istanbul's English-language weekly, the *Turkish Daily News*. He got half-way through an article about the staging of *Hamlet* outdoors in the grounds of the Topkapı Palace when he realized someone was standing in front of him. He glanced up. Those eyes, blue as the best Iznik tiles, were looking teasingly down at him.

'Hello,' said the girl. 'I noticed you while I was dancing here last night. I thought you looked nice. May I?'

She took the chair opposite him.

'You weren't in the dining room tonight,' she said. 'Did you eat out? You wouldn't ever buy a thirsty girl a drink, would you?'

You can buy almost any consumer item on the street in a city like Istanbul. The most visible things, hawked from cardboard box-lids and wooden folding tables, are the flashy modern items – digital diver-watches, personal stereos, sub-miniature cameras. Alongside these, often on the same tray but with no sense of incongruity, are such banalities as nylon socks, boot-laces, single cigarettes, chewing gum, hair-grips.

Dan pushed his way through the scrum of street merchants, tourists, beggars and idlers which always chokes up the main gate of the Grand Bazaar and checked his street map. He was on his way to find a more specialized dealer than any to be found here.

He started down a street going south from Divan Yolu towards the fishing quay of Kumkapı on the Sea of Marmara. About half-way down, he turned along a narrow street, counting the house and the shop numbers as he went. The name he had been given was Hasan Tutàr, electrical-goods seller. He found the shop at the second pass, the number being hidden by a girl standing outside the shop.

When she spotted Dan coming back to the shop the girl began babbling at him, and he saw that she was a mental defective. She was dressed like a child, in a short frock and knee-length socks, yet she was as tall as an adult, with a great expanse of forehead under her headscarf. Cinched as in a vice against her fully developed breasts was a brown plastic doll. She rocked her toy energetically, all the while directing a tumble of vowelly phrases towards Dan. He shook his head and shrugged, then indicated he would like to get past her into the shop.

Back in the winter Dan had briefly toyed with the idea of making surreptitious recordings of Blanchard, for use in his book. He'd asked around, and been given Tutar's name, as someone capable of supplying the necessary equipment. The notion had got no further than that, until now.

Tutar was standing behind a glass counter littered with electrical components. He had a jeweller's magnifier in his eye, and was making a minute examination of a small circuit-board. He was a slight man with an unnaturally round pot-belly and an incredibly thin moustache, painstakingly maintained by shaving most of his upper lip to leave only a fringe of bristles along the lower edge. Dan waited and looked around.

The inside of the shop was an utter shambles. The walls were hung with precariously bracketed shelves sagging under a higgledy-piggledy tangle of components. He saw coils, broken telephones, cathode-ray tubes, ancient radio valves, microchip circuits. There were unboxed loudspeakers, coils of wiring, transistors, condensers, plug boards, plugs, switches, pocket calculators, fractured microphones, disembowelled computers, tape-decks. There were hundreds of things whose uses Dan could only guess at, and everything was blanketed in a uniform layer of dust.

At last Hasan put down the circuitry and let the magnifier drop from his eyesocket neatly into his palm.

*'Iyi akşamlar, efendim.'*

'Excuse me. Do you speak English?'

Hasan tossed up his head and clicked his tongue. *'Kleine deutsch ich sprechen.'*

Dan thought his German would just be adequate. 'I need a microphone, which works by radio. I want to make tape recordings from it. Do you sell things like that?'

'How far away from the position of the microphone do you want to make these recordings?'

'I don't know. Maybe one hundred metres. And it needs to be a private, very *small* microphone – you know? Very secret.'

'Okay, I can sell such things. But it has to be a special order. Wait here. I must check my stock.'

Hasan disappeared through a dirty curtain into an even more unbelievably disordered back room. Almost at once the street door twanged open and the idiot girl came in from the street.

She leaned against the door as it clicked shut. Then she inserted a thumb into her mouth and eyed Dan. Feeling like a prize exhibit, he smiled nervously and moved towards a wall of crooked shelving to inspect some of the electrical junk on display. Still the girl stared at him, her eyes set round and small in her fleshy face. Picking up an electric motor and turning it over idly, Dan could hear the big child's mouth working on her thumb.

A minute later Hasan came back. He clucked gently when he saw the girl and hustled her into the inner room, returning with his face full of apology. Dan moved his hands fractionally in an emollient gesture. Hasan smiled.

'My daughter, she is –' He rolled his eyes and laughed. 'Do you want tea?'

'Yes, thank you.'

Hasan opened the street door and yelled. A boy came, and minutes later glasses of tea arrived swinging on a suspended salver. Hasan heaped sugar into his glass.

'Well, I can make this thing – I will make a microphone, a transmitter and a receiver. Have you a recorder?'

Dan nodded. 'Yes, Sony Walkman Professional. Is that okay?'

Hasan shrugged. 'Yes, it's okay. I will work on this for you tonight. You must come back tomorrow and we will test it. Is that good?'

'That's good.'

Hasan chinked glasses with him and drained his tea. It was a gesture he might have learned from watching Prussian officers drinking schnapps. Laughing, Dan did the same. He didn't quite know why, but he felt happy.

# 23

Dan was staying with Sarah now, sleeping on her living-room divan, cooking for her, watching her heroin intake. When he let her see the tiny unit Hasan Tutar had made she worried if it was capable of doing the job.

'What if it breaks down? What if it starts giving out an awful whistle or something?'

'It won't. It's a mike, not a speaker. A radio mike. It's much safer than wiring you up with the tape recorder, which Dorp would find if you had to strip.'

The microphone was fitted with cunning precision inside a ballpoint pen whose body was made of steel. This acted as the transmitting aerial, making the pen a completely self-contained unit. The mike and its receiver had cost Dan all the money he had left.

When they tested it the system worked. Sarah clipped the pen into her neckline and walked down to Eminönü to buy cigarettes. Following behind her with the receiver and tape, Dan recorded her progress: the footsteps, the street sounds, the Marlboro seller in front of the Yeni Cami giving her today's price, Sarah's self-conscious commentary.

'It's brilliant, Dan. It picks up everything.'

'Yes, we seem to be ready for tonight. But sticking the pen in your neckline like this isn't very natural.

You'll have to wear a jacket, and clip it into the handkerchief pocket. Have you got a jacket?'

She had. The jacket was rather old, but at least clean, and it fitted the image Sarah wanted to put over. For Dorp, she wouldn't play the hooker. She saw herself as a nice college girl, paying her way through a sabbatical year in Europe. She would wear cotton trousers with the jacket, and be demure.

So far Sarah had met Dorp twice. After that first drink in the Pera Palas bar she'd chatted him up one morning in the hotel lobby, and walked with him as far as Taksim Square. There he had sent her on her way, but not without an invitation to dinner the next evening, in the roof restaurant of the Sheraton Hotel.

'It's strange, Dan. I think he likes me. I don't know if he trusts me, or if he fancies me. But he does seem to like me. But there's more than that – something tells me he looks at me and sees his daughter.'

'Where do you get that from?'

'I don't know. Something tells me.'

'Well, just don't forget to turn the mike on, okay?'

When they invented the Walkman they had no idea what a service they were doing to electronic eavesdroppers. That little box is certainly a clever idea in the delivery of music, but it's a quantum leap in the war against secure conversation. It abolishes at one stroke the last great problem in surveillance, which is not where to plant a bug, but how to conceal the listening post. And it did it by bringing headphones out of the closet. People listen now on buses and trains, in waiting rooms and public parks, on bikes and in cars. Nowadays you can be almost anywhere, unashamedly tuned to some secret source, and no one looks twice at you.

Dan settled himself in the roof terrace bar of the Sheraton with a beer and tuned in to Sarah and Dorp, who were by now sitting at their table on the floor below. Her voice came through with sharp-edged clarity.

*'I learned belly dancing at Uni in Sydney, you know? There were evening classes and I took them. I just wanted to earn some pocket money – I danced at a Turkish restaurant near where I lived.'*

*'Wasn't it difficult to learn?'*

The South African's voice, too, was clear – not as loud as Sarah's, but every word was there.

Sarah laughed. *'My degree is Creative Arts. Dance is one of the options, so I'm not a complete bimbo at it.'*

She wasn't a bimbo at this either, thought Dan. Her creative arts teachers should see what she was creating here.

*'No, I could see that. You're very good, from what I saw.'*

Dorp didn't sound particularly sincere: but that was fine. As long as he bothered to pay Sarah lying compliments, she was probably getting somewhere.

*'I'll have this aubergine thingie, please. Aren't you having a starter, Jerry?'*

*'I never have starters. You go ahead. Just a bottle of mineral water for me. You have some wine?'*

*'Oh Jerry, be fair. I can't drink unless you do!'*

*'I don't drink.'*

*'No starters, no drinks. God, you're very hard on yourself. Just have a little drink, go on. I mean I'm not what you call a drinker myself, but I can do with a glass of wine now and then.'*

*'Just a little glass, then. You're a temptress, Sarah, you know that?'*

Dorp ordered the wine. He sounded reluctant, tense. Was Sarah overdoing it? She was acting like a daughter teasing Daddy – fine, so long as she was right about the pitch of Dorp's interest in her.

Dan took a book from his pocket and opened it. He could hardly sit in this bar for hours staring into space, and the last thing he wanted was to be buzzed by squadrons of hookers. When he tuned back into the dinner going on downstairs Dorp was drawing comparisons between their respective native lands.

*'Course you've got no blacks, not to speak of, that's your great advantage. Thank God for it, little girl. Just thank God for it. White South Africa can only survive on intimidating the blacks. As soon as we stop doing that . . .'*

Dan's mind supplied the finger drawn across the Adam's apple.

*'Have some more?'*

What was she offering? He heard the faint plock-plock of liquid passing from bottle into glass.

*'I shouldn't. Gave up drinking ten years ago, quack's instructions.'*

*'Oh, a couple of glasses won't do you any harm. Cheers. Now look here, Mr Dorp, sir. All we've been talking about is myself. What about you?'*

*'Oh, well, there's nothing to tell.'*

*'Rubbish! Of course there is. You're, well, a little bit older than me, am I right? Well then, you've been leading a life of fantastic interest, haven't you?'*

*'Not really.'*

*'Look, I'll help you gently along, okay? Are you married?'*

*'Yes, if you want to know. She's called Jean, English family.'*

*'And I reckon Jean doesn't understand you, does she, Jerry?'*

*'What do you mean?'*

*'Well, she stays at home and minds the kiddies, while you go out into the big bad world. She can't have an inkling of all the problems you meet up with.'*

Sarah really was fantastic. It was like listening to one of those personal problem radio shows, where the presenters are so skilled in drawing intimate revelations from their callers.

*'She doesn't get the chance to understand me.'*

*'Why not? Don't you talk to her?'*

*'Not about my work.'*

*'Why not about your work in particular?'*

*'Because my work is . . . well, it's classified. Secret. It's government work.'*

*'What? Secret even from your wife? Oh, come on! Nothing's that secret.'*

Again, Dan caught the plocky flow of more wine being poured. Dorp must have raised his glass, because Dan could hear him gulping wine in the middle of his next sentence. For a man who had not drunk alcohol for a decade, he was going some. Dan slipped the tape machine into record.

*'Well this* is *that secret.'*

*'Tell me.'*

*'Nope, can't.'*

*'Oh go on, I love secrets.'*

*'It's just buying things. Er – excuse me.'*

His tone had changed, his voice was being directed away from the mike. Who was he talking to? Must be the waiter. It was as if he had been a fish lightly hooked. He was just about to land slap in the bottom boards of the boat, when he'd spat out the fly just in time and plopped back into the water. He was saying, *'Another bottle of this, please, and – Ah! The food!'*

There was a hiatus in which plates and cutlery were the only noise. Dan stared at the page in front of him, but he had stopped following the printed lines. He was absorbed in the radio drama playing between his ears.

Sarah cast her line again. *'You were saying? Just – um – buying things?'*

This time Dorp seemed to miss her lure. He suddenly snatched at an earlier piece of bait. *'No, Sarah, as you so rightly surmise, Jean doesn't understand me. You know, she keeps wanting me to go into politics! Me! What a joke. I hate all politicians. They are treacherous, self-regarding shits. Oh, most of them have their foreign bank accounts, ready for the day when the black tide overruns us. Insurance, they call it. Bastards.'*

*'Perhaps she wants to see more of you at home. Less of this foreign travel?'*

*'She couldn't give a warthog's bollock for me, or my career. It's her father she listens to, the great Sir Sidney. He's a bigtime industrialist, used to be in politics until the National Party pinched his seat. He's all for selling out to the ANC, and he thinks I could be his mouthpiece. I'm a good Afrikaner boy, see? The Afrikaner only listens to his own kind, never to the bloody British. Anyway, I told her where to stick that idea.'*

*'Don't you love her?'*

*'We've been married fifteen years. What do you think?'*

*'Don't you even have a – a good sex life?'*

*'Sex? She probably has. Not with me. I go away, d'you see? I'm away a lot. But I don't know who she ruts with, and I don't care. Bitch.'*

*'Why do you stay together, then?'*

But the question was not answered, and conversation lapsed for a moment. With no visual clues Dan struggled to interpret the signals he was getting. He heard background murmur, of course, and then, straining, he picked out something which he assumed to be Dorp chewing his steak. The noise was a squelch, like boots walking across a saltmarsh.

*'Sarah, would you excuse me for a moment?'*

There was some disturbance, a rattle of steel and tableware, and then a further period of nothing bar the background effects. Dan became aware of something else, an underlying, faint but rapid thudding which, now that he thought about it, he realized had been there in the background throughout. It was the beating of Sarah's pulse. Hearing this so intimately, Dan suddenly felt close to Sarah. Plugged in to the sound of her blood pumping he felt especially privileged, a receiver of secrets.

*'Dan? Dan, can you hear me?'* She was whispering. *'Dan, he's gone to the toilet. Jesus, what a shithead, no wonder his wife hates him. This feels stupid talking at nothing. I wish it was two-way. Dan, how'm I doing? I thought we'd nearly got him opened up for a moment a while back, but then the fucking food came. He's getting nice and pissed though. If I can keep pouring it down him I live in hopes. He's coming back – oh no, he's talking to the maître d'. He's giving him some money. Now he really is coming back. He's stopped to talk to the wine waiter. I think he's ordered another bottle of wine. God, we haven't finished number two yet. Here he comes. Stay tuned.'*

For a non-drinker Dorp was suddenly putting away encouraging quantities of alcohol. His speech was getting slurred as he ranted about the political state of Southern Africa, how the ANC was getting the upper hand everywhere and the black states bordering South Africa were arming themselves, ready to sweep in at the first sign of weakness. Sarah said little, she just let it flow. Dan could hear the pauses Dorp made as he stopped talking to drink before resuming the diatribe. But then it stopped as suddenly as it began.

*'All right, change the subject. Tell me something else, Susan, I mean, Sarah.'*

*'Well, Jerry, I still want to know what this wonderful secret work of yours is. Jean might not be interested, but I am, you know. I'll bet it's something naughty to do with keeping out the blacks, isn't it?'*

*'Shhh! I can't go into this here. Not here, in public. All very hush-hush secret. Tell you what. Let's go somewhere private, know what I'm saying? 'S a terrific secret, what I do, state secret. Needs private accommodation. You'll be impressed, promise you that. Very impressed with Jerry. Privacy of my room. Come on now, you can bring your drink, order puddings in the room 'f you want. Let's go, hey?'*

*'Your room? But you're not staying here, Jerry! This is the Sheraton, you're at the Pera Palas!'*

*'Hate the fucking Pera Palas.'*

*'Maybe so, but that's where you're staying.'*

*'Not tonight. I'm staying here tonight. Just booked a room, 's matter of fact. You're staying here with me. We're going to do some very secret things together, whisper great secrets of the universe, jus' you and me. What d'you say?'*

*'Well I say – What do I say? I say yes, of course! Do you want to go now?'*

Dan thought, she ought to be pushing him harder. Suddenly she had become submissive, unsure, innocent. It made her more vulnerable – suppose he was the kind who liked to beat women.

Now Dan was hearing nothing but microphone noise,

as Sarah rose. Dan switched off the receiver, looked at his watch and got up. Almost quarter past eleven. The bar had filled up in the last hour, with the majority of drinkers clustered near the windows to admire the spectacular night view of the Bosporus. Dan moved out towards the lifts. It took him a second or two to orient himself back to reality after concentrating so hard on that unreal audio world of the transmitting microphone. He was above them, that's right, and they would be going further down to whatever room Dorp had reserved for his pleasure. He had to see where they went, otherwise they might go out of range of the transmitter and the whole set-up would be wasted.

There was one lift standing ready. He hopped inside and pressed the button for the next floor down. Just as the door jerked and began closing it slammed open again. An expensively dressed Turkish couple stepped inside. Dan willed the doors closed again, but Otis doors cannot be hurried. A cry from the corridor, and now the Turkish man jabbed the DOORS OPEN button with a stubby thumb. Another couple who looked like tourists joined them. The Turkish man looked up interrogatively.

'Ground, please.'

The Turk echoed the request. 'Ground.' He pressed that button.

Dan looked at the Turk properly for the first time, and realized to his horror who he was looking at. It was Nazım Ali Bey, General Manager of Anatolian

Airways. Dan swivelled away to avert his face. He should have taken the stairs. Had he been seen? No, Nazım Ali would have said something. It didn't matter about the girl who was with him – Dan didn't recognize her. She was beautiful and she wasn't Nazım Ali's wife, naturally.

Dan drummed his fingers against the steel walls. He would never know which room Dorp and Sarah were going to unless he could actually follow them. He needed to see them leave the dining room.

The lift started down at last. The passengers stood awkwardly, looking anywhere but at each other. Dan was thankful for this norm of lift protocol. Nazım Ali would have taken his presence in, of course, but he would merely see a European in glasses, before looking away. Dan knew if he was subjected to any closer examination at this distance, he would easily be recognized.

The doors opened at the restaurant level. Nazım Ali and his floozy stood their ground. So did the tourists. Dan, keeping his head down, stepped self-consciously out, but he couldn't stop himself from looking back at the last minute into Nazım Ali's face. The General Manager was staring directly at Dan. And, as the lift doors came together like two steel eyelids, the eyes of Nazım Ali Bey opened wide in disbelief.

It was because Dan had moved, of course. He remembered the wisdom of the crocodile: you recognize your prey a hundred times more sharply when it moves.

But it couldn't be helped. Nazım Ali might think he had seen a dead man walk, but more important matters were afoot. And soon enough, the attention of Nazım Ali's eyes and hands would be directed elsewhere.

Outside the restaurant there was no sign of either Dorp or Sarah. Stupid girl, why hadn't she given him more time, gone to the lavatory or something? He looked in through the door to the restaurant, which was slowly emptying.

He ran down a flight of stairs to the floor below and hunted along the featureless corridor. Then he tried the next floor and the next, all of which looked identical. His heart was galloping now, as he found no trace of Dorp and Sarah, so had no way of knowing into which room they had gone. Dorp was drunk, and he was three times stronger than Sarah. If he should find the transmitter . . .

For the first time since he'd left the bar he remembered the receiver, and switched it on, putting the light headphones back to his ears. There was a fizzing sound, then he could hear intermittent voices and laughter, and what seemed like a quick series of percussive shocks. But the reception was so poor it could have been almost anything – coughing, a door banging. Then suddenly he heard Sarah clearly. *'You can't do that! I'm your daughter, remember?'*

And Dorp's rough reply. *'I can, if I'm your father.'* And then more spluttering, which could have been interference or laughter. Dan turned his sound up and winced at a series of deafening microphone crumps.

He moved up the stairs, seeking better reception. In the stairwell itself there was none at all, and on the floor above it was faint. That meant he was moving away from them. There was a loud hum, under which he just made out a few confusing words.

'*... this is going to be the saving ... oh, I like that, that's the sign of a nice man ... yes, but how is it ... no, stop that, don't do that ... I'm not listening ... don't you want to? I really think ... tell me all about that deal, I mean I really wanted to ...*'

Sarah's voice – what he could hear of her – sounded calm, sweet and teasing, while Dorp's replies were virtually incomprehensible. These crumbs of the conversation came tantalizingly through, as if from some frantic kitchen filled with the sounds of sizzling and boiling.

Only once, in a sudden explosion, the South African came over clearly – a violent, signal-distorting bull roar. *'I'M GOING TO TRY TO BUY THAT STUFF, FOR CHRIST'S SAKE!'*

Dan ran down two flights, but could hear nothing there at all. His receiver was hissing permanently, and what voices there were could be heard only faintly. Perhaps the batteries were going flat. He switched off and changed them. But when he reassembled the apparatus he could hear nothing at all.

It was hopeless, he'd lost them. He'd not the first idea where they were. Not daring to think about what might be going on between Sarah and Dorp, he descended to the reception hall and sat down to wait.

Twenty minutes came to an end, during which his eyes met every lift. He forced himself to stop doing it and walked around, inspecting the glass cabinet of tourist souvenirs, the coffee-shop menu, the English and German paperbacks displayed in a revolving rack. He looked out at the night, a wide swathe of badly kept grass and the Republic Boulevard beyond.

He tried to quell himself into complete stillness. It was a fetish, a discipline with him, which he had learned in dentists' waiting rooms and crowded London tube trains, to gag the rising voice of panic. He sent every muscle in his body to sleep, working on them in groups – feet, calves, thighs and so on up to the neck and face. Oddly, it was often the face muscles which were the hardest to put under.

Dan had attained a satisfactory depth, almost a trance, when Sarah hurtled into the marble lobby. Aware at first only of a scuffling disturbance at his back, he was slow to respond. The next thing, she had thrown her arms about him and, in a dancer's effusion of relief, hung suspended from his neck while he revolved her slowly through three hundred and sixty degrees.

'Did you hear it, Dan? God, it was marvellous. He told me the whole bloody thing, from beginning to end, and then he passed out.'

# 24

Justin was in the Consulate chapel, praying.

When he'd first come to Istanbul he had loved the chapel. It was reassuring and familiar in the midst of an alien culture. It had straw-seated chairs, dust-puffing hassocks and brass flower vases. Its windows were leaded squares in dilute shades: rose-pink, lime and watery blue.

As a place of prayer it was close to his ideal. While muffled traffic churned away beyond the compound wall and the wind freshened the trees in the Consulate garden, here the protective force of stillness repelled intrusion. It was, he'd thought, a perfect trap for contemplation.

But things had changed. In his head they had changed, and the difference affected everything.

Now he could hear a continual background of noise, a buzzing and a bustling, like a cocktail party of his enemies in the next room. It angered and frustrated him. Tranquillity had died, and he had been born again in anger. He had been placed on war readiness.

There was a conspiracy afoot, and only he knew. Only he could do anything about it. His enemies whispered of it, planned for it, always just out of earshot, always in the next room. Yet he knew what it was. They wanted to foment war and so destroy the earth. And at the centre of their plans had been the late Dan Barry. John had been feeding him the details ever since that first, mind-ramming vision on Patmos. John did not talk in the poetic obscurity of the Book of Revelation. To suit an age of monosyllabic news values, John spoke like a tabloid newspaper.

*Love is a dodo, Juss.*

The coming war, he meant, would extinguish the world of love. So must Justin jettison what he had learned as a priest's tradecraft: self-deprecation, love for thy neighbour, patience, charity. Sometimes he was in a savage mood. He had given Mrs Harrison hell over her botched flower arrangement which had fallen over during Divine Service on Sunday, spilling water and blooms across the communion table. Eileen Harrison was the wife of the British vice-consul, a meek woman. He told her she was useless at flowers, and why didn't she concentrate on things she *was* good at, like collecting up the hymn books after Divine Service? Her face had twisted up like that of a whipped dog's, and he saw how necessary it was to despise a stupid, weak person. And how satisfying.

He didn't wish it. He wished he could have love spilling out, love to spare and to scatter promiscuously. He would like to have seen the sun shining even out of dull, pathetic Eileen Harrison's buttonholes.

*Can't afford it, mate. Chuck it. Love is crap, and it's each for himself. That's the norm now. New age, see?*

In this new state of alert, he was under orders. He was instructed to concentrate all of himself, like some laser beam, on the new source of power, on Lena. Then the beam could become a straw through which to suck back to himself hot pulses of energy, *dot . . . dash . . . dot*, energy needed to generate the anger and to carry out his mission. At any previous stage of his life he would have troubled his conscience endlessly over the way he spoke to Mrs Harrison. But now he did these things by direction: it was not a question of choice. He was *ordered.*

The back-room clergyman may need diplomatic skills, but Justin had been recruited into the secret soldiery. He had an encrypter fitted inside him, the kind that all special agents need to speak to their Control. The black box inside was safe. It was proof from the shock of revelation – indeed, it was charged up by it, like a dry cell battery. He used it more and more, seized as he was with the sense of being in training for a great spiritual commando mission.

*Zap! Pow! Biff! That's my boy, Juss. Knee in the crotch, don't ease up, boot in the ribs, slug between the eyes. Keep weaving, that's it, ducking and diving. That's IT!*

His coach was pleased with him, with his preparation and his commitment. The pride grew inside him, like a sweet tumour. He knew it was not purposeless, but whatever it was designed for remained in the hand of God. When the purpose was revealed, he would be ready.

A cough exploded drily behind his right ear.

'Padre? Could I have a word?'

Justin swung round. It took him some seconds to adjust to the idea of human contact.

'Who are you?'

'Name's Craike, British Ministry of Defence. May I have just a few minutes of your time?'

Craike sidled into a pew on the opposite side of the narrow aisle from the chaplain. He looked straight ahead, rather than at Justin, sweeping the altar, the candlesticks, the embroidered cloths with his cold eyes.

'Defence?'

There was a wild look in this big, red-haired padre's eyes, a match-flare of anticipation.

Craike looked around him. The polish-scented chapel felt impossibly alien. Too large, too public.

'Is there anywhere more private?'

'Nobody comes in here at this time, only me. No one's listening, no one except –'

He twitched his eyebrows upwards and smiled thinly.

'How can I help?'

'It's about a man I'm looking for, an Englishman, name of Dan Barry.'

A second match flared in the parson's eyes.

'Dan Barry? He was murdered in London last week.'

'Did you know him?'

'No, not exactly. I knew *of* him . . .'

'Padre, I must ask you to treat what I am going to tell you with the utmost confidence.'

'Why?'

'Because I have reason to think that Dan Barry is a very important criminal, part of a frightening conspiracy to import drugs and weapons into the UK. A conspiracy, if you like, against the fabric of our way of life. We are trying to catch him.'

'But Barry's dead.'

'No, he's here in Istanbul. Some Dutch kid spotted him over in the Old City. He's with a junkie dancer, an Australian girl. Now, the point is, you were, were you not, asked to take charge of his possessions, pending identification of a next-of-kin?'

Justin was nodding his head repeatedly. 'Yes, I was. I have them, I . . .'

'I want access to them. There may be important evidence.'

Justin's head arrested itself in the middle of a nod. The process of thought which had animated it seemed to freeze, and his whole manner changed. From being slightly fussed at the disturbance to his devotions, he suddenly appeared defensive, bland, inscrutable. Craike went on. 'Where have you got them? I'd only need perhaps an hour, two at most.'

'Mr – er – Craike, wasn't it? You'll have to let me think about this. I mean, I can't just let you rifle through all his stuff, not just like that. Wouldn't you need police permission or something?'

'I'm asking for *your* permission, you've got the things. I'm sure most of it's innocuous, but there's just the odd chance of a material discovery. I would expect a man of the cloth to have some sensitivity towards crimes of this kind, you know – drugs, violence.'

'Well, I am sensitive to those.'

Craike thought he saw a cunning look appear on the padre's face. Had he underestimated Fuller? He'd had Jenkinson check out the man's file at Church House, and it turned out there'd been some sob-story about his last job, up in the English Midlands. Had an emotional breakdown over a female parishioner. It sounded like he'd be a pushover. Craike hardened his voice.

'Look, Reverend, we are a hard-working and busy department and we can't afford the luxury of doubts and uncertainties. We want to nail this crook Dan Barry, and we shall do so, with or without your help.'

'What will you do with him?'

'Wait till he's next in London and pick him up. He'll be jailed for a very long time.'

'And he's a – a dealer in drugs and weapons, you said?'

'He's a courier, he used his job with the airline as cover. He's not the big fish. He's a sprat, but a knowledgeable one. We want to know what he knows.'

Craike could clearly see how Fuller was trembling. They both rose and faced each other. The priest seemed possessed by a powerful emotion, which was out of all proportion to what he was being asked to do.

'I may very well agree with your request, Mr Craike,' he said, tugging his earlobe as if this might switch off his shaking. 'Still, I must think about it. I shall sleep on it overnight.'

'You can call me at the Consulate, or come in and visit. I shall be there between nine and ten, I have an office.'

Craike pivoted on his heel and left.

Dan Barry was alive!

It was unbearable knowledge. How could he continue? While he knew Barry was dead, he could rejoice in the knowledge. Lena was free. He had wrestled – like Jacob with the angel – he had *fought down* his love for Lena. It had been a test, he knew that. A test which would teach him to give up his life in return for hers. Then she could be free. But Dan Barry's death, too, had been a part of the plan, or so he'd thought. Lena could not give herself to the world, to do her work of saving the world, of beating the conspiracy, if he were alive. So Dan Barry could not be alive, if she was to fulfil her destiny!

Justin's mind seethed. It was a beehive knocked over, aswarm with fear, pain and rebellion. He knew he was being told something now. Now was coming the call to action, and he didn't want to go. He felt the knotted stomach of the soldier, crouching in the trench with a silver whistle between his lips. He clenched his fists, shut his eyes, squeezed every muscle in his abdomen. He was being licked all over by fire.

*You scared, Justin my old son? What a turn up! I thought you was so big and strong. Go on! Get up there.*

*Kick the shit out of them.* John's voice was more than usually brutal.

'Yes, I'm scared. I wish the cup would pass.'

*But it can't pass, you know that. How can it pass? You're the one, you're elected, you've drawn the short straw.*

'Yes. To what?'

*Remember what I taught you? Forget yourself. Act. Do unto others before they do unto you. That's how you got to think.*

'I can't . . . I've lost the technique, I've forgotten how.'

*Nar, you ain't, Justin. You just making that up. I know you, boy. Do it. Do the business!*

Justin felt he was reedy and feeble – hardly a vehicle for world-shaking actions. His face had screwed up, and glistened with tears. His mouth was dragged down at the sides. He dragged in a great suck of air and opened his throat.

'BUT WHAT? WHAT MUST I DO?'

The voice reverberated in the chapel. It was terrible even to the ears of the man who spoke, like the howl of an Oedipus as he puts out his eyes. And at once the background noises, which he interpreted as static or atmospheric interference churning in his head, stopped. The calm was absolute, and he stood astounded by it. For the first time since he'd stood on that outcrop on Patmos, peace had settled inside him.

He stood for a long time. Later he realized he had been receiving messages via the encryption machine inside him. When he moved again his orders were all complete. They had come through in such glass-clear terms.

He left the chapel and, passing through the heavy iron gate of the compound which housed the Consulate, waved cheerfully to the two security guards. It took him ten minutes to walk briskly back to his flat, humming one of his favourite hymns, 'Rock of Ages'. His head was clear now, clear of confusing signals, misconnections and short-circuits. There was one bright path ahead of him, and all he had to do was follow it.

At the flat he quickly packed a small bag for overnight. He unscrewed the sweet jar where he kept housekeeping money and emptied it on to the bed. He filled his pockets with it. Then he opened a desk drawer and took out writing paper, envelopes and postage stamps, which he stuffed into the bag.

There was one more thing. In his spare bedroom was the pile of boxes packed with Dan Barry's possessions. On top of these was a towel wrapped up to make a bundle. Slowly, he unwrapped the gun which he had taken from Lena's refrigerator.

In the Old City, Justin found a small hotel called Merhaba. It was so seedy that no one would think of looking for him here. He asked among the knot of young men who sat around in the narrow hallway whether he could see a room.

The first he was shown had no table, but the second would do. It had an adequate chair and table where he could do his writing. He said he would take it.

When the boy had gone, Justin sat at the table and began writing. He wrote for sixteen hours, taking breaks only to sleep and to buy more paper.

At last it was done. He bundled the pages into a manila envelope and, after copying the address from his notebook, went out to the Yeni Postahane.

Lena and Georgette always took breakfast at a rustic café far up the beach, where only the most intrepid of the package tourists penetrated. Here the tea was a little less bitter than usual, and they served wonderful *börek* – envelopes of crisp, thin pastry filled with cheese. The two women would sit under the straw awning for most of the morning, reading, talking or simply looking out to sea, while the children ran between the café and the water.

There was a morning, about the time when Lena's ankle began to bear her weight without causing too much pain, when a boy came running towards them along the dusty track from town. Lena recognized Yusuf, the son of the *pansiyon* where they were staying. He was panting hard by the time he stood at their table.

'*Affedersin, Bayan* Lena. *Size bir mektup.*' He held out a large brown envelope, addressed in a sprawling hand which Lena did not recognize. She took it and weighed it in her hand. Georgette leaned forward.

'What on earth can it be?'

'Istanbul postmark, anyway.'

'Well go on, open it. I can't bear the suspense.'

Lena ripped open the flap and drew out a thick sheaf, half of which was letter paper, the other half sheets of lined A4. Both sides of every sheet were covered with the same rapid, untidy screed.

Lena scanned the first page back and front. 'I can't make it out. It's mostly wavy lines. It's like a stage letter. You know, designed to look all right from a distance, but when you see it close it's not real writing at all.'

She handed the first page to Georgette, while she hunted to the last page, looking for a name. 'It's not signed.'

She looked at Georgette, who did not look up. Her face was set in concern.

'What do you make of it, Georgie? Is it some kind of joke?'

Georgette took the rest of the pages from Lena's fingers and looked through them.

'If it is, it's in extremely bad taste. I can read some of it, just. It's all supposed to mean something, but it's the ravings of a madman. It's in English, I can tell that much. Seems to be written in some incredibly high-flown, apocalyptic prose. But who can it be from? Oh my God, look at this.'

She proffered a sheet, pointing to a passage where the writing was a little clearer. Lena read:

Dan Barry has returned from the dead, he has been seen here in Istanbul. I know this is incredible, but I have been told this by a man. A man from London who is hunting him. This man is an instrument, an unthinking vessel. He pretends to have his purposes, but he has not. I know the purpose. I have the knowledge and I am seeking the day when I will stand against Dan Barry face to face. He will not come between you and your mission. I must not, and nor must he!

'Someone,' Georgette said, 'thinks you have a mission to this world.'

'But all this about Dan being alive. Oh Georgie, I don't know how to *deal* with this.'

'Look, it's obviously a random loony. Someone's read about the whole story in the press, made something insane of it and felt they must write you.'

'But how did they know where I am?'

'The library?'

'They never give addresses out, it's security.'

'Then who *might* have?'

'I haven't an idea. The priest might have told somebody. It's someone who knows me who wrote this. I mean, look at this.'

She pointed out a sentence written in capitals:

BY ALLOWING ME TO LOVE YOU YOU HAVE LENT ME ENERGY FROM YOUR BOUNDLESS SUPPLY.

'So who loves you, Lena? Is anyone hot for you at the moment?'

'Don't be absurd, Georgie. It's so dumb.'

Lena stared at the sea. The letter writer talked about a man from London, who was hunting Dan.

'Georgie, I've just realized that this "man" from London must be Craike.'

'Who?'

'Craike. That Brit, the one who – the one who found me at the ruins. He was looking for Dan's associates, or people he said were his associates. If Dan *was* alive, he would know, wouldn't he? And I also think whoever wrote this wants to harm Dan!'

'Darling, Dan *can't* be harmed any more. Here, let me take that. It's shit.'

Georgie reached for the papers, but Lena held them out of her grasp.

'No, listen. Okay, they said Dan was dead. But it was an explosion. There was nothing left to identify! Suppose it was someone else and not Dan that died?'

'It's no use torturing yourself like this, Lena. Dan is dead, you've got to accept it.'

'That's what I did accept. Now I'm not so sure. I want to read this letter properly.'

With a sigh the older woman picked up her book while Lena went through the letter, page by page. She took a pencil out of her bag and began underlining words. Georgette was reminded of her husband poring over ancient texts. The area of modern Turkey is the oldest archaeological source of written texts – in fact, most people assume that writing was invented there – and when Con occasionally had Hittite or similar documents to decipher he worked on them the same way.

Suddenly, Lena threw down her pencil. 'Georgie, I've got to go back to Istanbul.'

'What are you talking about?'

'Georgie, listen to this. It says:

. . . the storm of love which I have inside me is transformed by Divine grace into a rage of hatred for the man who stands in your way. Dan Barry has returned for his punishment. I am his murderer. In the language of the detectives, I have the means and the motive, and all I seek now is the opportunity. He is already dead in the eyes of the world, he has still to die in the eye of God.'

She got up. 'Georgie, please! If I go back, will you stay down here and look after Annabel just for a couple of days?'

'Lena, what's got into you? You can't take this piece of raving nonsense seriously.'

'Georgie, I'll be back in two days. Now, please. Say you will.'

Two hours later, Lena was on her way to Antalya airport.

# 25

Yakup yawned mucously, reached under the sheet and scratched his belly. Then he rolled over and tugged the pillow into his face. He wished it was his darling Gül's body. Boss had made him send Gül away to their village for a week or two, with the boy. Yakup regretted it. He'd enjoyed having the priest's house to himself at first, but he was already getting tired of eating in sandwich bars, and he was missing the sex.

Maybe he should suggest to Boss that they go down to the *kerhane* tonight and have some women. Boss liked Yakup to go with him when he went there. And, as he paid for the two of them, Yakup was very happy to oblige. But then he remembered, Boss was down at Polonezköy today, not to be disturbed. Tomorrow was the big day, the Boss was resting up.

Yakup looked at his watch, and yawned again. Nearly five o'clock, and the afternoon was gone. Maybe he'd go down to the whorehouses himself later and, just for once, spend his own money. Boss said he'd get a big present after tomorrow, so why not? He rolled out of bed, pulled his trousers on, pushed his feet into some slippers and wandered outside.

The puppy greeted him with an exaggerated display of falling around. Normally Yakup kicked the creature, but today he felt tenderly towards it. It was all he had left of his family for now and he crouched to fondle its ears for a few moments, before opening up the church.

He entered the gloomy place. It was not, to Yakup's mind, a place in which to worship Allah. The stone walls were clothed neither with tiles nor even plaster, the floor was cold and lacked carpets. The mosque, now, was warm and homelike, even the grand ones like the *Suleymaniye* had a welcoming feeling. This place scared him. Perhaps that was why the Christians no longer used it. Perhaps it was inhabited by a *jinnee*.

Nervously he approached the big yellow bell-thing which stood in the middle of the church and put his palm flat against the side of it. It seemed to radiate a slight heat. Yakup fancied there was something alive in there. He hardly dared speculate what it might be like, but he had a vague notion of some jelly-like spawn of indefinite malignancy. He shuddered. When it was exposed to the air, what would it grow into?

Though he did quite a lot of Blanchard's driving, delivering people and packages to the airport, collecting them, Yakup could never form a clear picture of Boss's affairs. The flask, he had been told, contained some stuff for use in a weapon, and was very secret. Some men were competing to buy it. Yakup could see the round, lead plugs where special equipment had been used to drill into the side of the flask. The material was so vile you couldn't just open the lid and scoop some of it out to check the quality.

Tomorrow Boss would learn which of the men was

ready to pay the highest price. Yakup did his sweeping, then found some chairs and arranged them in the way Boss wanted, in front of the altar. He also found a small table which he placed in the centre of the circle of chairs. His finishing touch was a personal one. He ran into the house and doubled back with a bunch of chrysanthemums in a glass vase, bought that morning at the *Balik Pazarı*. He placed the flowers carefully in the centre of the table, then locked the great oak door and returned to the house.

He sat down, flipped on the television and lit a cigarette. It was American comedy. There was a talking horse in it, and Yakup watched for three or four minutes. Then he switched it off and stared at the wall.

He glanced at his watch, in a decisive manner. He washed at the sink, put on a shirt over his vest, wet his hair and ran a comb through it. With his appearance put to rights he secured the iron gate of the church compound, and set off around the side of the steep hill towards the Yüksek Kaldırım, off which ran the street of whorehouses. He did not notice the two young men who stepped from a doorway as he passed and sauntered along in his wake.

When Yakup had first arrived here from his village, before he'd even sent for Gül to follow him, he had found the street of whorehouses the most amazing of all the wonders in this wonderful city. Yes, the interiors of the great mosques were staggering in their size and beauty. But he could imagine a great mosque in his mind. The cars, the crowds of people, the glass buildings had all been imaginable. Only this had been unimaginable.

His knowledge of females, after all, had been confined to his mother and sisters, and to sweet little Gül – all good Turkish women and wives. True, there had been fat Yäsemin, who for a few *lira* would agree to go behind the village granary and let you play with her titties while she pulled you off. But how can you compare a single turnip to a truck-load of melons?

Yakup walked through the iron gates of the closed, cobbled street. It sloped gently down ahead of him for about a hundred metres before reaching a dead end. Along its whole length a crowd of men milled, their heads swivelling this way and that as they appraised the whores on view. On their faces played all the variations between jaw-hanging lechery and prurient disgust.

Yakup always walked slowly down one side, looking with care into each of the plate-glass windows. Behind these, under flaring neon lights, was the incomparable display of fruits. Every type of flesh was here. There was the white and the muddy, the black and the blonde. There were the hairy and the shaved, the fat-thighed and the bony-shinned. There were some whose breasts showed up delicate as peeled grapes and others with bubs like puddings.

They wore incredible, provocative underwear and they made kissing movements with their lips at him as he passed. Even an old hand like Yakup would find himself reaching the bottom of the street in a ferment of confused, drunken desire. He had to restrain himself then, because he must still trek back up the other side before he allowed himself to choose. He was meticulous about this, viewing all the available goods before he would buy.

He found himself first attracted by a thin little girl, dark and sad-looking. She wore black lace panties, and a brassiere that was a size too big for her pinched and tender breasts. She looked up at him with a yearning that was almost irresistible. The poor little soul seemed quite miserable, and Yakup wanted to cheer her up. Perhaps she hadn't had a client all day. It would make Yakup feel good to be her first.

But then, in a house a little further along, his eyes fell on a well-filled blonde in a fancy corset. She had vivid red lips that glistened passionately, and a great wobbly bottom. This she showed to him by deliberately bending over, and then peeping around the side so he didn't miss her heavily kohled and rolling eyes. He almost barged in through the door there and then. But he forced himself to stick to his custom of rigorous window-shopping before making his decision. By the time Yakup stood again at the top of the street, it was a straight choice between the two girls – the little waif or the big bum. He hesitated, pondering the dilemma. Now that he'd controlled the first rush of lust it was such a pleasant luxury, this sensuous debate. He didn't mind if it went on for a little while longer.

But Yakup's mind was destined never to be made

up. The pair of young men who had shadowed him all the way from the church now stepped in. One stood in front of him, obstructing his view of the street. He asked politely for a light and, as Yakup was pulling the matchbox from his shirt pocket, the other slapped him with a black-jack between shoulder and neck so hard that he staggered sideways, unable to help himself. His eyes fogged and, barely conscious of anything but the throbbing pain, he was hustled back to the street and into a taxi.

The milling crowds had not even noticed. They came and went, just as they always did, with eyes only for the purchasable women.

Dan came to the church early the next morning, so early that only a few bakers were awake, and a barber or two, sweeping out ready for the early shaving trade.

Sarah had clung to him as he left, like a child tugging at her father. Dan had wanted to go out before she awoke, but he had needed the alarm clock, and its shrill had brought her out of the bedroom just as he was pulling on his clothes.

'Give me some money. I'll have to score today. I don't think I can get through otherwise.'

'There are other ways, Sarah. Distract yourself.'

He was in the bathroom, carefully shaving off his moustache. His reply, semi-distracted, sounded so feeble, so schoolmarmish. He towelled his face, rubbed his upper lip with his fingers and felt better. He'd hated the moustache.

‘No good, Dan. I’ll just have to score, no two ways. But I’ll be all right. When this is over I’ll get a cure. I promise I will. You’ll take me away, won’t you, Dan?’

‘Yes,’ he said, ‘I’ll take you away.’

Yesterday in the Grand Bazaar he’d sold Ted Mills’s Amex card for a wad of banknotes. From his wallet he extracted a few large ones which he put on the table. He held her tightly for a few seconds. Then he quickly finished dressing, collected the backpack containing his equipment and slipped into the grey dawn.

He stood beside the gate which Yakup had locked some nine hours earlier. He could not safely climb the gate itself, as it was topped with a vicious tangle of barbed wire. Instead he had prepared a grappling hook on the end of twenty feet of nylon climber’s rope. He slung the hook upwards. It clinked against the stone of the fifteen-foot wall and fell back. He slung again, and this time it sailed high and over, giving a more muffled sound as it struck the other side. He pulled the rope back until the hook caught firmly against the parapet and then, gripping the rope as tightly as the muscles in his hands could manage, he shinned to the top. He sat astride between jags of broken glass that had been concreted into the wall, and used the hook to lower his backpack to the other side. Then he threw the rope after it and, with a teeth-snapping jolt, dropped to the ground.

In a matter of minutes a weak dawn wash would begin to appear across the sky. He could hear from somewhere a diesel engine labouring up some narrow hill, and behind it the more distant susurration of traffic beside the waterfront. But the sounds of the night had all but used themselves up, while the coming day still held its peace.

As he straightened, he found something whimpering and wriggling around his legs. At first he couldn't make out what it was, then realized these were the attentions of a small black puppy. He spent a few moments petting the animal, then set off, the dog scuffling at his heels, to scout round the church. So far, he had neither seen nor heard a human being anywhere near the place. But to be safe, he wanted to be inside before it was properly light.

He had worked out yesterday how he was going to gain entry, but he hadn't been able to get very close, and wasn't absolutely sure it was feasible. The next few minutes would tell, one way or the other.

Between the church's tower and the perimeter wall stood a high tree. He saw with relief that he could reach the lowest branches, without even the help of the rope. This he coiled and slung over his shoulder, and jumped for the first branch.

He began to climb steadily. He hadn't done this since childhood, but the sensation was the same as he remembered. At first it was all effort, heaving yourself between the well-spaced lower branches. Gradually, as you got higher, the branches became more numerous and a feeling of ease, lightness and exhilaration grew. Finally, nearer the top, you came to the younger shoots. These were smaller and closer together, which cramped your progress as you struggled to find the best upward route, swaying more wildly with each step up.

He was into this last phase of his climb when he saw he was now opposite the belfry. He had come to the first really dangerous juncture in the day's work.

The church tower had a pointed slate roof which surmounted the bell platform. Three unglazed Gothic apertures looked out from the belfry itself, and his idea had been, from the tree, to sling the hook into the gutter which ran under the tower roof, swing across and then rope-climb into the belfry. It hadn't seemed too daunting when he had contemplated this from the ground. Now, at sixty or seventy feet up, it was frankly terrifying. He looked at the gutter. Nathan Blanchard had replaced all the church guttering early in the spring, and it seemed to be fixed on with strong brackets drilled into the stone. But everything depended on the standard of workmanship employed by Blanchard's builders.

The sky over the city was getting palpably lighter now, and he knew he must make up his mind to do it. He dangled the hook at the end of about ten feet of rope and swung it like a pendulum several times before propelling it up towards the sloping roof. It cracked against the slates and slid down, dropping back into space. Dan realized he was a little too high, and moved a few feet down the tree before trying again. This time the hook slotted neatly into the gutter. He pulled the rope taut and yanked hard. The gutter seemed firm enough. Without another thought he reached up the rope at full stretch and lifted himself out of the tree.

Dan tried to cushion his impact against the tower wall by meeting it with his feet, but his body twisted in the air and he crashed against the stonework sideways. The blow knocked his breath away and it took a moment before he could review his position. He was dangling by a rope from a fragile plastic gutter, and if he didn't act soon something would start to give. He twisted his body, trying to bring his feet back to the wall so that he could walk up it. But suddenly he became afraid that if he pushed out too far the hook might slip out of the gutter. So, in desperation, he started to pull himself up hand over hand.

It was really no further than the climb he had already made over the churchyard wall. But at this height from the ground the thing seemed ten times more difficult. However, he made five feet without too much effort when he heard a crack like a rifle-shot above him. Either the gutter brackets were beginning to loosen, or the guttering itself was starting to splinter.

He was still another five feet from the belfry aperture. With his arm muscles now screaming in pain he strained against the downward drag of his own weight. But he had swung round and was facing the wall again, so had a little help from his feet and knees scrabbling for purchase on the jutting, semi-dressed stonework.

The last eighteen inches of the climb were accompanied by more splintering sounds from above, but just before the hook broke through the guttering Dan got an arm over the parapet and let go of the rope. For a further moment he hung and then, with a climactic effort of will over physique, he hauled himself into the belfry and sank down, gulping air into his searing lungs.

He sprawled on a dried carpet of pigeon shit, looking up at the clapper of the bronze bell, dull and brushed with verdigris. He didn't care how long he lay there. His mind was possessed by something stronger and more paralysing than muscle relief. He felt his life had been reprieved, and he was simply enjoying the moment.

The ecstasy subsided, Dan turned over and got to his feet. The musculature in his arms ached and felt weak, but he was otherwise intact. He began to work his way cautiously down the spiral stair which led to the body of the church.

At one point in the stair a narrow slit in the stone wall gave him a view over the church as a whole. He could see the nave and most of the sanctuary. Looking at the yellow flask, standing so massive down below him in the centre of the nave, he felt a new kind of fear begin to creep over him.

He completed his descent of the stairs which came out through a doorway in the corner of the nave. He walked across to the flask, his padding footsteps echoing on the stone flags, and touched it with his fingertips. The knowledge of what it contained gave him a peculiar, prickling sensation. He looked around.

He saw Yakup's arrangement of chairs and the low table with flowers. Dan studied them. He looked under the table. He ran his fingers around the overhanging edge of the altar slab, he looked into the niches and folds of the carved relief in the base of the altar. There were many places where he could conceal his bug, but most were far from the meeting.

He finally settled on the bunch of chrysanthemums itself. They were held together by a rubber band, so that if he pushed his microphone pen into the middle of the bunch it was completely concealed, and yet remained right in the centre of the discussions – at least, as long as everyone sat in the circle of chairs.

Dan took his receiver up the spiral staircase as far as the slit-window which looked out over the church interior. He switched on, flipped the Sony to record and returned to the sanctuary, where from various standpoints he spoke extracts from Shakespeare and Wordsworth learned years ago at school. When he listened back to the recording through headphones the results were good enough, although heavily reverberant. It was the best he could hope for. He retired to the top of the tower and lay down again to rest.

Blanchard believed he had earned this moment at the sty of Mary-Bel, his favourite pig. He had been neglecting his darling, with so many preparations and arrangements to make. Now they were done, and this was the morning when he'd find out how much richer he was going to be. He was entitled to enjoy the anticipation.

It had taken far longer than he'd allowed for all three of his customers to test the flask. They'd used fancy drill-samplers attached to remote-control 'wheelbarrows' – the name used for their robots, originally developed by the British army for bomb disposal in Northern Ireland. All had finally found, after their governments' tests, that this was the finest Plutonium 239, as, of course, he'd told them they would. 239 was the nuclear equivalent of number 4 heroin – the best. He felt he was out of the woods at last. He was going to make a nuclear sale. He had entered the big league.

He leaned on the gate of the sty and whispered endearments to his pig. 'Hey, Mary-Bel! My Queen. Have some corn.'

He sent a cob of sweetcorn wheeling through the air for Mary-Bel to catch.

He had been slightly disappointed with the take-up of his offer. When he'd got the stuff from that Brit Morrison, paying out two million cash in Spain, he'd been told to sit tight, that the buyers would come to him. Only two of them did, one broker representing South America and an Irishman agenting for a middle-eastern government. In the end Morrison suggested he contact the South Africans in person. If they agreed to come, he'd have three bidders, a nice number to start with – easy to control, anyway, for a first sale. Blanchard's original fantasies had featured an entire room full of people bidding frenziedly for his merchandise. Yeah, well. Next time.

He held out a second cob, not throwing it this time. Mary-Bel looked at him and shifted her bloated hocks warily. He shook the offering. 'C'mon, Mary-Bel! C'mon, sweetheart. Come to Nathan. That's right. Come for your corn, that's my girl!'

Mary-Bel had heaved herself on to her trotters and was moving towards him, never letting her pinched little eyes leave his. Nathan was holding the cob out in front of his face, and she could see it clearly. She crossed the sty and lifted her forefeet, first one and then the other, on to the lowest bar of the gate. With a grunt of effort, the sow lifted herself up until her snout quested within a few inches of the cob in Nathan's fingers. He bent his head and kissed her full on the damp, tough, glistering cartilage of her snout, then dropped the corn into her open mouth.

'G'bye, honey-pie. See yah!' He turned and walked to the waiting taxi.

The first thing Dan knew about Blanchard's arrival at the church was his shouting, and rattling on the gate.

'Yakup, you dozy bastard! Where are you? Open the fucking gate!'

Dan jumped to his feet and looked out cautiously from the tower. He had only a partial view of the gate but glimpsed Nathan Blanchard's ponderous form dancing in agitation over his servant's absence.

So where *was* Yakup? Dan had checked regularly from the tower and had not seen the man all morning.

Nathan must have brought his own set of keys because he now let himself into the churchyard, and then into the church itself. Dan crept down the tower stairs and peeped through the slit-window. Nathan was moving around restlessly, checking the chairs and the plutonium flask. He was muttering furiously to himself. 'Thanks a lot. Yakup, you bastard. Fine fucking time to go AWOL.'

Later, again from the tower, Dan saw Nathan sit down outside in the sunshine, on the steps of the priest's house. He looked at his watch, waiting for his customers to show up, and wiped his forehead with the back of his hand.

Dorp arrived first, erect and tidy in a panama hat. He removed the hat to wipe his bald head with a handkerchief, and the sun's rays bounced off his pate. Dan remembered Sarah's description of Dorp as she had last seen him, trousers around his ankles, sitting on the bed crying for his mother. That night he had lost all control. The man had turned out to be completely incapable of handling alcohol, which was Dan and Sarah's good fortune. Fortunately, too, he would have had little memory of what had been said to Sarah – how, in between the grief about his unsatisfactory marriage, he had revealed his government's redoubled programme of plutonium acquisition, and all his hopes that this sale would go well. He was buying from some crazy American amateur, and he thought there were chances of taking the plutonium at a pretty good discount on normal black-market rates. This of course would do wonders for his career. It would make his mother so proud if he could get promotion, he told Sarah, as he forlornly dropped his pants.

In truth, when he did this, he had already plunged into the self-pitying phase. He hadn't the heart, and certainly not the stomach, for a sexual sequel to the evening's alcoholic excess. Instead he sat on the bed, with clothes encumbering his ankles, and dissolved into tears. His face was stretched into a mask of self-abhorrence, as he babbled of his mother back home in Stellenbosch, and of his sweet little teenage daughter too, dressed all in white to go to church. That was when Sarah left.

Two other men arrived at the church gate and were admitted. They came separately, but within a few minutes of each other. Outside the church Dan didn't get a clear view of either newcomer: they were concealed by the angle of the building. He heard Nathan's voice, though. 'Guys, we are all assembled now. Shall we go in?'

Dan instantly moved down the stairs and took up his position beside his peephole. He saw Blanchard precede the others into the church.

'Now, you've already seen this here flask. Shall we take our seats on the other side? There's some chairs.'

They walked round the great yellow dome, staring up at it. A beam of red light from the stained glass window fell on each face in passing, first Blanchard's face, then Dorp's, and the face of a smaller man following him, and finally – Dan nearly slipped, perched as he was on the steeply sloping staircase. He gripped the lintel of the viewing slit to save himself. *What on earth – ?* He looked again. He could see the whole figure below him now. It was slightly foreshortened, but there was no doubt about it, none whatever. He was looking at Jack Bacon.

# 26

Justin felt sorry for himself. His head was again ringing with a confused cacophony of signals. Over and over he ordered his imperatives: clear the path for Lena's mission; find and kill Dan Barry.

He remembered what Craike had told him: *living with an Australian dancer in the Old City*. He wandered around the Old City, with little idea of where or how to look for an Australian dancer. He was hot and strung out, but kept on, asking everyone who would listen to him, asking with a persistence that had been born in him that day on Patmos. He was pushed and jostled by the shoppers as he stood in the entrance of the Grand Bazaar, repeating his question over and over before finally being moved on by the police. He wandered down to *Aya Sofya*, the world's most stupendous redundant church. He asked carpet dealers, trinket sellers, postcard boys. He surprised an elderly German coach tour by going among them, asking his question. *Has anyone seen? . . . Does anyone know . . .?*

One silver-haired old German, mistaking Justin for this Australian dancing girl's pimp, began applying for more details. Brutally his *frau* abridged the conversation. Justin kept on.

Only night temporarily defeated him. Then he crawled into his crummy hotel room and slept for hours, dreamlessly. The next morning he was back again, back to *Aya Sofya* and the Blue Mosque where, at least, the majority of people more or less understood English.

And it was here, at last, that he met the skinny lad with the gappy teeth. The boy overheard him asking his question, and came up to him.

'If you have any money, sir, I think I can help you.'

Justin ascended the stairs. He felt now only cold tranquillity as he pushed open the ajar door and found the scene which Dan had found a few days earlier: Sarah on her bed, nodding away.

Less gentle than Dan had been, Justin picked Sarah up, and shook her. 'Tell me where he is! This is a matter of world significance. Tell me where! Tell me where Dan Barry is! Tell me!'

It did not take long to break her down. She was in no state to resist manic terror-tactics. She had to be left alone, it wasn't fair. It wasn't *fair*.

She told him.

Perched in his eyrie above the quartet of men on the floor of the church, Dan collected his thoughts. For reasons which were perfectly obscure to him, he'd been set up. For Christ's sake, why was Jack here? What was he up to?

He knew where he'd previously seen the other man, the third bidder for the plutonium. It was the military type who had walked into the Transnational Hotel with Jack on the morning after Dan's supposed murder.

Dan activated his tape recorder, checked through the headphones that the mike was in order, and waited.

Blanchard sat down, as did the other three. They each selected chairs and shifted them until they were roughly equidistant from each other. Now they made an approximate square. At once Nathan reached into his armpit and drew out an automatic handgun. He rested it on his knee.

'I think we better come clean to this, okay? Is anyone else wearing any hardware?'

The others looked at each other and, like boys caught smuggling sweets into class, they drew out their various weapons.

Blanchard rose and moved up to the altar. He rested the gun on it, still keeping his hand loosely over the butt.

'Okay, I'm gonna put mine up here. Now what say we all do this at the same time?'

The others solemnly trooped up to the altar and placed their pistols beside Blanchard's. Before they each tripped back down the steps to their chairs, Blanchard held out his arms to the nearest of them, who happened to be Dorp. 'May I?'

Dorp raised his arms and Blanchard frisked him. He frisked the others in turn. Then Dorp frisked Blanchard, a performance less thorough and enthusiastic than Blanchard's own. The others seemed satisfied with Dorp's body-check of the American. They seemed embarrassed by the whole thing.

Sitting once again in their four-square formation, Blanchard laid down the ground rules. 'If you wanna bid, you jump in half-million steps. There's ten kilos of the shit in that flask, so I'm gonna start you off at two million dollars. Now, I got myself a reserve price, below which I ain't about to sell, but I ain't gonna tell you guys what it is unless you happen not to get past it. Now, I think it would be good if we introduced ourselves, just to show that this sale is being conducted on the basis of common trust.'

He looked around, expectantly. Dorp was quick to cut in. 'You said no names.'

Blanchard spread his hands. 'In general terms, right? Who's gonna start? Okay, *I'll* start. Well, you all know me, don't you? Name's no secret here, I'm Nathan Blanchard, I'm an international trader.'

There was a silence, followed by Jack Bacon clearing his throat.

'I don't think it'd be particularly useful to say more than that I'm a broker in certain . . . er, sensitive materials, here representing a sovereign government. I wouldn't be prepared to say any more.'

He was putting on some kind of phoney accent, which sounded like Irish. Nevertheless, Blanchard beamed at him. 'That's fine, my friend. You've broken the ice.'

Still smiling, he looked between Dorp and the British army man. The latter spoke next. 'I'm here on behalf of a government, a South American government.'

Blanchard nodded with avuncularity. Then he turned to Dorp. 'And you, buddy?'

'Well, Mr Blanchard, I think you know. I'm the servant of my own government, which is a certain African nation. Now, as this is not an encounter group, might I suggest we proceed?'

'Sure, sure. Like I said, I just wanted to break the ice here.' He rubbed his hands together briskly. 'Now. Who would care to start the bidding?'

They looked at each other. The ex-soldier said, 'I'll say two and a half.'

Jack Bacon came in with a bid. 'Three and a half million.'

'Four million,' said Dorp, looking down at his shoes.

There was a short silence, broken by Blanchard.

'Four million, for this here ten kilos of Plutonium 239. Is that *all*?'

The silence continued. Jack and the ex-soldier seemed to exchange a glance, while Dorp continued to look at the ground. Blanchard was about to speak again, when they all heard a curious squealing noise, and a scrabbling in another part of the church. Looking around, Dan saw the dark shape of the little dog, gambolling around near the yellow flask. Blanchard said, 'Pay that no mind. That's just Claudius, the pup that lives here, cute little feller. Now, I'm bid four million dollars, but surely I must hear more?'

Jack Bacon came back with another bid of four and a half, and the ex-soldier went to five. Jack said five and a half, at which point Dorp intervened again with a big jump. 'Seven. Seven million dollars.'

Now Blanchard was getting excited. 'Seven million. I have a bid of seven million dollars, you guys. Now, which of you's going to top that? It's still way off of the market rate, according to my information. Way, way off. Which of you two's gonna top our African friend with his seven million?'

Dan could hear Claudius snuffling his way over to the circle of chairs. He leaned over to get a better view and saw the pup was worrying at the leg of Dorp's chair. Claudius quickly transferred his attentions to the leg of Dorp himself, taking the cuff of the South African's trouser in his teeth and tugging at it. Dorp jumped up, and lashed out with his foot. 'For Christ's sake, man. Bloody control that dog, will you?'

Blanchard rose and made a threatening gesture at the dog. Claudius skipped two feet through the air and went careering round the church, yipping excitedly to himself. The men settled again, though Dorp looked ruffled. His dignity had been pushed askew.

'Now, I think the bid was seven million. But of course, you fellers ain't gonna leave it there. You can't! What do you say?'

This was followed by a further silence. Claudius was now sniffing around the side wall, on the scent of rats or mice. He was coming close to the opening at the base of the tower stairs, the entrance which had no door. If he climbed them he would be led directly to Dan. The dog disappeared from Dan's view immediately below him, as the others looked towards it. Dan quickly ducked down. He heard the sounds of the puppy coming up the stairwell, his incessant snuffling and then the click of his claws as they met the stone steps.

'What's that dog up to now? What's he found up there?' It was the Englishman who spoke.

Dan sat still on the stair. He heard Claudius coming nearer, as Blanchard's voice reassured the others. 'It's nothin', just rodents. Place is runnin' with the little bastards. Claudius catches a few, time to time. Can we get on, please?'

Dan saw the dog's nose now, gleaming a little in the pale illumination which came through the tiny slit. He continued to whimper, a friendly greeting this time, and began licking Dan's hand. They were noisy, slobbering licks.

'Have you got someone up there, Blanchard? I think the dog's found someone.'

It was the army type again, but now his voice was not coming from quite the same place. Dan heard the tap of his step on the church floor, and then a shoe scrape at the foot of the stairs. He stood up, but before he could do anything more, the man had sprinted up the stairs, seized the leg which Dan put out to ward him off, and was dragging it from under him. Dan crashed down, his face meeting the edge of one of the steps with painful force. The next moment he was being bumped down the spiral stair and hauled into the church.

'Just look what young Claudius has found, gentlemen! A spy! One of yours, Blanchard, or a freelance, I wonder?'

Jack jumped towards the altar and seized a pistol from the little heap of weapons. His move precipitated an unseemly scramble by the other two men for their own guns. Meanwhile the Englishman manoeuvred Dan, who didn't resist, into a half-nelson, forcing his right arm up behind his back. The result was excruciating.

Only Dorp did not recognize him. Jack Bacon did a smart double-take when he saw Dan, and Blanchard's mouth dropped open like a chocolate machine.

The Englishman said, coolly, 'Somebody check him for a weapon, will you?'

Nathan Blanchard's jowls quivered, his fists bunched and relaxed and bunched again. He would kill that bastard for sure this time. But he tried to level out his voice, appealing reasonably to the others. 'Okay, this boy's one of mine. He's out of line, I didn't ask him to be here. So if you guys would just let me take him into that room there –' He pointed to the vestry door.

'No, Blanchard. You won't take him anywhere.' The Englishman had assumed command with an ease that was conditioned in him. He pushed Dan towards a chair and made him sit. 'I know about this young man. He's a writer, an "investigative journalist", is that not how you describe yourself, son?'

Dan had no reply to make.

'Well, he is not denying it. So, one can only assume he is "investigating" our trade here. We do not know by what *right* he presumes to do so.'

Blanchard could no longer control himself. He jerked his body a step towards Dan. 'I'll pulp the bastard. Let me do it. Let me take him.'

The Englishman pushed Blanchard back. Blanchard stuck out his lips in a furious grimace. 'Don't push me, you sonofa–'

'Leave it. We can't kill him. We don't know how he might have deployed the information he surely already has against us. We have no choice, we have to deal, offer him an arrangement.'

Blanchard did not agree. He began to raise his gun, but was arrested by a click beside his temple. He turned. He was looking up the snub nose of Jack Bacon's handgun. Bacon took Blanchard's own weapon as the Englishman spoke to Dan. 'I really rather detest your type, Barry. *News*paper men. I would not be too distraught if Mr Blanchard here were to have his way. But I am a realist. You are not working alone, are you?'

Dan thought of Sarah. 'Yes, I am. I –'

'You have a – what would you call him, a collaborator, an accomplice? Moustached fellow.'

Moustache? Who was he talking about? Then Dan's head tripped into comprehension. 'Oh! You mean Mills?'

'Well! That's progress. We have a name. But it's a name I already know, Barry. I know the name, but not the person, if you get my drift.'

'What do you want me to tell you?'

'Who is Mills, where is he, what does he know?'

Dan shrugged. 'He's my partner in this. He knows everything I know.'

'Is he in Istanbul?'

'Yes.'

'Can you contact him, get him here for us?'

'I could.'

'Will you?'

Dan hesitated, as if considering. 'What do I get?'

'You get to live a little.'

Dan sought Jack's eyes but his former friend, the man who practically put him up to this in the first place, would not look at him.

'I'll think about it,' said Dan.

'You do that. You think, while the rest of us finish our little bit of business.'

He looked at Blanchard, who seemed nonplussed, as if he couldn't remember what little bit of business that might be. But with a slight shake of the head, he brought it to mind. 'What you mean, we get on with the auction, with this punk here?'

'Why not, he was here before and didn't bother us.'

Blanchard's glower began to change. Then he was smiling. 'Sure. Why not? So, gentlemen, where were we? Ah, yeah, seven million I think you said, feller. Now, is there any more advance on –'

But Dorp butted in. 'Jesus, man. You can't expect me to go ahead with this, not after what just happened.'

Blanchard looked at him pityingly. 'Guy's just a lone nut, okay? This Mills is probably some asshole he borrowed money from. If he was important, I'd know about him, okay? Now, any advance on seven million?'

Dorp settled in his seat with a sigh. Jack Bacon lowered himself back into his chair, still resting the gun on his thigh.

'Jees, c'mon, fellers, this stuff's worth more'n seven million!'

He searched their faces but found no response, no chink of encouragement. He sighed and thumped the edge of his chair-seat. 'Okay, so I'm selling to the gentleman for seven million dollars, cash. I'm selling now.'

He raised his fist to strike the chair seat again, intoning in a voice grim with disappointment, 'Going once . . . going twice . . . going for the third and last time –'

Blanchard never finished the formula, because at that moment, in the nave of the church, a firing-pin pecked down and exploded an 8mm shell whose projectile smashed a hole high in the stained glass window, right through St George's left cheek. Blanchard's chair went clattering backwards as he floundered to the floor. At once the church's hollow space was filled by a volley of gunshots – three, four in rapid succession. The bullets were ricocheting too fast to comprehend, and chips flew from the stonework. Beside the yellow flask in the centre of the nave smoke was spreading like a white blot in the dim air.

More shots came immediately, one of which smashed into the marble pulpit, sending up a small puff of white gravel. Another burst into the altar itself, gouging out a wedge of stone which dropped to the floor and disintegrated.

The group sitting in the circle of chairs had reacted like frogs jumping from a stone. Dan crawled into the narrow space behind the altar. Jack Bacon was firing back and Dan heard shouting. It was a voice he did not recognize. He stood and peered through the marble ornamentation which rose from the back of the altar table. He saw a large man dressed in a pair of old jeans and a sweat-soaked T-shirt, his red hair matted and a look of almost beatific fulfilment on his face. The man advanced into the open space between the yellow flask and the altar.

'Mr Blanchard, I have no quarrel with you. You are a respected business man. I am only interested in Barry, Dan Barry, who has a place waiting for him in hell.'

He levelled the gun again and blasted away at the altar. Dan ducked, but in the corner of his vision he could see the crown of the pulpit, a semi-circular marble balustrade with a gap for the lectern. The Englishman who had claimed to represent a South American state was crawling up the curl of the steps. He sprang to his feet. With a clear field of fire, and both hands steadying the butt of his gun at arm's length, he drew a bead on the head of this very amateur attacker, then put a coolly precise single shot at a downward angle into the gunman's forehead. The shell must have collected a good part of the brainstem as it ploughed through, exiting at the back of the neck and spending itself on the floor.

Justin continued to stand for a count of three, his face setting in an expression of stunned astonishment. Then, like a detonated factory chimney, he toppled. Dan heard the crunch of fracturing bone as his dead weight hit the floor.

The Englishman lowered his automatic and dropped his chin into his chest for a moment. Jack and Blanchard stood up stiffly. They drifted back towards the circle of chairs but Dan stayed where he was. From the pulpit, the South American agent said, 'Now, *please* can we conclude this business?'

He looked across the church. Jack Bacon was shaking his head. 'It's over, Ed. We'll never finish it now.'

He pointed down towards the bottom of the tower steps. Protruding from the entrance were two legs clad in light-coloured sports slacks. When they turned him over, Dorp was dead.

# 27

The survivors stood in a group around Dorp's body, watching the sticky puddle of his blood seeping on to the stone floor. He had been hit in the upper chest. The puddle spread to the edge of the sanctuary steps and, as it began to drip from step to step, Dan found himself obscurely grieving. He'd known more about the South African than any of the others, and he felt now as if a mild acquaintance had fallen under his car at speed. Over were the Dorps' marital warfare, the rows about the man's career, the cuckoldry. Dorp had died without even knowing he'd died, and his egg-head lay at a crooked angle like a discarded puppet of Humpty-Dumpty.

Blanchard stood beside Dan, eyes popping, his breath coming and going in wheezing, asthmatic periods. But he was more interested in the other body than this one. He pointed back to it, jabbing the air. 'That was the preacher! That was Fuller, the fuckin' preacher!'

The Englishman pulled a long face at Dan. 'You *have* got a lot of enemies, Dan Barry,' he said. 'How do you manage it?'

Blanchard lumbered over to the priest's body and kicked it half-heartedly, muttering to himself. He turned and spread his arms and fingers wide. He searched the others' faces.

'Okay, the South African's dead.' He gestured at Dan. 'The preacher was nuts but he meant to kill that shithead over there, not Dorp. He didn't know shit about this plutonium. Listen, I can dispose of these bodies, no problem, I can get Yakup to–' He stopped for the length of a beat, remembering Yakup was missing. Shit, he'd turn up. He continued. 'So what say we finish the auction, then we can all go home and forget this mess? Okay?'

Jack Bacon's lips trembled. He began to laugh, his shoulders shaking, his head lifting involuntarily.

His colleague snapped out, 'Stop that, Jack. Shut it!'

'Sorry, Craike.' Bacon fell silent. But the tone of the exchange brought Blanchard up short. He crossed his arms, and lifted a finger to scratch his chin. Then he raised the same finger and wagged it at Craike.

'Hey! Wait a minute. You givin' that guy the orders? Wait a fuckin' minute. You two guys know each other, you're working together on this. Now, what the fuck is this? You're in cahoots. You're –' He fell silent, dropped his arms to his side. His wrists and hands swung limply. He was watching Craike who moved swiftly around the church, collecting together the fire-arms. He detached Justin's crooked forefinger from the trigger-guard of his piece. The metal was still hot, and Craike snatched his hand away with a hiss of surprise as he touched the barrel. He lifted the gun by its butt and moved back to Dorp whom he lifted, discovering the small automatic wedged beneath his stomach. Craike straightened and sighed wearily. He half-shut his eyes in a mock smile, as he took in Blanchard's blank, uncomprehending face.

'It's a set-up, Blanchard. You've been the victim of a little scheme – well, not the victim, the unwitting tool.' He laid the guns back on the altar, carefully placing them as if in a shop display. 'Unfortunately, the scheme's gone awry. Not your fault, of course.'

'Scheme? Whose scheme?' Blanchard still had his gun in his fist. He raised it in Craike's direction. He wasn't exactly aiming it, but using it for emphasis. Anyone could see that Blanchard was not at ease with a gun. 'What scheme? What set-up?'

But Craike merely held out a hand, palm upwards. 'Give me it, Blanchard. Jack here's a very good marksman. Give me the piece.'

Still trying to suppress his mirth, Jack had levelled a gun at Blanchard's heart. The American's scowl wilted. 'What's funny, asshole? Is nobody gonna explain all this?'

But he gave up his pistol to Craike without another murmur. Craike said, 'Sit down. And you, Barry.'

Craike himself did not sit. He paced around as he talked. 'It was a good scheme. It was my scheme. Now that it's gone phut, I'll be needing your help to scuff over the tracks.' Craike was in complete control of himself. He sounded like a lecturer in staff college, outlining a programme of study.

Dan found the urbanity monstrous. He didn't bother to disguise his dislike. '*You're* in a fix. Why should we help?'

Craike's eyebrows arched upwards. 'Be patient. I'm going to tell you. When word gets out about all this' – he indicated the two bodies, still lying where they'd fallen – 'well, you can probably imagine the consequences. Okay, I'll be chopped from my job. But I'm lucky, I have diplomatic privilege. For you, Barry, and Blanchard here, a very much ruder scenario awaits – shall we say a long, a very long lease on a Turkish prison cell? Or worse, perhaps. They still have the death penalty, don't they, Jack? So let's say it's in all our interests to cooperate together, yes?'

Dan interrupted. 'Before we get on to cooperation, I *would* like to know where my friend Jack fits into all this? What was the idea, Jack? Are you a natural hypocrite, or did you learn the art?'

But Jack would not look at Dan. Instead he gazed towards the stained glass window, with its bullet holes, silently whistling a tune through pursed lips.

Blanchard shifted uneasily. This was a nightmare, in which nothing anybody said made any sense. 'I just wish someone would spill what this is all about. What job you gonna lose, you – what's your real name, anyway?'

'Craike.'

'I thought you were in business for yourself, Craike. I thought you brokered that stuff.'

He jerked a thumb at the yellow flask. Craike shook his head.

'I work for the British government. I'm entrusted with the implementation of special policy.'

'Then what you doin' buyin' plutonium for Chile, or wherever it was?'

'I'm not. The whole point was not to buy. I mean, to buy would look pretty daft when it was me who sold it to you in the first place, wouldn't it?'

Dan heard the plop of Blanchard's slug lips, as they parted in surprise.

'*You* sold it to me? Like hell you did. I got it from a guy named Morrison, in Spain.'

'Morrison was my man. I arranged for the plutonium to go to you.'

'But . . . I mean, I don't get it. For what?'

'Because I wanted you to sell it on the black market.'

'Ah, come on! You wanted me to sell it on the black market, so you and your buddy could turn up and buy it back? I ain't *that* stupid!'

Craike reacted crisply. 'Nor are we. As I just said, the whole *point* was not to buy it. We wanted poor dead Dorp here to buy it.'

'You mean you and this prick here were working for the British government, but Dorp wasn't?'

'No, of course not. He was exactly what he said he was – worked for Pretoria, their chief buyer in nuclear material, or was. He went all over the world. Bought in tons of the stuff over the past few years.'

Blanchard shook his head, defeated. 'This is crazy.'

But Dan had begun to understand. 'You wanted South Africa to get the plutonium?'

Craike nodded. 'As I said.'

'But you just told us your job was implementing policy – or was that ironic? I mean, South Africa is not a signatory of the nuclear non-proliferation treaty, so it *can't* be *government* policy to sell them plutonium. It's against the treaty.'

'Well, of course it's not *official* policy. If it was, we wouldn't need all these shenanigans, would we? Officially South Africa is a nuclear pariah. But that hasn't stopped them developing a bomb. Anyway, our support for non-proliferation contradicts some of our other policies, such as supporting the current government in South Africa. It's a question of priorities.'

'You mean, you're selling South Africa the bomb to shore up the apartheid government?'

'Well, not exactly. In public we're against apartheid. But South Africa needs a settlement which will continue to safeguard white interests. That means strong armed forces – the ability if necessary to intimidate the country's black neighbours. But most of all it's a matter of giving the whites confidence, of boosting morale. We pay golfers and cricketers to go and play out there. We oppose sanctions. We make sure they get the best military supplies. It's all part of the same effort.'

Blanchard's face was screwed up in frank disbelief. 'I don't get it. You wanna sell this plutonium to the South Africans, right? So why in the name of Jesus do you go this way? Why not just sell it to the suckers straight out?'

Craike looked at him pityingly. 'Because we don't

want them to *know*, do we? Think what their propaganda machine could do with it. It could make Ollie North look like a choirboy. They'd have us right there. Do what they like with us. Naturally we can't afford that. The plutonium sales had to be covert, even as far as the buyers are concerned. They had to believe they were getting it black market.'

Dan interrupted with a shake of the head. 'Look, come on. There's no real shortage of nuclear material around the world. I mean, why get involved at all, when you can leave it to the free market? Windscale leaks like a colander, doesn't it? South Africa gets all the plutonium it wants, doesn't it?'

'It used to. That's the point. Thanks to this new idea that politics can be any colour so long as they're green, we're being forced to plug the leakages out of Windscale. We've got new and very tight systems coming into use. They're very secret and they work. As most of the rest of this stuff comes from the French and they're doing exactly the same, there's a big squeeze coming up on black market supplies. The ante on unofficial nuclear bombs is going through the roof, South Africa could be priced out of the 239 market by people we'd really rather didn't get any at all. This system had the double plus of keeping the Arabs and Argies out, and getting the stuff to South Africa at a cut rate.'

Blanchard almost rose to his feet, then thought better of it. But his anger bubbled up just the same. 'A *cut* rate? On top of everything, you bastards tried to cheat me!'

Now Craike's smile was real, a thin, smirking elongation of the lips. 'You were doing all right. You pay two million, you sell for seven. Five mill profit doesn't seem too bad to me, chum!'

'Yeah, when I was counting on a minimum seven. Jesus!'

His lips moved in discontent. Dan watched him warily. Blanchard, he knew, was more formidable than, perhaps, Craike would allow for. Now he was smouldering, and Dan was waiting for the detonation.

'So what're you going to do, Ed?' It was Jack Bacon, his voice languid, as if he was enjoying the situation.

'That depends on Mr Blanchard here. How would he react to a proposal? An offer he can hardly spurn, under the circumstances.'

'Which is?' Blanchard growled.

'Which is that we buy back the plutonium at cost. We take it away with us, and you get your original two million returned intact.'

There was a pause, in which Dan held his breath. Then Craike added, 'We *might* be able to throw in a few thousand interest, just so you're not out of pocket. Shall we call it handling charges?'

'Handling charges? Handling charges? By Christ, I'll give you handling charges!' With a sound that was half-snort, half-roar, and moving his bulk faster than would seem possible, Blanchard lunged forward. Long before Jack Bacon could begin to react he had reached Craike, and was closing his hands around the Englishman's throat.

Blanchard was putting every muscle in his body into the strangling of Craike, who writhed in his massive grip like a worm trapped in a door. The blood vessels which ran down on both sides of Blanchard's neck stood out, even through the layers of fat. Both men suffered a change of complexion. Blanchard's skin was puce with effort, as Craike's face turned from red to blue, the eyes rolling up to show only their bloodshot whites. Jack Bacon sprinted across to help his chief, raising the pistol, but Blanchard lifted Craike clean into the air and planted him in the line of Jack's fire.

Craike was losing the battle for life, grunting and kicking futilely with his heels. Blanchard pulled him backwards to a pillar at the edge of the sanctuary while Jack Bacon, jinking to left and right, tried to get an opening where he could strike a blow. But he was continually frustrated by Blanchard heaving his struggling victim in the way. Dan suddenly saw that Blanchard's bare-handed ferocity gave him the diversion he needed.

He started to move towards the main door of the church, his eyes all the time darting back to the group of three in the sanctuary. He made five, ten, then fifteen feet and reached the yellow plutonium flask, unnoticed. Once he was in its shelter, his retreat through the main church door was covered.

The great oak door had been left a crack open by Fuller when he'd let himself in. Dan crossed the remaining space between flask and door, hooked his fingers into the crack, widened it no more than was sufficient and slipped through.

The church's interior had been gloomy, no more than a half-light. Now his eyes met sunlight that seemed so intense he could see no depth. His field of vision was like a coruscating screen. He blinked and started along the earthen path to the gate.

It was incredibly quiet and normal, which Dan found hard to understand. Had none of the shooting been heard? Why was there no curious crowd? Then he thought, shots inside a space like that would come through like the noises of construction work, hammer-blows or something, if heard at all. Normal sounds, nothing to be suspicious of. He smiled and breathed in the peace of normality. Then a hand was clamped over his mouth from behind, yanking his head back with brutal ferocity.

Without speaking two more men approached him, hooked their arms through his and lifted him. The other, whose hand gagged him, shuffled backwards. In a few seconds he was being deposited in the church porch.

A group of men joined them here, a dozen at least, jostling together to fit into the porch. They were about his age or younger, in jeans, training shoes and polo shirts, grinning to each other in shared excitement. They could have been any Sunday-morning park football team, except that they carried assault rifles and grenades.

Dan was pulled to the side of the porch. He shut his

eyes. His mouth tasted the palm – salty sweat with a trace of engine oil. When he opened his eyes again, the rest of the party had funnelled into the church.

Dan heard shouting, scrambling feet, the clunk of steel on stone, as he was dragged back with them.

Lena arrived at the airport and took a taxi straight to the Anadolu Hava Yolları office in town. Her feeling – it was no more than that – of Dan's return to life had grown, and she now went on the assumption that he was in the city: it was only a question of where to find him.

Nazım Ali's secretary received her with friendly concern. 'Nazım Ali Bey is busy for the next ten minutes, Miss Priestley. Will you wait?'

Lena waited. She flipped through the selection of glossy magazines whose posed models, with lips sipping the air, irritated her with their irrelevance. But then, so did the rest of the material in the magazines. At last she was taken through to Nazım Ali's office.

'Miss Priestley, it is good to see you looking better. The last time we met you were not yourself, understandably I think . . .' He had a way of making the skin on his forehead ripple in an interrogative way.

'Thanks, Nazım Ali Bey. Yes, I am better because I have had some news. It's about Dan.'

Nazım Ali placed his elbows on the desk, and with delicacy brought his hands together so that the fingertips just kissed. 'About Dan?'

'Yes. You see, he's not dead – it's a mistake. I had a

letter from the Reverend Fuller. Dan's in Istanbul again. He's in some kind of trouble though. I came straight to you in case he'd contacted you.'

It sounded daft, as if Nazım Ali had been any kind of confidant of Dan's, whereas Dan hardly knew the man.

'Well, I hoped you might have heard something . . .'

Nazım Ali looked down, and then up again at Lena. 'Dan *isn't* dead, you say?'

'Well, I don't know. I mean I can't prove it, I haven't seen him. But Mr Fuller has told me he is alive and here in Istanbul.'

Nazım Ali blinked. He straightened the telephone near his right elbow. He pulled the points of his moustache. He had not told anyone of his encounter in the lift at the Sheraton Hotel, because he did not want to imperil the honour of the beautiful girl he had been dining with. But how tempted he had been once or twice, in the *hamam* and the golf club with his friends! When you know something for sure, some secret, it's no problem to keep it to yourself. You wait with a pleasant sense of anticipation for the secret to unfold. When you only half know it, but you're not sure if it's a phantasm or a mirage, a creation of dust-motes on the eye or the emanation of a tired brain – then you need to talk it through with some person. You need assurances that you are not mad or hallucinating.

Nazım Ali hesitated too long. Lena read his uncertainty. 'Did you know he was here? You haven't seen him, have you?'

'Miss Priestley, you say Dan is alive and here in Istanbul. But it's impossible–'

Lena rose briskly. 'No it's not, you just confirmed it. Thank you, Nazım Ali Bey.' She looked down at the General Manager's pristine desk. 'I can see you're busy. Goodbye.' Then she left.

She would go straight home. Dan must be in trouble, but he would contact her. She took a taxi to Emirgan.

A Murat saloon was parked beside the entrance to the flats. As Lena handed money to the taxi driver, she saw a fresh-faced young man in a light suit get out and take up position just in front of the plate-glass doors. Lena took her change and passed a tip back, glancing aside at the man. Yes, he was undoubtedly hovering.

Lena could have asked the driver to wait. She could have climbed in and told him to drive away, to drive any place. Yet she straightened and, as the accelerating taxi churned up the dust, walked towards the apartment block. The young man stood perfectly still, watching her, and she was close enough to him now to feel his eyes on her body. She flicked a look around, but there was no one. It was past midday, when the heat had driven everybody indoors.

She was ten feet from where the man was waiting when he stepped smartly forward and spoke in accented English. 'Miss Lena Priestley? Please would you mind coming with me?'

Lena did not resist as she was led by the crook of her elbow towards the Murat.

# 28

One of them was in the pulpit, another in the tower and two in the organ loft which hung above the church door. They looked like children, cradling their assault rifles and Uzi machine guns like soft toys. The others were busy about the yellow flask, directed by their leader. They were unpacking the contents of their rucksacks, laying the contents out in neat mosaic on the floor.

Dan was watching the leader. He was physically no older than the rest of them, but he had the authority of an operational veteran leading a crew of first-timers. He murmured orders in quiet, level tones, and was obeyed with scurrying alacrity.

Facing towards the nave, with his back against the altar, Dan sat on the stone flags beside Blanchard, Craike and Jack Bacon. The young man set to cover them from the pulpit eyed the captives with a kind of fearful astonishment, as if they might at any moment change shape or explode.

The leader of the Musa Dağ group had laughed when he'd come upon Blanchard wringing Craike's neck, and it had taken four of his men to separate them. Both Craike and Blanchard had immediately slumped to the ground, and it was difficult to see who was the more seriously affected, Craike by his near-strangulation or Blanchard by the effort of carrying it out. It was Craike who recovered first, however, his neck marked by vicious bruises, yet as ever maintaining his sang-froid. Blanchard was less inhibited, rolling this way and that on the ground and breathing stertorously, like a sea mammal. Now he was lying still, rubbing his breastbone, complaining of chest pains, muttering threats. 'I ever get out of this, Craike you bastard, I'm gonna finish your neck, you hear?'

Craike didn't look at Blanchard. He was watching the activity around the flask. 'I doubt you'll get the chance. Look at that.'

'What? What are they doing? I can't see.'

The leader of the gunmen turned from the flask and walked back to the altar with an unhurried, fluid gait. He nodded down at the fat man. 'You are Nathan Blanchard?'

'Damn right I am. Who the fuck're you?'

Blanchard heaved himself sideways and upwards, and almost got to his feet. But the effort petered out and he subsided into a sitting position, from which he looked up pugnaciously.

'You took our name in vain, *Mister* Blanchard. You used us. We don't like that.'

'What you talkin' about, took your name? Never even seen you.'

'But you have seen our name, written up all over this town. Our messages for the Turkish people, our appeals for the release of our inspirer and leader, Krikorian. We are Musa Dağ, Mister Blanchard, and I repeat: you took our name and abused it.'

'I don't know what you're talking about.'

Jack Bacon broke in. 'Course you do, Nathan. London, hotel room, blood everywhere, two words written on the mirror. You tried to put them in the frame for your dirty work. You're in the shit, Blanchard. These guys don't piss about.'

'You're *all* in the same shit, as this gentleman has impolitely called it, because I regret to inform you that you are now my hostages.'

The leader squatted down a few feet from them and looked at his watch.

'My name is Hagop, by the way. Are there any questions at all? I have time for a little pleasantness.' Hagop smiled invitingly.

Blanchard broke the silence with a grunt. He indicated the plutonium flask. Hagop's men were now stacking paper-covered packages, the size of small bricks, around its base.

'What you doing with my property?'

'Laying charges. Semtex. We're preparing to blow that thing through the roof.'

Blanchard looked wildly from Hagop's face to those of his fellow hostages.

'Jesus Christ! You know what that'll do, don't you? I mean, you know what's in there? That dust gets in the air, it'll poison the ground this motherfuckin' city's standing on for the next thousand years – more!'

Hagop nodded, smiling modestly. 'Oh sure, I know. I know what it contains, because Yakup, your poor servant, told me. I also know what it can do. It can bring these Turks to their senses, then they will release our leader. It's their choice.'

Craike turned his head, although the effort seemed to pain the damaged neck. 'You'll need a negotiator, Hagop. It'll be very hard. You'll need someone to convince them you mean business.'

'Do you mean yourself? And who *are* you exactly?'

'Craike, British diplomatic corps. I can help – I'm trained, after all.'

'Mister Craike, I think you are trained for war, not discussion. It should be *Major* Craike, should it not? Originally of the Brigade of Guards, later the Special Air Service, and now Defence Ministry executive operations – is this not so?'

Craike's face did its best not to register surprise at the terrorist's knowledge of him. 'I repeat, I am trained to negotiate in situations like this.'

'Let me tell you a story, Major, which might put my refusal of your offer in perspective. On 24 August 1896, twenty-six of my countrymen, led by a seventeen-year-old hero called Babken Siuni, carried out an operation not unlike this one. Persecution of my people in this country had reached such a pitch that Siuni decided to attack where it hurt most. He took over the Osmanlı Bankası, the Ottoman Bank, and said he would blow it up, together with the stupendous reserves contained in its vaults, unless his demands were met. They were very reasonable demands, demands for fair treatment, that is all. The bank's director, Sir Edgar Vincent – an Englishman like you,

Mister Craike – convinced Siuni and his comrades that something would be done. He was very kind. He obtained safe conduct for them out of the country on his private yacht – think of that! And no sooner had they gone' – Hagop brought his hand down in a chopping motion – 'no sooner had they gone than the Sultan unleashed his revenge, a massacre of the Armenian civilians on the streets of Constantinople . . . this city, Major Craike.'

Standing up, Hagop flexed and stretched his legs.

'The Western powers were strong here in those days, I mean *strong*. But they stood aside while eight thousand died – eight thousand innocent people killed in their homes, and running in the street, by Muslim fanatics and Ottoman soldiers. You see? The world hasn't changed much, has it? America, England, the EEC – they are not to be trusted by small peoples like us. We do our own bargaining now.'

He turned and went back towards the flask. As he passed the pulpit he spoke to his man stationed there. He spoke in English, for the hostages' benefit. 'If any of them gets up, or moves more than one metre, kill him.'

'Think, Miss Priestley, please think.'

The chair she sat in was of bentwood, with a cracked ply seat. The interview room was painted institutional green. It had a window and a desk, and a concrete floor. She saw, along the wall, a shallow gully running into a drain in the corner.

'I don't know why you're asking me. I don't know anything.'

He was a standard-issue policeman – wiry, ill-shaven. His thick moustache, curling inwards, gave his face a sad-dog expression. He chainsmoked Marlboros.

'Look, we have had a warning from these terrorists. They name your friend Dan Barry as one of their hostages, along with Nathan Blanchard. We know that Mister Barry has been working for Blanchard. We know now that they were trying to sell plutonium on the black market. Yes, Miss Priestley, plutonium. You know how serious that is? We need to find out where this plutonium is stored.'

'I don't know this guy Blanchard. I've never even heard about any plutonium. Look, that's not stuff Dan would get involved in. I know him. He wouldn't.'

When they had told her Dan was alive, she had fallen to the floor. She hadn't fainted or lost consciousness or even closed her eyes. But her legs had been so tired that she'd flopped down. Nevertheless, they had begun the interrogation immediately, though she still felt weak. She was not in shape for this.

A uniformed man entered with a glass of tea. Lena sipped it eagerly and shuddered as the sharp, brackish taste flooded her mouth.

The interrogator's voice hardened. 'Miss Priestley, I don't think you have any choice except to tell me. You will be charged as an accessory to trafficking in drugs and contraband, and for bringing toxic materials into the country. Under the Turkish penal code you are heading for a life sentence.'

She gathered her power to shout at him, but it came out more like a whisper. 'Don't you see? Can't you get it? I thought he was dead, I thought he'd been murdered in London by these terrorists. Now you tell me they've got him hostage here in Istanbul. I don't . . . I just don't understand. I haven't done anything. I'm accessory to nothing. I'm just completely confused now.'

An hour later the interrogator gave up. He gave orders for her to be released.

Blanchard seemed to be asleep, and Craike and Jack Bacon were whispering together. Dan kept thinking of Beirut – of the many hostages buried in the maw of that churned-up city, of Waite and McCarthy, and the others like them. Like himself, now.

He contemplated the hostage's predicament: the months of interrogations; bargaining through intermediaries; constant anxiety; moving from safe-house to safe-house; lying in greasy nylon sleeping-bags, cuffed to the heat-pipes. Once, for an article, he'd interviewed a former hostage of *Hezbollah*, a professor of literature from the American University. There comes a point, he had said, when you lack the will to be released. You still want it, sure. But you don't have the courage to believe in it. It gets to be easier to think of things going on as they have been, as they are, forever.

Dan saw again the professor's face which displayed

the lines and folds of two years' captivity, and his hands which would not stay still, fiddling remorselessly with anything in reach.

Dan looked at his own hands. They rested inert on his knees. Istanbul was not Beirut, and this would not be that type of captivity. It would be short and sharp – a sudden release, a quick death.

The gunmen not on guard were having a meal. They'd finished setting the explosive charges around the flask. Dan knew containers like that to be incredibly strong, tested in hundred-mile-an-hour rail accidents, shot with field-guns. But nothing was completely indestructible, and Dan had a fair idea of the power of Semtex. The explosive he could see in front of him, packed like miniature sandbags around Blanchard's plutonium, looked enough to blow the entire Pan Am and British Airways fleets out of the air. It would almost certainly do the job asked of it by the terrorists.

Dan watched them, sitting in a circle eating fish balls and rice. They were tense and subdued, although every now and then a remark would be passed and they would all laugh together.

Hours went aimlessly by. The hostages were moved into the vestry so they could be more securely guarded. They were given food, and allowed occasionally to stand and stretch their limbs, but mostly kept lying or sitting on the floor.

In the one corner of the small room, propped together against a wall in the same sitting posture as the living prisoners, were the cadavers of Dorp and Justin Fuller. They leaned shoulder to shoulder like two drunken bums at a city railway station, their flesh greyed and heavy, their hands resting palm upwards on the ground. Dorp's sports shirt was filthy with clotted blood. His head had dropped down and sideways and rested on Fuller's collar bone, the crown of his porcelain head being jacked under the clergyman's jaw.

Fuller's head was cocked back, and the face was directly displayed to the room. At first Dan could not look, but later he began to get accustomed to the body's presence, and to examine it more closely. The mouth was open, in the position a baby uses to invite a spoonful of food. The face itself was streaked by seepages of blood and cerebral fluid and the eyes were open, glassy, fixed on infinity. The hole in Fuller's forehead where Craike's bullet had entered looked like a parody of another, third eye, but puckered and winking and clogged with dark matter.

It had felt almost like a kind of test, an interrogation, to sit under Fuller's pitiless gaze. Jack Bacon had been the first to crack. He slid forward and, with the guard's nodded permission, attempted to close the eyes by pulling at the lids. But Fuller had been dead more than five hours and, with the face muscles hardening already, the lids simply flipped open again.

After this failure the others behaved as if the corpses were not there. No one had tied or chained the prisoners and from time to time Dan heard Craike and Jack

Bacon arguing in undertones about whether they should try to break out. There was no communication between Dan and Jack.

For much of the time Blanchard sat rocking, a cigar in his fingers or else between his lips, muttering to himself. Sometimes he lit it for a few puffs, but would let it go out immediately. 'Only got two more a these durned things,' he explained. 'No knowing how long we're gonna be cooped up.'

The rest of the time, Blanchard simply dozed. At first Dan could not sleep but gradually, worn down by boredom, his concentration wandered, then his head dropped to his chest. His day had started early: it could not go on interminably. Under the gaze of Fuller's unseeing eyes he fell asleep.

He was woken by a sharp commotion in the main part of the church but it was now dark and, opening his eyes, Dan could see nothing. Feet scuffled outside the vestry door. A hinge squeaked, someone was bundled towards the doorway and, with a violent push, sent staggering into the confined space.

The newcomer sprawled across Dan's knees, cursing and lashing out with fists and feet. They could tell at once from the voice that it was a woman. Yet only Dan put out his hand and touched her, because only he immediately recognized the voice. He said, 'Lena? Is that you?'

When the police let her go Lena walked at first without

any purpose, until she found a neglected little park. Here a few iron seats were ranged beneath some unhealthy-looking trees, and she chose one with a distant view, between blocks of flats, of the waterway below. Here she sat as the evening darkened and tried to clear her head. She felt she'd hardly used her brain since first realizing that Dan must be still alive. Now she needed to put things straight.

Whatever she'd said had not been able to shake the policeman's belief that Dan was part of some illegal arms deal – black market plutonium, was it? Lena thought she'd never heard such crap. Dan was an airline steward with a fantasy of becoming a writer. Still, they seemed convinced plutonium was being stored somewhere in the city by this man Blanchard, and that Dan would know exactly where.

All right. Suppose Dan was in this up to his neck. Suppose he got into it with the dumb idea of researching his novel. It was all about smuggling, wasn't it? Shit! Maybe he was.

Between the buildings she glimpsed the lights of a cruise ship manoeuvring on to the right approach line for the quayside. Her decks would be lined with people in bright clothes, waving and clapping. Who knows who they were – Americans, Russians? She suddenly felt desolate. Who could she talk to? She thought of Conrad Hamilton, but dismissed the idea. He was essentially unsympathetic, didn't like Dan and had his mind full of other things, mostly concerned with re-migration back to the States. The last thing he'd want would be this.

There was, in fact, nobody.

*The Nobody Men.* She recalled Dan's book title. She still couldn't figure out why he thought it so smart. *Nobody*. Or should it be *No Body*? Both equally depressing. Then she sat up with a start. She had remembered what he'd written on that sheet of draft, the one she'd picked up and read on the last morning she'd seen him. Something about working for a man who *styled himself church warden*. What if the American businessman that Justin Fuller had told her about, the one who rented the church as a warehouse, what if *he* were Nathan Blanchard? That would make him guardian of the church – church warden.

She rose sharply and left the park.

As Lena approached the gate of the English church in the darkness, she missed her footing and stepped into a hole in the cobbled surface, which had remained unfilled by the city authorities for months. With a yelp she plunged downwards, banging her knee on the jags of cobblestone which jutted round the edge.

Cursing the pain under her breath, Lena pulled herself up. She went straight to the churchyard gate and found it locked, so stared at the church through the bars. It was dark: there was no one here, anyway. The house, round to the right, was dark also. Lena sighed. She hung on for a few moments but saw no change. Then, as she was about to give up and turn away, an unmistakable flash passed across the three-light Gothic window which rose above the church porch. The way in which the illumination slid from window-light to window-light, moving down and across at an angle, made her sure it was not the reflection of a passing car.

Afterwards, Lena wouldn't have been able to say how she climbed that gate. She swarmed up the iron-work and somehow rolled over the protective barbed-wire coil, ripping her clothes, and her flesh beneath, in many places. When she thought she was clear she dropped to the ground and tumbled like a skydiver meeting the earth. As she'd fallen away from the barbed wire the tearing of her shirt had seemed as loud as a chainsaw. She crouched and listened.

Then she was edging along the side of the church, keeping within the shadows. The night was clear with no low cloud to reflect the city lights and, glancing up, she picked out the zigzag stars of Cassiopeia. She was still looking up when her tilted chin rammed into a man's chest and she gave out a little, vocal gasp of surprise.

She hardly had time to comprehend what was happening when she was whisked off the ground and carried into a large, booming space – the nave of the church. Metal rattled against metal and feet pattered urgently around her, as the man in whose arms she dangled shouted words in a language she did not know.

Lena was dropped to the ground and she lay there for a few seconds, curled up. She got to her knees, then all fours and tried to scramble away, but a foot came down on the small of her back and forced her down to the cool, tiled floor. This time the foot stayed where it was and a small group of men held a near-hysterical conversation above her. The hysteria was immediately arrested by the intervention of another man, who was unquestionably a figure of authority. A torch flashed briefly on her, then he issued a couple of orders, and turned away.

One of the other men seemed to disagree with his leader. He spoke passionately, in a gush of argument, for the best part of a minute. The man in authority cut him off with a single word and stalked away. Then she was taken to the small room in which she found Dan.

Throughout the rest of the darkness, she had clung to him, whispered with him, cried. There were occasional interjections from Blanchard, but she was only intermittently aware that others were present in the room. When morning came, she knew everything Dan knew.

# 29

*A field in South Armagh. Rain, bloody incessant Irish rain, and Craike was in a ditch, having the shit kicked out of him by a gunman in a British army uniform.*

*'For Christ's sake,' he was saying, trying to shield himself with his arms, 'whose fucking side are you on?'*

Like a bird transferring from one branch to the next, his brain hopped into consciousness. But, even though he was awake, persistent kicks were still banging against his calf. He sat up with a jerk. A hand reached down, grasped his arm above the elbow, and pulled him to his feet.

'Come. You are wanted.' Silently, the Armenian led him out of the vestry, stepping over the other four hostages and past the young gunman who stood sentry outside.

It was dawn. Across the city mullahs robed for prayers, muezzins switched on their public address systems. At any moment the ululating conversations would begin to curl like smoke across the rooftops.

Hagop was waiting for them in the church porch. He was talking rapidly on a portable telephone. He ended his conversation abruptly when Craike and his escort approached. 'I've changed my mind, Major Craike. They still have not responded to my demand. So I've decided to accept your kind offer to talk to them, as you said you were trained to do.'

He dropped the mobile phone into an inside pocket, and from another drew out a small box in black plastic, the size of a cigarette packet.

'What made you change your mind?' asked Craike.

'They are running out of time. I want them to make sure they realize it. I want them to talk to someone who has met me, knows what kind of man I am.'

'The kind that doesn't back down?'

Hagop chopped the side of his right hand into the palm of his left. 'Exactly as you say. No backing down, no alteration of deadlines. One chance. They take Krikorian from jail. They take him to the airport. They put him on the nine o'clock flight from Ankara to America. They do it this *morning*.'

'And for you people?'

Hagop looked at him, as if he didn't understand.

'Do you want safe-conduct for yourselves? And where to?'

Hagop hesitated. He shook his head, as if to dislodge something. 'It doesn't matter what happens to us. We can think about this later. And please, Major. I have good communications with people who observe what is happening in Ankara. Not just this.' He tapped the portable phone in his breast pocket. Then he held up the plastic unit in front of Craike's eyes. 'And this is tuned to the right frequency. Make sure they understand. I am not afraid to press the switch. Now go.'

Craike believed him. The man was an informed fanatic, that most powerful, rare and dangerous type. Twice before he'd talked face to face with such a man:

in the desert in Oman, and in the Divis Flats, West Belfast. You could tell from looking in their eyes, from a coldness like some shard of ice buried there, that they would order the destruction of the world if they thought they had to. Oh, yes, Craike believed Hagop would do this.

The gunman who had woken him up unbarred the church doors, and took Craike to the outer gate. He unlocked and pushed Craike through, silently closing it again between them. Hagop, Craike thought, must be surprised not to have been discovered yet, not to be at this moment under siege. By sending Craike out, he was effectively arranging this. It must have been a part of the plan.

Craike began to hurry, stumbling uphill to Istiklâl. He would convey this message from the safety of the British Consulate-General. He would get on to Schultz and the French, too. The Turks must be convinced to free Krikorian.

When the others awoke there was no guard in the room with them, and no Craike. Blanchard lumbered across to the door and drummed on it with the heel of his bunched fist. 'Hey! Get your ass in here. I wanna take a leak. Hey!'

There was no answer. He looked at the others, his glance darting among them nervously. 'Hey, where's Craike?' He licked his dry lips. Then he turned and hammered on the door again.

Jack Bacon rose also and stood behind Blanchard. 'Open it, Nathan. Open the door.'

Blanchard turned. 'You think I'm stupid? Could be a guy the other side of that door with an AK-47 ready to cut me in half.'

Bacon said, 'I don't think so.'

Blanchard stepped to one side and permitted Bacon with a sweep of his hand to move in front of him. 'Go ahead, you open it. *You* open it. And where the fuck's Craike?'

'I heard them come for him. I don't know, I think they let him go, take a message, probably. It's standard practice. All right, Nathan. Stand back, will you?'

In spite of everything Bacon had a sense of what was right. It was nothing to do with morality, since in every other way he was amoral – a liar, a *spy*. But originally he'd been an army officer and, as he'd been told and told again at Sandhurst, a good officer leads. Especially if he's got a bunch of rookies in his command he must, literally, lead, precede, go first, stick his neck above the parapet, play the man. Playing the man is the British military counterpart of machismo and British officers are conditioned to it. Bacon played the man. He extended his fingers until they touched the doorhandle. The circle of barley-twist iron clinked as he grasped it.

Dan pulled Lena away from the sightline of anyone standing outside the door. They crouched beside the pair of corpses, too near for the woman, who had earlier covered their heads with a ragged tea-towel she'd found in the vestment cupboard. The towel had a number of holes in it and – as she now noticed – through one of these Fuller's left eye could be seen staring, like a madman at a keyhole.

Bacon looked around one final time, as if to check if the others were ready. Blanchard shuffled backwards to a position where he would be placed, as the door swung open, behind it. With the faint ghost of an ironic smile playing as usual on his mouth, Bacon turned the handle of the heavy door and walked it open, like a groom turning a horse. When it was at ninety degrees he leaned slightly backwards and looked into the church.

There was no guard on the other side of the door. Bacon stepped forward and, bending slightly in the get-set position, checked to right and left. There was no one in the nave or the apse. He walked forward until he was in front of the altar, standing at the focal point of the church.

'I think you can safely come out. I think they've all gone.'

They had gone. The belfry tower was vacant, and so was the organ loft. They'd gone.

They stood in front of the yellow flask, whose lower half was lagged all around by the little wall of miniature sandbags. On the floor at the base of the wall were six cigar boxes, out of which wires snaked and buried themselves in the plastic explosive immediately above. A message was taped on to the upper part of the plutonium flask. It was in a confident hand, the hand of the British-educated terrorist. It said simply DO NOT BE A BOOBY!

'What the fuck's that mean?' said Blanchard. 'What kinda shit is that?'

'It means these detonators are booby-trapped,' said Jack Bacon. 'We touch the wires, or try to cut them, we go up in a cloud of plutonium dust.'

Lena said, 'But why have they gone away and left all this?'

Jack Bacon swivelled round, as if noticing the woman for the first time. He put up a hand.

'Lena! Fancy seeing you again after all this time.'

Dan came forward and encircled Lena's waist from behind. 'Shut it, Jack. Unless you can answer Lena's question, shut it.'

Jack Bacon was looking up and down Lena's body appreciatively. But he seemed only half distracted by it. 'The question? Oh yes, well, I imagine they left it all here because they've got a radio detonator. They don't actually need to be here, could be anywhere within range of a decent signal. They could simply overfly this building in a chopper and blow it as they pass.'

Blanchard was lighting a cigar. 'Wish someone'd give me a chopper, 'cause boy, I'm fucking off out of this. I'm getting out of this *country*. Thought I was going to *die* back there. Jesus!'

Dan knelt in front of one of the detonators. He lowered his head until the cheek rested on the floor and squinted sideways at the hinged box. 'There's something . . . I don't know . . . there's something not quite right about this.'

He raised himself, resting on his elbows, his face just three inches from the wall of Semtex. It was a smell, a thick, almost spicy smell. And it tickled some remote pigeon-hole of his memory. He put out a finger and prodded one of the lumps of explosive. Jack Bacon almost screamed at him, 'For fuck's sake, Dan! Don't! Christ almighty, it'll blow!'

But Dan was smiling. He reached to the top of the stack and picked up one of the Semtex bricks. The others shrank back, even Lena.

The explosive was wrapped in a thick greaseproof paper. Dan began to unwrap it. He took out the orange-coloured oblong and pressed it to his nose, then he started working it with his fingers, pressing and moulding it, pulling it out, rolling it between his palms.

'Don't you remember? At nursery school – don't you remember, any of you? Blanchard won't, I shouldn't think. Don't suppose he ever went to nursery school, don't suppose he was ever four years old.'

'Have you flipped, boy?' Blanchard retorted. 'Honest to Pete, this is no time to do the qualifying time for the funny farm olympics.'

Dan jerked the wad of plastic through the air towards Blanchard. Clumsily the fat man caught it, sharply exhaling, acting like he'd saved a rare porcelain tea bowl.

'The point is –' said Dan, picking up another brick

from the wall and tossing it casually to Jack Bacon, '– the point is, if this stuff is Semtex, then the Pope's a Protestant. This isn't plastic explosive, this is Plasticine.'

He picked down a third piece and pitched it to Lena. 'Just cop the smell. Don't you *remember*?'

They were all smelling it. Then Jack Bacon began to laugh. 'Come on,' he said. 'Let's get out of here.'

He was still chuckling as he tugged open the door of the church. The others were at the big door too, but Bacon had elbowed his way to be first into the warmth and light. He felt, as they all felt, an unspeakable relief, and now he was greedy for the air and the sun.

He heaved the great door back and strode out into the morning, still holding the lump of modelling clay, slapping it from hand to hand. For a moment he blinked, dazzled by the brightness. There were strange, unexpected shapes in front of him. Men in grey and olive green, armour-plated vehicles, camouflage nets. He hesitated, half-turned and, at the church doorway, Dan saw his face drop from the upward pressure of pure enjoyment to the slackness of uncertainty.

The thing must have happened almost instantaneously, but it seemed to Dan to occur slowly, disjointedly, like a video advancing frame by frame. Fire spat from one of the vehicles. Bullets ricocheted off the stone arch behind Jack. He had started to turn back towards the church and his frame continued in its turn, but falling now, going down in what might have been the beginning of a gymnast's shoulder-roll. He had taken two lines of shots, machined across his ribcage. His fall appeared to last seconds, then he hit the ground and lay still. The lump of Plasticine flew from his hand and pitched into a dry, hard-baked flower bed under the church wall.

There was a pause, in which everyone listened to the dying echo of the shots. The soldiers realized the error at once, but were waiting numbly for some backlash to take them. One of their number had shot reflexively, that was all. He'd assumed his target to be armed and a member of Musa Dağ. He had seen in his mind an Armenian criminal terrorist breaking from the stake-out, someone to be shot down, or what were these guns for? But when they looked again, he and his comrades did not see a dead Armenian bandit, but the corpse of a tall European in a tropical suit and with pale-pink skin. They saw, in other words, the worst outcome of a hostage-taking siege: a dead hostage.

They came round from the trance, were shouting, moving forward. They knelt over the corpse, arguing, blaming each other for the mistake. One of them, seeing Dan, Lena and Blanchard in the church porch, waved them towards him. He still kept them covered, but he was not going to shoot.

They came out with their hands held out from their sides, cautiously.

# 30

Lena stood at the french windows in the living room. It was becoming dark. Soon it would be necessary to turn on the lights, and then the last of the garden would vanish behind the black mirrors of the window-glass.

It had taken forty-eight hours for the Turkish authorities to decide what to do. At length deportation papers were drawn up and signed, and she and Dan were put on a DC-10 belonging to Andolu Hava Yolları, Istanbul to London. They were given to understand that they had barely escaped a trial – with a virtual certainty of conviction – and the mandatory sixteen-year prison sentences which would have followed. As it was, they were warned never to set foot in the Republic of Turkey again. Two days later Georgette Hamilton brought Annabel to them here at Dan's mother's house, in England.

The wind was whisking up a susurrus in the plane tree beyond the small lawn. The sky was a canopy of baggy, leaden cloud. Rain was coming.

The thought of rain made Lena's spirits lift. The last months in Turkey had been so interminably dry, and now she was here in this well-watered, viridian country. It held out the unmistakable promise of a new beginning, new life. This was such a strong feeling she'd even mentioned it to Dan's mother.

‘Well, autumn’s coming, isn’t it?’ Phillipa Barry had said. ‘Though *I* always associate new life with a different season altogether.’

Lena had laughed. ‘Then perhaps it’s winter wheat we’re planting.’

The whole Blanchard business should have been behind them, but it still appropriated most of Dan’s attention. He had begun to make notes again for his book, and he’d been trying to contact Sarah McAskey. There had been no way to get in touch with her from the jail cell in which he’d been held pending a decision about prosecution, and now Dan had grown almost morbidly worried about her. Most recently he had asked Georgette to go to Sarah’s house and, if possible, persuade the girl to come to England.

‘She needs a cure – she *promised* she would get one. We must help her.’

‘Must we?’ Lena had asked. She didn’t particularly want this burden.

‘Of course we must. I owe her, she helped me. She did more than I had any right to ask.’

‘I suppose so.’

But Georgette’s letter had contained no good news. She had written:

Dear reunited lovebirds, Sorry, I’ve got bad tidings as regards Sarah McAskey. I did go to the flat, and found it occupied by a very loud American from Philadelphia named Donna Lubomir. She had only recently moved in there, and was living with a frankly terrifying-looking Iranian guy, who looked like he probably committed murder daily. Lubomir knows Sarah, of course, but hasn't seen her for a few weeks. Apparently the girl just flew the coop, owing the landlord rent: the usual story with junkies. Sorry not to be more up-beat. I'll keep on asking around in the couple of weeks we've got left here. After that, Conrad and I are flying back to the States (oh Glory!) to take up a new job in good ol' Sacramento. Okay, it's not Berkeley, but it's California, and that's something!

You keep in touch, you hear?

Lena turned. She heard Dan coming down from Annabel's room; he'd been reading her a bedtime story. He turned at the bottom of the stairs, drifted past the living-room door and went into the kitchen where his mother was cooking. She heard the clink of bottle on glass as he poured out drinks.

Normality. Quiet, orderly, North of England suburban normality. New life. It *was* what she wanted, of course it was. Swiftly, Lena moved across the room and put her hand on the light switch.

'Mary-Bel! C'mere, you sweet sow. Your sugar-daddy's got something nice for you. Daddy's got a big, juicy peach for his Mary-Bel. Come to Daddy now.'

Nathan held out the peach with one hand and, with his other, propped the shotgun on the outside of the sty's wall, where the pig couldn't see it.

Nathan's lawyer had told him he had no chance of acquittal. His best hope was to invest in bribes and a huge bail-bond. Then he might just be allowed to slip quietly out of the country, past blind eyes.

It had cost him every penny, and every bit of real estate, he possessed. And now it was time to say goodbye to his own ones, to the family he could not take with him.

'Come to Nathan, angel toes, come here now. C'mon now.'

But Mary-Bel kept obstinately to the rear of the sty. She watched the coveted fruit through her spoilt-child eyes, willing him to throw it at her. She would not be enticed forward, and Nathan had no choice but to slide back the bolt on the gate and slip inside.

'Like I said, Mary-Bel, I got somethin' real nice for ya. Real nice.' He kept talking and holding out the fruit, and, as he crouched down, he felt behind him through the lower bars of the gate. He found the stock of the shotgun with his finger and thumb, and jerked the weapon until it fell sideways. Then he pulled it through the gate into the sty, turning his body as he did so to mask it from his old girl. He broke open the gun, checked it had two cartridges in the breach, snapped it shut and flipped the safety catch off.

'See, you and I got a few things to discuss. I got to go away on a little vacation, and there's no way I can take my little Mary-Bel, see?' He straightened up, holding the gun tight against the seam of his trousers, barrel between thumb and forefinger and the stock in the mud. He began edging towards her. He was sweating heavily, and tears had begun to bother his eyesight.

The pig recognized his distress as something abnormal. In her whole life she had never seen the man behave like this, so tense and edgy. With a squeal and a little run she doubled capriciously into the sleeping-house. Nathan bent and followed her.

When he mucked-out the sleeping-house Mary-Bel was always in the yard. Now, with the two of them in there together, the place was hot and congested. Mary-Bel's nose, wet with a film of mucus, pointed towards him questioningly, but canted at a howitzer's angle of fire. He would give her the peach and then, while she was eating, do it. His stomach was leaden and there was a pronounced shake in his hands and wrists. He leaned the shotgun against his leg and swept the perspiration from his forehead with the back of his hand. Then he squeezed the tears from his eyes. His other hand still proffered the untasted peach.

It was at this moment that Mary-Bel's patience ran out, and she decided to go for the peach. She did it at the charge, head raised, eyes narrowed, mouth extended, ready to close on the furry, luscious globe presented to her.

Nathan jerked back, and lost his footing on the slimed concrete. As his legs slid from under him, the stock of the shotgun too began to slide outwards, bringing the end of the barrel in towards Nathan. He groped wildly downwards to catch the slipping gun, but was already himself off balance and going irreversibly down towards the shit-strewn floor. His fingers did catch something, however: they caught at a protuberance of the gun, a protuberance placed roughly one-third of the way along its length. Both barrels discharged, almost simultaneously.

The blitz of lead ripped into Nathan's cheek, shattering all his teeth, obliterating the palate and pushing out one of his eyeballs. Meanwhile the shot spread as it flayed into the fat man's brain, and was still separating when it exploded out of the top of his skull. Then the hundreds of balls of lead-shot, each pushing ahead of it a shred of Nathan's brain, buried their little portions of him deep in the plaster wall behind.

Mary-Bel was alone. After the shock of the loud noise had worn off, she began to feel hungry. She rooted for the peach, which had rolled from the man's fist into a corner of the sty. She bit the peach, with a shiver of delight as the juice ran. Then she found the peachstone with her tongue. Mary-Bel manoeuvred it between two molars and crunched with satisfaction.

She did not stay satisfied for long. Mary-Bel had not yet had her bucketful of swill today. Where would it come from now? No one had heard the report, and no one would be coming near the pig-sties for days. She grunted, and her head began swaying from side to side. As Nathan's carcass lay among the urine-soaked straw and accumulating ordure, Mary-Bel looked about her for something more to eat.